THE BURNT COUNTRY

Also by Joy Rhoades

The Woolgrower's Companion

THE BURNT COUNTRY

JOY RHOADES

BANTAM
SYDNEY AUCKLAND TORONTO NEW YORK LONDON

BANTAM

UK | USA | Canada | Ireland | Australia
India | New Zealand | South Africa | China

Addresses for the Penguin Random House group of companies can be found at global.penguinrandomhouse.com.

First published by Bantam, 2019

Cover photography/illustrations by Arcangel
Cover design by Louisa Maggio © Penguin Random House Australia Pty Ltd

Typeset in 12.5/15 pt Bembo by Post Pre-press Group, Brisbane
Printed and bound in Australia by Griffin Press, part of Ovato, an accredited
ISO AS/NZS 14001 Environmental Management Systems printer

A catalogue record for this book is available from the National Library of Australia

ISBN 978 0 14379 372 4

penguin.com.au

For my family

CHAPTER 1

When engaging an overseer for stock work, the prudent woolgrower shall first make discreet and specific enquiry, before any personal interview might be conducted, to form solid notions as to the character of the applicant. 'Repent at leisure' is an apothegm for the yards, as much as for the household.

THE WOOLGROWER'S COMPANION, 1906

Amiens, via Longhope, New South Wales
November 1948

Afterwards, Kate Dowd believed that if luck had been with her, if Jack had been unable to find his way that night, things would have been different. But as it was, her husband had made it to Amiens, all of the sixteen miles out from Longhope.

It had been a quiet night, hot, the household off to sleep early as usual. Before turning in, Kate had curled up for a few minutes in one of the verandah wicker chairs, wrapped in a sheet she'd pulled off her bed. She loved to sit there. Even in the black milk of that night, Amiens was beautiful. Kate made out the hills along the horizon and the creek line marked with myalls. She preferred moonlight, of course. But there was none tonight, just some slivers of light from the Milky Way. *Dust from a witch's housekeeping*, her father used to say.

She smiled, thinking of him, and pulled the sheet closer around her to ward off the mosquitoes. He'd built Amiens's thirty thousand acres and seven thousand head of sheep from nothing, and he was proud of his 'bit of dirt'. Her father loved the Milky Way too, even as he got older, as he got sicker. He'd stand on this verandah and show the stars to her, the saucepan and the Southern Cross. He taught her, when she was only seven or eight, how to find the two stars a bit to the side, the pointers for the Southern Cross. *If you run a line*, he'd say, *out perpendicular from the pointers, and one out from the bottom of the Southern Cross, where they meet? That's south. You can always find y'way, now, Katie.*

Finding her way was hard. And it was hard, too, to think of her father without sadness, even now, years after his death. She pushed that out of her head and looked up again. There was something peaceful about that night sky, Amiens under it, as though the land itself slept too, along with the handful of souls in the homestead – the children, Daisy, Mrs Walters, the new housekeeper – and the men in the workers' cottages half a mile off down the flats. Amiens was a little community, struggling to stay afloat, but good people, finding their way.

Calmed of her worries by the sky and the land, Kate took herself to bed, and, despite the heat, was soon asleep. But not for long.

It was the crash that woke her, a chair going over in the dark.

'*Bugger.*'

Kate was jolted upright. 'Jack?' she guessed, fearful. The air smelled of grog. She pulled the sheet up. 'Jack? Is that you? Are you all right?'

'Never bloody better.' His words were thick, angry even. Kate worried for the four others asleep in the house. Jack had a temper when sober, and now he was drunk.

'Cup of tea, Jack?' Kate said. It sounded ridiculous, even to her.

His voice came back through the darkness. 'You know what I want. We're selling up.'

She listened hard in the dark. Was he moving? Coming towards her?

She went to get up but suddenly Jack was on her, pushing her back onto the bed, the stink of stale beer around them. She knew not to struggle. His breathing came through the dark but calmed a little against her stillness. He released her and flicked on the light.

He seemed to fill the room with coiled energy. A fair head taller than her, with a solid build, he looked ragged, older than his twenty-eight years.

Unsteady, he fished about and pulled a dog-eared piece of paper, folded longways, from his back pocket and threw it in her lap. *Contract of sale* filled the top of one side.

'Sign it.'

She didn't move.

'For a wife, I bloody drew the short straw.'

Kate didn't speak.

'Well? You have to sign.'

'I can't. I have to help Daisy and Pearl. They've no one else.'

'Pearl?' He almost spat the word. 'There's at least ten blokes in this district with black kids running round. You think they acknowledge those kids? Much less *raise* em.'

'I must. Because Dad—'

'Must? Your duty is to *me*. Duty, Kate. You don't know the first thing about it.'

She knew to be quiet.

'Honour and obey. O-*bloody*-bey. What if womenfolk didn't do as they were told? Jesus H. Christ.'

Kate listened, hearing nothing in the rest of the homestead. Hoping they'd stay asleep.

'You do as you please, as if you were a bloke.' He was incredulous. 'And don't think I don't know about that Eye-tie bastard sniffing around you during the war.'

Kate steeled herself again not to react. She was now deeply ashamed of herself, of her wartime affair with Luca, even as brief as it was. The years since had shown her her madness.

'I'm bloody away doing my bit in the war, and he's here having a go.'

She cried then, trying not to make any sound for fear of getting him angrier. Jack had left her and gone to work in the Islands three years before. Why was he back now?

'The bloody war put ideas in your head. And you're burning off too much, I hear.'

'No—'

'You think you can run this place? You! Now you do something right for bloody once. Sign.' He jabbed at the contract in her lap.

A wet circle formed on the deed, a tear fallen on the paper. Very slowly, firmly, Kate shook her head.

Backhanding her, he knocked her across the bedside table. She crashed onto the floor, the lamp with her.

'You're a bloody disgrace.' His voice was thick with grog and anger.

Her face burnt, from shame and pain. In shock, her mind moved slowly. *Please God, let the others stay away. Safe.*

Jack picked up the deed. '*Sign*,' he said again.

She shook her head. She couldn't.

'You'll sign, all right.' He started to unbuckle his belt.

Suddenly there was the sound of a shotgun breech snapped shut. Jack's head spun round to the barrel as it was pushed into the room.

'Mrs Walters.' Kate's voice was hoarse with fear, afraid for what Jack would do if he got to the housekeeper.

He moved towards the gun. The barrel swung away from

him to point out the open verandah doors. *BANG.* A single shot filled the room, deafening them.

Kate could hear nothing. But she could see. Jack lurched back, fumbling with his belt, his eyes still on the gun. The shooter was hidden in the hallway but the gun barrel jerked, motioning Jack away, gone. He stumbled out the open doors.

Her ears still ringing, Kate followed onto the verandah and with a shaking hand threw on the yard lights, daylighting the homestead garden and yards of the house paddocks. Even lit up, Jack didn't look back. He went over the homestead fence, running on towards the creek. Soon headlights shot into the darkness from the gully as a car swerved round and off towards the main road.

She turned inside, shocked to find it was Harry, not Mrs Walters, cradling the shotgun. Kate felt ill at what might have happened. Harry was just thirteen.

But he was grinning, a mouthful of bright white teeth. He was as tall as Kate but skinny, his blond hair in a short crew cut. 'I showed im, eh?' she heard through the ringing. Behind him was Daisy with little Pearl in her arms, and Mrs Walters in curlers and dressing gown.

'You all right, Missus?' Daisy rubbed one ear as Pearl cried, her head of dark curls against her young mother's brown shoulder.

Kate nodded. Daisy might be seventeen, but she was resourceful. She had woken Pearl, scooped the two-year-old into her arms, ready to run.

Everyone was safe. 'Is there another cartridge in it?' she asked Harry.

'Nuh.'

She reached out for the shotgun and he handed it over, reluctantly.

'Back to bed then.' Mrs Walters's voice shook but she took charge and shepherded them all into the house.

Kate turned off the yard lights, her face still stinging from the blow. For now, at least, Jack was gone. But she would never forgive him for tonight. Nor he, her.

What had become of them?

CHAPTER 2

It may be laid down as a rule that the most important traits for a woolgrower are fortitude and a stoic turn of mind, in the face of the inevitable vagaries of fortune which will be visited upon his endeavours.

THE WOOLGROWER'S COMPANION, 1906

The next morning Kate woke in the heat, groggy with tiredness, glad of the gentle rhythm of the day, of breakfast noises carrying to her from the homestead kitchen. She dressed, then took her sore cheek to the bathroom to inspect the damage.

The mirror above the basin was tizzy, its frame a laurel of exotic leaves, all painted over in a now-chipped gold colour. Her mother had found it in a junk shop somewhere, years and years before, but Kate's father had observed it was 'fit for a bordello', so it had ended up here, hidden away in the bathroom. Kate wished she could hide away for the day, out of sight, as well.

Today, with her cut lip and bruised cheek, off-balance from Jack's visit, she almost didn't recognise the woman looking back at her in the mirror. Youngish – twenty-five – with an oval face, short brown hair, a quick smile and a watchful expression. She wondered how others saw her, if they spotted her wariness. Sometimes, the hardest person to see clearly is yourself.

Kate went to the kitchen, busy with Harry and Daisy and Pearl. She took a potato from the basket in the pantry and sliced it in two, pressing one side against her bruised cheek. She tried to sip tea with her cut lip.

'Tea leaves, Missus, eh. For ya cheek.' Daisy smiled at her in sympathy and held out a tiny trussed pudding cloth. Kate accepted the poultice gratefully and winced as she applied it. It always struck Kate how pretty Daisy was, with her deep brown eyes and head of full curls. No wonder Ed was keen.

Beside Kate, Harry attacked a plate of Vegemite toast. 'You ever been hit, Dais?' he asked.

'Harry!' Kate hissed.

Daisy carried on with the breakfast.

'At that Home, eh, in town, I bet. The bastards.' Harry went back to his toast.

Kate gave him a stern look from under her pudding cloth.

Mrs Walters came through the kitchen door, her petite frame almost hidden by the basket of laundry in her covered arms. She avoided Kate's eye and Kate knew she had a problem. She'd not told the new housekeeper any of the scandal about Amiens, about Jack leaving, about her father. After last night there was no sweeping it under the carpets they didn't have. She just hoped this housekeeper wouldn't up and quit, like the last one.

Outside, Gunner barked and a truck door banged shut.

'Damn,' Kate said, remembering. 'It's mail day.' She got up quickly.

'No swearing,' Harry crowed virtuously.

Kate was almost into the hall when Mick Maguire's voice boomed behind her. She had to stop but was careful to keep her back to the postman.

'Morning, all. How the hell are youse?'

Harry replied, a mouthful of food and greeting. 'All right, eh.'

'What about you, Mrs D?'

Kate had no choice. She turned, annoyed with herself for being too slow to escape.

The postman filled the doorway. A big man, more than six feet, with a girth and a booming voice to match his size.

'Jeez. That's a beauty. Tea leaves and whatnot'll never work. Put porridge on it.'

Maguire was always giving Kate instructions – whether on bruises, like today, or on any and every aspect of the management of the sheep property Kate had run successfully since her father died. Maguire told her what to do and she ignored him.

'How'd ya get that?' Maguire asked, putting the post on the table in front of Harry.

'The yards.' Kate said the first thing that came into her head.

'Yeah?'

She wondered if the postman knew Jack was in town, and had been on a bender. And whether he might then put two and two together. Jack was still popular in Longhope, his charm effective on men and women alike.

'Loose rail come down,' Harry said conversationally, smart enough to know they couldn't tell the truth. 'You see my wallaroo on ya way in?'

Maguire grinned. 'Hissed at me from under the tank stand.'

'Doesn't like strangers. Watch you shut the gate on your way out.'

'Where'd you get him?'

'The mum was hit by the side of the main road and Ed checked her pouch.'

Maguire smiled. 'What's his name, then?'

'Donald. For Bradman, eh.'

Maguire laughed. 'Your wallaroo gunna be a cricketer?'

'Mebbe.' Harry grinned.

'You seen your uncle, young Harry? Y'know he's back?'

Harry was suddenly serious but not surprised.

'No secrets in a country town. I saw im yesterday.'

Harry threw a filthy look. 'He's not m'uncle.' He got his school case and was gone.

Maguire took a mug of tea, nodding thanks at Daisy. 'No love lost there, eh? Grimesy's not a man who's easy to like, I'll give you all that.'

'It's his great-uncle,' Kate said needlessly. Either way, she wasn't pleased. Grimes had been gone from the district – and from Amiens where he'd been manager – for three years now. Maybe he was only passing through? Harry's reaction surprised her too. She wondered if he had already heard. Harry had an unfortunate tendency to eavesdrop.

The stack of mail caught her eye, a handwritten letter addressed to Daisy on the top.

'Any chance of a scone?' Maguire asked, watching her.

'Sorry,' Kate said, not sounding sorry. 'Bit early today. Mrs Walters hasn't had a chance.' Maguire should count himself lucky. Mrs Walters had many good points. Cooking was not one of them.

'So ya gettin that yard-rail fixed, Mrs D?' Maguire asked.

'What's that?'

'The yard-rail. Mebbe you could borrow that Eye-tie, Luca Canali, from the Rileys t'fix it.'

Kate didn't react. Maguire had tried that trick on her before, in the months since Luca had been back in Australia. She'd been shocked when she first heard that he had returned. It could only mean that there was no family in Italy to keep him there. No one left. She grew horrified, too, that he may have come back for her, and shaken that Luca could still move her.

'He's a handy bloke to have about the place, isn't he?' Maguire grinned, trying again. Kate smiled politely.

She still hadn't heard, but half hoped that Luca had brought a wife with him from Italy. Many of the former POWs had done so when they came back. But that thought palled and she was relieved he hadn't tried to see her. A swirl of emotions, of wistfulness and denial, still plagued her, but now at least she was better at putting on a poker face for Maguire.

The postman was watching her closely. 'The rail,' Kate said. 'Ed's fixing it.' Ed Storch, her head stockman, *would* have it fixed too, if it had ever been broken.

'Hey Dais, how is Ed, anyhow?' Maguire grinned as Daisy fled, embarrassed, to the laundry.

'Any bread for us today?' Kate asked, wanting to shut him up. That sort of ribbing was dangerous. To look at, Ed passed for white. But there was gossip that he was part Aboriginal. And no self-respecting white man would fall in love with an Aboriginal girl.

'No bread t'day. The oven's had it, 'parently. They waitin on a new element from Armidale.' Maguire drained the last of his tea and put the mug on the sink. 'You had any rain?'

'Not this week,' Kate said. 'Still, I count my blessings after this run of good seasons.'

'Yeah, well. This sort of pasture means fire, sooner or later. You people are burnin off?'

Kate paused before answering. 'A bit.'

'That's what I hear, round and about.'

Kate knew Maguire's mail run took him all over the district, including to her difficult neighbour, John Fleming on Longhope Downs. She was casual when she spoke. 'We back onto the State Forest. And we do nothing out of the ordinary in the way of burning off.'

'Is that right?' Maguire wasn't convinced, and his was probably Fleming's view. 'Better not let it get away on youse, eh.'

Kate watched the big postman saunter back across the lawn to the mail truck under a bright blue sky. She would warn Ed that there was talk in town about the unusual burning off on

Amiens. He'd need to be ready if someone had a go at him over it, in the street.

She put that out of her head; she needed to get to the yards and went to get a hat. But back on the verandah, as the truck went down into the gully, she saw a police car pass it and come on towards the homestead.

'Daisy!' Kate called urgently into the kitchen.

'I seen im, Missus,' Daisy said. With Pearl in her arms she ran through the laundry and out the back door, her flight hidden by the trees along the house paddock fence. Heaven only knew what Mrs Walters would think of that. But it was necessary. The sergeant, among other things, was the representative of the Aborigines Welfare Board for the district.

Yet what if Daisy and Pearl weren't the reason for his visit? Had something happened to Jack overnight? Kate dismissed that. Maguire would have known. Maguire would have also seen the police car, and it would be all around the district soon, that the police were at Amiens.

The sergeant got out of the car and put his hat on, trapping his large ears. He was known as Wingnut on account of those ears, and Kate always had to think hard to remember his real name. Withers, that was it. At least he was alone. In her experience, he brought reinforcements for arrests and for serving court papers. She waited on the verandah, working to stay calm.

CHAPTER 3

Mouthing is a means by which a sheep's age may be immediately established. For decrepitude sets in, from just four years of age, on dry, harsh pastures, manifesting itself in gaps and falling teeth.

THE WOOLGROWER'S COMPANION, 1906

Kate still felt odd going into her father's office. *Her* office, now. But it was private, and that's what she needed today for the policeman. She led Wingnut into the cool of the room and shut the door, keeping Mrs Walters out of hearing.

The visitor's chair creaked as Wingnut sat, his hat in his hands, his ears free. She sat too, facing him across the old desk, its big top bare apart from her much-thumbed guide to woolgrowing, *The Woolgrower's Companion*, open where she'd left it.

'All well, Mrs D?' Wingnut looked closely at her bruised cheek.

'Oh,' she said, making herself smile but wincing instead with the pain. 'A yard-rail came down on me.'

He nodded; like Maguire, not buying that. 'I see you got the *Companion*.'

Kate wondered when he'd get to the point. She'd been looking in vain for anything on preparation for bushfire. There was a lot on what to do after a fire. Nothing else. And she was embarrassed in case Wingnut thought she needed to study. 'Can I get you some tea?'

'No. Thanks. I won't stay long. I come about the Board. They been onto me from Sydney. Daisy's gotta give up Pearl.'

Kate held her breath as he went on and on.

'They've had enough, Mrs D. Daisy's an unmarried half-caste, with a toddler born out of wedlock. She's gotta give up that child to be brung up by a white family. It's Board policy. She shoulda give her up at birth. As you know.'

Kate did know. Wingnut had told her often enough. If Pearl had been born in hospital, she would have been taken by the Board then. Daisy too would have been transferred to another employer, away from Kate and from her baby. Instead, Daisy, heavily pregnant, had absconded and made her way to Longhope and to Amiens, where Pearl had been born. Kate and Daisy had spent the three years since trying to fend off the Board.

Wingnut sighed. 'You've heard this said before, Mrs D. The Board says for the good of the child, it's gotta be raised right.'

Kate started to protest but he held up a hand.

'I know youse are doin a good job. But rules are rules. The Board's tellin me now either you deliver Pearl, or they'll transfer Daisy to another employer – one or the other, by the end of the month.'

Kate stared at him.

'End of the month, it is.' He nodded. 'I think ya stirred em up with that wages nonsense, if ya don't mind me sayin so.'

Kate looked down at her hands. 'I shouldn't have mentioned it. But Daisy got that letter, saying that they still hold money for her. I just asked for it.'

'They lookin after it, Mrs D. For all the Abos. Not just Daisy. That's their job, eh. They don't take kindly to people poking into their business.'

Kate wished she'd never raised the damn wages.

'They've been pretty patient, what with your father passing away and so on. But that was three years ago.' Wingnut stood up, turning his hat in his hands. 'Righto.' He saw the gun-rack on the wall, and its padlock. 'Good that you keep it locked.' His voice was soft, sympathetic.

'I had it put in, you know. After—'

'Your father's accident,' he said.

'Yes.' It had been Wingnut who'd determined that her father's death was accidental when he was 'cleaning his gun', although both of them knew otherwise. The district knew too.

'The trick is to hide the key from Harry,' Kate said.

She saw Wingnut out then. He strode across the lawn, startling Donald. The wallaroo bounded away in fright from the stranger. But it was Pearl Kate thought of, and worry wormed its way in. Kate and Daisy seemed to have run out of options.

At a brisk pace, you could make it over the hill from the homestead to the yards in only six minutes. Harry had timed it once. As she went, Kate watched where she put each booted foot on the track. Mating season for snakes was over, but that didn't mean she could avoid a bite if she trod on one.

Kate walked fast, not wanting to miss John Fleming or his man coming for the sheep. She needed the cheque, and she needed to get it to Addison. The bank manager had approved the sale of this stock, on condition the cheque was banked, of course. She'd made that beginner's mistake only once, forgetting to get his OK, forgetting that the stock, like the land, was mortgaged to the bank. Most graziers just sold and told the bank after. But Addison had a long history with Kate; he was another one who refused to believe a woman could run the place. He used any means he could to threaten her with default. It was wise, then, always to get his approval first to sell her stock.

It was a glorious morning: that bright sky and some clouds so wispy they'd come to nothing, rain-wise. Birds shrieked from the ringbarked tree that stood like a dead sentinel by the gate, its trunk smooth and grey with age. A flock of galahs festooned the bare branches like Christmas decorations. Her mother had loved them, these beautiful birds, with their pale crests, dark pink breasts, and grey wings like a cloak over the top. They watched as Kate walked by, squawking at her like men propping up the bar at a pub in town.

The bird noise receded behind her, soon replaced by a dusty air full of bleated thirst and hunger, the smell of dung and urine. The sheep had been yarded since the night before, to empty out, ready to be trucked today. Water and feed waited for them at their new home.

'Mornin, Mrs D.' Ed, her manager, smiled a greeting at Kate, his eyes stopping on her bruised cheek. He said nothing. Daisy had probably told him. He was a good egg. They were about the same age, she and Ed. Together they'd somehow managed to keep Amiens afloat since Kate's father had died.

Ed manoeuvred his gammy leg between the rails and stepped neatly into the yards. He'd hurt one leg as a kid, rolled on by a horse he was breaking, but he compensated somehow. Put him *on* a horse and you'd never know. Kate was forever surprised by his agility.

'They ready for truckin,' Ed said. He moved through the throng of sheep, arms out a bit in case of a knock, and also to pat a sheep's head, scratch its ear. He loved 'his girls'. 'Maguire been this mornin?'

'Just left. There's talk in town about us doing too much burning off.'

'Yeah?' He sounded annoyed.

'My thoughts exactly.' Every grazier who was any good burnt off. But Amiens's process was a bit different. Their very methodical approach had been Ed's quiet idea, way back, as soon as the drought broke in '45 to '46 and the good pasture came on. She wasn't sure how he knew about fire but suspected he was taught as a boy, growing up on a place outside Wilcannia, not far from Daisy's home of Broken Hill.

Burning off generally just made sense. No area got too overgrown, and that prevented a build-up of fuel, so a bushfire might be slowed or even stopped.

Most local graziers were sensible about the fire risk, but not many went about it as often or as carefully. Some, the worst, were all-or-nothing types. They'd have big, infrequent, widespread burns, and those graziers had long since stopped those. Others, the more prudent types like Kate, were still doing small patches. They chose where and when carefully. Neat. Methodical. Controlled.

She looked off towards the State Forest with some satisfaction. Up to that boundary the pasture had not been allowed to build up or get unmanageable. Kate suspected she was being singled out for criticism for the usual reasons. She was a woman. What did she know about burning off, or sheep for that matter? And her father, never an easy man, had made enemies in his lifetime. Small towns have long memories. Some visited that ill will on Kate, when they got the chance.

'Did ya hear Grimesy's back? Fleming's hired him as manager, 'parently.'

'Manager?' Kate looked at Ed across the platform of sheep backs. 'What about Mr Tonkin?'

'Word is Fleming told him he could lump it or walk.'

An unhappy thought occurred to Kate. 'It won't be Grimes today, will it? Coming for Fleming's stock?' It was common knowledge in the district that after her father died, Grimes didn't like working for Kate so he'd quit. And she was worried about Harry.

'We're bout t'find out.' The Flemings' truck was visible now on the track in from the main road.

'Even if it's Grimes, he'll still have to pay,' Kate said. 'I mean, it's Fleming.' She needed that money. They always needed money. And Fleming, oddly, was known around the district as a slow payer.

The truck pulled up, the man's hat making it hard to see his face. But then out of the cabin, at a leisurely pace, came Amiens's former manager, Keith Grimes. Kate's bruised cheek throbbed.

She'd forgotten how tall he was – over six foot – and broad, solid from a lifetime of hard yakka. Grimes's thick eyebrows were more white than grey now, and he clearly still liked his blue work shirts. He reminded Kate of her father – they'd been the same vintage – and suddenly she missed him. He could always handle this man.

'Mornin,' Grimes said. 'Took one to the mouth, Mrs D?'

The heat went to her face and her lip throbbed. 'It was an accident.'

'That a fact?'

'You're working for Fleming,' she said flatly. If he was not to offer pleasantries after years away, then neither would she.

'Yup. I'm here to get his wethers.'

They're not his yet went through Kate's mind.

'How ya been?' Ed called from inside the yards.

Grimes ignored him.

'Pretty good. How you been, Ed?' Ed parroted the reply that should have been given, gently needling his old boss.

But Grimes just approached the yards and climbed in.

'If you back her up t'the ramp, I'll load,' Ed said.

'I'll see em first.'

'Woddaya mean?'

'Gunna go over em. Can't trust any old bloke these days.'

They half thought he was joking. But to make his point, he caught a wether, forcing open its mouth to inspect the teeth. Satisfied with that one at least, he moved across the yards towards the drafting race, where he could check them one by one.

By insisting on checking the stock, he was implying that Kate and Ed would include ring-ins – a few lame, old or poorly animals – with the rest. The *bloke* business was a dig at Kate. Grimes had hated working for a woman, even the woman who owned the best Merino flock in the district.

The next wether shook its head unhappily, as Grimes counted its incisors to check the age. Kate hoped one of them would give a good nip to his hand.

'Get em organised,' Grimes called to Ed, issuing the orders.

Ed's face set and Kate's with it. Grimes meant to check every animal. Kate knew she should refuse to sell at all, cheque or no cheque. She should. But they needed the money.

Ed whistled up the dogs and started the long process of putting the wethers, one at a time, into the race for Grimes to examine.

'Be a while, Mrs D,' Grimes said without looking up, dismissing her. 'I'll come to the house on m'way out.'

Bastard was what her father would have said. But then Grimes would never have done this to him. Kate stalked back to the house, her boots throwing up tiny breaths of dust on the track. She was angry with herself for being rattled by Grimes, but glad that Harry was at school. She and Ed might withstand Amiens's former manager, but Grimes and Harry together were combustible.

CHAPTER 4

The woolgrower shall be mindful that quiet demeanour and good temper are worthy traits of rams and ewes. A beast of true value does not possess virility or strength of line alone.

THE WOOLGROWER'S COMPANION, 1906

As Kate walked in from the yards, she could see Mrs Walters in the homestead garden under the clothes line. Cross as Kate was with Grimes, she knew she had to speak to the new housekeeper about Jack. Kate's calm persuasion was needed.

Mrs Walters was hauling damp white sheets onto the lines in the hot breeze. She was a slight thing, no more than five feet two, and had to stretch up to peg. She reminded Kate of a wallaroo, compact and industrious. Kate had made the mistake of mentioning that to Harry, when Mrs Walters first arrived. Harry hoped that Mrs Walters wouldn't deposit piles of manure everywhere in the garden, like Donald.

Kate took one end of an unruly sheet and helped haul it up over the line, trying to get up the gumption to say something. The previous housekeeper hadn't lasted a week, shocked at what she found at Amiens. An absent husband, a half-caste child, gossip about Kate's father's death. And she hadn't even suffered a visit from Jack.

This time, with a new agency, Kate had tried the other tack.

She just got Mrs Walters up from Sydney on the train and would let her work all that out. Mrs Walters, a widow, needed to support herself, and in the ten days she'd been with them, she seemed to have accepted the circumstances. Until Jack's visit.

'It's warm for this time of year,' Kate began.

'Yes?' Mrs Walters kept pegging. A sheen of perspiration shone on her face in the heat.

'The old-timers will tell you a hot November brings a dry summer out here.' Bushfire too, only Kate didn't add that.

Overhead, a family of lorikeets screeched and swooped. Daisy's lorikeets; she loved their noise and colour.

'I'm very sorry, Mrs Walters, about last night. I'm sorry I didn't tell you.' The small woman frowned, and Kate hurried on. 'He – my husband – doesn't live in the district. He'll be gone soon. Back to the Islands. To his work there.' The words came out in a rush. Last night had shaken Kate too. The woman kept pegging, unmoved. 'We need you, Mrs Walters. Very much.'

She stopped pegging then and hugged a damp sheet to her like a child. 'Can I ask you about Pearl, Mrs Dowd?'

Kate looked off towards the horizon and the weary pasture. 'She's my half-sister.'

'Your father's child.' Mrs Walters's voice was soft.

'Yes.' It had been so hard once to say that. 'But he. My father. He – Daisy didn't want—'

Lips pursed, Mrs Walters shook her head and dropped her eyes to the sheet in her arms.

Kate waited for the outrage, for the *I can't stay under this roof a minute longer* speech. The previous housekeeper had been shocked that Kate would acknowledge a black baby sister. That was the line that Longhope took too, that Kate was foolhardy, unhinged, even, to embrace Pearl as family. Deny the rape, deny the child. Why hadn't she done that? they thought.

Kate sighed, remembering the awfulness of that time, and worse, the shunning since. People were not uncivil in the street of Longhope. They'd nod. But no one stopped to speak to her. Now, she had only the Rileys, and her own people on Amiens.

Suddenly, the housekeeper went back to pegging. 'It's all right, Mrs Dowd,' she said, her eyes on the sheet.

'Really?' Kate could not believe her luck.

Mrs Walters nodded, a bird-like twitch. 'But there's something I must tell you. I wasn't truthful.'

'Oh?' Kate probably wouldn't mind, so long as Mrs Walters stayed.

'On the application form. Next to religion, I put Church of England. But it's not true. I'm Catholic, you see.' Mrs Walters's face grew pink. 'I didn't think you'd give me the job, since I live in the house with you.'

Kate was confused. While it was worrying that Mrs Walters had lied, it wasn't such a terrible one. Catholicism was an affliction Kate could handle. 'That's all right. You're here now.'

Almost heady with relief, Kate walked across the lawn to the house. Mrs Walters was staying. One problem solved.

Her relief did not last long. She found Daisy in the kitchen, tears in her eyes, that letter in her hand. 'Missus—' Each time Daisy tried to speak, her voice caught. She held the letter out to Kate. 'Please.'

The letter, in a neat, round hand, was from Daisy's mother in Broken Hill.

I hope you are safe and good.

I am very sick. The doctor says I only got one month.

I am longing to see you my Daughter. I am waiting for you to come soon.

Kate read the letter again, her heart breaking for Daisy and for her mother. 'I'm so sorry. You must go to see her, as soon as you can. We'll pay for your train ticket. Don't worry about that.'

'Pearl, Missus? Who look after her?'

'We'll manage. Truly. Between Mrs Walters and me.'

'Wingnut come, Missus?'

Kate paused. 'He says there's a time limit the Board has set. The end of the month.'

'Me or Pearl, eh?'

'Yes. But we'll think of something,' Kate said.

Daisy nodded, unconvinced. Afraid.

Outside a dog barked, as a truck pulled to a stop and its engine was shut down.

Kate frowned. 'That'll be Grimes.'

'Mr Grimes, Missus?' Daisy asked, alarmed.

'Yes, he's back. Stay inside, all right? Keep Pearl out of sight too, won't you?'

Kate was thinking of what had happened a few weeks before. A visiting mechanic had come to the homestead to be paid. But while Kate was inside getting her cheque-book, Pearl ran onto the verandah. This awful man had sworn at the toddler, and told her to get out, not realising she lived in the homestead. With Pearl crying in Daisy's arms in the laundry, it was all Kate could do to even pay the man. Grimes would be worse. He knew Daisy, and of Pearl's birth.

'I'll have to go and speak to him.' Kate touched Daisy's hand lightly. 'But we'll talk again about this. All right? I promise. We'll get things organised.'

Daisy sniffed the air. She went straight to the stove and pulled the door open. A breath of smoke wafted across the kitchen from Mrs Walters' cooking. As Kate went out onto the verandah, Mrs Walters passed her, going the other way at speed. It occurred to Kate that perhaps Daisy should take care of the cooking, and Mrs Walters might do the cleaning and laundry. An easy dividing line. Kate suspected this housekeeper would not baulk at Daisy cooking. Some households forbade their Aboriginal girls from touching or preparing food, but Kate had dropped that years before.

She went out as Grimes came up the verandah stairs, and could not help but think of the last time he'd stood there, when he'd quit all those months before. Kate had been more than pleased to hand over his wages and see him go. But today, he had her money.

'The cheque, please, Mr Grimes.'

'You people still short of a quid, Mrs D?'

'The cheque,' she said again. Kate would not be rankled.

The smell of burnt scones wafted out from the kitchen. 'Somethin on fire? I hear there's a bit of that out this way.' He laughed.

Kate frowned. 'Careful and often is how we burn off. No cause for alarm.'

Now Mrs Walters came onto the verandah. 'Shall I get the gentleman some tea, Mrs Dowd?'

'He's not staying.'

The housekeeper retreated inside.

Grimes looked out across Amiens's hills. 'Bloody Canali's around too. But I reckon ya know that.' He smiled. 'The Eye-ties. Good to hear they shipped that Buconti fella back though. The commie. One down.'

'The cheque, and then you will leave,' Kate said firmly. She was annoyed; this cheque business was underhand.

'Hold on, Mrs D. I come to talk business with you.'

'Give me my cheque.'

'Don't have it. You'll have to ask John Fleming. It's his money.'

'Good day, Mr Grimes.' Kate headed for the kitchen.

'I need to talk t'ya bout Harry,' Grimes said to her back.

Kate turned in the kitchen doorway.

Donald chose that moment to hop round the corner of the

house. He stopped on the lawn and looked up at Kate and the visitor.

'Harry should be with family,' Grimes continued.

Kate doubted very much that Grimes cared anything about family. He just wanted to get at her. 'I'll let him know you were here,' she said.

'Let im *know*? No, Mrs D, the boy's comin to me and that's final.'

'He won't want to live with you. He never did.'

'I'm his uncle.'

'Great-uncle,' Kate corrected automatically.

'I'll come back here with the coppers. With the sergeant. I will, I'm tellin ya.'

So. Grimes was serious. 'This is not your decision,' she said.

'It's not bloody Harry's, if that's what ya thinkin.'

Kate was silent.

'Righto. I'll be back with Wingnut.' Grimes went for the steps.

'Harry's grandmother is the person who should decide,' she said.

'What?'

'Mrs Grimes. She should decide.'

He mulled over her suggestion.

'Well?' Kate said, sensing her advantage.

'All right.' Grimes planted his hat on his head and marched across the green lawn.

From what Kate knew of Harry's grandmother, she was a practical woman. Four years before, when she'd been too elderly to care for Harry, she'd rung Amiens looking for her brother-in-law. Kate's father had answered the phone. Without consulting Grimes, Kate's father had agreed on the spot to take Harry. So Harry came to live on Amiens.

But it was Kate who'd ended up caring for the boy. He'd spent almost all of his waking time at the homestead with her and Daisy, not at Grimes's cottage. When Grimes had quit and left the district, trying to take Harry with him, the boy absconded and returned to Kate.

What Grimes didn't know was that Harry had been writing to his grandmother once a month for the years he'd been gone. After all those letters of happiness, there was no way Mrs Grimes would make Harry leave Amiens now.

CHAPTER 5

Although unfashionable amongst the less discerning, it is this writer's firm belief that the demeanour of the woolgrower has an exceptional influence on those about him and is duty-bound to show a deep interest in all who claim the patronage of the holding.

THE WOOLGROWER'S COMPANION, 1906

'Tony's made the first eleven, eh. For the district.' Harry announced the news at the end of the kitchen table, through a mouthful of one of Daisy's scones. Mrs Walters had ceded the day's baking to her.

'What's that?' Kate was distracted, still thinking about Grimes's visit. She had to tell Harry somehow.

'I'm a better batter. Yet bloody Tony got in the team.'

'No swearing,' Kate said, pouring herself a cup of tea. Behind her, the two-way radio squawked, and she listened with half an ear. It was the Rileys' men. Not Amiens. Ed had found a set of ex-Army two-ways just after the war. He'd talked her into buying them, and she couldn't imagine how they'd cope without them now. One at the house, one at Ed's – the manager's cottage – one at the shed and one in the truck.

'He couldn't hit a cricket ball with a shovel.'

Cricket. Harry was talking about cricket. 'You'll get in

sooner or later, Harry. I know you will.' She looked at his hair. 'Are you wet? Did you swim on the way home?'

'Mebbe. Mebbe not.'

She touched his hair. 'Wet.'

'Greasy.'

'You can swim. But you must promise me you won't swing off that dead tree. It'll come down for sure.' The tree had died soon after the dam filled, its roots drowned.

Harry extracted a shiny green box from his school case.

'Gosh! Is that a Meccano set? Who gave you that?'

Harry smiled, proud of gift and giver. 'Luca.'

'Oh.' Kate turned away.

'It's the bee's knees. Bit puke green though,' Harry said. He opened the box on the kitchen table and began to place piece after tiny piece in neat rows.

Daisy frowned. 'Gunna make the tea there, eh. Verandah, mebbe?'

Kate saw her chance. 'Tell ya what, Harry. You want to come to the dam paddock with me? Ed's started to shift mobs in towards the shed for shearing.'

He was up in a flash, any homework forgotten. Harry would have to handle the news that Grimes wanted to raise him, so Kate could live with unfinished homework.

They went out the gate, careful to shut Donald in and keep the dog out.

'What you doin, Gunner? Ed'll have your guts for garters if he finds out ya not workin.' Harry roused on the dog. Gunner loped round them on the short walk to the vehicle.

Kate climbed into the car and fired up the ignition. As they drove, Harry asked, 'Why they startin so early? Shearin's not for a coupla weeks.'

She slowed the car to shudder over the grid, out of the house paddock. 'You know that Amiens is long and thin. So it takes a bit of manoeuvring to get the mobs in from the ends.'

'Can't ya walk em in? They'd do it in no time.' A crow watched them from a ringbarked tree as the car passed.

'It's a bit of a risk, to try to get them in, with no time to spare. Because if the temperature's up – like it is at the moment – they can't walk as far or as fast in a day. There has to be pasture and water for them too, till shearing.'

'The dam paddock's gotta lot of both, eh. Water and grass,' Harry said.

'Yes. But we've got a lot of mobs to be moved in, in time. We can't mix mobs without messing up the blood lines.'

'Tricky.'

'It's like a big puzzle, where you can only move one piece at a time—' Kate began.

'And that has to be empty, anyhow, to move em into?'

'Exactly.' Kate loved talking sheep with Harry. Loved teaching him.

'Tony reckons there'll be a lotta bushfires this year. Big ones, his dad says.' Harry nodded at the rolling hills of yellowed pasture that was now Amiens.

Kate tried to think how best to raise the news about Grimes. Harry had had such a rough trot in his life: he'd lost both parents. Grimes, the only relative able to take him in, was a rotter.

'Tones is jealous of my Meccano.'

'That's a generous gift, Harry.' Kate tried not to think about Luca. It just made her sad.

Harry produced a smug half-smile.

'Did you say thank you?' Kate asked.

He grinned at her. 'Nuh. Mebbe Thursday. Mrs Riley says I can visit the pups on Thursdays. After school.'

Kate remembered that a litter of puppies had been delivered a month before to one of the Rileys' work dogs. Mrs Riley was the owner, with her husband, of a stud called Tindale. A lovely couple, older, in their forties, they had no children and a soft spot for Harry – and Luca. They'd sponsored him to emigrate from Italy. Luca and the puppies were a powerful magnet for Harry.

'Old Luca, eh?' Harry said, watching her.

She kept her eyes to the front as she drove.

'You keen on Luca, Mrs D?'

'No, Harry. Not at all.' She sounded tired. She was tired.

'I reckon he's sweet on you.'

From Harry's voice, she knew he was grinning. Fighting a weird burst of pain and pleasure, Kate swallowed, and focused on the dam wall on the far side of the paddock. 'I'm married, Harry,' she said. It came out sounding hollow. 'I'm married,' she repeated, more forceful this time, glancing across.

Harry looked left then right, like Charlie Chaplin. 'Where's your old man, then?' He laughed.

Kate brought the car to a halt at the bottom of the dam wall, and Harry got out, still grinning.

Had Luca said something to Harry? She hoped not. Poor Luca, if he still felt anything for her, if he thought that there was a chance for them. Not now. That was long dead. But she wasn't surprised in some ways that he'd come back. He always had drive, wanting to make something of his life.

They walked together, she and Harry, towards the dam wall, but Kate's mind was still on Luca. She *had* loved him, that she was sure of. But after the war, after he was shipped home and as time passed, she wondered more and more how it had even been possible. How could she, a married woman then and still, have allowed herself to fall in love with him? Ashamed, she'd done her best to work Luca out of her head and her heart, making herself imagine him in Italy, married with children, doting on his family. Painful, but necessary. Duty came first.

Because in those same postwar months and years, Kate began to understand just how hard the Aborigines Welfare Board would fight to separate Daisy from Pearl. She realised that she'd have to be devoted to both mother and child to help them at all. Her father's terrible rape of Daisy had decided Kate's duty and her future.

After the war, when Jack came back, he'd wanted them to sell Amiens and move to the Islands, to escape the shame of her father's suicide. Pride and his good name had always been everything to Jack. But Kate could not take Daisy or Pearl with them to the Islands; the Aborigines Welfare Board would never allow it and they'd snatch both, sending them, apart, to some unknown and difficult future.

So Kate said no to Jack. He could not believe it. But for her it was easy. Yes, she was a bad wife to him. That was true. But now she had to look after Daisy and Pearl, and Harry as well. Jack had said, *I have to look after myself?* She'd shrugged, immovable, but secretly afraid in the face of his anger.

Hopefully Jack was gone again, back to the Islands, at least for now.

She followed Harry up the dam wall towards the general direction of the dust, the bleating of the mob, the shouts of men and dogs barking.

Kate and Harry stood on the top, looking across the spread of the dam water to the men and the mobs beyond. Kate loved to watch them shift stock, a remarkable flow of linked pieces, like a flock of birds, separate yet connected, wheeling and moving with their brethren.

'A murmuration, my dad called it,' Kate said, her eyes fixed on the movement of the stock, the mob turning as one as the stockmen forced them this way, then that, towards the gate.

'A murmur-what?'

'Murmuration. Birds and fish do it. Dad reckoned sheep do it too. Swarm behaviour.'

But Harry wasn't impressed; he was looking at the dam water. 'Can sheep swim?'

'If they have to. If there's a flood or they fall in or something.'

He considered that. Harry's curiosity was a good thing, Kate reminded herself. He wanted to learn. Amiens might be his one day. Pearl popped into Kate's head. *What about Pearl?*

'Miss Parkin told us camels can't swim. But I reckon that's bull dust. Armadillos can't though.'

Kate was hard-pressed to know what an armadillo looked like. Armour, she guessed. It was probably heavy.

'Why don't you help at the gate?'

Harry ran down the dam wall and off across the paddock, to duck through the fence wire. Part of the mob was through, with a bit still to come. They'd want to be one flock, at the end of the day.

Kate waved a hello to Robbo, the new stockman, on horseback on the other side of the fence. He touched his hat but looked away. They'd been peers of a sort, both progeny of local graziers, but when Robbo came home from the war, the father and son had fallen out badly. Robbo had trouble holding down a job so, despite Ed's resistance, Kate had put him on.

As she watched Harry at the gate, Kate cursed herself for not telling him about Grimes as they were driving up from the homestead. Idiot that she was, she'd been distracted by Harry's talk of Luca.

Ed signalled for Harry to shut the gate and he did so, hopping on to catch a ride as it swung. The mob flowed out evenly, like water poured from a jug. Ed had taught her that Merinos stay close, in a pretty tight mob, day or night. They stuck together, following the leader, and struck out across the open paddock and off towards the distant trees and the creek. Kate watched them go, so proud of them as they gathered in the dusk at the edge of the paddock. Kate liked this time of day best, with work almost done and the sky a swirl of orange and pink, the dam's surface a mirror for the vivid colours.

Harry climbed back up to her. 'Red sky at bloody night,' he ribbed.

'Red sky at night,' she corrected.

'Shepherd's bloody delight.' He laughed.

'Dad would not have approved of your little variation.'

'*He* learnt me.' Harry laughed again.

Kate smiled. It did sound like her father. 'Taught, not learnt. And please don't swing off that trunk, Harry. It'll come down on you.' She pointed at the hollow tree trunk halfway up the dam wall, the only shade tree that had been left when the dam was built.

As they walked back to the car, Kate tried to find the words to tell him about Grimes.

'What's got ya goat?' Harry asked as Kate moved the car off.

'What?'

'Ya stewin on somethin.'

Kate looked at him.

'I'm right, eh?'

'We had a visit today. From your uncle.'

'Great-uncle,' he corrected.

Gunner had appeared, to run shotgun alongside the car. He was smart enough not to get hit somehow. He'd be in big trouble with Ed, for disappearing from the muster.

'So he really is back?' Harry said.

'Yeah. He's working for John Fleming now. On Longhope Downs.'

'Well, that's a mistake. What did he want?'

'He was picking up the wethers I'd sold to Fleming.'

'Uh.' Harry lost interest.

'But also—'

'What also?' Harry looked at her.

'He . . . He wants you to go and live with him.' She looked back at him, a boy-man silhouetted against the sky, with the last of the sun draining into the west.

'He's in for a disappointment, then,' Harry said. 'You told him?'

'Yes, but—'

'But?' Harry said flatly.

'He insisted. I said we should ask your grandmother. You know, go to Sydney to see her.' Kate was thinking they'd go soon, to get the trip in before shearing started in just under two weeks' time.

'Why the bloody hell'd ya say that?'

'He's. He's—'

'Dead set on raisin me.'

'Yes.'

He dropped his head forward, and he was again the small boy who'd come to them years before, tired and alone.

Harry looked up. 'Smart, eh.'

'What?'

'She's smart, my nan. No flies on the old lady. She knows Grimesy's a bastard –'

Kate let the swearword go.

'– an I reckon she'll be sweet.' He started to nod. 'Yeah. I reckon that's pretty smart of ya. An I get a trip to Sydney!'

She smiled, hoping they were right – for Harry's sake and for her own.

A little later, back at the homestead, Kate was pleased to see the Rileys' car coming to a stop outside.

'Hello!' She walked down to the fence as Mrs Riley got out of the car.

'Kate, dear. How are you?' Mrs Riley smiled quickly, and collected her hat and a small packet from the back seat. Always immaculately turned out, even for an impromptu visit, she was a big lady, both tall and 'broad of beam'.

'I do feel terrible, Kate dear, dropping in like this, unannounced, but I was passing and you may need these for the wallaroo.'

Kate accepted what appeared to be three beautifully ironed pillow cases, slightly worn but pressed, with a faint scent of starch.

'Harry told us that you might be short of cases for him to sleep in? I thought I'd best drop them off. They were destined for the ragbag, otherwise.'

'Thank you.' Kate smiled at her. 'Harry will be pleased. But please do stay for a cup of tea?'

'Truly, I shan't, dear. I am already intruding.' She kissed Kate farewell, removed the hat, placed it on the back seat and departed.

Kate had no choice but to wave her off.

Just over an hour later, Kate stood with a mug of tea, the verandah upright post still warm against her back, and watched the sun sink from a clear sky into the Amiens hills. The pasture dried out a little more, every week without rain. It was not yet a drought sort of dry. But bushfire-dry, for sure.

Outside the homestead fence, Gunner paced, pleading with her. Ed would have one of the boys feed all the dogs soon, but Gunner always tried his luck at the homestead anyway.

'You can go on your way, my friend,' Kate called to the dog. 'Nothing for you here.'

As she sipped her tea, something smallish and dark that looked like a chop bone sailed over the fence from behind the house, landing just beyond the dog. Another followed, and Gunner was on them in a second.

'Harry!' Kate called. There was silence, and no more bones.

Her crossness was interrupted by headlights from an unknown car poking up out of the gully. With Amiens and all on it pariahs in the district, they got no casual callers. Had Jack come back? Her fear was automatic. But this couldn't be Jack; he'd be driving fast, and she suspected he was gone now from the district. For a bit, anyway.

Kate hurled the remnants of her tea onto the garden and put the cup in the kitchen. She wanted to be back out on the verandah, three feet above the visitor, when whoever it was arrived. Home pitch advantage.

But then she saw. The verandah steps would be no help with this visitor.

It was Luca.

CHAPTER 6

While the greatest regard for animal husbandry is an essential, on no account shall the woolgrower allow vestiges of endearment to impede his clarity of purpose. A hapless poddy lamb, hand-raised but long since weaned and put out to pasture, must nonetheless be culled when its time encroaches.

THE WOOLGROWER'S COMPANION, 1906

In the twilight, Luca got out of the Rileys' car and straightened up, putting a hand through that thick black hair. He was just the same: her height but broad, his face a rich brown, deepened by his work in the sun. She knew all of him, from how he moved and how he felt, even down to the scar ridges on his back.

He closed the gate behind him and glanced around. Harry must have told him about the wallaroo.

From the lawn, he looked up at her, taking her in.

'Luca,' she said.

He almost smiled.

Kate had to be sensible, and to breathe. She wanted the security of the kitchen, the bustling calm of Daisy. 'Come in.' Her traitorous voice was hoarse.

In the kitchen, Luca stood looking at her across the expanse of the table. Up close, he was the same too. A little older, some flecks of grey in his hair, yet the same handsome Luca, with those pale green eyes and milk-tea skin. Her hand went to smooth her hair, and his eyes followed. He smiled again. They knew each other so well that she felt a physical pain in her chest. This would be much harder than she'd imagined.

Embarrassed, she sat down. Luca sat too, and his familiar scent wafted over to Kate: soap, and sump oil, and him.

Daisy bundled in from the laundry and he was on his feet. 'Mister Luca!' She grinned, as pleased as he was. 'Pearl! Pearl!' Daisy called. 'I get her for youse,' she said, disappearing again into the hall.

The silence pressed on Kate as they looked at each other across the kitchen table, Luca smiling, Kate anxious.

Then Daisy was back, carrying a bathed Pearl in pyjamas, and she shuffled the still-damp toddler into Luca's arms.

'S'Luca, eh, littlie? He know youse forever. Since you was born.' Daisy beamed at them both.

Pearl didn't take to strangers, usually. But she just sat in Luca's arms, thoughtful, observing him and her mother's smiling face. Then Pearl reached out and patted Luca's head as if he were a dog. Daisy and Luca laughed. Pearl's fingers dropped to touch the beads of perspiration on his forehead. 'Wet,' she said to her mother.

Daisy laughed again and took the toddler back. 'Bed, Pearl, now.'

Luca wiped his forehead with the back of his hand. Kate hoped Daisy would put Pearl to bed and return to them, but there was an unusual silence in the house.

Mrs Walters appeared then, all bright eyes and neat curls.

'Our new housekeeper. Mrs Walters,' Kate said.

Luca dropped his head briefly and smiled.

Kate had forgotten that. His way of greeting. 'This is Luca Canali. He worked here. During the war. He's a POW. Was. Was a POW.'

'Before,' he said. 'Now I work at Mr Riley.'

'How do you do,' Mrs Walters said politely, then disappeared into the hall again. In the silence, the kitchen clock ticked on, and Luca seemed not the slightest bit uncomfortable, happy to look at her.

Kate started to shift in her chair. Where was Harry? Missing. Had he known Luca was coming?

He startled her when he spoke. 'Perhaps out, *Signora*? It is possible?' It was *his* voice this time that was hoarse.

The house seemed too quiet after all. They went onto the verandah, and Kate sat, immediately wishing she hadn't, as Luca stayed standing. She had a sudden irrational terror that he was leaving. Then he spoke.

'You are good.'

'Yes. Well. Thank you.' But Kate realised then it was a statement, not a question. She was an idiot. She pulled at the rattan of the chair seat, and then stopped herself.

Luca walked to and fro on the verandah and she was fearful of her pleasure at the sight of him.

'Before, in August, I come back,' he said, waggling his head, trying to start.

'You did,' Kate said softly. He must hear the regret.

She didn't ask about his family. Harry had told her bits already. Both Luca's brother and father were dead by the end of the war, his sisters married and settled. There'd been little to keep him in Italy. He'd accepted the Rileys' invitation to sponsor him. So here he was. What Harry had not said – and what Kate had not asked – was whether he was married. *Please God, let there be a wife.* But he wouldn't be here if he had a wife.

She wondered if it was Jack's appearance that had prompted Luca to come and see her. Jack would be staying at his mate Biggsy's pub; the whole town must know by now Jack had left her for good.

'I come back. I hope . . .' As he walked, his voice trailed off and he couldn't finish. Eventually, he stopped pacing and stood on the edge of the verandah, looking out across Amiens. 'Much grass,' he said.

'Three good years of rain since you've been gone.'

He nodded, impressed, as though Kate had conjured up the rains.

'It's drying out now though.'

'*Sì*.' He could see that.

He came then to stand beside her.

She tensed, not wanting him to be so close. 'You were kind to buy the Meccano for Harry.'

'Yes. Mrs Riley, she go in the shop for me.'

Kate looked at him.

'Mr Nettiford not like the Eye-ties. He explain me.'

Poor Luca. He would get a lot of that in town. Even the boom times since the end of the war – it was hard to get workers to fill all the jobs going in Longhope – had not erased the way Australians felt about the Italian immigrants. Foreigners were bad enough, but former POWs were the worst of the lot.

'After, Mrs Riley, she buy for me.'

That sounded like her. A silence passed between them. Not uncomfortable, within reach of each other, their eyes on Amiens.

It made Kate remember their days at the end of the war. Each night Luca would come, bringing her a meal that the other POW had cooked for them all. They would eat together, in the Amiens kitchen, just the two of them alone in the homestead in gentle and remarkable domesticity. Then Luca would stay. They would make love. All for a few short, glorious days. What madness was that?

'Today I come to you,' Luca said. He took her hand in his and the heat of his fingers sent something through her. His eyes serious, he leant in, his mouth towards hers.

Kate pulled away.

Luca stopped still, his eyes on hers, but she got up, pushing past him.

'*Signora*?'

Kate suddenly felt the weight of what she had to do and dropped back into her chair. No matter that it was the right thing, the best thing, the *only* thing, despite the pain it would cause him.

Luca walked – paced – in front of her, hands behind his back, eyes on the verandah boards. She knew him so well, his gait, his smile.

He stopped pacing and looked at her. 'I know, *Signora*. Your wedding – it is dead.'

She looked away, ashamed.

'I am sorry for this,' Luca said. Suddenly, he pulled the other wicker chair up close to hers and sat. He took her hands, their faces only inches apart. 'I am sorry, yes. But happy. For me.' Luca spoke intently, the roughness of his fingers firm around her hands.

Dear Luca. She extracted her hands gently and stood up.

But he kept speaking. 'I say you, *Signora* – Kate – I ask you.' He stopped and thought again. '*I* ask you. To marry. After. Soon.'

She shook her head, very slowly. She willed, willed, willed herself not to cry, and she shut her eyes to hold in the tears.

'You think on this?' Luca said with panic. He was watching her – she knew it.

She shook her head again. Then she spoke, hearing her voice sounding old. 'I'm not going to get married, Luca.'

'I wait.'

'It's not that.' Kate hated herself. She'd never imagined he would come back. She opened her eyes, the disloyal tears in check.

'It is me.' He looked stricken, as if he'd expected that she might say no. 'I have nothing. Not the land. But you?' He spread his arms and caught all of Amiens.

'No, no. It's not that. I just can't. I'm a bad wife.'

'Perhaps, to Jack.' He shrugged. Jack deserved it, he seemed to say.

She shook her head, sadness crushing her. 'I have responsibilities, duties to Daisy and to Pearl. I have to protect them.'

He looked at her, puzzled. She watched him wrestle with the realisation that she was serious. 'We've managed so far, you see? The Board has not been able to take Daisy or Pearl. But it will always be a struggle, especially if – when – Jack divorces me. They will argue I'm unqualified. Unfit.'

She looked down. In her heart, she didn't feel like a bad woman. But if everyone believes something, how is it not true?

'The local businesses too. Those men continue to deal with me, grudgingly. That will change after a divorce, let alone a remarriage. I'm a woman running a place on her own. That alone is not the done thing. I'll be punished, you see.'

He shrugged. 'I help this. Much help to you.'

'I know. You would. But I still can't marry you,' she said simply. 'Or anyone.' Those words then were a kind of weight off her.

Kate felt herself on the edge of a huge sea, as the ebb began and all of the power and strength that was Luca began to draw away from her. 'You think I'm a coward,' she said.

He waggled his head once, slowly, sadly. 'No, not *vigliacca, Signora*.'

'It might seem silly. But I have to look after Daisy and Pearl. It's a duty.' She was embarrassed to use the word to a former soldier.

Luca said nothing for a moment. 'There is other duty also. I know this,' he said softly. He took her hand and placed her palm flat on her sternum, and she felt her own heart beating hard within her chest. The heat of his fingers on her hand shot through her. 'Your duty to you.'

She shook her head and tears fell from her eyes. Then, finding strength, and with trembling fingers, she gently removed his hand.

Luca turned and looked out across the paddocks, not wanting her to see his devastation.

They stood for a long moment like that, each with their own grief.

Luca nodded. 'I go,' he said, his voice thick.

She could not speak for fear of breaking down. But she knew she was right.

Kate watched him walk away through glassy tears with the same terrible sense of loss she'd felt when he got on the POW train to leave the district at the end of the war. Then she'd truly believed she'd never see him again. And the pain burnt.

CHAPTER 7

It was written by those most observant of Englishmen, our earliest explorers, that frequent conflagrations were undertaken by the Aborigines, the smoke and cinders visible for many miles.

THE WOOLGROWER'S COMPANION, 1906

Kate pulled herself through the days by force of will. She knew that she'd had to reject Luca. She was convinced it was the right thing. But she'd think of him, and immediately of her loss. Their loss.

By the third day, Saturday, she felt something, a change in herself, like a snake sloughing off an old skin, doing what was necessary to survive. She got herself ready for the day's burning off, and accepted a cup of tea and some toast from Mrs Walters. But weariness lingered.

Kate usually liked to be about in the paddocks first thing, in the cool of an early morning. But not today, for some reason. She told herself it was just tiredness, as she walked in the paddock with the Amiens men around her. She was worried about what they had to do, worried that it would go wrong. At least she was ready: a scarf at her neck for the smoke, the fire-beater in her hand. The beater was a feeble thing, really, but better than nothing: a long shovel handle with a flat canvas flap attached, the canvas measuring a foot by a foot, a quarter of an inch thick.

Ed walked in front, carrying a metal fire torch as well as his beater. Harry, and the stockmen Robbo, Johnno and Spinksy, followed behind. Kate worked to keep up. She was almost woozy with tiredness.

Ahead of them all was a planned burn-off in Deadman's paddock. It ran parallel to the creek that divided Amiens from her difficult neighbour, John Fleming on Longhope Downs. A double hex of sorts, if Kate thought about how dry it was.

Ed stopped them at the edge of the flat by the creek, and they formed an odd semi-circle around him, ready for instructions.

'Youse look like cowboys,' Harry said, grinning at their faces, scarves round their necks, ready to be pulled up over mouth and nose when the fire was lit.

Ed brushed a fly away from his mouth. 'Once we light her, keep yer eyes on the fire. How high, where it's goin, what the wind's doin.' He spoke softly and they listened carefully.

'We burnin off up to the break at the creek line. We got the firebreak there now, that Robbo done with the grader blade. But watch it. If the wind gets up and the fire gets away, Flemin'll have our guts for garters.'

Kate was willing to risk this burning off today, a piece of the fire plan she and Ed followed. They burnt for pasture control but also to remove vegetation to provide a green flush with the seasonal rains. They burnt regularly, the frequency for a particular paddock or patch determined by the vegetation. Quick-growing grasses or ones with a high oil content – Ed knew these things – got burnt more frequently than, say, a bare paddock. Deadman's had few trees so got burnt less often. But it needed a burn now, especially as across the boundary on Fleming's Longhope Downs, the pasture was long and dead. A fire there would be well fuelled to come on to Amiens. Only Robbo's firebreak would stand between an oncoming fire and the rest of Kate's property. That and the burning off they'd already done.

This was the last burn though. They'd lay up then until there was rain.

'Keep in sight of each other? Mrs D with Harry, and so on.'

Harry frowned. He would not be coddled.

Ed squatted to unscrew the brass cap off the top of the drip-torch barrel. From inside the canister he levered out the wick, a thread about ten inches long and a quarter of an inch in diameter. With the top back on, he tipped the canister forward, away from the group, to spread a little fuel on the ground.

'Ya reckon it'll light?' Harry asked.

Ed smiled. 'Don't get none on your boots.'

Harry stepped back. 'Would it explode?'

'Pure petrol would. But she's a mix, mate. Three parts diesel to one o'petrol.'

Harry stored that away.

Ed pulled his scarf up over his mouth, and the others did the same. He put a lighter flame to the fuel-wet ground, and it went up with a *woof*. 'Right,' he said, and he moved off to the fence line, driptorch angled down, a low line of flame following him. But the men and Kate and Harry fanned out to track him, an emu parade a hundred or so yards apart, following the gentle crackle of dry grass shafts.

Kate, her scarf up, sent silent prayers into the still sky.

At first Ed's driptorch did little, the narrow line of fire behind him just visible against the pasture. But then it took, a sudden flame that went up along the torch path, and out from it. Kate stopped, checked. That thin red line was now a wall of flame, licking up into the sky. Soon Ed was just a shadow ahead of them, appearing and disappearing in billowing black smoke at the front of the flames. The sound changed then too; crackling, hissing, blowing, the fire eating its way across the paddock, gorging itself as it grew.

Kate looked for Harry through the smoke. He gave her a lazy wave. *It'll be all right.* Dear Harry. A curse on Grimes.

A sudden breeze fed the flames and the fire moved even faster across the paddock. For a moment, Kate panicked that it might get away. But it stayed on course, picking up speed until it reached the bare dirt where Robbo had 'dozed ahead of the burn. He'd gone back and forward with the grader, turning over the pasture to dirt and roots, depriving the flames of now-buried fuel.

Ed had planned well, for when the flames reached the empty soil, they were checked. The roar that had grown and grown across the paddock softened, as the fire sought something else to burn. But there was no more fuel and, slowly, the flames dropped and fell.

Harry and the stockmen waited well behind the blackened ground, watching the last of the flames. Soon, just spirals of smoke remained, here and there drifting off over the barren dirt.

They got to work then, using the fire-beaters to put out the last of the embers. Kate put her back into it, getting a sort of pleasure from giving the dirt a hiding. But it was heavy going, and the beaters threw up ash and dust. The scarf across Kate's face protected her mouth a little, but her eyes were exposed. She kept on; their work meant no spark could float off to catch elsewhere.

'Mrs D,' Ed called, pointing off to the other side of the creek. 'Here come the cavalry.' The Longhope Downs truck was making its way slowly cross-country, parallel to them. Mr Tonkin, the former manager now usurped by Grimes, was driving, one elbow resting lazily on the cab window.

The truck tray was packed; a full contingent of stockmen, rouseabouts and others, although, tellingly, neither Fleming himself nor Grimes was there. Still, Fleming was making a point. *Your fire's going to get away but we'll be ready.*

'Bloody idiot,' Harry said, matter of fact, beside Kate. She was just glad there was no Grimes.

'Truck's movin slow, eh,' he added.

'Pasture's long,' Ed explained. 'Ya can't see a rabbit hole in that lot.'

'They shoulda burnt off,' Harry said.

Ed held up an arm in greeting. Tonkin raised a slow hand in reply, but the truck didn't stop.

CHAPTER 8

A novel means of undertaking a routine matter or procedure is not to be disparaged out of hand by the prudent woolgrower. In this new age, men of science have made remarkable advances in arenas both new and old.

THE WOOLGROWER'S COMPANION, 1906

It was good for Kate to be in the quiet of the garden at the end of the day. Quiet was relative, though. The cicadas were still at it, even as the day ended. It needed to be seventy degrees or above before they'd sing. Kate dropped her knee mat on the lawn next to the fence and knelt. A noise right behind made her turn. Donald hopped quietly towards her from under the tank stand.

Harry had volunteered to raise him when Ed had appeared at the fence, the month before, with a very sad and sorry orphaned joey.

Kate and Daisy had each warned Harry that raising a wallaroo was like raising a baby: a lot of hard work. But he insisted he'd look after it. They'd been dubious but Donald, who seemed to have a knack for timing, chose that moment to stick his head out of the hessian sack that Ed had put him into, to keep him warm. Long ears and his black triangle of a nose pad were set off by large black eyes and generous eyelashes to match. All three of them, Kate, Daisy and Harry, had fallen for Donald at that moment. So he'd joined the household, although they regretted it from time to time. Donald would give you a good nip if you were late with his bottle.

The boys and Harry had rigged up a roo-door, so the little wallaroo could go in and out of the laundry during the day. A foot square of gauze on a plywood frame, hinged at the top, it was set about six inches off the floor to discourage snakes. Donald would nudge the flap open with his head, put his front paws inside, lean on them and lift his back legs through.

He was out of his pillowcase more and more, as he started to mature. He still liked to be off in the shade, out of sight during the day, unless there was a friendly soul about, doing something. In which case, Donald would be there to assist.

Kate smiled at the wallaroo. She was ridiculously fond of him. This was a treat, too. Usually, Donald was too canny to be near the fence in case one of the dogs was about. But the dogs were out in the run with the men today.

She leant forward to bang the garden gloves on the lawn, and let them lie there for a moment, to allow any spiders time to depart. Donald hopped in close and bent down to sniff at the gloves. She gently pushed the soft fur of his muzzle away.

As the gloves went on, Kate asked him, 'Are you going to be a problem, my friend? Will you go all manly on me and we'll have to turn you out?' He'd want to be off soon enough, to find a mate. It worried her, though. He might get taken by a fox, although hopefully he was too big now.

She set to work, weeding her way along the bed, ridding it of anything that might not be earning its keep – weeds and even native grasses. There was something about gardening, about being with her *treesanshrubs*, that calmed her.

She was so engrossed in her work she was startled when Ed appeared on the other side of the fence. 'Can I've a word, Mrs D?'

But he said nothing else so Kate spoke. 'Robbo settling down?'

Ed cocked his head to one side.

'I know you think I was mad to put him on. But where would he go if we didn't take him in?'

Ed shrugged. Perhaps he thought Robbo, son of a local grazier, was getting a second chance not offered to a bloke without that sort of pedigree.

But what was on Ed's mind? 'Will we be ready for shearing on the fifteenth?' she fished.

'Yup. The blokes are cleanin up the yards.'

Kate waited, giving him time.

'Harry says you're going to Sydney?' Ed said eventually.

'On the Wednesday train. We need to see his grandmother. Get her say-so, for the record, for Harry to stay here. Rather than go to Grimes.'

'Harry likes her,' Ed said. 'His granny.'

'She seems kind and sensible. I wrote to her, years ago, when Harry jumped off that train and came back to us.'

Ed smiled at the memory.

'When I wrote then, she was quite happy to have him stay here. So I think this is just a formality. But I want to ask her in person rather than by letter,' Kate said. 'In Sydney.'

'I come to talk t'ya bout Sydney. About the Board,' Ed said, sounding relieved to have an opening. 'Daisy's worried, eh.'

Kate didn't know what to say, but was glad to speak to someone with Daisy's interests at heart. 'I've never seen the Board in person. The Aborigines Welfare Board, I mean. I might see them in Sydney. Try to get them to let Pearl stay with Daisy.'

'They're never gunna do that, Mrs D.'

He was right. She was grasping at straws.

Ed faced her, serious. 'C'n I tell ya something?'

'Is anything wrong?'

'No.' His Adam's apple bobbed as he swallowed hard and

looked away. 'It's Daisy 'n' me. I wanna . . . We wanna . . . We wanna git . . .'

'Married? You want to get married?'

'Yeah.' Ed exhaled, glad to have it off his chest. 'Daisy'll be eighteen soon, real soon. So we could, then. Would you be all right with that, Mrs D?'

'All right? I'd be thrilled.' She smiled, resisting the urge to hug him. 'But you'd need—'

'The Board's approval for the wedding. Yeah.' Ed looked worried again.

'Wait. If she's married, Daisy might be able to keep Pearl . . . ?' Kate was catching up.

'Yeah. That's what we hopin.'

'But that'd be wonderful, Ed,' Kate said. 'They don't object to the girls marrying, if the man is reliable. I know that from before.'

She recalled her conversation with the matron at the Domestic Training Home for Aboriginal Girls in Longhope, when Daisy was first pregnant with Pearl. The matron had made clear that the Home's first aim was for Daisy to marry the 'responsible young man'. If he was white. Daisy had refused to say who the father was, and would not consider marrying him.

Kate felt the weight of guilt for what her father had done. But she knew that the Board, on paper, should be pleased with the idea of Ed marrying Daisy.

'Mrs D, there's another thing too. The Board still shifts em away sometimes. The girls. Outa the district – even when they're married.'

'Really?' As she thought about it, Kate wasn't surprised. Policy came before everything.

'But, see, there's a paper they can give now. The Board. A certificate of exemption.'

'Exemption from what?'

'From the laws for Abos. If she had this certificate, the Board couldn't move her about.'

'Heavens.' Be free of the Board? Kate had never heard of such a thing.

'It's pretty new, this certificate business, apparently. But the Board gotta say yes. To the weddin and to the certificate.' Ed swallowed, their future rolled up in forms and unsympathetic administration hundreds of miles away in Sydney.

'You're a good man with a stable job. If they won't say yes to Daisy marrying you, who on earth would they approve of?'

He smiled, embarrassed. 'Daisy's gotta show stuff too. To get the certificate. That she's a good girl. Reliable. Doesn't touch the grog.'

'I can vouch for you both. I'll go ahead and see the Board when I'm in Sydney. Sound them out about the wedding and the certificate thing.'

'Thanks, Mrs D.' Ed exhaled. It must have been preying on his mind for a while.

'If Daisy is released by the Board, they should pay all her wages to her.'

'Ya reckon it's wise t'go down that road again, Mrs D?'

He was being tactful, but he was right to be wary. Kate still smarted over the mistake she had made just a few months before. It was all over wages. Employers had to pay all wages to the Board. And the girls, like Daisy, had to apply to the Board for any money and convince them it was for a proper purpose. But spending money on a coat and a pair of shoes (to replace both, which were worn out) was not considered proper.

Out of the blue, Daisy had received a letter from the Board confirming that it held money for her. The gossip was that a new Aboriginal Board member had forced the Board to write, to acknowledge that it had all this money for the Aboriginal people who'd earned it.

When she saw the letter, Kate had decided to pay the wages direct to Daisy. She wrote cordially to the Board to let them know and received an immediate reply. The Board blamed Daisy for what they saw as an outrageous challenge to their authority from an Aboriginal girl. They crisply instructed Kate to continue to pay direct to the Board all of Daisy's wages. Worst of all, the Board now saw Daisy as a troublemaker. So they'd stepped up their attempts to force her to give up her daughter. Kate bitterly regretted drawing their attention.

'You're right, Ed. I won't mention wages.'

Donald had slowly built up the courage to come out from under the tank stand, and he hopped back across the lawn, to Kate at the fence. Ed squatted and put his fingers through the wire netting. The wallaroo leant on his paws and moved one hop in, to sniff the fingertips held out for him. 'He's grown, eh?' Ed said.

Kate nodded. 'Also, you won't burn off till we get more rain, will you?'

'Nuh. Too dry now.'

'Good. If a fire got away while I was in Sydney, there'd be hell to pay.'

'There be hell to pay even if ya here, Mrs D.'

Ed stood up and, with a wave and a smile, headed towards the workmen's cottages. Kate felt a weight lifted. Ed just might have solved the fearful problem: of losing Daisy and her darling Pearl, of the separation of mother from child.

Kate's relief was punctured when she heard the phone ringing. Since her father's death and her claiming Pearl as her sister, no one rang just to chat. She ran inside to catch it.

'Mrs Dowd? This is Mr Prior. Of Philbeach and Trout Solicitors.'

Solicitors?

'Mrs Dowd? Mrs Katherine Dowd?'

Jack. He must be going to divorce me.

'Mrs Dowd? Are you there?'

'Yes.' Her voice sounded strangled. What would this man say? On the party line?

'Might I arrange an appointment with you at Amiens? A routine matter, Mrs Dowd. I promise I won't take up much of your time.'

'Yes,' she said, her voice still thick.

'Tuesday? This Tuesday the ninth? Nine in the morning?'

'Yes,' she said, unable to say anything else.

Tuesday was the day before she would take the train to Sydney. She was almost glad. To have to wait until after her trip would have been painful. She'd pushed a divorce out of her mind these past three years, out of sheer force of will, hoping, stupidly, that Jack might never do it. Now, it seemed, it was coming.

CHAPTER 9

A woolgrower, engaged in the careful improvement of his lines, must consider that some priority within a flock shall be established. Certain animals shall always endeavour to impose their will on their brethren.

THE WOOLGROWER'S COMPANION, 1906

The days that followed seemed to pass slowly, although Kate was busy preparing to go to Sydney. But she carried her sadness about Luca with her, and her worry about the solicitor's impending visit.

She was unsure why the man might need to see her; she imagined divorce matters were done in court. But then she had no idea, really. Kate knew no one, not a soul, who was divorced, not in the town of Longhope itself and not even in the wider district. The shame of it ate away at her as the solicitor's visit drew nearer. More scandal from Amiens. Yet she felt something else, too. Relief. At last this burden of uncertainty might be lifted, albeit at a terrible price.

Early on the morning of Mr Prior's visit, Kate dressed carefully, as if she were meeting the bank manager: neat but not too prosperous, well-tended but not fashionable. She'd use the same firm manner on him too. That was her plan.

Mrs Walters had the kettle on, the tray of tea things prepared, when they heard a car coming up out of the gully just before nine.

Kate went to stand on the verandah, trying to quiet her nerves. *I can survive this shame. I can.* But the butterflies in her stomach fluttered in panic.

The suited man who same up the stairs was both very short and very young – younger than Kate. He was taking pains, she noticed, to grow a pale moustache. He would not meet her eye when she shook his hand, cool and damp in her own, and she felt an unexpected rush of pity for him. That would prove to be misplaced.

Mrs Walters stood at the kitchen door, at the ready.

'Tea, Mr Prior?' Kate offered.

'No, thank you.' He cleared his throat. 'Tea doesn't agree with me. An allergy.'

'Really?'

Mr Prior blushed then, and she felt guilty. It occurred to her that he had still not looked her in the eye. An odd fish indeed.

They sat, Kate still half a head taller than this Mr Prior who was allergic to tea. She began to feel better.

'I come on behalf of my client, your husband, Mr Jack Dowd.' He produced some half-glasses from a pocket of his suit and perched them on his nose. Mouse-like. He was mouse-like. 'I begin by conveying my condolences.' He spoke almost mechanically as he opened a large ledger-style notebook.

'Thank you,' Kate said, off-kilter. 'But my father has been dead some time now.'

The mouse turned puce. 'I'm so sorry, Mrs Dowd,' he said, clearing his throat again. 'I was referring, in my condolences, to the untimely demise of your relations with, and marriage to, my client, Mr Jack Dowd.'

It was Kate's turn to colour.

'Mrs Dowd, I must tell you that you have a right to have your own solicitor present, and that in continuing, you waive that right.'

Kate felt a chill, and immediately she was on guard, suddenly realising that without her own solicitor she was at a disadvantage in meeting with Jack's.

'I will record that at this moment, before we begin.' He smiled briefly, without warmth and without looking at her, and wrote in his notebook. His eyes on the ledger, he spoke again. 'I am to convey to you that Mr Dowd wishes to commence divorce proceedings.'

Kate nodded and looked down. She'd guessed it was coming but reacted just the same. She felt her face flush again.

'I will propose some steps and then request that you kindly consider them. We ask that you notify us by the end of this month, the thirtieth of November, so that we may proceed. This gives you a full twenty-one days, Mrs Dowd.' He wrote again, then flicked his eyes past her, only for an instant. 'Do you know the procedure for a divorce, Mrs Dowd?'

She tried to speak. When words would not come out, she shook her head.

'Ordinarily in these circumstances a petition is got up. One party to the marriage is called the applicant and the other, the respondent. The petitioner instigates – begins – the divorce. As a courtesy, the gentleman is willing, in appropriate circumstances, for the lady to act as petitioner.'

Kate nodded, not really understanding.

'There are no children in this case, so that makes the dissolution of the marriage somewhat more straightforward.'

That she understood, and even after all that had gone on between them, she felt the familiar sense of defeat at having failed to bear a child for Jack.

'Where there are no children, a court will grant a divorce if certain circumstances are met: fault must be established,

Mrs Dowd. The fault of one party, namely infidelity, mental cruelty and abandonment.'

Kate willed herself to remain calm.

'The least worrisome, from a publicity perspective, is usually abandonment. Also, it is the simplest to provide the necessary proof that the court requires.' He glanced for a millisecond at Kate.

She nodded, sure that the horror she was feeling must be written across her face.

'If abandonment were to be adopted as the appropriate grounds, the court would require an affidavit from your good self, and one from Mr Dowd, as to those circumstances. Such divorce petitions typically go through with a minimum of fuss. The newspapers are uninterested in the mundane sadnesses of others.'

Mundane sadnesses. The shame of divorce would never be mundane to her. Kate would be crushed when it happened. It appalled her that there might be a report of the divorce in the *Longhope Clarion.*

'I hope you won't find it too painful. Duty requires me to enquire as to the circumstances of abandonment.' Kate stared at her hands in her lap. 'As I understand it, Mr Dowd was demobilised in December 1945, and he returned from Kogarah Camp in Sydney to Amiens for a period of four days. Is that your recollection, Mrs Dowd?'

Kate nodded.

'I understand Mr Dowd had already by that date obtained a position in the Islands, on Bougainville, as a plantation manager for Burns Philp.'

'Yes.' She could hardly hear her own voice, pulled back to the awfulness of those few short terrible days; Jack insisting she sell Amiens and go with him, and his slow realisation that she would never leave the property, nor Daisy and Pearl.

'I also understand that you refused your husband's lawful instruction that you accompany him to Bougainville?'

Lawful instruction?

'Mrs Dowd?'

'Yes. I wanted to . . . This place.' She gestured weakly at the hills of Amiens. The farm gave her the ability to keep Daisy and Pearl.

'You are attached to your property, Mrs Dowd.'

'My father made this place. All of this. He was a soldier-settler, yet he built Amiens into the largest holding in the district, and from nothing.' She realised she was going on. Perhaps it was her shock. That Jack would do it, that he would divorce her.

Mr Prior removed his glasses. With a bright white handkerchief, he methodically polished one half-moon, then the next. 'I understand your father bred fine Merinos. You must be proud.'

'Proud? No.' There was so much of which to be ashamed. Now there would be more.

The solicitor cleared his throat again. 'To conclude, after filing of the petition and the evidentiary affidavits, the court sits and considers the case. Assuming all is in order, a decree nisi will be granted, ending the marriage.'

'I see,' Kate said, although she didn't. Not really. 'Will you prepare the paperwork?'

Mr Prior looked perplexed. 'The paperwork?'

'The form you mentioned. The . . . petition?'

'No, no, Mrs Dowd. Your solicitor will do that. You need to appoint one as soon as possible.'

That would be expensive. She cursed Jack.

Mr Prior continued. 'In any event, Mr Dowd will allow you to take the role of petitioner. If certain requirements are met.'

Kate's heart stopped. Jack wanted something.

'Mr Dowd is starting afresh in the Islands. For that he must have capital.'

Money. That was it. He wanted money. She could not believe it.

'You are a woman of means, Mrs Dowd. Significant means.' Mr Prior waved a hand at Amiens's many acres and its fine Merinos. Kate braced herself.

'Mr Dowd is not an unreasonable man. He requires ten thousand pounds.'

CHAPTER 10

The woolgrower may take comfort from the sheep's natural avoidance of snakes in the paddock. Much, however, of this advantage is obviated when stock are forced into yards by dogs. Whilst sheep will trample any unfortunate snake therein, they may be bitten in the process.

THE WOOLGROWER'S COMPANION, 1906

'Ten *thousand* pounds?' Kate gasped.

'Amiens is worth five times that, at least, Mrs Dowd. So, a small amount, relative to what you enjoy.'

'How will I possibly find that sort of money? We are mortgaged, Mr Prior. Heavily.' That wasn't strictly true, as Kate had paid off some of the mortgage – but Jack wasn't to know that. Regardless, it would be difficult to get all this money.

The solicitor cleared his throat again. 'My client is confident the amount is more than well within your means, Mrs Dowd.'

'His confidence and my circumstances are quite different things,' Kate said. Fleetingly, it occurred to her that Jack was not allowed to do this. She rejected that thought. This solicitor would only ask her if it was legal, surely?

Mr Prior went on smoothly. 'I understand there is an undrawn overdraft of which you could avail yourself.'

Bloody Jack. He knew she'd just managed to repay the

overdraft her father had so quickly and dangerously exhausted before he died.

'The bank manager will never allow me to borrow. Not for this.' And Addison would never permit her to use the equity she'd built up in Amiens for anything but the purest business purposes, and possibly not even then.

'Perhaps you underestimate your bank manager, Mrs Dowd.'

She shook her head. 'Sadly not.'

Mr Prior stared out at the Amiens paddocks. 'It would be best to remember, Mrs Dowd, that in return my client is willing to allow *you* to act as petitioner.'

Kate didn't completely understand. She knew she was being threatened, but how?

There was more throat-clearing. 'If agreement can't be reached on this amount, Mr Dowd must proceed as petitioner himself. On other grounds, of course. Rather than abandonment.'

She still didn't see. 'What other grounds?'

'Adultery, Mrs Dowd.'

Why would Jack, to whom his name meant everything, be willing to blacken it? Then Kate gasped as the truth hit her. 'You mean *me*? *I* would be the adulterer?'

Mr Prior nodded. 'It is somewhat indelicate, but I must point out that the other party to the adultery is routinely named in the court documents.'

Sick to her stomach, Kate could not speak. Jack would blackmail her. If she refused to pay him, then her affair with Luca would come out.

Mr Prior went on, to be completely sure she understood. 'Mr Cannally would be identified publicly as the other party to the infidelity. The co-respondent.'

'Canali.' The name was barely audible. 'It's pronounced Can-*nah*-li.' She found her voice then. 'You have no proof of this. It would be Jack's word against mine.'

'On the contrary, Mrs Dowd. We have a fine witness, a man in an excellent position to observe the immoderate *conduct*' – he said the word with a hint of distaste – 'over a long period.'

Kate made a guess, and she was right.

'Your former manager, Mrs Dowd. Mr Keith Grimes.'

The solicitor reminded Kate 'to appoint her own representation', and to have him respond by the end of the month. Then he left.

CHAPTER 11

It is to the greatest good fortune that Australia hosts that most bountiful of sheep, the Merino. The woolgrower, then, is first among men who must fulfil his duty to his country and the Empire, in protecting and improving upon such a munificent animal.

THE WOOLGROWER'S COMPANION, 1906

'Is Luna Park the goods, Mrs D?' Harry was shifting about, unable to sit still even in the back seat of the Amiens car. He tugged at the unfamiliar tie at his neck – a small price to get to Sydney and the amusement park.

Ed was silent as ever as he drove them in to catch the train. A sleepless night had left Kate dreading the long trip ahead, and Harry's chatter wasn't helping.

'Will you be long? At Fleming's?' He was dead keen to get on the train.

'No. And I've got to go to the service station too, after Fleming,' Kate said. She spoke softly. Yesterday's visit from Jack's solicitor had left her wounded. Now she had to handle Fleming.

Harry knew the grazier was difficult. 'Gotta gird ya loins, Mrs D? For Fleming,' he said. 'Do girls have loins?'

Kate played a straight bat and replied as if it were a serious question. 'I believe so. Pork loins come from sows as well as boars and barrows.' Best to get Harry off the topic of nether regions.

'How d'ya gird em? Tie the dangly bits up? That'd be boys only?'

Kate rolled her eyes. 'Have you ever been to Sydney, Ed?' She was keen to change the subject.

'Me? No, Mrs D. Never.' Ed was smiling, possibly about the loins. But he'd been smiling a lot these past few days. Daisy seemed happy too. Now Kate just had to get the Board onside.

'Ya reckon I can go on all three?' Harry asked.

Kate wasn't really listening. Grimes. Jack. Daisy. Luca. Fleming. She felt she had a full plate.

'*Can* I go on all three rides, Mrs D?' Thankfully, Harry was off loins and back on Luna Park.

'We're really going to Sydney to see your grandmother, Harry. Luna Park is a sideshow.'

'Oh yes it is!' Harry almost shouted with excitement. 'Best sideshow out there, I hear.'

Kate shook her head. She was concerned about what she'd say to the old lady regarding Jack. She couldn't imagine how she'd put it. *My husband has left me.* But then, what if Mrs Grimes already knew? It would look bad for Kate not to say anything.

She remembered something then. Her mother had given her some cryptic advice just before Kate got married. *Hold your ground at the start, dear, and a good deal more. If you accommodate then, you're lost. Later? Perhaps.*

Kate had not really understood at the time, especially as her mother was normally a firm believer in a lady's place being in the homestead. But she thought she did now. Kate had given in to Jack from the start, deferring to him on all things when they were courting and then after they were married. He probably had no idea that she had a will of iron. But then she didn't know that either when she married him, just as she had no idea that he could be cruel.

Harry brought her back to the present. 'So I can go on all of em? The rides?'

'What?'

'Luna Park.'

'Harry.' Kate frowned. She gave up on thinking about Mrs Grimes. 'All three rides? No. They'll be expensive. We have a long time on the train first,' she said, as they drove on. She shifted her thoughts to John Fleming, and whether today he might give her the cheque. Why was he being difficult? He wasn't short of money.

'How long d'ya reckon each ride'll go for, Ed? Half an hour, mebbe?'

Ed gave the question consideration. 'Half an hour? That's a good bit of fuel, mate. I reckon it'd be short. Like a ride on that poor Shetland at the show.'

'Struth,' Harry said in disgust. The Shetland came with the travelling attractions attached to the annual agricultural show. The pony was thin and bad-tempered, avoided by any self-respecting bushman on account of its poor condition.

'We're almost there,' Kate said.

'Pretty grand, eh? Fleming's,' Harry said. He was looking at the expensive fencing along the road.

'Mrs D's got more dirt than this bloke, mate,' Ed said mildly. 'By a long shot.'

Kate smiled at his pride. Ed was right, though. Amiens was just over thirty thousand acres and Longhope Downs closer to twenty thousand. Her father had actually disliked the Flemings, on principle. John Fleming had inherited his place, while Ralph Stimson had built his up, acre by acre. For the same reason, her father respected the Rileys. A bit younger than him, they'd made what they had, not inherited it. That, and the fact that Mrs Riley would talk to anyone, from Kate's mother to the Aboriginal ladies at the reserve, where she was helping them start a Country

Women's Association group. She helped the CWA do a lot of good in the district.

Ed steered the big Humber off the main road onto Fleming land.

'That's quite a gate.' Harry turned as they went through. The gateposts were stacked stone; the only stone walls in the district, to Kate's knowledge. From one hung a large sign – glossy black lettering on crisp white – announcing *Longhope Downs* in Old English font.

Ahead of them, the long straight road that led up to the homestead was lined with poplars. It struck Kate that her mother, always wanting to be respectable, may have copied this avenue of trees on Amiens. As they sped by, Kate felt a rush of sympathy. Her mother had lived her life fraught with feelings of not being as worthy as 'the good families' like the Flemings. For a time, she'd managed to elevate Kate to be accepted. Elizabeth Fleming had even invited Kate to tea when Kate was a newlywed, pointedly inviting only her. But her mother had been thrilled, not slighted. Later, even ill as she was, Kate's mother had died with the satisfaction that her only daughter was *someone* in the district.

Kate exhaled, remembering. It was not so long after that her father had died and Kate had claimed Pearl as a sister. Everything changed then, and Kate was back where her mother had started, disowned by all of the good families – apart from the Rileys, bless them. Kate had not been invited to Longhope Downs since. That was quite all right, she told herself, and meant it.

The view pulled her away from her thoughts. As they went over a small rise, the Longhope Downs homestead stood to attention in front of them. Kate had forgotten it was quite so beautiful: a low central building with a short wing angled off on each side, like arms open in welcome.

Harry was wide-eyed. 'It's like *Gone with the* bloody *Wind*.'

'It's only a house, mate,' Ed said. 'It'd burn like any other.'

CHAPTER 12

A ram of fine outward appearance, full in wool and excellent lineage, may yet hide ill temper or weak shoulders.

THE WOOLGROWER'S COMPANION, 1906

John Fleming came out onto the verandah to the top of the steps. At least ten years older than Kate and a tall man, tending to bald, he had quite pronounced front teeth. He was kitted out like the well-to-do grazier he was: trousers the colour of stone, plaited kangaroo-leather belt, blue countryman shirt, double-pocketed, with R. M. Williams riding boots. Her father had worn the same uniform.

Ed got the door for Kate, which she thought unnecessary. He gave her a nod.

'I'll wait here, Mrs Dowd,' he said. Kate noticed too that Ed used *Dowd* rather than his usual *Mrs D*, giving her respect in front of this man. In case Fleming was tempted not to do the same.

'Mrs Dowd.' John Fleming's voice was even, commanding, almost melodious. Generations of money and private schools will do that.

They sat on the verandah, off to one side of the wide homestead entrance. The chairs were of woven rattan, with expensive cushions that had to be Sanderson chintz. Kate guessed that

Elizabeth had chosen the pattern. She was a Sydney girl. More expensive school fees.

'I hope Elizabeth is well?' Kate asked.

'Yes. She's sorry to miss you. At bridge.'

Kate didn't play bridge. It was one thing her mother hadn't been able to teach her.

There was no offer of tea from Fleming and Kate was sorry, only because she'd have no chance to refuse it. 'The wethers are settled in?' she asked.

'I haven't heard they're not.' He smiled.

'I'm pleased. So I hope it's not too indelicate to ask for payment.'

Fleming laughed, teeth on display. 'You do get straight to the point, Mrs Dowd.'

Kate wished he would as well. Instead he looked out across his land.

'Thank you for coming. I wanted a word, you see.'

She waited. Where was her cheque?

'We're fortunate that we've had a run of good seasons here on Longhope Downs,' Fleming said, managing to imply that his skill had produced the rains. 'With careful husbandry of the land . . .'

Was that deliberate? Kate, effectively husbandless, felt the heat in her face. *Get a grip*, she told herself.

'Your family is newer to the district –'

I was born here, she thought but did not say. He was hinting, with disapproval, at the fact that Kate's father was a soldier-settler.

'– but you'll know Longhope Downs has a long history of good management. Over many generations. Good husbandry is essential everywhere, Mrs Dowd.'

He'd said it again. John Fleming, Kate decided, was a ratbag. But she needed her cheque.

'I don't mean in the sense of stocking rates. We'll agree to disagree on that.'

She forced a smile. Now he was on about the fact that Kate carried less stock per acre than some others. Than him, specifically. But too many stock destroyed the pasture. She resisted the urge to tell him that good graziers loved their land and looked after it.

'A number of the graziers in the district have spoken to me about something. Asked me to lead, as it were. When I see a neighbour in trouble, it's my duty to help.'

'But we're not in any trouble,' she said with surprise.

He shook his head slowly and exhaled. 'There's two things, Mrs Dowd. First, the burning off in such dry conditions. We both back onto the State Forest. That would burn if one of your fires got away. You're risking livelihoods, not just your own but others' too.'

Kate fought to keep her voice measured. 'Our burning is always well controlled. We all know burning off will save us from a big fire. It's much what other graziers do.'

'No, Mrs Dowd, you don't have their expertise. That's the difference. I've been a grazier all my life, my father and grandfather before me.' He spoke kindly. Slowly. 'I tell you this from my experience and theirs. You must stop immediately.'

'We have stopped.' It was true. Albeit recently.

He raised an eyebrow, reminding Kate of the cowboy baddie in Harry's comic.

'There's something else, Mrs Dowd. I'm hearing there's been repeated damage to the fencing on our boundary. The boundary between Longhope Downs and Amiens.'

'The men check our fences. I'm sure your men do too.'

Fleming laughed, teeth exposed, and he shook his head. 'Your men do as they please, Mrs Dowd. That's what I hear.'

Kate's set mouth should have told him she was angry.

He didn't seem to notice. 'I can afford to lose a few sheep through downed fences. But it's the principle of the thing. If you don't have a firm hand on your men on Amiens,

Mrs Dowd, this is what happens.' He stood up. The conversation was over.

She could see Ed at the car, talking to Harry, keeping a close eye on her. 'My cheque,' she said, her voice strangled.

'I'm going to hold on to it for now. Help you understand the seriousness. If there's no burning off until, say, the end of the month, you can come and get it. Have a cup of tea with Elizabeth then, and pick up your cheque.'

'You can't do that!' Kate was aghast.

'I'm doing it for your own good. Someone has to help you learn, Mrs Dowd. Safe trip to Sydney, now.' Fleming went into the house and left Kate open-mouthed on the verandah.

CHAPTER 13

The stewing of mutton may effect a pleasant change on this weak meat. The cut dissolves into a soft mass when subjected to heat by a sustained simmering.

THE WOOLGROWER'S COMPANION, 1906

'He could eat an apple through a tennis racquet, with those teeth.' Harry greeted Kate at the car. 'Where's the cheque?'

She got in. It took her a moment to speak. 'Fleming wouldn't give it to me. He will, but only if we don't burn off till the end of the month.'

'Struth,' Ed said, as he steered the Humber back out along the straight track to the big gates and the main road.

'But it's our money,' Harry said, outraged.

Kate nodded. She'd been snookered. *Get the cash on the nose*, her father had always said. It was the first time she'd done business with Fleming.

Ed shook his head sympathetically. Kate knew the same rules didn't apply to her as to other graziers, to the men. If she did anything that was disapproved of, the town felt, without exception, that she needed to be taught a lesson, as if she were a child.

The rest of the trip into town passed in silence, with even Harry unusually quiet.

'You want me to come in?' Ed asked, as she climbed out of the car at Hayward's. He was on alert, aware she might have trouble anywhere today, now that Fleming had held back the cheque.

'No. I won't be long,' she said. The service station was the best in the district. George Hayward was a natural with engines. And he was no trouble.

Kate went into the small fibro office at the back of the shed, behind the pumps. Hayward was on the phone, although he was having difficulty getting a word in.

'We ordered em . . .' He trailed off. 'I'm tellin ya, they sent the wrong part. I rung em up Saturday. Rung em up, John. A trunk call. No, you won't be payin . . .'

The voice on the other end of the line wasn't mollified, and Kate wondered if the ladies on the telephone exchange were getting the full story.

'Look, you're a good customer, John. Longhope Downs's been with us since Dad started up.'

George Hayward was talking to John Fleming; an annoyed John Fleming by all accounts.

It was then that Hayward noticed Kate, and rolled his eyes. He wasn't getting het up, even if Fleming was.

'The spark plugs'll be up on today's train. We'll put em in for ya straight away. Soon as ya pay ya bill. John? John?' Fleming must have hung up, because Hayward pulled the receiver away from his ear and looked at it. He set it back on the cradle and smiled thinly. 'Kate, you gunna chew me ear too?'

She smiled. She'd been at school with George and he was all right.

'Bloody Fleming's takin a piece outa m'hide. Sydney sent me the wrong parts. All that's holdin the bloody Longhope Downs truck t'gether is fencin wire, I reckon. Now it's the electrics givin him trouble.' He shook his head. 'Anyhow, what can I do f'ya?'

'I have your cheque.' She always budgeted with care and made sure to pay the essential people early.

'Always happy to take y'money.' He smiled back, looking at it. He compared the figure on the cheque carefully against the invoice.

'All up to date now,' Kate said. 'I'm going on the train today. To Sydney.'

'Let's hope the buggers send up the right spark plugs, otherwise I might hafta come with ya.'

Kate went on her way to the car, to the station and to Sydney – to see Harry's grandmother, and to the Aborigines Welfare Board. She wished she knew how to gird her loins.

CHAPTER 14

Honesty and sobriety be the boots in which the very great responsibility which attaches to the position of woolgrower may be borne without disfiguring his reputation.

THE WOOLGROWER'S COMPANION, 1906

Kate was still a bit weary from the long train trip the day before, and an unsettled night at the Country Women's hostel. The last time she stayed there, during the war, it was American servicemen carousing in the early hours that had kept her awake, the exotic accent floating up from the street. But perhaps Potts Point was always lively, because again, the noise of patrons after closing, of empty kegs and rubbish trucks, had disturbed her sleep. Not so Harry, who slept through everything. He, as ever, was full of beans, excited to be in Sydney with its bright blue harbour and promise of Luna Park fun. He flicked a yo-yo backwards and forwards across the aisle of the bus, which luckily was almost empty.

'Can we go to Luna Park this arvo?'

'We'll see,' Kate said by reflex. Outside, the Northern Beaches suburbs ran lazily down the hill from Pittwater Road to the Pacific. 'I don't know how long it will take to see your grandma at the home.'

'Is it a home like in Longhope? That dump Dais was stuck in?'

'No, no. This is a nice place. It's a home for returned servicemen.'

'Gran weren't a soldier.' Harry was bored, his yo-yo flicking perilously close to the seat in front.

'Her husband was. It's a home for widows too, clever clogs.'

The bus came to a halt with a squeak of brakes, and the driver called out to Kate, 'This is your stop, love. Ocean Street. For the RSL home.'

Harry went on yo-yoing while getting off the bus. Kate was half annoyed and half pleased. It kept him occupied.

'So where is it, then?'

'There, for sure.' Kate pointed. Up the hill sat a squat brick building with tall Norfolk Island pine trees in front, and an Australian flag flying on a shiny pole at half-mast. White cockatoos screeched and wheeled around the pines.

'Why's the flag not up?' Harry asked.

'Armistice Day. It's the eleventh today.'

'It's Remembrance Day, now. Not Armistice Day.' He nudged her in the ribs, momentarily forgetting his yo-yo. 'They won't have to change it again, will they?'

'What do you mean?'

'When there's another war, Remembrance Day'll still be all right as a name for the day.'

Another war. It was unthinkable.

They reached the threshold of the home. 'Now, very best behaviour, Harry. Promise me?' Kate said.

'She's my nan. You're the one who's gotta impress.' He winked at her.

Kate only just persuaded Harry to stop flicking the yo-yo at the building's entrance. A nurse took them right through and out the other side, onto a verandah overlooking Narrabeen beach. The home had a breathtaking view: a Wedgwood Blue sea, with a broad swathe of bright sand. More Norfolk Island pines lined the esplanade, reaching high into the air, above all the other trees and houses.

At the far end of the verandah, a small woman sat quite erect on a bench facing the sea, a walking stick in her hands, and a dillybag on the floor near her feet. Birds screeched nearby.

'Visitors, Mrs Grimes.' The nurse left them with a wave.

'So good of you to come all this way.' Mrs Grimes smiled at Kate and her grandson. She was petite, probably even smaller than she'd been as a young woman, with very white hair cut bluntly at her chin, and skin mottled and stained with blotches from decades of sun.

She was rather frail, shifting herself with difficulty on the bench. 'You're so tall, Harry, dear. Come here,' Mrs Grimes said softly. 'Let me kiss you.'

Kate held her breath. Harry did as he was told, and the old lady pecked him lightly on the cheek. It couldn't have been too much of an ordeal because he smiled and plonked himself on the ground next to her, like a puppy. She smiled backwards and forwards between Kate and Harry.

'Ya usin a stick now?'

The old lady gave a sort of resigned shrug, not unhappy. 'It helps. Now, somewhere I have a present for you, Harry, dear.' She struggled to reach into the dillybag so Kate passed it to her.

Mrs Grimes produced a parcel wrapped in brown paper, and delivered it with shaking hands. Harry was up on his feet at once, keen to get into it. 'So that Mrs Dowd and I may speak, perhaps you could open it there.' His grandmother pointed to another bench, this one on the far side of the lawn. Harry took the present and was off.

'It's not an easy thing, to decide between you and my brother-in-law. I thought you might tell me a little more about yourself, dear,' she said to Kate.

Kate was surprised, and hoped she covered it well. Mrs Grimes must know a lot from the letters that Harry wrote to her each month. Kate had to stand over him to get him to write them. She cleared her throat and began. 'Of course. Well, I like looking after Harry. He's a lovely boy and we're very happy to have him grow up on Amiens.' Kate felt her face become warm after the *we*. She had to tell Mrs Grimes that Jack had left. He'd lived away so long, there'd need to be a lie in there somewhere.

'I do so enjoy Harry's letters, Mrs Dowd.' The old lady watched the boy across the lawn. 'Although they're rather brief.'

That gentle criticism landed on Kate but she said nothing. She would do nothing, either. Getting Harry to write at all was already a Herculean task.

'And his spelling . . .' Mrs Grimes shook her head sadly.

Kate bit her lip, then. That, she could have helped with. She tried to check every letter – it was only once a month, for heaven's sake – but sometimes there was just too much on. She'd never thought she might have to beg Mrs Grimes to let Harry stay on Amiens. For the first time, she felt a chill, a worry, that the old lady might say no.

'I must say, Mrs Dowd, that Harry seems very happy with you.'

Relief flooded through Kate. 'I think so. He's doing well at school now.' *After Grimes left.* She should have said so, but that might be laying it on too thick. 'His spelling needs a bit of polish.'

Mrs Grimes started to ask questions about Amiens. How many sheep did it carry? Did Harry really ride to school? Was that common? How many children attended his school? This was all easy, and Kate threw in a mention of Harry whenever she could – how much he loved the land and how he was learning so much.

There was a pause finally, the old lady no doubt thinking through all she'd heard.

'I love Harry as if he were mine,' Kate said. Then she stopped. She should have said *we*.

'I can see that, dear. I know that you both, you and my brother-in-law, want what's best for Harry.'

Kate said nothing.

'I'm glad to have spoken with you at last, dear. I'm grateful, you know. For what you do. It's remarkable for a young person to take on a boy like Harry.'

Suddenly, Harry himself was back, beaming, holding out the largest hand catapult Kate had ever seen.

Mrs Grimes nodded at him. 'Harry, dear, there's one condition attached to that catapult: lizards and snakes? They're fair game. But no birds or possums and whatnot. Promise?'

Harry's face clouded. 'All right.'

'Can I show you both something?' Mrs Grimes asked, struggling to her feet. They helped her across the short lawn, back to the verandah to a fernery enclosure at the far end. The screeching told the real story: the structure was for birds, not people.

Mrs Grimes's face lit up as they made their way into the fernery, hung with potted plants and large birdcages, a white cockatoo in each. 'One of the servicemen started it, years ago, apparently. Now we have nine birds,' she said proudly.

Harry moved up close to one cage, putting a finger to the cockatoo bobbing up and down on its perch.

'Careful, dear. He'll give a nasty bite.'

The cage floors were lined with newspaper to catch the droppings, and a piece of cuttlefish was wired to the side.

Kate smiled politely but felt sad for the caged birds. Their free brethren were looping and screeching in earshot and eyeshot between the Norfolk Island pines along the beach.

'Thank you for coming, my dears.' The old lady kissed both of them as they left, and Kate felt the weight of that worry, at least, lift off her. It had gone very well.

'I'll write soon,' Mrs Grimes promised.

CHAPTER 15

This writer is unfortunately compelled to warn a prudent woolgrower that the qualification as a man of exceptional and strong opinion does not of itself alone render such opinion of value.

THE WOOLGROWER'S COMPANION, 1906

They took a ferry that afternoon, the *Lady Denman*, from Circular Quay across the short stretch of water to Milsons Point on the lower north shore: to Luna Park.

'Lady Denman's a lucky old bird.' Harry's wide eyes took in the two decks, the central funnel and the smart paintwork. 'Imagine ownin y'own boat?'

'It's not hers—' Kate started, but Harry had gone. He'd never been on a boat before and was zipping backwards and forwards, from bow to stern, not wanting to miss a single fishing seagull or the wake of a passing boat. As soon as the *Lady Denman* took her long elegant self under the towering Harbour Bridge, Harry was ready for land. It was all Kate could do to keep him from jumping to the pier as the ferry docked.

Luna Park had opened just before the war in 1935, but Kate had never been. It was quite, quite famous, and Kate felt a rush of happiness for Harry as he pointed up with excitement. 'Look, look, Mrs D! That's a big head! An the mouth? We gunna walk right into it!'

That mouth and Luna Park did not come cheap. Kate took a deep breath and paid their entry fees: a shilling for her, half that for Harry. Special treat, she kept telling herself, a once in a blue moon sort of thing.

'Mrs Riley reckons once you're in, it's free,' Harry explained, trying to smooth over her concern about the cost. She smiled too. How Mrs Riley knew about the entrance fee at Luna Park in Sydney, Kate did not know. But she had taken the time to find out (from the *Women's Weekly*, perhaps), and to talk to Harry about his excitement at the coming visit. She was such a lovely lady, and it almost made Kate sad to think on it. There weren't too many Mrs Rileys in the district now, who cared about Kate and Harry and Luca. Perhaps it was because they had no children of their own that the Rileys had taken them to heart, or perhaps they felt sorry for them. It didn't matter to Kate.

Harry ran on ahead to the first of the rides. It was a sort of little train, which moved up and down tiny hills made of narrow scaffolding no wider than a wheelbarrow. The tracks arched high into the air, almost as far as the giant mouth. Harry persuaded her into the first of the wagons of this ridiculous rickety train, something called a 'roller-coaster'. Kate could see no coasting going on, and she clutched the round metal bar in front of her as the train moved off. The line of small open carriages slowly climbed up to the first peak.

As they hurtled down Kate was ashamed to find herself screaming along with the other passengers, Harry included – but his were shrieks of joy.

I'm paying for this? was what ran through her mind; not just then, but on the next ride and the next.

But Harry was happy as Larry, and he hooted and cheered with every lurch on every ride. For that Kate was grateful, as she clung on, up and down, round and round, oblivious to the glint and sweep of beautiful Sydney Harbour laid out before them.

The next morning a serious Kate was in her best frock and hat, and on time for her appointment, although the reception room was soon empty. The young lady who had recorded Kate's arrival and asked her to wait had disappeared.

A large sign on the wall proclaimed *Aborigines Welfare Board.* But she could see that *Welfare* had been painted over something else: *Protection.* It was tragic for Kate to recall her father's old joke about the Board's original name: *Who's protecting who from what?*

It was meaningless, anyway. She'd failed to protect Daisy from her father. Kate gripped her handbag, her work-beaten hands safely hidden today by unfamiliar gloves.

The minutes passed, measured by the clicks of the wall clock, a smaller version of the one Kate had seen at Central railway station. She wondered if all the clocks in the Public Service were the same, just different sizes.

On the table in front of Kate, three magazine-size documents were arranged in a fan of neat precision. *ANNUAL REPORT of the ABORIGINES WELFARE BOARD for Year ended 30th June, 1947* shouted the cover of the first one. She flipped it open and began to read, her eyes soon lighting with relief on: *one of the principal features of the Board's policy is the assimilation of the better-class aborigines, particularly those of lighter caste, into the general community.*

That boded well, sort of, for Daisy marrying Ed. Kate kept turning the pages, but there seemed nothing else that might help their case. Then she stopped, and read and reread under the heading *EXEMPTION CERTIFICATES FOR ABORIGINES*, that the Board may *issue to any aborigines, or person apparently having a mixture of aboriginal blood, a Certificate . . . to enable the more advanced types of aborigines to . . . secure full status as citizens of the State.*

Surely this meant Ed and Daisy were right. Kate kept turning the pages, looking next for anything on the wages held in safekeeping for all of the Aboriginal domestics in service around the state. There was no mention of it, not even in the accounts of the Board in the appendix to the report. Kate wasn't sure if that was a good or a bad thing. It certainly meant that the Board wasn't counting it as its own money. Yet it wasn't upfront about holding it, either. It was 1947's report. This year's, when it came, might have more on wages.

The main thing was to get Daisy free of this lot. Kate tried not to be nervous. She went over and over what she planned to say. She'd first show respect for the Board and its work.

She was mid-speech in her head when a man in a suit appeared, seemingly out of nowhere.

'Mrs Dowd? This way, please.' He was gone again just as quickly, and Kate hurried down a hall after him.

In his office, he sat down, motioning her to do the same. He was older, perhaps late forties, and quite slender but otherwise unremarkable. As interesting as an ironing board.

'How do you do, Mrs Dowd. I'm Mr Wosel. Head of Welfare Officer Oversight.'

Wosel. Was that a German name? Kate sneaked a closer look at him and wondered. He was quite fair. Harry would christen him Weasel and make jokes about *weasoning* with him.

'Your journey went well?' His eyes were on the file in front of him.

Kate tried not to judge him too soon; it was one of her bad habits.

'So which date is it to be, Mrs Dowd? To deliver the toddler to us.'

'Oh. No.' Kate sat forward in her chair and gripped her handbag. 'I have other news, Mr Wosel, to discuss with you.'

He sat back and exhaled. 'Mrs Dowd. The Board has waited patiently for too long for the delivery of this child into its care. That time has come.'

'I understand. The Board has been patient. But I have a proposal that I believe will please all concerned.'

'With respect, Mrs Dowd, I cannot imagine what proposal you might have which could possibly improve upon what the Board has planned for the child. She has a hope for a life in civilised society, a hope that her mother is denying her. She will be placed with a good family – a white family, of course – and raised with strong values, values that will enable her to take *her* place in civilised society. A chance that was denied her mother, I might add.'

Kate knew she had to persuade him. 'Hear me out, Mr Wosel. Please.' She picked her words carefully. 'A young man in our employ, an excellent young man, advises me that he wishes to marry Daisy.'

'A white man?' Mr Wosel seemed surprised.

'Yes,' Kate said smoothly. Anything else was just talk. 'His name is Edward Storch and he is our head stockman. He's an excellent horseman, and a most steady young man.'

'How old is Daisy?' Mr Wosel scanned the file then, and Kate tried not to hope.

'She turns eighteen next year, as far as we can tell. She'll be of age to marry then. I believe that Daisy cares greatly for Ed. Edward.'

'First, Mrs Dowd, the Board would be most unlikely to approve marriage for one of our girls before she turned twenty-one, let alone eighteen.' Mr Wosel was hunting through Daisy's file. 'Is Daisy full-blood or mixed-blood?'

'Mixed. Her mother was Aboriginal and her father was a drover. Irish.'

A shadow crossed Mr Wosel's face. Kate should not have mentioned the Irish part; another mark against Daisy.

'Is she very dark, Mrs Dowd? She doesn't appear to be.' He peered at the photograph in the file.

'No. Very much of lighter caste.' Kate deliberately used the words from the Board's own report.

'You see, Mrs Dowd, a new process has been put in place by the Board, to help as many of these girls into civilised society as possible. Where the girl fits the bill.'

'Do you mean the certificate of exemption? It sounds marvellous.'

He looked up from the file. 'Yes. Exactly. The girl applies, agrees to the conditions, and then may even marry.'

'And she could keep her child?' Kate could hardly breathe.

Mr Wosel pressed his lips together as he thought. 'It's possible. It would depend on the character and circumstances of the girl herself, and on the young man.'

'He's a fine young man, and she's a solid, reliable girl.'

'I see. Even if she were to be approved by the Board for a certificate, any breach of a condition and it would be revoked. So there must be general cleanliness, no public drunkenness—'

'Oh, Daisy more than meets such criteria. And she's most anxious to—' Kate was about to say *keep her child*, but thought better of it. 'To assimilate into the general community. A deserving case, it seems to me.'

Mr Wosel looked up sharply, and Kate smiled at him warmly. Perhaps she was overdoing her use of the report's wording.

After her previous misstep with the Board over Daisy's pay, Kate was afraid to raise Daisy's indenture now, in case this miraculous new solution might evaporate. But she forced herself. 'Daisy's indenture to the Board, Mr Wosel. What happens to that if she gets this certificate?' Kate knew just how bitterly the Board chased every penny of the wages that Daisy earned. They'd be letting that go if they released her early.

Mr Wosel cleared his throat. 'Assimilation is the Board's new priority, Mrs Dowd. If Daisy were to apply for a certificate of exemption, that would include her early release from indenture. If she chooses to apply, then the local welfare officer –'

Kate knew that was Wingnut.

'– would prepare a report on her. For the Board to consider. She couldn't reside on a reserve, of course, and would need prior approval to visit one.'

'I see.' Kate worked to keep her tone neutral. In the pause that followed, she could hardly believe Sydney was being so kind to them. She couldn't wait to get back to Amiens to tell Daisy and Ed. What's more, Harry's grandmother was indeed a delight, and Kate felt hopeful she would let Harry stay with them. Kate felt a rush of gratitude and an unfamiliar elation, a sense that things might be all right.

'I want to thank you, Mr Wosel. This is most helpful.' Kate stood up to leave. Then she remembered. 'One last thing I must tell you. Daisy's mother is sick. Mortally so. I will be allowing Daisy to journey to see her very soon, for a short time. To be sure she sees her mother before she passes away.'

Mr Wosel frowned again. 'No, no, Mrs Dowd. On no account can our girls be traipsing off across the countryside.'

Kate was so surprised she sat down again. 'But Daisy's mother is *dying*.'

'That's as it may be, but frankly we don't put great store by what these girls say. The Board's duty is to haul them out of their circumstances. Pave the way for a better life for them or their children. Enforced segregation of the girl from the bad influence of her family is a pillar of the Board's work.'

Kate was struggling to understand. 'Daisy's mother is dying,' she said again.

'So she says. That is not relevant to the Board.'

'Will this be different if Daisy has a certificate of exemption?'

He began tidying the papers, apparently sorting the pages in date order into the file. 'Not at all. In that case, the girl may only go onto a reserve, or see any family elsewhere, after proper approval from the—' He stopped speaking suddenly, staring at the page in his hand. 'I'm so sorry, Mrs Dowd. I didn't realise . . .' Wosel's brow knitted in disapproval. 'The Board would not entertain any special treatment of this girl. At any time.'

'Why not?'

'She's a troublemaker, Mrs Dowd. Of the first order. Don't you recall? She agitated for her wages. And she absconded from a Home while awaiting the birth of her child.'

'No, Mr Wosel. The wages are a misunderstanding. I approached the Board. I made an enquiry, that's all.'

Wosel smiled benevolently. 'It is gallant of you to take on the blame for this girl's shortcomings.'

'But it's the truth. I applied for the wages, not Daisy. It wasn't her idea.'

He went on as if she hadn't spoken. 'Gallant but wrong-headed, Mrs Dowd. This sort of girl understands nothing but a firm hand. Allowances will only lead to further problems. No, no, she has to be an example to the others.'

'But—'

'You must decide which it is to be, and by the end of this month: the girl goes to another posting or the toddler is adopted by a deserving family. Both, preferably, although I appreciate that may inconvenience you briefly in your domestic staffing.' He tidied the file again. 'The Board has been more than patient, Mrs Dowd. We've indulged your clear affection for this girl, yet there are real concerns. The child, Pearl, will very shortly be three.'

'This month,' Kate said.

'There had been some sympathy for your circumstances – at the time of the loss of your father – but years have now passed. You must choose: Pearl or Daisy, and by the end of the month. You understand?'

CHAPTER 16

For the dedicated woolgrower, there is little more fulfilling or rewarding than a return to his flock after a rare absence.

THE WOOLGROWER'S COMPANION, 1906

Ed met a tired Kate and Harry at Longhope train station late on the Saturday afternoon. He helped Kate down with her bag, then did the same for the lady behind her, the only other passenger alighting at Longhope.

Kate smiled at her. And Alice Wilson, the sole daughter among a clutch of Wilson sons, smiled back. The Wilson family sailed close to the wind, and were probably quite well known to Wingnut, from pub fights and most recently, some kerfuffle over a missing horse. No doubt Alice understood just what it was like, being on the edge of Longhope's respectable society.

'All good, Mrs D?' Ed asked.

She bobbed her head, not wanting to discuss Mr Wosel and the Board in front of Harry. 'Harry's grandmother is lovely. Isn't she, Harry?'

'Yeah,' he said. The yo-yo had been found and was at work as they walked across the flat to the Amiens car.

'Any news here?' Kate asked, as she got into the front passenger seat.

'Nothin to speak of.'

Kate was pleased enough with that.

When Ed dropped Kate and Harry back at the Amiens homestead, Daisy was in the kitchen with Pearl to welcome them, along with Mrs Walters.

'Tea, Missus?' Daisy asked as Pearl climbed into Kate's arms, causing an almost physical constriction of Kate's heartstrings. It wasn't until much later, when the children were in bed and Mrs Walters herself had retired for the night, that Kate and Daisy were alone to talk. Ed would also be wanting to know.

'I saw the Board,' Kate said evenly, as she put away the last of the drying-up and Daisy wiped the kitchen table.

She looked at Kate, and paused. 'They say no, Missus?'

When Kate nodded, Daisy's face fell.

Her heart went out to her. 'Can I tell you about it, Daisy?'

There was another pause before she answered. 'No, Missus. Ed, eh?'

She could see Daisy was close to tears. Kate was too.

The kitchen clean, Daisy went off to bed. She must be terribly worried, and Kate could understand her need to open wounds as little as possible. Kate would talk to Ed and then Ed to Daisy.

It was not until the Monday morning, at the shearing shed, that Kate would finally see poor Ed. Kate watched where she put her feet on the track as she walked towards the shed. She was without a dog to scare off the snakes today as they were all with the men. A screech sent her eyes upwards. Daisy's lorikeets swooped and catcalled above her, their bright greens vivid against the blue of the cloudless sky.

Kate walked on, to the hive of the shearing shed, encircled by its moving mass of sheep and men and dogs. A light haze of dust hung over the shed, thrown up by hundreds of hooves. Sheep were yarded to void themselves of dung and urine before they were put into the shed.

The unmistakable drone of the Lister carried across the flat. The engine drove the overhead gear for the stands, powering each handpiece used to shear. The noise would only cut out when the shearing team knocked off for smoko: their mid-morning tea, damper and a smoke. Kate stopped at the outer gate to the yards and waited for Ed. Shearers were a prickly lot and a woman in their shed might set them off, even if the woman happened to own the shed and all the sheep. Kate could ill afford a walkout. A persistent fly buzzed about her mouth and she waved it off.

The engine spluttered into a shutdown, and soon, on the far side of the shed, a throng of shearers ambled off towards the quarters, to take their tea and damper.

Ed came down the ramp and headed her way. Kate waved that fly away again.

'Mrs D.' Ed climbed through the rails, gammy leg first. Every time she dealt with Ed, she was grateful he was both a kind man and a good stockman. The shearers liked Ed. He had a slow fuse.

'Things all right?' Kate asked.

'No fights yet. But it's early days.'

Kate smiled. 'Grateful for small mercies?'

'Yeah. There's one new bugger, Wiggin. Thinks he can take the ringer.' Ed shook his head.

'Isn't the ringer Laracy? His boss?'

'Yep.' He smiled then. 'He's got no chance of beatin Laracy, but he'll have a go, f'sure. Bit of shovin already.'

'What if they fight?' Kate was thinking about the lost time.

Ed laughed. 'They're shearers, Mrs D. They're gunna fight.'

She frowned. That sounded ominous.

'S'all right now. The other blokes'll down tools to watch only if they can afford it. When they got most of the mob sheared.'

'Nothing we can do?'

'Nuh.'

Kate nodded, trying to find the right words to tell Ed about Sydney. 'I saw the Board, Ed.'

He looked off towards the homestead. 'They said no, eh? They said we can't get the certificate for Daisy?' There was no disappointment in his voice, just resignation. Daisy had told him.

'I think it would have been possible, only . . .' Kate said.

'Only?'

'Only they think Daisy's a troublemaker. Because I applied for her wages. I'm so sorry, Ed.'

He said nothing and looked away to the creek. 'You weren't to know, Mrs D. Maybe it were a pipe dream, anyhow. I heard yesterday the mob call em "dog-tags" up in Queensland. The certificates. The Board up there has ya on a lead like a dog.'

'There's more,' Kate said. 'Daisy can't go to see her mother. Not until she's released from the Board.'

'Her old lady's real crook.'

'I told them. I said she was dying.'

'But—'

'They think the family is a bad influence. Daisy can't see them.'

'Struth.'

'The man said they would make an example of her.'

'Struth,' Ed said again, shaking his head. 'They never gunna let her go, are they?' He walked away and Kate felt the weight of his helplessness.

CHAPTER 17

The sole reliable constant in a woolgrower's lot is the variability in the impediments to his endeavours and industries.

THE WOOLGROWER'S COMPANION, 1906

Much of the next day Kate spent walking fence lines, looking for holes and cursing the Board, herself and especially Fleming. She couldn't find his jolly fence holes.

The Amiens homestead kitchen was busy when she got in at about four that afternoon. A pleased Pearl was at one end of the table, Harry at the other, working his way through a glass of cordial and some bikkies. Mrs Walters and Daisy were in the laundry, folding washing.

'Harry bin t'school,' Pearl explained to Kate. The little girl loved to have afternoon tea with him.

Kate put her hat on its peg. 'How was school?'

'All right.' Harry had a biscuit in one hand and was sifting through the pile of post with his other.

'Truly?' Kate asked.

He ignored her, waving a letter instead. 'It's for you. From my nan. Read it out.'

Thank heavens. That good news would be more than welcome. Kate tore open the envelope and read aloud.

'*Dear Mrs Dowd—*'

'Not me too? That's a bit stiff,' Harry said, with his mouth full. Pearl picked up the empty envelope and carefully began to put the remains of her biscuit into it.

'*I begin by thanking you sincerely for all you have done for Harry. He is growing into a lovely boy and –*'

Harry frowned.

'*– I can see that you have great affection for him, as he does for you too.*'

'Bleugh.' Harry made a vomiting noise and Pearl giggled, delighted.

Kate read on.

'*I have thought a great deal about where it is best for Harry to be, from this time forward. I was most disappointed –*'

Kate stopped.

'Struth. What'd she say?' Harry was up, next to Kate. He continued reading.

'*I was most disappointed to learn by chance that your husband, Mr Dowd, is away in the Islands, and not to have heard this from you. I know you, in turn, will now be disappointed. I have decided that Harry is best to live with his great-uncle, Keith Grimes, Harry's flesh and blood, and a good and forthright man.*

'*I suggest December first is the best date for the move, to give time for accommodation changes to be . . .*'

The silence in the kitchen was broken only by the hum of Longhope Downs traffic on the two-way. No one spoke. Even Pearl was quiet, looking wide-eyed from Harry to Kate.

Then Harry was gone, out the kitchen door, banging it so hard he startled Pearl, who began to cry.

'Harry!' Kate called after him.

'I'm goin ta the Rileys',' he yelled at her, and didn't look back.

Daisy appeared from the laundry and picked up the toddler, but Pearl would not be consoled.

Kate sat down at the kitchen table and stared, unbelieving,

at the letter. It was her own fault. She had not mentioned that Jack was gone, and the old lady had found out. Kate was ashamed and appalled. She'd caused this.

'We're stuffed,' Harry said repeatedly in the days after the letter. He was right.

There'd been times before in Kate's short life when she'd felt overwhelmed and panicked: her mother's illness and passing, her father's death a few years later, Jack's leaving her at the end of the war. Yet after each, in hindsight, she felt a small kernel of hope, because she'd survived, gone on, got on with her day and her work.

This too will pass, she'd always told herself, something her mother had said. But as she faced Harry's removal to Keith Grimes, and no easy means for Daisy and Ed to marry or for Daisy and Pearl to stay together, the saying now left Kate cold. She felt she'd failed them all. She could see no answers.

CHAPTER 18

Whilst prudent selection of men and stock will protect the woolgrower from any other than occasional malfeasance, it is a fact that the ill-natured inevitably swarm to their own, with dire consequences.

THE WOOLGROWER'S COMPANION, 1906

On Saturday afternoon, the problems in the shed boiled over. Raised voices carried to Kate, clear across the yards, even full of stock. A fight – had to be. She dipped below the rail cross-pieces to push her way through the sea of sheep and on, up the shed ramp. Inside, a ring of shearers bayed and cheered two men at their centre. Ed was held off, pinned by a couple of the shearers who wanted the fighters to have a go.

Kate tried to force herself through the crowd, but she was blocked by men, shoulder to shoulder, the smell of sweat and wool all round her. She caught glimpses of Laracy and Wiggin as they circled, throwing punches, landing one to the crowd's roar.

The hooter sounded in two long full blasts. The noise echoed round the shed, enough to stop the shouting. In that second, Ed pulled free of the shearers holding him back, and latched on to Wiggin's nearest arm. Even hampered by Ed, Wiggin threw another punch with his right.

A third blast of the hooter stopped them though, and someone cut the engine.

'Afternoon, ladies.' Grimes grinned.

Kate was relieved and appalled at the same time.

'I see you allow women in your shed, Laracy,' he said.

Laracy forgot Wiggin and moved towards Grimes. The jibe was for Kate too. It was her shed.

Grimes ignored the approaching Laracy. 'I want a word with you, Mrs D. Now. Outside.' Grimes spoke as if she worked for him.

Kate was suddenly afraid that he had come early for Harry.

Laracy saw her fear. He moved in, just a foot from Grimes, and his shearers lined up behind him. 'I don't believe the lady wants ya on her place, mate,' Laracy said, cordially enough, yet his words were laced with threat.

Ed pushed forward to intervene. 'Grimesy's leavin.'

'Ya leavin, mate,' Laracy repeated.

'I'm here to see Mrs D. Not this rabble,' Grimes said, without force.

'Ya seen her now. On yer way.'

'I'm getting the boy on the first. No monkey business, Mrs D,' he said. But he backed out of the shed then, and skittered down the ramp.

Laracy spoke to Kate. 'You want the boys to have a word with him for ya?'

'No. Thank you. Truly,' Kate said. 'I'm sorry I came into the shed, Mr Laracy.'

'Your shed, Mrs D,' he replied. 'Let me know if ya change ya mind bout Grimesy.' The shearers moved slowly to their stands and returned to work.

Kate left, back down the ramp, not wanting to push her luck. Ed caught up with her in the yards.

'Laracy saw off Grimes.' Kate couldn't believe it.

'He has no time for him,' Ed said. 'An he and Wiggin have that in common.'

Kate walked to the homestead, feeling the heat of the sun on her neck. Laracy had got rid of Grimes this time. She was sure he'd come to tell her he was serious about taking Harry. On the first of December, just ten days away, Harry had to go to live with that man.

CHAPTER 19

The principal predators of lambs are feral pigs, foxes, domestic dogs and crows. But a careful and methodical working through of each problem shall significantly reduce losses, whether through lambing in tussocky shelterbelts or lambing at different times to others.

THE WOOLGROWER'S COMPANION, 1906

Kate was more than usually relieved to get into the garden that afternoon. It was work, yet she switched off there. Her shrubs and veggies, the birds and the dirt. They were like a salve. She did her rounds, walking a circuit of the homestead, checking on anything that needed some water or a bit of sheep manure (the week before, the stockmen had, under sufferance, brought her a load from the woolshed).

After Luca left, it had taken Kate a long time to garden without grief. She smiled, remembering. Luca had worked with her in this garden every day for almost ten months, all the months he was assigned to Amiens. Each afternoon he'd appear, whistling quietly, after a hard day's work out in the paddocks. He was a good gardener, careful and attentive. That was Luca. Kind, even to plants. It almost hurt her physically to think about him.

A piece of cat's claw creeper had the temerity to stretch along the fence netting. Wrenching it out was satisfying, even if another would appear soon. It was rampant. Back then, she'd been afraid of Luca at first. But over time, they'd become friends. She'd shared her worries with him; about her father when he was still alive, about managing the place, about how she could possibly keep both Pearl and Daisy from the clutches of the Aborigines Welfare Board. He'd listened to it all, as they quietly weeded and clipped and pruned their way around the garden.

And then, at the end of the war, immediately before he was repatriated to Italy, it happened. They became lovers, for just four glorious, secret days. Amiens had been unusually quiet, deserted even. Ed had gone to see his father, injured in an accident, and Daisy was busy with newborn Pearl. So Kate and Luca had Amiens almost to themselves. They worked, walking those fence lines, looking for gaps ahead of the coming shearing. But mostly they talked and laughed. And made love.

Looking back, Kate could not imagine how they'd found themselves in such madness. How she of all people, who so believed in duty and loyalty, could have done it. But that one moment, that late afternoon at the dam, there'd been no hesitation from either of them. Ironically, it wasn't those glorious days that made Grimes suspect the affair, for by then he was long gone. It was earlier, as she and Luca worked together. Luca had not hidden his regard for her. And Grimes had seen that.

Outside the fence, Gunner yawned and rolled onto his side to sleep. As she moved her weeding mat, Luca crept into Kate's thoughts. What would he suggest she do? *Wrong then wrong*, he used to say. She smiled just thinking of it. He meant problem by problem, to solve things one by one. That's how she should think about things. One at a time.

First, the Aborigines Welfare Board. She needed to tell them that Daisy would not apply for the certificate of exemption. But if she told them, then they'd come to take Pearl.

Damn the Board. She just wouldn't reply. Let them chase her. That might get her a few more weeks to think of another plan to fend them off again. Wingnut would be slow to act, even if they asked him. He didn't like paperwork or being told what to do.

Next, Fleming. She needed that cheque. She would have to go and see him again. But how could she *make* him give it to her? He was a bully, knowing she could hardly fight him for it. He really only respected money or force. Her father would have gone over and threatened to fight him until he gave up the cheque.

Maybe she should ask Mr Laracy to have a word with him? She laughed at herself – hiring a heavy to extract the money she was owed. Anyway, Laracy wouldn't do it. Fleming was an important customer of his.

Ed? She couldn't ask him. With suspicions round town that Ed had some Aboriginal blood, he could never take on one of the wealthiest men in the district. Ed had enough problems of his own.

Damn. There was nothing for it. Kate would just have to try herself.

Harry was the next problem. The old lady had said Harry must go to live with Grimes at the start of December, just ten days away. Kate had no answer to that, and a familiar fear lurched in her stomach.

She pushed herself on to the last problem on her long list. Bloody Jack. Kate could not think about Jack's demand for money, the *blackmail*, without fury rising up.

But how could she avoid bringing embarrassment on Luca and the Rileys, and even more shame on herself as a scarlet woman, unless she paid? And how could she find ten thousand pounds? Addison would never agree to her drawing down on the overdraft as Jack had suggested.

Kate had a small cheque due in soon; a grazier from Broken Hill, one Mr Perry, was coming to buy some young rams. He'd pay a deposit, then the rest when Ed delivered them. But even together, that wasn't much. Good for an injection of cash, but a fraction of what she needed for Jack.

What else could she do? Sell a paddock, maybe. But that would break her heart. Her father never sold any land; he just bought and bought, bits, parcels, paddocks, neighbouring places. So to sell now, to sell anything, was hard to imagine. And who would buy a paddock? Fleming, her neighbour, was the only logical purchaser. Or perhaps old Mr Wilson, who had little paddocks all over. Kate didn't relish either prospect.

Jack had her boxed in. If she could not find the money, in court he would name Luca as her lover. After that sort of scandal, even Mr Babbin, the only stock and station agent in town, might find it hard to keep dealing with her; his other customers would complain. News of Kate's affair would confirm everything that slimy snake Addison had ever thought about her. She needed the bank, above all the business people. What a mess.

A bad pong wafted across from the dog. 'Ugh, Gunner,' she called. 'What have you been eating?' The dog lifted his head off the ground to look at her, then laid it down.

Kate went back to her thinking. Addison. She had to see the man and ask: ask for a loan, even if he would say no. She had no other options.

CHAPTER 20

The new-chum woolgrower may learn as much from the composure and deportment of his elder peers as from any book on the Merino; even, this writer concedes, The Woolgrower's Companion.

THE WOOLGROWER'S COMPANION, 1906

Two days later, Kate was in the office going through *The Woolgrower's Companion* for something, anything, on bushfires, when Daisy called to her.

'Someone comin, Missus. A car.'

Kate went straight onto the verandah. 'It's all right, Daisy. It's not the sergeant.'

In the middle of the afternoon, Kate wasn't expecting anyone except Harry in a bit, home from school on horseback.

It turned out to be the unpleasant Mr Nettiford. When not fighting fires, he ran the only haberdashery in town. He tended to be longwinded, yet curt with some. He made up for his numerous limitations entirely with over-confidence. Uriah Heep, he was called, because he fawned a bit on the big graziers in the district. Worse, he was slimy with Kate.

Nettiford squared his hat and walked up to the house, a man with a purpose. Kate's first thought was that she'd forgotten to pay her bill. But she rarely shopped there now and paid cash when she did, so it couldn't be that.

On the verandah, he took off his hat and smiled at her. 'Good afternoon, Mrs Dowd. An official visit, I'm afraid.' He must have seen her confusion. 'Fire business. You'll recall I'm the captain.' He came so close, she was obliged to step out and round the wicker chair.

'How can I help you?' It was less than two weeks since Fleming had given her a dressing down for back-burning, after she'd stopped. Perhaps it was Nettiford's turn.

'I reckon it's how I can help ya, Mrs Dowd. We're in for a long, hot summer. After the run of good years of rain, that dry pasture and all that heat mean the highest fire risk in years.' His words made sense but he held eye contact with her for a little too long.

Kate knew Daisy had taken Pearl off to the chooks, just in case the visitor turned out to be from the Aborigines Welfare Board. But she wished Mrs Walters would appear in the kitchen. She remembered then that the housekeeper was in town at a prayer meeting, something Kate felt she couldn't refuse, envious that the woman still had her faith. So Kate was alone with this man.

'We've known each other long enough' – he smiled – 'that I know I can be straight with you. I'm told ya still back-burning.'

'Not any more. We stopped a while back.' She smiled to soften the abruptness of her reply.

'You sure, Mrs Dowd? Not just telling me what ya know your captain wants to hear?'

Oh, for goodness' sake. 'We don't burn more country than anyone else. We've stopped, anyway. As I said.' She heard the frustration in her voice.

'It must be hard, Mrs Dowd, to be a lady on your own.'

Kate worked hard not to sigh. Because truly, honestly, she was so tired of the idea, popular with a certain sort of man, that as Jack had left her she was fair game; and more than that, probably desperate for a man's embrace.

'I can help you, Mrs Dowd. In my position, I have responsibilities to the people of this district. To preserve life and property, to protect from the savagery of fire.'

When you're not selling socks was what occurred to Kate. She arranged her face in an appropriately agnostic fashion, without enthusiasm but without disrespect, either.

As he went on, she realised she was in some peril. As with the one or two other men who had tried something similar since Jack left, Kate had a complicated dance to perform. She had to make clear to the man that she had no interest in him of any kind, while also preserving the facade that he had never expressed any interest in her. She'd been luckier the last time. It had been a travelling salesman, and Mr Maguire had appeared just in time to save face all round.

But the postman would not save her today.

'Mrs Dowd, might I point out some of the features of ya property that are at especial risk to fire?' Unasked, he *took her hand* and led her into the kitchen, carefully closing the door behind him. She half thought she saw movement out of the window, but there was silence.

'Now, ya wood stove, Mrs Dowd.' He stood close behind her, his hands on her arms now. 'Ya need to store your wood at an appreciable distance from the stove itself. Heat,' he almost whispered into her ear, 'is a dangerous thing.'

She was starting to panic. If she had to push him, to shove him off, there'd be no hope of preserving the pretence and he'd have it in for her, for good. She might well need him and his other fire volunteers one day.

An overloud clomping on the verandah stairs saved her. Mr Nettiford moved at a pace to the respectable side of the kitchen table.

'G'day.' Harry came in the gauze door and leant two cricket bats, one new, one quite knocked about, against the wood stove.

After a brief but respectable interval, Mr Nettiford took his leave, citing fire duties.

'No rest for the wicked,' Harry quipped.

Kate smiled cordially when Nettiford departed, as though his was the most appropriate visit in the world. They saw him off.

Harry stood beside her on the verandah, spinning the new cricket bat vertically on the floor boards.

'Heat is a dangerous thing,' Harry whispered hoarsely, and laughed.

'Harry! You heard him?'

He went to the verandah stairs. '*Clomp-clomp-clomp*,' he said, and walked the bats up the steps like feet.

'I'm cross with you, Harry. You should have come in at once. Not waited so long!'

He laughed and laughed, as he went across the lawn to hit a ball against the water tank with his cricket bat. 'No secrets in a country town,' Harry called back, quoting Maguire.

CHAPTER 21

Whilst the quest for consistent range and tensile strength must be the primary aim of the woolgrower, he must also be a man of commerce, with a most thorough understanding of the sums and figures of the accounts of his concern.

THE WOOLGROWER'S COMPANION, 1906

The next morning, as Kate parked the Humber outside the bank, it occurred to her that she drove quite comfortably now, even in heels, her driving skills acquired by necessity during the war. But what she had ahead this morning would not be comfortable. From the car, she checked the big clock on the town hall opposite. One minute to ten. Now, she had to face Addison. It had taken her a long while to realise that he made an effort to frighten her. But even so, she was nervous. At least she'd received Mr Perry's deposit cheque, small as it was, though Addison was expecting the money that Fleming was keeping back.

The Wilson boy – Bill? – nodded a greeting at Kate through the glass door as he unlocked it. He never looked happy, and it always struck Kate as odd that he worked in town. He was as wild as his older brothers. Unlike them though, he'd finished high school. Kate suspected his mother had insisted, with all his schooling, that he get a job. He boarded with his older sister, the girl Kate had seen at the station. She worked as a cleaner in the Lands Department offices. But office work was a kind of punishment for a boy who'd rather be on a horse, or fixing fences. She smiled at him, and he looked away.

Kate clicked her way in those unaccustomed heels across the marble floor to the manager's secretary and his office, in the far corner of the bank. The new secretary was an older lady. *A hundred not out* was Harry's description. She'd transferred in to Longhope only two months before with her husband, who was with the Department of Main Roads. His unlikely surname was End, and the locals quickly nicknamed him 'Dead'.

Mrs End was typing but stopped. 'Can I help you?' She peered at Kate in surprise, as if customers were a novelty.

'I'm Kate Dowd. I have an appointment.'

Mrs End took a deep breath. She looked slowly over a large bound diary on the desk beside the typewriter. 'Nothing there,' she said cheerfully, and went back to typing.

'I do have an appointment, Mrs End. I'm a customer.'

The typing stopped again. 'I checked the diary. Nothing there.'

'I'll just pop in,' Kate said. Mrs End's eyes opened wide. Kate was already past her and she tapped on the manager's door.

'Come,' sounded from the other side.

Mr Addison, at his desk, was openly surprised at an unannounced visitor. But only for a second, and he hid it well. 'Sit,' he said.

Sit? Kate stifled her annoyance but did as she was told. It occurred to her that she usually did as she was told. 'I have an appointment,' she said. There was no response. He'd never forgiven her for rebuffing him when he'd made a pass, years before.

Kate watched Mr Addison as he worked, his eyes on a single sheet of paper on the desk in front of him. A very slender man, with a pale complexion and fine hair tending to ginger. Skinny almost. With his head forward, bent over his work, Kate had a clear view of a shiny scalp. He combed his thinning hair across the bald bit.

He looked up sharply. 'Mrs Dowd. Good day. You've come to deposit the cheque from Mr Fleming, I assume. Payment for the wethers?'

Kate opened her mouth but he went straight on. 'You're most welcome to use a teller, Mrs Dowd. To make a simple deposit. It is that for which they are employed.'

It took her a moment to process his last sentence. 'Of course I would do that usually, Mr Addison. I don't want to waste your time . . .' Her words came in a rush. 'However . . .' She sounded like an idiot. She *was* an idiot.

'However . . . ?'

'I don't have the cheque.'

Addison sat back, incredulous. 'Mrs Dowd, you'd best go home and fetch that cheque. To come but forget it?' He shook his head, disappointed but not surprised. He was, as Harry always said, a drongo.

Kate looked down at her hands again. 'I didn't forget it, Mr Addison. Mr Fleming wouldn't give me the payment.'

For the first time, Addison seemed unsure. 'Mr Fleming?'

'Yes.'

'He is a reputable man, Mrs Dowd, a fair man. He must have had his reasons. Did he say why?'

It struck Kate that Addison was afraid of Fleming. Perhaps the world was like that; each bully afraid of one that was worse, and so on. She wished she was the orca, not the minnow.

'I hope I'll be able to collect it this week,' she said. She certainly wasn't telling him that Fleming had kept the cheque over back-burning.

'*Hope*?' Addison repeated. He straightened the single page on his desk. 'I do appreciate that you came in person to tell me. But to be frank, I'd prefer no visit and a cheque banked with a teller.' He laughed. It wasn't funny to either of them.

'Good day then, Mrs Dowd,' he said, and he went back to work, his eyes on that single paper on the otherwise empty desk.

'There's another reason that I needed to see you.'

'Oh?' He looked at his watch.

'I must borrow some money.'

Addison leant back in his chair and shook his head slowly.

Kate wanted to tell him to cut the amateur dramatics but she was too afraid. She made herself say it. 'I need ten thousand pounds.'

He laughed, as if she'd made a joke.

'I mean it. Ten thousand pounds.'

'And the *purpose* for such an amount?'

'The purpose?' Her voice dropped. 'My husband is divorcing me.'

'What's that?' he said sharply.

'Divorce.' It came out as a whisper, her shame strangling her voice.

Addison looked at her, mystified. 'I am truly sorry for you, Mrs Dowd. But I do not see the connection between such a sad event and your banking arrangements.'

She'd not seen it either. 'My . . . My husband has asked – requires – that I pay him.'

'I see,' Addison said. Kate suspected he did not see at all but in any event was relishing this gossip, even if he could tell no one but Mrs Addison. He stood and took a green file from the cabinet behind him. Kate's hopes rose when he put it on the desk and began to write in it. But then he put his pen down and rested clasped hands on the open file.

'Mrs Dowd. The bank's shareholders can approve only those advances in pursuit of legitimate business consistent with the interests of its borrowers. This, this *idea* of yours? That is not something that would ever be approved.'

Kate couldn't speak.

'I'm sorry,' he said automatically.

They both knew he wasn't sorry at all.

'Might I give you some advice, Mrs Dowd?'

She inhaled. *Primary . . .*

'Primary production is a challenging endeavour. Very challenging, even for the most competent grazier.'

For a lady, alone . . .

'For a lady, alone, it is especially difficult. Unguided.' He shrugged. 'I can only encourage you to—'

'Sell. I know, Mr Addison.'

'I believe there are one or two buyers, good solid men, with the resources and experience to acquire a sheep property as large as Amiens. Sell out, Mrs Dowd. Wool prices are up. The '39 drought is long broken. Sell while you can. For the love of all that is sacred: get out.'

Kate pushed her fingernails into her palms to stop herself telling him to mind his own business.

'One last thing, Mrs Dowd. I hear you are burning off when there's been no rain for some time. I am no grazier –'

That's the truth.

'– but I speak as your bank manager. So, to burn off now? You risk your stock and pasture, Mrs Dowd, and the bank's security. What are in effect our assets. A catastrophe is waiting to happen.'

Kate saw red. 'Look, we *have* stopped burning, if you must know. Yes, because of the fire risk now. But we were burning off to prevent a catastrophe. And at least I did something. If only my neighbours were as *neighbourly*.'

Addison's lips grew thin, and he snapped the file shut. 'I understand the volunteer brigade will shortly call a meeting of all graziers. So everyone – *everyone* – understands their duties to the district. Duty, Mrs Dowd. Something you'd do well to think a little more about.'

Bastard. 'I want to apply for that loan,' Kate said.

He looked at her as if she was mad. 'I tell you no, no and no again. Head office in Sydney will not even consider an application if not supported by me, and I will not support it.'

'I *will* apply. I'll be back in to sign the form.' Kate rose to leave. 'Good day to you, Mr Addison.'

'You should sell!' His voice followed her out the door. She kept walking, but her mind reeled. He'd actually *yelled* at her.

CHAPTER 22

Survival of the enterprise is at the heart of the woolgrower's experience. Drastic measures may be required in the face of financial adversity, but each should be studied and considered in good time.

THE WOOLGROWER'S COMPANION, 1906

Kate sat on the edge of her chair on the wide Longhope Downs verandah, opposite John Fleming. Behind him, huge vertical banks of cloud filled the sky. Thunderheads, they were called, yet their rain disappeared before it hit the ground.

'Always spectacular, those clouds,' Kate said, making small talk.

Fleming glanced at the horizon. 'All noise, Mrs Dowd. The rain evaporates in the air.'

'Ah.' She tried to sound impressed.

'But I'm sure you didn't come to learn about the weather.'

Kate felt herself getting cross for the second time that day. Addison, and now this.

'Young Harry Grimes is better off here,' Fleming said. 'On Longhope Downs. No doubt in time you'll agree.'

'Mr Fleming, Mrs Grimes has said Harry will live with Mr Grimes. I accept that.' *For now.* She wanted Fleming off the topic of Harry and onto something less explosive. But things got worse.

'It's not you that I object to, Mrs Dowd, you understand. It's all the blacks you keep about.'

Kate clenched her hands in her lap and stayed quiet. She'd found it was always better to let people vent if they got onto the topic of Aborigines. They were not to be persuaded.

'Your father set an example. There were no black children loose on Amiens in his day.'

Fleming knew that her father had sired Pearl; the whole district did. It was not uncommon. Yet Fleming saw no responsibility in that? She fumed.

'He knew that, your father. For the good of this country, graziers must stand up for what's right, Mrs Dowd.'

There was a pause. Fleming looked at her. 'I imagine you've come for a cheque?'

Kate felt her stomach turn.

'Yes. Please. But first, I have a proposal for you.' After his talk of all the blacks on Amiens, it was probably useless to try to sell him anything. But she would try.

His smile somehow had the effect of making his face hard. 'A proposal?' He knew about her impending divorce. As Maguire said, there were no secrets in a small town.

'I am thinking of selling Riflebutt,' Kate said. 'You know the paddock well. It's on the boundary with Longhope Downs. I wanted to give you the first chance to buy it.'

'First chance, Mrs Dowd? Is there a queue?' He laughed then, as harsh as the noon sunlight in which they sat.

She knew from her father to resist the bait. Keep to the script. 'Riflebutt is good country. It runs along the watercourse. It's well drained.'

Fleming said nothing for a bit. 'Just Riflebutt?'

'Yes.'

He shook his head. 'It's not worth the trouble, for a bit of dirt like that. No. Not interested.' He folded his arms.

'But having someone else, a new grazier, own Riflebutt

might be difficult for you. Leaving gates open and so on.'

He laughed again. 'With respect, Mrs Dowd, even a melon grazier couldn't be worse than where we are now.'

So Kate was a bad neighbour, no better than someone new to the land. The man was obnoxious. Poor Elizabeth, having to live with this.

'I'm still losing stock,' he said. 'Holes like cheese, that boundary. Fast as we fix em, new ones appear.'

'Sorry to hear that.' She didn't challenge him and tried again. 'As a favour, I wanted to let you know first that I'm selling.'

'I'd be doing you the favour,' he said. 'As you're short of cash.'

'I'm not short of money.'

'But it seems you have to sell, Mrs Dowd.'

'I don't have to sell,' she said evenly. 'I'm willing to sell for the right price. It's a good block. A good size.'

He frowned. 'I suppose I could give you a hundred pounds.'

Kate was trying hard, and failing, not to be affronted. 'It's worth three times that. At least.'

'It's worth what you can get for it, Mrs Dowd. It's you who needs the money. It is neither here nor there to me.'

He wasn't buying. Kate stood up.

'I expect I'll see you at the end of the month, Mrs Dowd. For your cheque,' he added, with a sly smile.

She couldn't believe she'd forgotten about that bloody cheque. 'But you have my wethers.'

'I told you before. Stop burning off.'

'We *have* stopped.'

'I'm afraid that's not what I understand. You're risking people's stock and fences, the fire threat being what it is.'

She left him. Kate was more than angry. No cheque and no sale. If Fleming didn't want to buy Riflebutt, it would be a hard sell to anyone else: a small block wedged between two big places. He'd offered a pittance, almost too little to even think he might one day buy. She certainly wasn't going to give it away, not when the amount was nowhere near what she needed for Jack.

CHAPTER 23

The prudent woolgrower should overlook an occasional expression of ire in his peers, an entirely understandable expression of the natural virility of men. However, it is of benefit to consider that ladies who allow similar bad temper to be displayed should be avoided as difficult and likely unable to run a household.

THE WOOLGROWER'S COMPANION, 1906

On the way home, still hot under the collar from her run-in with Fleming, Kate made a spontaneous stop at the bank in Longhope. Twice in one day; two times too often for her liking.

Mrs End seemed to be suffering from the heat. She turned the pages of the appointment ledger with wide eyes and sloth-like slowness. 'You had your appointment this morning, dear. I remember.'

'I must see Mr Addison again.'

'Mr Addison holds no more appointments today. Perhaps next week? Or the week after?' Mrs End's face was shiny. November wasn't usually so hot. Hot and tinder dry.

Kate glanced about to see who was in earshot and then said firmly to Mrs End, 'I want to sign an application for a loan. Today.'

The woman looked up at Kate in surprise. 'Here?'

'Here. At the bank. An application.'

'Oh,' Mrs End said, smiling kindly. She bent forward to tidy the stacked tray of papers on her desk, then clasped her hands in front of her.

That did it. Kate walked passed the secretary's desk, rapped on Mr Addison's office door and went in. Later, she would tell Harry about the delicious look on Addison's face, his shock as he registered that she had walked in *again* without an announcement. But her pleasure was short-lived.

'Mrs Dowd!' the bank manager yelled at her. Again.

'Mr Addison.' She spoke politely, if a little menacingly, and sat without waiting to be asked. 'I've come to sign that application.'

'I beg your pardon?'

'The application for a loan. I've come to sign it.' She gripped her handbag in front of her like a shield.

'I told you, Mrs Dowd. I cannot support such an application.'

'Still, I insist on applying.'

Addison took in that information carefully, like a cat testing whether a still rat is just playing dead.

'I have no other choices, Mr Addison. I will be applying today.'

He leant back in his chair, wistful concern on his face, as if to say *If only I could help.*

Kate remained calm. 'You can't in good conscience refuse to accept my application. We're the biggest sheep place in the district, only modestly mortgaged now, and we have no overdraft.' What she didn't mention was that Addison had almost cancelled the overdraft in 1945, the minute Kate paid it off.

Addison actually rolled his eyes. 'A pretty speech, Mrs Dowd. But you've had the luck of a run of good seasons and strong wool prices. There is much more to good grazing than luck.'

'Prudent management is essential too, wouldn't you say? You know that Amiens is carefully managed and performing well.' She set her mouth, almost daring him to refuse to let her apply.

He shook his head. 'I cannot allow this.'

Kate saw red. She stood and banged a finger on his pristine desk. 'I run Amiens well. You know it. I *will* apply today.'

Mrs End unknowingly saved the day. Her head appeared round the door. 'Excuse me, Mr Addison.' Oblivious to the tension in the office, she held out a form to Kate. 'Is this the one, dear?' She hummed, holding out a printed form marked *APPLICATION FOR A LOAN.*

Kate took the single page from her, trying not to snatch it, and Mrs End withdrew, still humming.

Kate sat back down, lifted the smart ink pen from its holder on Mr Addison's empty desk, and worked her way briskly through the questions, trying to still her breathing and calm her scribble. *Number of acres, stock per acre, value of recent improvements, value of annual wool cheque, average wool grading at last clip.* She knew it all off the top of her head. Finally she signed at the bottom, under *Applicant.* The bank manager watched in shock, it seemed. He sat quite upright in his chair, his hands squeezed together in two fists in front of him.

'Your turn, Mr Addison.' She pushed the form across his tidy desk and held out the pen. The clenched knuckles turned white on the desk, but Kate did not blink, and slowly, slowly, his right hand extended to take the pen to sign.

CHAPTER 24

Woolgrowers shall always remember that a stratagem for specific adversities, from fire to flood, should invariably be on hand, kept precisely and revised punctually.

THE WOOLGROWER'S COMPANION, 1906

On Thursday evening, fire prevention got the attention of the local graziers. The district's great and the good, along with those graziers of novelty value, like Kate, assembled somewhat unwillingly at the RSL hall, called together by Mr Nettiford in his official capacity as captain of the district's volunteer brigade. Kate had not seen him since his unfortunate visit to Amiens a few days before.

There'd been 'fire prep' meetings called just like this in the past, years before, whenever conditions, weather and pasture meant a bushfire or fires were likely in the season. On this occasion, Mr Nettiford stood at the front, legs slightly apart, hands on his hips, surveying the packed hall with satisfaction. She avoided his eye and suspected he did hers.

Each man, and Kate, had been given a typed sheet on the way in, and she fanned herself with it. Even with all the windows open, the hall was hot, so full of people. She and Ed had been lucky to find seats – although in the back row – a warm sea of blue countryman shirts and sun-mottled necks in front. At least at the back Kate, the only woman in the room, was less conspicuous.

Mr Riley arrived, and he waved a greeting. Kate smiled back, disappointed but not surprised that Mrs Riley had not come with him. Just pleased that he hadn't brought Luca. Thinking of Luca made her feel sad; for them both. She knew she was a coward, not willing to take on one more battle, the long fight for acceptance in the district, let alone respectability, if she married Luca. That was too much. No, her first duty, her sole duty, had to be to Pearl and Daisy.

The mood in the sweltering hall was unsettled. Unusually, the local police sergeant, Wingnut, had joined Mr Nettiford at the front. The fact that he was there was important. If that didn't tell this crowd they had to toe the line, Kate didn't know what would.

Any kerfuffle tonight would be over who should do what in a bushfire. For as long as the people in this hall could remember, graziers had dealt with fires on their own, helping out their immediate neighbours and anyone else within cooee who might need a hand. The volunteer brigade was relatively new. So far it operated in much the same way, extending this neighbourly courtesy to cover the district.

That was likely to change. Just before the war, big bushfires down south in Victoria had done a lot of damage and some graziers, whole families, lost their lives. Another bout of fires in Victoria in '44, again with loss of life, meant that all the state governments were nervous, and keen to act once the war was over. Now, there was serious talk that they'd take over the running of firefighting from the graziers. Which made Mr Nettiford happy, but not the graziers.

Yet it wasn't slimy Mr Nettiford or the government that was worrying Kate. She was nervous at all-male gatherings, having learnt that certain men, when in numbers, will go for the most vulnerable. In this room that meant her: a woman, with an absent or absconded husband to boot, who kept burning off when everyone else had stopped. They never let the truth get in the way of a good story.

She shifted in the hard wooden chair. Judging by the rising level of talk and the rustle of paper, the rest of the crowd was also keen to get this over with.

Mr Nettiford cleared his throat. 'Good evening, gents. And lady.' He smiled, embarrassing Kate.

Wingnut glanced her way and nodded a greeting.

Nettiford cleared his throat again. Was he nervous too? These men in front of him were his customers. While it made sense to avoid having one of the graziers as head of the volunteer brigade – so there could be no allegations of favouritism as to where the firefighters should be sent – it still made for a tricky relationship. Mr Nettiford could hardly tell his customers what to do. The government was yet to make those new laws. All he could do was make suggestions.

'Right, gentlemen. We all know the risk of fire is pretty high, a Shire ban in place. If it stays this hot, and specially if a wind gets up, we'll be lucky to stop a fire should one start. Tonight we're gunna discuss bushfire preparedness.' That brought some muttering.

'Nettiford. I got one for ya.' The speaker was old Mr Wilson, father of all those wild boys and Alice. The graziers didn't count him as one of their own, as he didn't have one big place, just bits of dirt here and there around the district.

'Ya gunna tell us what to do, when a fire comes?' Mr Wilson said. 'Put it out, d'ya reckon? Or keep it goin for ya? Till your blokes can get there?'

A titter rippled through the hall.

Kate was surprised when John Fleming's voice filled the room. 'The captain is here to assist the graziers of the district. To help us help ourselves, if you will. We ought to give him a fair hearing.'

Mr Wilson raised both his hands in surrender, an older version of all those lookalike sons.

'Thank you, John.' Nettiford almost dipped his head in deference. He looked back across the crowd. 'For the record, I repeat that a complete fire ban is in place. So for them that don't understand that, *no back-burning*.'

Some turning around told Kate that last comment was directed at her and she felt heat come to her face.

'All right then. To planning. For starters, I wanna count of the fire trucks we got in the district.'

Kate regretted that her father had never bought an old clunker to refit as a water truck. He'd been lucky enough to have good seasons early on, and not to need one. As he got older . . . well, he wasn't himself. So she had no water truck.

'How many of youse have got a truck ready? Show of hands. I mean anything ya use: a trailer with water tanks, or 44-gallon drums of water – anything like that.'

From the back row, Kate could see about eight hands raised.

'Good. I know about you blokes already. For those that got em, I'm not teachin ya to suck eggs. But ya better get ya trucks ready. Outa the shed. Run em and get em fuelled. Fill the water tanks too, o'course.'

More laughter in the crowd. 'You'd be amazed the number of blokes who leave the fillin till it's too late. Oh, an keep em ready right through the summer, eh.'

Kate was surprised to find herself impressed. Mr Nettiford might be slimy and these might be his customers, yet he was taking his job seriously.

'While ya filling ya truck, check ya hoses for length and holes. An make sure ya creek or dam access is checked and clear. So it's all sweet. All right?'

The murmur wasn't one of disagreement, so he went on. 'All right. Next, all of you gotta think about ya plans. You gotta have a fire plan now. Remember? Ya gotta have a plan.'

There was another murmur then. This fire-plan business was quite new and the graziers always resented being told what to do. But Mr Nettiford didn't give in. 'Plan. Prepare and respond. Remember?' More mutterings. 'So what's a plan then? Have a look at the paper.' He waved his copy above his head. 'Y'all got one as you come in.'

Sheets rustled in the hall.

'*PREPARE*. See? It's at the top. So that's everything from shiftin ya woodpiles, if need be, away from the house, to slashin ya house paddocks. Cut down anything dead nearby too.' Nettiford seemed to know his stuff. 'Cut em, mow em. Specially if ya got a lot of buffel grass. It burns faster'n anythin.'

'Bugger,' carried across the hall.

Mr Nettiford looked for the speaker. 'Was that a question?' But there was no response.

'That reminds me. You blokes gotta look at ya wife's garden. Not popular, but if ya got shrubs right up against the house, or overhangin, you're like a box of matches.'

'Ya getting a bit antsy, aren't ya? Might not even be a fire.' That was old Mr Wilson again.

'We've had a long run this past week of high temperatures. After seasons of good rains. Heat and fuel. So this week or later this summer? Good conditions for a fire outbreak.'

Murmuring in the crowd showed some were not convinced. But Mr Nettiford was adamant. 'You gotta be prepared. Take ya gardens. Ya gotta get rid of ya shrubs up against the house.'

There was quiet then, those men who thought they'd act on this considering exactly how they'd approach that with their better halves. Gardens were usually a rare source of comfort to a lady in the bush, and sacrosanct. No men were generally involved in the decision-making as to where to plant the next jasmine or whether to shift the wisteria.

'I appreciate that's not simple but it's a fact. Them trees and shrubs gotta come down, anything against or overhanging the house, if ya think there's a chance a fire could reach em.'

'We're a good three-quarters of a mile of clear paddocks to the nearest trees. I don't reckon I'll be chopping anything down.' That was a voice Kate didn't recognise.

'You got a line of trees up to the house?'

'Nope,' came the reply. 'I'm a cocky, mate. Not a bloody grazier.'

An uncomfortable laugh followed. Just like their cockatoo namesakes, farmers on smallholdings scratched a living from their land and resented the graziers, who had more dirt and a less precarious living.

'If any of youse do – have trees linin ya road in – I recommend they go too, dependin on what they are. Fire'll walk along em. From a patch of bush a mile off, it'll get to ya house, no worries. Jump tree to tree.'

There was open laughter then. Who would chop down an avenue of trees just in case? Nettiford had a kangaroo loose in the top paddock.

But Kate didn't laugh. The fire captain was making sense. She thought immediately of her mother's trees, of her beloved poplars leading up to the Amiens homestead. The shrubs in the garden, the ones up against the house, would have to go as well. They were too big, too close to the homestead.

'All right, all right. But I say again, *ya gotta have a plan*.' Mr Nettiford raised one hand high above his head to stop the noise. It worked, sort of.

'You blokes can read the rest of it there on the *PREPARE* part.' He waved the sheet of paper again. 'What to do about stock: get those gates open. Move ya stud animals into the town yards for a bit. Or to a neighbour who's closer to town, better situated. There's stuff too about ya house itself. Wet ya verandahs and so on, if you know it's comin. An only if ya got time.'

'But most important—' He stopped until there was silence. 'Most important is the last bit. *RESPOND.* Ya gotta watch what's goin on, keep in touch on the party line. Withers – the sergeant here – will be manning the lines while I'm with the brigade. But he'll be quick to keep the lines clear.'

Wingnut nodded, his arms still folded across the pale blue of his uniform shirt.

Nettiford went on. 'Leaving early is the key. Leaving when things are calm and you got plenty of time. When there's no threat of fire reaching you on the road. If ya find ya need to think on ya feet it's already too late to leave. If ya can smell smoke, it's too late.'

There was an outbreak of unhappy talk. Nettiford didn't know anything about fighting fires.

'I'm tellin ya. The families down south that copped it, going back a few years? They waited too long and got killed on the road.'

This time there was silence.

'An if ya leave? Where ya goin? Ya gotta have a plan. What ya gotta have?' he asked.

A plan. The hall filled with voices. 'I know, I know. Youse wanna stay and protect ya property. It's worth nothin if ya dead.'

Groans followed.

'But if ya caught out in it, find an area that won't burn, the bigger the better. So that's a road or a firebreak. Ground heavily trampled by stock. A creek bed or a dam, if ya lucky enough to have a big one.' His eyes settled on Kate. Small towns had long memories. Her father had dammed their creek and cut off water to the neighbouring properties downstream.

There was more talk then.

'Righto. It's gunna be a long summer. So get movin. *Plan and prepare. Leave early.* Thank you all.' Mr Nettiford turned to answer a facetious question from someone in the front row.

Kate left quickly, to avoid Nettiford and not wanting to hang around in case someone tried their luck, one on one. She and Ed had a lot of work to do.

CHAPTER 25

The woolgrower's flock is protected not only by his good self, but also by the munificence that is a sheep's fleece, for it protects the animal in the cold, in the heat, and, remarkably, does not support flame.

THE WOOLGROWER'S COMPANION, 1906

The hot, dry westerly winds hung on. To Kate, they felt like portents of doom. She hoped she was wrong and the district would get through the summer without a bushfire. But Nettiford was right. They should be prepared. And there was no room for sentimentality.

Thunk.

Kate winced as Ed's axe bit hard into the first forty-foot poplar trunk. She couldn't help it. She remembered the day her mother had planted these trees. She must have been eight or nine and they'd walked together, her mother and her, inspecting each sapling set on either side of the road up the hill from the creek to the homestead. They'd grown and grown, and were like tall giraffes, guarding the road in. But now every one of these graceful trees would be brought down.

Ed hacked a small wedge into the trunk, with blows to the top and then the bottom. Chips flew as the axe blade cut through the outer bark. Above them, the branches shook; their leaves quivered, a mass of deep green triangles.

'C'nivva go?' Harry carried his own smaller axe, a tomahawk. Ed stepped back and Harry replaced him. His first blow was misaimed and he struck the bark outside the pale cream of the exposed sapwood.

'Follow my line, mate.' Ed pointed.

Harry tried again, and the blade hit right in the V of the wedge.

'Better. Now go for the outside edges. Ya not cutting mutton, mate.'

Harry laughed and swung again, taking a divot off the side of the widening wedge. He kept at it, until Ed called halt when there was an open wedge of a third or so of the trunk's diameter. They shifted round to the other side of the poplar. Then Ed started work there, taking an identical wedge, piece by piece.

'Gunna take a while, eh,' Harry said to Kate, looking along the line of poplars. 'Why'd ya mum plant em if she knew they might hafta come down one day?' he asked, ever practical.

'It's like joining. You join even in a drought. Because you hope for the best.'

'Well, they're coming down today,' Harry said, watching Ed. 'Not all today, mind. I reckon it'll take us a while.'

Sweat flew from Ed's arms as he swung the axe.

Kate thought again about her mother. She'd married Kate's father and then set about getting her family some respectability, some standing in the district. Expensive poplars were just one outlay on that climb, along with devoted study of the *Women's Weekly* for tips on what 'good families' did. Kate's father might whinge – and he did, about the doilies and the serviettes – but his wife worked on. And she'd done it; Kate had grown up accepted by everyone in the district, until – well, until her father died, and Kate claimed Pearl as her sister.

And there was worse to come. Her mother would be ashamed, so ashamed, of Kate's coming divorce. A blessing that she'd not lived to see it, any of it: first her father's disgrace, and now Kate's disgrace.

'Clear!' Ed yelled, as the poplar started to shudder. He backed away nimbly, gammy leg and all, as the poplar came down opposite him. It landed with a wallop and a cloud of dust, the soon-dead trunk lined up parallel to the track up to the house. Kate dropped her head. *One down.*

'It didn't land on the road, Ed. Well done.' Kate admired his handiwork.

He grinned at her. 'I better get that right, eh, Mrs D?'

She knew what he meant. In case they had to leave in a hurry. Other preparation work had already been done. Ed had cleared the creek paddocks, the ones bordering Longhope Downs, a week or so back, knowing if a fire came, chances were it would come from there.

Ed picked up the spare axe and moved on to the next tree in the avenue. 'Now, young Harry, you remember what t'do?' He lined up to cut into the next tree. 'Woddaya do if ya get caught in the paddock with a fire?'

Harry rolled his eyes. 'Ya take cover. Creek bed or some such.' Harry was sick of being asked but Kate was glad Ed was drumming it into him, into all of them.

'What if it might be comin' – the axe blade hit the trunk – 'for the homestead?'

'Go to the dam. Take a jumper.' Harry sighed.

'What sorta jumper? Cotton?'

'Nuh. Wool.'

'Why'd it best be wool?'

'Cos the wool holds the water and won't burn good. Not for a while anyway.'

'Yep. How d'ya breathe?'

'From under ya jumper. Use it like a tent. In the water on all sides.'

'What's gunna get ya? Fire or heat?'

'The heat, probly.'

Ed nodded. Fair enough.

They worked their way along the avenue all that day, and the two days that followed. With every tree that came down, Kate died a little. Her poor mother would have wept, but Kate tried not to, at least not in front of the boys. This was bush life; shed a few quiet tears then get back into the paddocks.

Spinksy, Johnno and Robbo worked with them then, cutting up each downed trunk one by one, loading the blocks into the truck tray. They'd store the cut timber far from the homestead, in small separate stacks on open ground, where it might not fuel a bushfire too much or for too long.

It was not until late on the third day, as Ed and Harry worked on the last of the poplars, that Kate was relieved to see a bank of cloud in the sky to the east. 'You reckon we'll get some rain out of that?'

'Nah. Smoke and mirrors. No rain.' Ed spoke quietly to her. 'I reckon we gotta set the gates open early t'morra, Mrs D. Cos if a fire comes . . .'

'You think it's that likely?'

'Mebbe. This heat . . .'

Just as the poplars had had to come down, now the time had come to make the last preparations for the stock. Opening the gates, all across Amiens, would mean the stock could move anywhere. But it would mean they might have a chance to get away from a following fire.

'It'll take some sorting out.' Everything would end up mixed together. But Kate knew Ed was right. 'Thank heavens the Rileys will take our rams. At least till we get some good rain and the risk goes down.' The Rileys' fire risk was very low. They had far less land than Amiens, and their paddocks had long since been cleared, the trees ringbarked and poison pushed into the axed crevices.

'Yeah. And I'm due t'truck Son of Basil and the other young rams out to Broken Hill, to old Mr Perry. Day after t'morra anyhow.'

'That's right. Look sharp round Basil himself, won't you?'

Ed laughed, remembering. The ram, Basil, had chased Kate and Harry once, when he was just out of lambhood. He was scary even then. But at that time Basil was still young and light enough that Kate had managed to throw him on his back to fend off a charge. She'd earned Harry's wide-eyed respect for it ever after.

She pulled her thoughts back to fire prep. Her *fire plan* – Mr Nettiford would be proud. 'What about the horses?'

'I'll open the gates and push em through towards the road paddocks. Safest there.'

'You think a fire'd really go across Amiens? After all the burning off we've done? All the grazing in the creek-side paddocks?'

Ed sucked in a breath between his teeth. 'I reckon we're not too bad. Here on Amiens . . .'

'But?'

'The bugger of it is your mate Fleming, Mrs D. He hasn't burnt off in months. He's got a bloody bonfire ready to go. Specially where Longhope Downs fronts the State Forest.'

'But would it come through here?'

Ed squinted unhappily. 'If a fire gets a go on in Longhope Downs – if the fire's big enough – it'll come through us anyhow, specially if the wind's behind it. Question is, have we done enough to stop it? The creek paddocks are pretty much eaten away. We burnt off good. We got the firebreaks ploughed. But places burn, Mrs D. Ya just never know how much.'

Kate struggled to imagine it. She'd grown up mostly with drought, not so much with the risk of bushfire. Ed, on the other hand, had been taught about fire as a boy. It was ironic, really, given Wilcannia, way out west where he grew up, had much lower rainfall and so much less vegetation than Longhope. He'd ended up working for Kate's father by happenstance. He was only fourteen, and on a drove passing through, when Kate's father saw him working stock. He had offered Ed a job and he'd been on Amiens since.

'An we gotta bring the homestead trees down, Mrs D. Them ones up close.'

'I can do it. Harry and I. You get the rams to the Rileys' first thing.' She watched the clouds, huge nimbus thunderheads, building up. If only those clouds could deliver rain, then tomorrow would be a lot less worrying.

CHAPTER 26

It is an oft-overlooked truth that whilst a battle plan is always in the armoury of the victor, such plan may become useless once the fight is on.

THE WOOLGROWER'S COMPANION, 1906

Days on end of hot westerlies had made the air crackly dry, with no relief in the nights. Even by midday, Kate felt weary from the heat.

Harry was sitting at the end of the kitchen table eating lunch, Pearl in the highchair next to him. School had been cancelled for that day and possibly the next so the children could be at home, not so much for safety as to help with fire preparation. Having Harry home pleased Pearl, who had not taken her eyes off him; hardly believing that she had him for the whole day. In the laundry, Daisy folded washing.

'Will they be all right?' Harry asked.

Kate was in her socks, back from dropping off food first thing at the stockmen's hut on the old yards near the escarpment. As she'd pulled up, Kate could have sworn she'd seen Fleming's truck, disappearing into the heavy timber forest that dwindled into sparse bush on their side of the boundary. Yet it was rough country up there and hard to get a truck along that track. She had no time to think about it now. She was just glad the hut was stocked and ready.

'Will they?' Harry asked again.

'Will who what?' Kate was drying up dishes.

'Ben and Donald.'

Ben had been Kate's pony, now appropriated by Harry, his mount to ride to school each day.

Harry stopped eating and put his fork down on his plate. With him distracted, Pearl reached over from her highchair, delicately removed Harry's fork and put it into her mouth.

'We'll put Donald in the laundry, if we have to leave the homestead. But that won't happen.'

'What about Ben?'

'Ed opened up all the gates today, on his way to town. He took the rams to the Rileys' and Mrs Walters in to do the shopping. With the gates open, Ben and all the stock will be able to move about. If they need to,' Kate added. 'It's a *just in case* sort of thing. Stop worrying and do eat up. We've got to get down the last of the garden trees.'

Harry took the fork back from Pearl, who frowned. Her own food, the same as Harry's, was apparently much less tasty.

'How's Ben gunna know the gates are open? Specially if there's smoke everywhere.'

'Animals know,' Kate said. It sounded weak.

'Yeah?'

'Come outside. I want to show you something.'

He followed her onto the verandah, carrying Pearl on his hip. The homestead garden looked almost naked, unfamiliar gaps along the fence line where Ed and the stockmen had taken down the biggest trees.

They stood together, the three of them, at the edge of the verandah looking out at the yellowed paddocks of Amiens, its ridges and hills hot and still, the sky almost cloudless, that bank of empty nothing still making its way in from the east, borne by strong hot winds. 'Listen,' Kate said.

'Birds?'

'Exactly. I'm sure they'd go if a fire was really coming.' Kate didn't know how else to convince Harry that Ben would be all right.

'Ya reckon?'

'I reckon.'

'That's bull, Mrs D,' Harry observed without rancour.

She was silent. He wasn't wrong. The odd thing was, she could swear she smelled smoke too. The faintest scent, only now and then. She had to be imagining it.

'Daisy, did you do the jumpers?' Kate called.

'Yeah, Missus. I get em.'

Daisy was out in a second from the laundry with four jumpers, neatly folded and stacked. 'I did them necklines. With string. Tied em up.'

'Thanks, Daisy.' Kate was grateful. At least they were ready. *Prepare for the worst.*

Harry rolled his eyes when Daisy went in and put the jumpers on the kitchen table. As if they'd ever get stuck where they'd need those jumper-tent things. He took himself and Pearl back inside, and Kate heard him ask Daisy for the sugar pot.

Then, still outside, Kate saw with horror a scrap of ash floating in the air.

The shrill ping of the telephone broke into her thoughts. She ran in and picked up the heavy receiver. Harry pressed his ear against her head to listen in, while Daisy cuddled Pearl to keep her quiet.

'Longhope switch here.' It was Barrel, on the party line. 'Please listen for your name. Then I have the sergeant for you.'

Kate heard each of the graziers answer by name, a rollcall of the men whose properties filled the land between Amiens and

Longhope. All of them had stayed close to their homesteads, just in case. Kate too; Amiens was the last on this party line.

There was a muffled shuffling as Barrel passed the receiver to the policeman. 'They all on?' Wingnut asked. After a pause, he cleared his throat. 'Sergeant Withers here. We have a grass fire. I repeat, a grass fire. An outbreak thirty minutes or so ago at the triway. I just got off the blower to the Longhope Downs people. Nettiford reckons it's burnt a good few acres already. Moving south, south-west. That'll take it down the Longhope Downs and Amiens boundary.'

'Where did it start? Which of the three?' Kate asked. Longhope Downs, Amiens and the State Forest met at the triway. Knowing where it started would help to fight it, and to predict where it would go.

'I can tell ya that you blokes on Amiens will be next, if the wind keeps up and they can't stop the fire.'

'They got bugger all chance of stoppin it on Longhope Downs,' Harry said quietly to Kate. He was right. If the fire got into the Downs, all that dead pasture would carry it on to Amiens.

Wingnut said again: 'I repeat: Fire at the triway. You all get that?'

A masculine *yes* went back down the party line to the policeman.

'Where's Nettiford?' a voice asked.

'They're fighting the front at the triway now. Siren went off for all the volunteer fire fellas soon as we got the report. On the Longhope Downs side, near Myall Creek.'

Kate hoped the volunteers would be safe. Her father had considered the land round Myall Creek bad luck, after a massacre of Aborigines in the early days of settlement. It half annoyed Kate that they weren't fighting it on the Amiens side, but Longhope Downs faced the bigger threat. It had more fuel, because Fleming had not burnt off much.

Wingnut finished up. 'Err on the side, you hear me? And we might get a southerly change. It'd turn the fire when you're not expecting.'

There was silence.

'All right. Good luck, gents. An Mrs D? Can you stay on the line?'

Kate felt her heart fall. A series of clicks told them the men had left.

'You got a man on the place, Mrs D? Is Ed there?'

'He's on his way back now, probably.'

'Where's he comin from? How long will he be?'

'Town. He delivered our rams to the Rileys first thing then dropped off our housekeeper in town. That was at eleven.'

What they didn't know, and wouldn't know until a full day later, was that Ed and Mrs Walters had not yet even reached Longhope. In the morning light of the drive in, the truck had hit a roo, a big one. It took Ed more than an hour to untangle the carcass and shift the bent mudguard back off the front tyre. An hour to get back on the road. He was out of range of Amiens's two-way radio.

'Where are ya Abos?' Wingnut asked.

'Out in our southern blocks. They're opening the gates. Ed had them to keep as much stock as possible in those paddocks.'

'At least down there they'll not be caught up in it. Likely see it comin.' After some muffled conversation with the mouthpiece covered, Wingnut's voice came back down the line. 'You got wheels, though, haven't ya?'

'Yes. We have the car.'

'Don't think about goin up there. Let Nettiford and his blokes tackle the fire. They don't need to be bloody rescuing womenfolk.'

Wingnut was right, but for the wrong reasons. Longhope Downs was a tinderbox. There'd be no fighting it, if it got a go on.

'Get out, eh? Early. If in doubt. All right. Good luck, Mrs D.' The line went dead.

For once, Harry said nothing. Daisy looked out of the kitchen door, Pearl on her hip.

'Ed's home soon.' That was for Harry's sake.

Daisy's eyes were on the gusty paddocks. 'S'hot, eh, Missus.'

'Yes.' Kate didn't try to reassure Daisy. 'We better cut that cypress pine down and hose the verandahs.' Both were up against the homestead.

'I'll get Ben outa that horse paddock,' Harry said.

'No need, Harry. Ed would have checked Ben on his way through. You know Ed.' And Kate didn't want Harry anywhere but right here, with her. She was sure now that she could smell smoke. She'd kept a sharp eye on the horizon to the north-east.

In the homestead garden, the pair of them walked down to the gates, Harry with his tomahawk, Kate with an axe. When a curious chook followed, Kate cursed herself for forgetting. She should have shut them all in the shed, first thing.

They went first to the cypress pine near the gates. It was six feet or so high, and Kate pushed aside its dense lower branches to get at the trunk. She aimed the blade about eighteen inches off the ground and swung, but it glanced off. Kate could chop wood well enough to cut smallish bits for the fireplace. But this sideways business was harder, especially with the branches pressing in on her. She tried again.

'Ya bloody hopeless,' Harry observed. He held out a palm and a smut of ash floated gently into it. 'And I smell smoke,' he said, matter of fact.

Kate did too. But Nettiford had to be wrong about that, about leaving as soon as you smelled smoke. She turned back to the tree, shaken.

'Let me have a go, Mrs D,' Harry said.

She backed out then to let him in, but kept an eye on the

horizon to the north-east, and on the gully for the truck. A sooty gum leaf fell out of the sky, then another, swirling about with each tug and pull of the gusting wind. *Where the heck was Ed?*

Harry took her axe and set to. He was strong, even at thirteen, and just those few days spent felling poplars with Ed had made their mark. The cypress pine came down with a thump across the lawn and that lone chook went into the air in fright, air dusted with embers now.

From then on, Harry chopped and Kate hauled back the downed branches. They worked their way around the garden, tree after tree, shrub after shrub. Cinders were everywhere, circling like crows at a carcass. The sky was almost overcast too, as a bank of storm cloud moved right across. The cloud was a weird colour, almost dark green, and thunder rumbled from it. More smoke than cloud. They had to hurry.

Harry moved on with the axe to the other side of the house, and they kept going under the darkening sky. The fire was moving and moving fast; Kate felt it in her bones. She tried to stifle that foreboding feeling.

Harry brought down the last tree, a jacaranda sucker. He sat on its narrow trunk and looked back at the house. 'She's pretty bare now, eh?'

Kate didn't want to see that, and kept her eyes on the branch she was pulling. She wished Ed was home.

From his seat, Harry held out his palm to catch another piece of floating ash. 'I reckon I'll check on Ben.'

'Harry. I said no. You have to stay here.' She dropped a downed branch outside the gate, and he gave her a dirty look as she came back.

'What about them wisteria?'

Kate looked back towards the verandah trellis, suddenly transfixed. Her eyes went up and up. The western sky was full of grey smoke. A distinct plume rose from the mass, black-grey smoke at the bottom, white at the top. A bushfire giving birth to its own storm.

'We have to go.' She said it quietly, almost to herself at first, then started to run for the house. 'Harry!' she yelled. 'We have to go!'

CHAPTER 27

From the profusion of references to sheep in the Bible, this writer holds the following most dear: 'My sheep listen to my voice; I know them, and they follow me.' (John 10:27)

THE WOOLGROWER'S COMPANION, 1906

'*Now. To the dam!*' Kate ran round the house towards the kitchen door. On the verandah, Daisy was hosing down the boards with Pearl on her hip.

'The dam, Dais. We have to go now!' Kate shouted.

Daisy put the hose end against the house wall and left the water flowing.

In the kitchen, Kate was shoving scones and bikkies and anything edible to hand into a knapsack. Then she stopped still, listening. She heard the low hum of the diesel. *Thank God.* It must be Ed. She moved round the table, still stuffing things into the knapsack, to look out the kitchen door. But it was the Rileys' truck, lights on.

Luca jumped down from the cab, left the door open and ran across the lawn towards her.

'*Signora*!' he called, pointing to the bank of cloud and smoke. 'We go to the water, *Signora*. Now.'

'Yes.' She turned and shouted into the hall, 'Daisy! Harry! To the truck!'

Luca came into the kitchen and the sight of him gave her comfort. 'Can we get out to the main road?' she asked.

Luca shook his head. 'The fire, he come soon. We go *now*.'

The telephone was ringing as Daisy went by them with dillybags in one arm and Pearl in the other. 'Where is Harry?' Luca asked.

'In the garden. On the other side.' Kate picked their hats off the peg.

'Harry!' Luca yelled. 'Harry. We go now!' He took the two wicker chairs off the verandah and across the lawn, hurling them into the truck tray, then filled the water bag at the rain-water tank. Daisy was at the truck with Pearl, and Luca helped them up into the cabin.

'Harry!' Kate yelled again. She ran to the far side of the house to grab him. But the garden was empty, just cut down shrubs and Harry's axe abandoned by the fence. She went in again, searching, room by room, calling him. 'Harry! Harry!'

Then she stopped, stricken, sick to her stomach. Harry had gone to Ben. For sure. Woollen pullovers and hats in her arms, she ran, almost ignoring the phone that was still ringing in the kitchen. But it might be help.

'Fire's comin your way fast, Mrs D.' Wingnut's voice came down the line, worried. 'Ed's here.'

'What? We're going to the dam. Luca will take us. But Harry's gone.' She hung up and ran outside.

Luca was slinging tarps into the truck tray and moved to help Kate into the cabin. 'Harry?'

Kate shook her head. 'We can't leave him!' she cried, terrified.

'We rest here' – Luca pointed at the ground – 'we burn.' He lifted Kate up into the cab and shut the door behind her. She put an arm across Daisy and Pearl to steady them. Then Luca climbed in, firing up the engine. The big truck wheels spun in the dust as they moved off.

'Oh no. Donald!' Kate cried. She'd not found the wallaroo. Harry would be so cross with her.

'S'all right, Missus. I caught him,' Daisy said. 'He's in the laundry.'

Kate scanned the paddocks and the mirrors for Harry but there was nothing, just shifting smoke.

The truck rattled over the corrugations so hard that Pearl started to cry. Daisy held Pearl's head to her chest but the toddler would not be consoled. She'd picked up the fear in her mother, in all of them.

'Keep the shoes in the water,' Luca said, pointing at Kate's feet. 'Yes? For after.'

At the dam, Luca pulled the truck to a stop close to the water and left the engine running. Kate and Daisy got themselves, Pearl and their gear out fast. Luca unloaded the two wicker chairs, and ran with them held high, wading out into the water until he was waist-deep. He pushed each under the surface until their feet sank into the mud, and then he leant on them with his full weight to force them down even further. As he waded back out, Kate remembered a fleeting image of Luca years before, in this same water with her. *Another life.*

A distant hum brought her back with a start. Fire. It was getting closer, but they had no way of knowing how much time they had. Or whether it would pass them by. Luca was looking hard at the trees round the dam. Most were far back, cleared when the dam wall was built. The water level was down too, making the bare earth round it wider than usual. All good things in a fire.

But one damn tree remained. It was the trunk she'd forbidden Harry to climb. She'd forgotten to ask Ed to bring it down. It stood now, a slender grey bone against that terrible sky.

'It'll reach us, won't it?' Kate realised with horror. 'If it burns and falls?'

Luca waggled his head. 'Perhaps. You must watch.' He took her hand. 'I go now. Search Harry.'

Kate inhaled sharply. She might lose them both.

'I come back.' Luca straightened her hat and touched her lips with a finger. Then he left her, running for the truck.

'Luca,' she called in terror, her voice drowned out by the roar of the truck engine as it pulled away, its tail-lights drifting in and out of sight through the smoke.

'Missus.' Daisy touched her arm and spoke softly. 'We gotta go inna the water, Missus.'

Kate pulled her eyes away and, with a shaking hand, took a jumper from Daisy. A hot gust hit them, and she pulled the felt hat down hard on her head. Pearl, in Daisy's arms, stopped crying and looked at Kate in her funny hat.

'One for you too,' Kate said, putting the hat on Pearl's strong hair. She gently tied it on with a bow under the toddler's chin.

They waded in then, hand in hand. The dam water was cool against Kate's legs, deeper as they approached the half-submerged wicker chairs.

They got themselves into the chairs, water up to their armpits, tightly holding hands under the dirt-coloured water.

Kate looked back over her shoulder and gasped. A tiny patch of blue sky appeared but it was quickly swallowed by smoke and cloud, and the horizon was lit with bursts of orange as far-off flames lunged into the air, bits of the sun come down to earth. It was like something from the Bible.

Kate, long an unbeliever, prayed for Harry and Luca, for Daisy and Pearl, and for herself.

CHAPTER 28

The Merino is generally a stolid, reliable animal, most unlikely to take fright, to run hither and thither, or to stampede, unless desperate of thirst, or fleeing danger.

THE WOOLGROWER'S COMPANION, 1906

Harry had left the homestead garden by hopping the back fence and heading straight to the shed to get a bridle. With the smoke and maybe fire too, he knew he'd have to haul Ben out.

Now Harry ran and ran, his hat in one hand, the bridle in the other.

The horse paddock was not that far from the homestead. Usually, Harry would've cut straight across the ram paddock, but there was so much smoke about he didn't want to chance getting lost. He followed the track that ran parallel to the fence although it added a good few minutes. He'd tried to keep running flat strap, but got buggered quickly. It was too far and the smoke was too thick. He was down to a jog.

The horse paddock cocky gate was pulled back. Mrs D'd been right; Ed must have opened up the gates on his way into town, so the stock would get away. Harry thought that was a load of bull. Sheep were dumber than their own manure. If the fire came through, he reckoned a mob'd cram against the fence, right next to an open gate, even. Then . . . then? He didn't want to think about that.

'Ben!' he yelled into the smoke. Bits of the paddock came in and out of view.

Bloody horse. 'Ben!' He cupped his hands round his mouth and yelled again. Ben didn't like to come at the best of times. When Harry went to catch him in the morning before school, the horse would trot off and stick his head in a bush as soon as he heard Harry's call. Just his head. If Ben couldn't see Harry, then Ben's horse brain told him that Harry couldn't see Ben either.

Harry walked the paddock then, down one fence line. He got to the corner, a T in the fence.

'Ben!' Still nothing. He turned left, along the bottom of the paddock. The smoke was getting thicker now, and he was glad he had the fence to tell him where he was.

'Ben!' he yelled again, listening for the sound of hooves. Nothing. Just the noise, far off, of a low hum, like a two-way radio off channel. That must be the bloody fire.

Harry broke into a jog past a startled mob of sheep. 'Run, ya idiots,' he said. But they stayed still, staring at him. Harry started to panic. He jogged on and suddenly he was back at the gate, with a mirage in front of him. There, twenty feet away and shifting nervously, was bloody Ben.

'G'day, mate,' Harry said softly, walking in real slow. 'Where ya been, eh?'

Ben was snorting, unhappy. He was a lot smarter than the stupid sheep. He knew they were in trouble.

'You gotta come with me, mate. All right?' Harry came on, step by step, fifteen feet left between them, always fearful flighty Ben would take off.

Harry kept patting his pocket. 'Yeah. Sugar, mate.'

The horse eyed him nervously. Ten feet.

'It's right here. In m'pocket. Ya want some?'

Ben snorted, wide-eyed, skittish.

Harry held out a flat hand, one little lump of sugar on it. *C'mon, Ben.*

Eyes on that lump, the horse took a step towards Harry and, as he did, the boy moved as well. He got his shoulder under the horse's neck and slid the bridle over the ears, pushing the bit into the flabby mouth. Ben's big lips were warm and soft against his palm, and wet with spit.

'Righto,' Harry said, slapping Ben's hard neck with affection. Smoke circled around them. He couldn't see more than fifteen feet in any direction. 'Now what, eh? Now bloody what?'

CHAPTER 29

The prudent woolgrower shall grasp that preparation; above all, preparation of mind, as well as of pasture and stock, must be understood as the marrow of the bones of his success.

THE WOOLGROWER'S COMPANION, 1906

The time seemed to crawl by, with Kate and Daisy half submerged. Pearl, unfazed, climbed from one lap to the other. 'Swim,' Pearl explained solemnly, touching the wicker. 'Chair swim.'

Kate couldn't guess how many minutes had passed. The haze and smoke were suffocating, the air heavy with the ash and cinder swirling about them. She felt the weight of the missing, Harry and Luca, just glad Ed was safe in town. If Luca or Harry died, she was to blame. She should never have let Harry out of her sight.

Worse, the temperature was rising.

Daisy practised submerging, showing Pearl how to take a big breath, puff out her cheeks, and hold it in to go under. They did it together, and up they'd come; slowly, brown dam water dripping like tea off their hats. Daisy did it again and again until Pearl refused to practise any more. But could Pearl do it under a sodden jumper? Kate prayed so.

The toddler gently tidied a strand of her mother's hair,

tucking it into her hat, droplets of water still dripping from the brim. But Kate could see, even with the dunkings, that a layer of black cinder was soon settling again on Daisy's hat. She looked hard at the dead trunk. If the wind changed, if the trunk burnt, the only flammable thing for a good hundred yards might reach them if it fell the wrong way.

Kate coughed again, her lungs sick already with the fumes.

'Reckon they all right, Missus?' Daisy said.

'They're smart, aren't they.' Kate sounded pathetic, even to herself.

'Yeah. An Ed's all right. Got hisself stuck in town.' Kate could hear Daisy almost smiling.

'Will you be all right?' Kate asked, her voice cracking with worry.

'Yeah, Missus. Right as rain, eh.'

Kate felt Daisy's hand gently squeeze her own. She prayed again.

CHAPTER 30

The woolgrower would be wise to heed a sudden urge by his flock, or indeed, any cloven-hoofed animal in his charge, to flee.

THE WOOLGROWER'S COMPANION, 1906

In dense smoke, Harry led the flighty Ben through the cocky gate and into the rams' paddock. It was hard to get his bearings, and he had to brush charred leaves from his face as they fell out of the sky.

'We be all right, mate. Just get to the homestead, eh?' On a tight rein, the pony pulled back. That spooked Harry. Ben wasn't coming of his own accord. Were they heading *into* the fire? The falling leaves burnt Harry's skin and he knew they'd be hurting Ben too.

The thick smoke shifted here and there, when a gust blew through. Only there wasn't a wind, none that Harry could feel. The smoke just moved around him and branches popped and exploded, closer and closer, showing themselves only by the flash of sparks through the haze.

Harry heard a low hum then, like a two-stroke at first, but it grew and grew into the deep whine of an engine, a huge one. Then it hit him. *That's the fire, the noise of the fire front.*

He and Ben might die out here. Mrs D'd tear strips off him too. But he'd be dead, so it'd be all right if she got mad at him. Still. She was going to be ropeable. He hoped Mrs D and Daisy and Pearl were safe in the dam. Luca'd take care of them, for sure. Harry had seen him come in the truck. He'd slipped out, then, to get Ben.

The ground was suddenly bare under his feet, trampled by a hundred hooves. 'Bugger!' Harry hit something in the thick smoke and almost fell into it. The water trough – and it was full, the surface reflecting the weird greyness of their tiny world, hemmed in by eddying smoke.

Suddenly, Harry gripped a fistful of Ben's mane and clamped the bridle with his other hand. Beyond, even through the banks of smoke, he could see it. The fire, the front of the fire. It was coming towards them – in roughly their direction, anyway.

Harry thought fast. Behind them was only fence. Like a drongo, he'd brought no wire-cutters so he couldn't get Ben through it. The other direction? They'd never reach the gate at the end of the paddock neither.

The fire front came on.

Ben pulled hard at the bridle; he wanted to run. But Harry knew there was nowhere to go. His head swam. They would bloody die here, like stupid sheep.

Harry's eyes lit on the ground at his feet. Better they stick here by the trough, the pasture all dead and gone. Nothing to burn.

Ben pulled his head up again and again, panicking in the smoke, the coming flames.

'We gunna try'n get ya into the trough, mate.'

Even as he said that, Harry knew it was nuts. On a good day, he might have kidded Ben into lying down on the dirt for him, with a lot of coaxing and sugar. But that was not this day. They were stuffed. The fire must have got into the State Forest, and that was going up like petrol.

Harry put the bridle under his foot and, with his hat, started ladling water over Ben. The pony pulled back but Harry talked him down. 'S'all right, fella. Eh? S'all right.'

Hatful after hatful, Harry threw trough water over the horse. The heat got worse and worse until it was hard to breathe as the flames advanced. The blaze would not go right over them but it would come bloody close. When Harry could bear it no longer, he grabbed the bridle up from under his foot in the dirt and pulled Ben closer. Harry got into the trough, the green slime making his grip on the side slippery. Ben lurched up again with the movement of the water, but Harry held on tight.

'C'mon, mate,' Harry called, again bailing water with his hat onto Ben's head and as much of the pony's body as he could reach. But the heat was getting stronger and stronger. It became too much, and Harry wrenched his shirt off over his head, ready to make the stupid tent Ed kept going on about, to breathe through. Gripping the shirt in one hand, he took a big breath and put his whole body under the water, hat and all, eyes wide to the fire around him, one wrist exposed, his other hand clamped on Ben's bridle to stop the horse from bolting. They had little enough chance here. But running? Ben'd die for sure. He'd never outpace the fire.

Harry took another breath and went under, struggling in the trough, sliding against the slimy sides. His lungs bursting, cheeks full of air, he pulled his exposed arm with the reins under the surface, eyes still open, looking up, and the watery sky above him flashed orange like the sun.

CHAPTER 31

It is a regrettable that lightning may travel down a tree and still alight upon a hapless flock sheltering beneath.

THE WOOLGROWER'S COMPANION, 1906

Pearl coughed, and Kate patted her head against her, the smoke swirling about them. The toddler held out her arms to go to her mother and Daisy took her through the water, quickly getting all but her head back under the surface. Pearl rubbed at her eyes, sore from the smoke.

Kate's shoulder ached from the cold and from holding Pearl, and her bottom hurt from the wicker chairs, even with the jumpers around her. Every part of her exposed – her head, neck and face – was hot, cooled only by a dunk under the surface.

The fire was nearer; Kate knew it from the thick air, the dense smoke and the sound. It was like the wind, at first, a far-off breeze through trees. Then it changed to something alive, something moving, the flames jumping from one tree to the next, a hum of destruction.

Sometimes, through her fright, Kate recognised a sound amid the roar: the pop and spit of eucalypt leaf oil igniting; the crash of a burning trunk, off in the escarpment. But the pace of the fire kept on, up and up, the dead and now live embers raining all around them.

'It's comin, Missus,' Daisy gasped, terrified.

Kate pulled the first woollen jumper up through the water and helped Daisy drag it, sopping, over her head. The toddler stared at her mother and Kate made herself grin for Pearl's benefit. Daisy looked like a soggy ghost. 'Can you see anything?' Kate's voice was strangled with fear.

'Nuh. A bit, mebbe,' came from under the wet wool.

'You all right, Daisy?'

The shape nodded.

'Now, Pearl, you're going to be a ghost too! Under there with your mum.'

Pearl gave her an arch look, but didn't protest as Kate pulled the expanse of wet wool up and over her as well. More and more embers fell about them, carried on gusts coming from nowhere, from all over and with an unnatural force.

Kate found the second jumper and went under the water to work it onto her own head, the sopping wool scratchy against her skin. She could see little through it and she reached out in the water, finding Daisy's hand once more.

Suddenly, through the wool, Kate saw a red light. She lifted her jumper to see the tongues of flame licking up from the horizon. That red grew and grew, up and outwards, as if a giant had winged his way, airborne, along the hill curve, lit torch behind him, lighting up the line of the horizon.

Death. She saw her death, Daisy and Pearl with her. Luca and Harry. They were caught too and would die.

In that moment, Kate knew, with as much certainty that she knew she might well die in the next minutes. She loved Luca, and she wanted to be with him. He was right. She owed a duty to herself too, along with her duty to Pearl and Daisy. They would fight the district together. If they lived.

'Go unna, Missus,' Daisy said. The three inhaled and submerged, Daisy counting to five with each squeeze of Kate's hand. They burst up, desperate for a breath, the air hotter than before, even through the wet fabric.

Pearl's whimper became a cry and Kate heard Daisy whisper to her, consoling her. Kate worried then for the Amiens sheep, and prayed they'd got themselves away from the fire front, through the open gates.

The heat intensified, gusts wafting over them as the front grew closer. The wind had swung round.

'Unna, Missus.' They went down again, counting and counting, then up.

Daisy coughed and spluttered, and Kate squeezed her hand through the water.

'Got a cramp, Missus,' Daisy said urgently.

Kate pushed her sodden wool covering up and back onto her head, and lifted up Daisy's too, Pearl's frightened eyes looking back at her. 'Give me Pearl. Rub hard. Hard.'

Daisy lifted the crying toddler across to Kate, and Pearl continued to wail.

Behind Daisy, the whole crown of a box gum at the edge of the dam paddock burst into flames, the fire swallowing its trunk-line V, like a giant worshipper opening fiery arms. Its neighbour followed, then the next and the next, until the dead tree trunk near the dam edge caught with a shower of sparks, a massive ember storm spewing ahead of the front.

'Go deeper, Missus!'

'Stay under your jumper,' Kate said. 'I'll lead you.' She took one step towards the middle of the dam, still holding Pearl, heading away from the chairs. But Daisy's cramp hobbled her and she barely moved.

'Into the deep. I've got you!' She dragged Daisy on, gripping her with one arm, the other round Pearl, to the deepest water in which they could stand, their covered woolly heads just above the surface. Daisy hopped back and forth, trying to rub the cramp. Kate clung to her hand and they dunked under together, gasping as they came up to breathe smoke-filled air, willing the front to pass them by.

At that moment, the dead tree split with a crack like a gunshot. 'Look out! Look out!' Kate shouted, clutching Pearl. Daisy screamed as the trunk crashed down.

CHAPTER 32

An apparently very slight effect on a flock may have the direst of results. For sheep subjected to worrying by dogs, or other panic, may die within a short matter of hours from shock.

THE WOOLGROWER'S COMPANION, 1906

Shaking, Kate staggered with Pearl out of the water through drifting smoke. She made herself walk away from the dam, one step, another, on black dirt. Numb, she could think only of Luca and Harry. And of Daisy.

In halting steps, she followed the track across an unknown paddock, scorched of landmarks, always wanting to look back, towards the dam.

Something moved just ahead and Kate lurched away. A sheep, burnt black, its muzzle and legs blistered.

Let Harry and Luca live.

She walked on, staring through the smoke.

The truck. *Please God, let them be alive.*

She put Pearl down, placing each small foot on top of her own, protecting the child from the hot earth.

Kate, as blackened as the paddock in which she stood, raised a hand. *I am here.*

A man got out of the vehicle, and Kate moaned. She swayed, her knees buckling, as she clutched at Pearl.

Luca started to run. He caught them both, kissing Kate's hair, her blackened face, her throat.

'Harry?'

Luca shook his head. 'Not yet. They look. They look him now,' he said. Her tears dampened his shirt.

'Mumma,' Pearl said, and Kate stroked her cindered hair.

'Daisy?' Luca asked.

Kate could not bring herself to speak. She willed herself not to look back towards the dam.

Pearl began to cry.

Later, Kate would remember just parts of the next hour. Flashes in her head: Luca; coming out of the scorched Amiens paddocks to the unburnt country; seeing the homestead untouched, only naked of its trees; Donald in the garden as if nothing had changed, bounding about, spooked by all the people.

She remembered telling them too about Daisy; the shocked faces; the concern for her and for Pearl. *It's Daisy who's gone*, Kate wanted to shout. She remembered crying then, with relief that they believed her and with shock. She remembered weeping, clutching Luca, knowing he was alive. Being carried into her room. Wanting to help search for Harry. Mrs Riley persuading her, telling her over and over that Ed and Mrs Walters were truly safe.

Being given a tablet.

Something.

The fog of sleep and, even in sleep, weeping with relief for Luca, and in desperation too.

CHAPTER 33

The prudent woolgrower shall remain vigilant, in the hours and days following a panic in his sheep. A lack of interest in grazing, an unwillingness to return to the mob, or a turning in circles; all are grave signs of distress to which the woolgrower must be alert.

THE WOOLGROWER'S COMPANION, 1906

It was the rasp and buzz of the two-way radio that shook itself into Kate's sleep, and slowly, slowly, she stirred as the blaring carried throughout the homestead.

The light in the window told her it was early evening but her head felt heavy, as though she'd woken in the night. Her swimming eyes found the alarm clock by her bed. Almost eight. She'd been asleep for hours.

Harry. She sat bolt upright and was out of bed at once. Where were her jodhpurs? Hopping on one foot in her hurry to get them on, she pulled a hand through her hair and went down the hall towards the sound of the two-way.

The kitchen was a blur of people. Mrs Riley stood in the laundry doorway, bouncing a fraught Pearl on her hip. She was elegant as ever, but dressed down today, without her usual pearls.

Mrs Walters was making tea. Kate smiled automatically at the housekeeper, grateful for her calm efficiency in all the activity.

Wingnut, Mr Nettiford and Mr Riley were bent over a map spread out across the table. Even groggy as she was, Kate was glad of that, glad there were many people in the kitchen today. Outside, cars and trucks were drawn up to the homestead fence like flies on a dead animal, as men moved about them, coming and going. Searching.

'Mrs D.' Wingnut's voice was clear to Kate, even through the fog of her head. 'We runnin the searches from here.'

'Of course.' Kate took Pearl and the child gently laid her head on her shoulder. 'Harry?'

'Not yet.'

But then a shout from outside told her otherwise.

'Harry!' Luca's voice carried. 'Harry!'

Soon Luca came into the kitchen, his arm round Harry. The boy's head was down, one hand tucked into his armpit like a broken wing. But he wouldn't look up and his face, streaked with soot and tears, was broken.

'Is OK,' Luca said to Kate softly.

'I couldn't save im,' Harry said, his face crumpling. Kate folded him into a hug and he sobbed silently against her and Pearl.

Mrs Riley hugged Harry long and hard, and he endured it like a trooper.

Wingnut went to Kate. He spoke softly, his eyes on the laundry. 'There's just one missin now. It's Grimes, Mrs D.'

'Two,' Kate corrected him. 'Daisy. Daisy Nunn.'

The kitchen fell silent. 'Oh, yeah. Your Abo girl.'

'But she's not missing. She's—'

'All right,' Wingnut said, taking out his notebook.

'Where's Ed?' Kate asked.

Mrs Walters, her hands in the sink washing teacups, tipped her head towards the garden.

'Outside.' Wingnut spoke. 'He's pretty cut up.'

Kate went out and Luca followed, stopping her on the steps.

'You are OK?' Luca asked her, worried. 'I say this?'

'No. I must tell Ed.'

Luca nodded. He smiled at her and she felt more tears come to her eyes. Despite their loss, despite everything, she was so grateful that they were both alive, every moment treasured.

She went across the lawn to Ed as Luca went back into the kitchen.

'Mrs D.' Ed looked at her, fear across his face, each aware of the kitchen full of people not far away.

'Walk with me, Ed.'

They moved slowly away – around the house, out of earshot – and the murmur of talk sprouted again in the kitchen.

CHAPTER 34

An injured animal, if it be judged likely to survive, is best assisted by all such things as are commonplace for uninjured stock. Grazing, water, shade, rest and sleep shall be as unremarkable as they are abundant.

THE WOOLGROWER'S COMPANION, 1906

Kate walked slowly back to the kitchen steps, leaving Ed alone on the far side of the garden. Ed loved Daisy. They both did. Now he and Kate had to be brave over the coming days, fearless in the face of what they had to do.

Inside, Kate scooped up Pearl and kissed her cheek. 'Ed wants a moment by himself,' she said, to no one in particular. Mrs Riley had moved Harry back to the kitchen, where the light was better.

Kate stood watching. She hugged Pearl in her arms, conscious that Harry sat in front of her and Luca stood just behind. Alive. Both alive. She gulped aloud, a choke of tears and relief.

Mrs Riley said nothing, just patted Kate's back gently. She took Harry's arm then, turning it gently to examine each side of the burn that extended from the back of his hand all the way up past his elbow. She'd trained as a nurse before she was married and was the closest thing they had to a medic, until Dr King could be found.

Her eyes on the burn, Mrs Riley spoke casually, as if in passing. 'Reginald, dear. Have we heard when the doctor might be coming?'

'What's that?' Her husband looked up from the map.

'Dr King?' Over Harry's head, she arched an eyebrow at him.

'I'll enquire.' Mr Riley motioned to Wingnut to step outside onto the verandah. Kate, still cradling Pearl, followed, as did Luca.

'How did you manage to survive, young Harry?' Mrs Riley's voice carried out to them. Kate knew it was intentional; chatter to distract from his pain.

'Mumma.' Pearl started to cry for her mother. Kate rocked her, pressing her lips against her cheek, but she would not be soothed. Tears collected in Kate's eyes too as Pearl hiccupped and wept.

'Mumma loves you,' Kate said, not knowing what else to say. 'But she's gone now.'

Outside, Mr Riley walked Wingnut to the far end of the verandah. 'The boy's burn might become serious, I'm told by my better half. Do we have word on Dr King?'

Wingnut scratched behind one of his large ears. 'He's gone to ground somewhere. Longhope Downs, they reckon.'

'Is someone hurt?' Kate asked. She'd heard nothing on the two-way traffic.

'Nuh,' Wingnut said. 'Nobody's too crook there, far as I can tell. A dislocated thumb is what I hear. I'll see what I can do.' He spoke to his junior, Constable Hartwell. The junior got on the radio at once, the crackle drifting back to Kate and Mr Riley on the verandah, out from the two-way speaker in the office.

They heard the reply together. '*We'll get the doc. An they found Grimesy's truck, Sarge. In the Longhope Downs creek paddock. Over.*'

'You're on an open channel, so watch y'self,' Wingnut said. 'Is Grimes there?'

'*Negative. I say again, negative.*'

Wingnut hung the handset in its cradle and looked away to the sky.

'We're out of light, Mrs D,' he called. 'We'll have to start again first thing.'

The night was long. The rest of the household was in bed, if not asleep, but Kate was patting a restless Pearl in her cot. Hours after her bedtime, she was still awake, fraught with tiredness and grief.

'Mumma,' Pearl said. She couldn't understand why her mother didn't come. She asked over and over, and Kate replied gently, over and over, that Daisy wasn't coming back. When Kate could not comfort her in her cot, she picked the toddler up and took her outside onto the verandah.

The change stilled Pearl's sobs for a minute and Kate started to talk, filling that silence to stop her from crying again.

'Where's the moon?'

From Kate's arms, Pearl looked up, searching the empty sky, a fist in her mouth for comfort.

'The moon's out there, you know. We just can't see him. A brand new moon, so shy it's hiding away.'

Pearl threw Kate a look, a sort of toddler eye-roll. It was such a grown-up look that Kate smiled, feeling an odd pang of happiness in the hushed grief of that night.

Pearl smiled then too, just for an instant.

Kate walked on round the house on its wide verandah. She stood next to the laundry door, looking out up the hill.

She was conscious that Donald, light sleeper that he was, was very close, in his pillowcase in the laundry. Her voice might carry through the roo-door gauze. She spoke very softly.

'The chooks are asleep. Over the hill.'

Pearl leant her head against Kate's shoulder, and Kate kept talking.

'We can get the eggs together tomorrow if you like.' It hit Kate with a pang that egg-collecting was something that Daisy did with Pearl. She rushed on to something else.

'They must be nice and snug, the chooks, on the straw and with their feathers round them.'

She stopped, feeling Pearl's regular breaths against her collarbone. Might she be asleep? From the other side of the laundry door came some thumping and wriggling. Donald was trying to get out of his pillowslip, for sure.

Kate stood, waiting, listening. Hoping. There was quiet. Both Donald and Pearl were asleep.

Kate retraced her steps, tiptoeing along the verandah. She stopped near the kitchen door and looked out across Amiens, the dim line of the silent hills, the country sleeping. She thought of Daisy and a lump came to her throat, Pearl's warm breath against her cheek.

CHAPTER 35

In the unhappy circumstance that a woolgrower must determine from an injured flock which are to be culled, he must identify, with most speed and care, those for immediate culling; those which might be slaughtered within a matter of days; and those which might be saved with nursing and ministrations.

THE WOOLGROWER'S COMPANION, 1906

At first light, the search for Grimes was back underway. Wingnut had sent Ed and Luca out to search the Amiens side of the boundary, 'in case he come over from Longhope Downs'.

It was Luca who drove. He kept one eye on Ed – beside him in the truck cab, pale and short of sleep – and one eye on the track. They made their way through the unburnt paddocks, past the yards and the woolshed, and then on down towards the creek. Luca remembered this track. He'd come this way three years before, taking Kate to Daisy to help with Pearl's birth.

They approached the burn line then, passing from the ordinariness of Amiens's regular pasture to the still-smoking footprint of the fire.

'*Cazzo*,' Luca said softly, shaking his head at the smoke drifting from the remains of a charred hay-bale stack.

They drove past a crush of sheep caught in the corner of a paddock, up against what was left of the fences. Luca looked hard for any sign of some poor beast still alive. But there was nothing, just the movement of flies, like a haze over the carcasses.

'You wouldn't credit it,' Ed said quietly. Just beyond the mass of dead sheep was the open gate. They could have got away.

Luca exhaled. '*Stupidi animali*.'

'They're not bright, poor buggers,' Ed said.

Soon the track was blocked by a fallen branch, smoke lifting from it like an afterthought. Luca jumped from the truck and dragged it away. They went on. But only a minute later they came up against a downed trunk right across the track, and Luca knew they'd never move it. Beyond was another trunk, and another. 'We must walk,' Luca called to Ed.

He unhooked the canvas water bag from the truck and slung it on its strap round his shoulder. 'We start at the fence,' he said, keeping an eye on Ed, who followed. Luca marvelled at Ed. He had seen many men lose their reason after a death, their limbs moving but their minds hollow. But Ed? He was strong. He carried on.

Little was left of the fence, just blackened uprights like grave markers. 'Grimes!' Luca called, hands cupped, his throat already dry from the smoke haze.

The going was slow over still-smoking ground and stumps. Luca was hampered too by dry lungs, breathing hard even at their sluggish pace. He'd been spared the worst of the fire. After he had left Kate at the dam, he'd headed towards the horse paddock but had been forced back to the homestead, and had to watch, powerless, as the fire front moved up the small hill and beyond: towards Harry and Ben.

The fire had missed the Amiens homestead, the ploughed firebreaks holding in the end. Instead, the front went down the boundary, fuelled by the pasture on the Longhope Downs side, and on towards the dam. Luca had spent some terrible hours, not knowing if Kate – and Daisy and Pearl – or Harry were alive.

Burnt pasture gave way under Luca to a rabbit hole and he pulled up, forced to extract his boot. He worked through in his head where Grimes might have gone. If he'd made it across the creek, he would have headed for the cover of the Amiens homestead. But Luca suspected he'd never have got that far; that the fire coming down the boundary would have cut him off.

Grimes knew both places well, Longhope Downs and Amiens. So where would he go, if he got caught in the open with the fire approaching? Luca turned slowly on the spot, searching for cover, scouring all 360 degrees of burnt pasture and the smoking stumps of trees long dead from ringbarking.

One line of trees stood out, their trunks blackened but still standing. The creek. It had to be. 'Ed!' he called. 'Come. We go here.'

Luca went down the creek bank, between two scorched trunks, and Ed followed.

'Gum ghost,' Luca said, pointing to a thick trunk.

'No, mate,' Ed replied. 'You mean ghost gums, in point of fact.' The thick trunks of the trees were far from their usual mottled white.

They searched slowly, carefully. 'Grimes!' Luca called out, as he tracked along the creek bed. Even here, in the protection of the gully, a layer of ash covered the sand like black snow. No one could survive this. Luca walked on, water bag on his back, the sand shifting under his boots.

He turned a bend in the creek and suddenly saw where he was. It was the downed trunk that reminded him. The huge gum across the creek was like a dam wall. It was here that Daisy had given birth to Pearl. A special place. He was glad the old trunk had somehow survived the worst of the fire.

Luca stood for a moment, almost reluctant to leave the spot. Ed was a way behind him now. But he climbed up and over the trunk, for it effectively blocked the creek, dropping down onto the sand on the other side.

He went round the next bend and was startled when a sheep, unharmed other than for a light dusting of ash and soot, wandered past him, followed by another. There were four of them in all, holed up, safe in this little corner of the creek bed, trapped on one side by the fallen tree trunk.

He was almost surprised they were smart enough to get themselves down into the creek bed to safety. But scanning the opening, he saw a muddy pool a bit further along. Perhaps the water had brought them.

He caught some movement, and he stopped and looked again. But what was it?

Luca narrowed his eyes, searching. Something up against the creek bank. It was alive, struggling to breathe. He went towards it and the thing shifted. Living, it was living.

'*Gesù, Giuseppe e Maria*,' Luca whispered. He dropped to his knees, his eyes struggling to recognise the figure, yet knowing this was a man.

The body was crammed sideways under the shelter of the overhang, the gum's roots burnt black where they were exposed from the dirt, the man's trousers and boots almost covered, burrowed under the creek bed's sand. At the other end, Luca could now make out the remnants of a leather hat, blackened but whole and, under that, protected by it, some tiny threads of blue cotton. It was Grimes.

Below, the man's back was a vast, terrible mix of charred flesh, patches of oozing white where the skin had burnt away completely, ash and dirt pushing painfully into the exposed layers.

Luca straightened up on his knees, turned away, and cupped his hands at his mouth. 'Ed!' he yelled. 'Ed!'

Grimes groaned then, responding to the noise. Luca unslung the water bag from his back and set it beside him, staring at Grimes's body, trying to choose where to grip, whether to even put him on his back to give him water. The pain would be intense, as the skin that was not blistered was burnt away. But Luca knew burnt soldiers died of many things, and one was *disidratazione*. They had to get him to drink water. But first, they had to turn him over.

He was about to shout again when Ed came around the creek bend.

'You help,' Luca said, and motioned for Ed to get alongside Grimes's body. 'We must turn. Yes?'

But Ed was frozen, shocked by the thing that was once Grimes.

Luca got up and went to Ed, shaking his arm. 'You listen me.'

His face ashen, Ed tore his eyes away from Grimes to Luca.

Luca was back on his knees in the sand, and he pulled Ed over to him.

There was nothing to protect Grimes's exposed skin from the dirt, so Luca unbuttoned his shirt and pulled it off, laying it carefully beside Grimes's chest. He looked at Ed, who was still staring mutely. 'Together. Now.'

Ed nodded slowly and got down on his knees.

'We shift you, Mr Grimes. For the water. OK?' Luca said gently. The *Mr* was to show respect.

'Can he hear us?' Ed whispered.

Luca waggled his head, uncertain. Together, gingerly, the two men turned Grimes onto his back. The front of his blue shirt was intact.

A long sound escaped his lips, more like a breath exhaled than a groan.

'Did we kill im?' Ed's face was stricken with guilt and shock.

Luca shook his head. He was relieved to see that Grimes's

face, his torso and the front of his arms were largely unburnt. He must have shielded that side of his body. But his back had taken the full force. Luca reached for the water bag. 'Water now. OK?'

Grimes didn't respond. Luca gently took Grimes's hand, the palm oddly smooth against his own. 'You hear me, Mr Grimes? Show this me.'

But Grimes's hand was limp in Luca's own. Luca hoped there were no other injuries they didn't know about, no blow to the head that might stop him swallowing.

He tried again. 'You want the water?'

A tiny pressure. *Yes.*

'Give him, now. Little, little bit,' he instructed Ed.

'It come,' Luca said to Grimes again, and carefully Ed dribbled some water into the mouth. Grimes rasped and coughed, the movement bringing more pain.

Ed saw it: the throat bulged. 'Yes, it went down!'

'You try. See if he talk at you,' Luca said.

Ed made himself get close, looking nowhere but at Grimes's face, avoiding sight of anything else. 'Grimesy. Can y'hear me, mate?'

'He push my hand. Good, good,' Luca said. Grimes might not be able to talk but he was conscious. He knew they were there.

Luca said to Ed, 'Go. In the radio. Tell them of Grimes. Tell them.' He motioned up, his hands behind and below his hips. *Tell them about the burns. Tell them where.*

'Yeah. I'll get on the two-way.' But Ed didn't move. 'Maybe there's grog in the truck? Robbo might have a stash.'

'*Va bene*,' Luca said, his voice firm. 'Now go.'

Ed turned, stumbling away. Then he ran, jumping some part-burnt branches on to the downed tree trunk, then up and over it, running until his lungs burnt with every stride.

CHAPTER 36

A great if sober point to be remembered in the particular circumstances that follow a bushfire is that those animals showing circumlocution of air passages or other impediments respiratory in nature should be humanely destroyed without delay.

THE WOOLGROWER'S COMPANION, 1906

Luca had sat beside injured men before. He'd waited with them for help or for death on broken battlefields, some burning still, not unlike this place. It occurred to Luca that Grimes would have done the same. Grimes had been a soldier too, *nella Grande Guerra*.

In the silence, Luca remembered an Army doctor shouting at him once, while he waited with a badly wounded friend: *You! Talk, man! Talk to that soldier.*

So now, Luca talked to Grimes. 'Ed, he go. For the help.'

Grimes's eyes swivelled to Luca's face, his chest rising and falling with painful breaths, fear written across his features. He shifted his hand, the one by Luca, and Luca took it.

'The doctor come. Soon.'

Grimes's eyes flickered. His breaths, laboured when Luca had first found him, were slower. But he was still alive.

'She is a good country here, Amiens. Good grass. Her trees.'

The breaths rasped on, Grimes's hand resting on Luca's.

'Gum ghosts, yes, these trees. He know much, Ed.'

It would take time. For Wingnut to find the doctor. To bring him to Amiens. For Ed to get him out here. But they would try. He knew they would all try. He hoped Grimes would last.

'Trees of Lombardy, they is different. Much rain there. Much, much rain.' Luca felt the faintest pressure on his hand.

'These ghost trees? Black now, not white. Before, she is beautiful, no? God love these trees.'

Luca had not thought of God in a long time. There was no place for God in the war. In what Luca had done.

Grimes rasped. Luca carefully tipped some droplets of water into his mouth, surprised again that the man's face could be undamaged when his back was so bad. He gently took up Grimes's hand again. 'Soon the doctor, he come,' Luca said. 'He give this *morfina*. For you.'

A crow circled above them, the first bird Luca had seen since the fire, its wings shiny in the sunlight as it settled on a charred branch to watch. Luca knew what they did, these birds. He'd seen them take the eyes out of newborn lambs.

'*Va via*!' he hissed. The bird didn't move.

Just then, Ed appeared round the creek bend. He was dragging a makeshift stretcher: two long fire-beater handles with a tarp tied between. Luca could see at once that it would do, and he nodded his approval as Ed gently positioned the stretcher next to Grimes, careful not to touch him.

'Mate, can I've a word with ya?' Ed indicated with his head that they should move away from Grimes, out of earshot.

'*Sì, sì*. I help this.' Luca loosened his hand very gently from Grimes's and got up, stiff from sitting still for so long. They moved off just out of sight, behind the bend.

Ed spoke softly. 'They're huntin for the doc. Still can't find him. They reckon they got the Flying Doctor Service comin too.'

'We bring him now? To the homestead?'

'Nuh. Wingnut told me on the two-way: just keep him comfortable. Till Dr King gets here.'

'*Comfortable*?' Luca waggled his head. '*Cazzo*. He need *morfina*.'

'Yeah. I'm goin now. T'get the morphine outa the medical chest at the homestead. Dressins and bandages too. But I got this from the truck.' Ed pulled a small hip flask of rum from his back pocket.

Luca smiled and took the bottle. '*Gesù, Giuseppe e Maria*. Good. Very good.' Only a third or so was left. It was something, though.

Ed nodded unhappily. 'I guessed Robbo mighta had one stashed. Poor bugger.'

'He is sick, this Robbo?'

'Nuh. Can't get off the grog. After the war.'

'Ah.' Luca waved a fly away from his bare chest.

'I'll get ya a shirt too, from the homestead.'

'*Grazie*. When he come? *Il medico*?'

'The doc'll be here in a bit, they hope. Flying Doctors? Soon as they can. But that'll be late. Late this arvo. Tonight even. They're comin all the way from Charleville in Queensland. That's the closest.'

'We need the *medico* soon, Ed.' What was this doctor *doing*?

'Yeah. I told em, eh. From the two-way, sounds like Mrs D's ropeable. She'll be tearin strips off im when he does get here.'

They exchanged a look, worried about how long Grimes would last without help.

'I'll stay on the two-way at the truck, anyhow. Bring the doc straight in when he gets here.'

Luca looked at the morning sky, hazy with smoke, and spoke softly. 'Maybe you rest with Grimes? No love last.'

Ed grinned. 'No love *lost*, mate.'

'You stay?'

Ed avoided Luca's eyes and almost whispered, 'I can't bloody stomach it, mate.'

Luca nodded slowly and held out his hand. They shook, before Ed retreated along the creek bed.

Luca walked back to Grimes. 'This Ed, he is the good bloke, no?' He held the flask in front of Grimes's eyes. 'Rum.'

Luca uncorked the bottle and squatted, carefully dripping some into Grimes's mouth. Then he took up the man's hand again, and a slight pressure told him Grimes knew he was there.

With his free hand, Luca took a tiny swig himself; to keep Grimes company, to have something to do with the injured man. 'She is good, no?' he said. 'Ed, he go back to the truck. The doctor come soon. Also, this plane. They come for you.'

CHAPTER 37

While an unpopular theory, this writer vouchsafes for the benefits of a careful attention to all those who appear to possess knowledge, regardless of class. Sound advice comes not exclusively from the best regarded of men.

THE WOOLGROWER'S COMPANION, 1906

The homestead kitchen was full. Kate, Mr Riley and Harry were all silent, listening to Wingnut on the phone, as he relayed information from Kate to the Flying Doctor Service in Charleville, four hundred miles north-west of them.

'Confirmed that the *Dragon*'s airborne. Is there an airstrip on the place?' The Flying Doctor's voice crackled down the phone line.

'Not as such,' Wingnut said.

'A straight flat road will do us, Sergeant. Six hundred yards is what we need.'

Kate nodded at Wingnut, who spoke into the receiver. 'Roger that.'

She just wished he'd give her the telephone.

'Location, relative to the homestead or woolshed?'

Kate whispered urgently. 'The Box Ridge paddock is one over from where Grimes is. It's three-quarters of a mile—'

Wingnut held up a hand and spoke to the Flying Doctor.

'Three-quarters of a mile—'

'South-east—'

'Three-quarters of a mile, south-east—'

Harry rolled his whole head, not just his eyes. 'Mrs D, you should just bloody talk to em.'

Wingnut frowned, unsure, and disapproving of the boy swearing too. He put his hand over the receiver. 'You be all right with that, Mrs D?'

Mrs Walters passed behind him with a tray of tea things, and the ghost of a smile. She'd managed to put Pearl to bed.

'I'll be all right.' Kate held out a hand for the receiver and Wingnut gave it up, reluctantly.

Kate spoke. 'The paddock with the nearest and longest straight flat road is three-quarters of a mile south-east of the Amiens homestead.'

'Is the place name painted on the roof?'

'On the woolshed. Amiens. Letters are fifteen feet.' Her father had done that. Her mother had thought it showy, but he'd been right to do it.

'Flat road? Length of the straight?'

'Flat and a straight run of at least five hundred yards. Best we got.'

There was a short silence. Kate wondered if it was long enough for them to land, and then to take off with the extra load of a patient on board.

They must have decided it would do. 'Current condition of that road? Any trees down on it after the fire?'

'My men are out there now. But they'll clear things in time.'

'What's at each end of the paddock? Trees? Scrub? Hills?'

'Open paddocks both sides. That bit of road slopes up towards the northern end, once it gets into the next paddock.'

'Visibility at the moment? Smoke cleared?'

Kate pulled the receiver cord with her and moved across to the doorway. 'Yes. So you've got three miles at least, I'd say.'

Wingnut nodded in agreement.

Silence. Then: 'Stock in the paddock? You'll get them off the track for us?'

'Those paddocks were cleared before the fire. But we'll check,' Kate said.

'Do you have two-way down there?'

'Yes. In the truck.' God bless Ed for making Kate buy their two-ways.

'Right. What's the condition of the patient now?'

Kate covered the mouthpiece. 'Harry, you go to Pearl,' she instructed.

When he didn't move, Wingnut half manhandled Harry out of the kitchen.

'Our last report was less than an hour ago. Moving in and out of consciousness. In a lot of pain.'

'Burns to what parts of the body?'

Kate cupped one hand around the mouthpiece to stop her words carrying. 'I'm told they're on his back. He must have protected his head, his face and chest, even his legs. The back's very bad.'

'Please have the burns dressed and bandaged. Use the morphine from your medical chest. Keep the fluids up. Keep him in shade. Is that clear? Until your local doctor arrives.'

'Yes. We're hoping Dr King can be found.' Where the hell *was* he?

'All right. Tonight, if the pilot reckons he's got enough light to land, he'll dip his wings. If he doesn't, it means he won't land. Understood?'

'Clear.'

'The Bureau says last light at 19.39. The plane'll refuel in Lightning Ridge. ETA at about 19.15. Can you light the place up, the woolshed and the homestead, so we can find you?'

'Will do. Understood.'

'And the strip itself? We must have lights. Can you get

vehicles down there? Shining into the wind. Down the perimeters too.'

'We'll have perimeter lights for you,' Kate said. She just didn't know how.

The sound of a vehicle got their attention. The Amiens truck, its fender bent. Through the window, Kate saw Ed drop from the cabin and lope across the lawn. She went out to him.

'Ed!' Kate looked about for Harry. If Grimes had died, God forbid, she didn't want him to hear it like this, in front of all these people.

'S'all right, Mrs D. No change. I come for the morphine and such, eh.'

'Come in, Ed. Please. I have things ready for you.' Kate had taken the morphine out of the Flying Doctor medical chest. Every homestead worth its salt had one, stocked with emergency supplies. 'And Mrs Walters has food for you all too.'

'And we need a shirt,' Ed said.

Kate looked at him.

'Luca took his shirt off to put it under Grimesy's back. Keep him outa the dirt.'

'I'll get you something.' Kate went to the laundry, to the sack of clean rags they kept for odds and sods. *Yes*, she had just one of her father's old shirts; it hadn't been fit to give away.

She came back, shirt in hand. Harry grinned. 'Old Luca without a shirt, eh?' He wiggled his eyebrows up and down at her, and she gave him a stern look. His great-uncle was badly injured. This was not the time for jokes.

'No sign of the doc?' Ed asked on his way out.

Kate shook her head.

'Jesus. And we don't move the poor bugger outa the creek?'

'No. Has he said anything?'

'Nuh. He can't talk, Mrs D.' Ed turned back to the truck.

'Will you help Luca bandage him up? Do the dressings?' Kate asked.

Ed blanched.

'Don't worry, I'll go.' Kate turned to Wingnut. 'Luca needs help down there. With the bandages.'

'I reckon you're needed here, Mrs D,' the sergeant said. 'In case the Flying Doc wants more info. You'll go, Ed, mate, won't ya?'

Ed nodded slowly.

By the middle of the afternoon, Luca was sore from sitting so long. He shifted a bit in the sand of the creek bed. But he kept on speaking, his voice even. '*Un gran Paese*, he is. *Un gran Paese*.' He was talking of Australia, of everything and nothing, stopping only when the pressure on his hand lessened, and Grimes slept.

It was hard work to keep the flies off the man. Luca knew they might kill him. *Germi, infezioni*. He worried each time a fly got through, landing on the rawness of the burns, where the barrier of the skin was gone. Grimes rested easier now, the morphine that Ed had delivered taking away some of the pain.

Luca had injected Grimes, jabbing the needle like a dart into the thick of the upper arm. They'd bandaged him up, with clean dressings and pads on the burns, and then Ed supported Grimes's torso as Luca wound bandages around to hold the dressings on the back. Luca worried that they would have to be undone as soon as the doctor arrived, but orders were orders. It was on more orders that Ed went back to the truck to sit by the two-way for news of the doctor.

When Grimes stirred, Luca gave him more water, his hand gently behind the man's neck, lifting him up to take in the droplets. The sun was climbing and the shade from the creek banks would soon be gone. Luca rigged up the tarp that Ed had brought, as a shade for them both. Each time he moved though, he came back to his position next to Grimes, taking the man's hand in his.

The hours crawled into the afternoon, Luca watching the sun slowly move across the sky. He stretched, trying to keep the cramps at bay and his mind alert. When he was a soldier, sometimes he would whittle to pass the time – a toy or a whistle or even a person's likeness. But today Grimes needed his hand. Otherwise he was not uncomfortable. This new shirt was old but good; it fitted him a bit. He smiled. A clean smell, a laundry smell, *sapone*, clung to it, and made him think of her.

Kate. He leant his head back and closed his eyes. Everything was wrong for them. He was *italiano*. He was before a prisoner. No land. No *inglese*. But still, they loved each other. He struggled with it: madness, *follia*, that he wanted this woman, this difficult woman, from the other side of the world. And hope that she might want him back.

She's gotta lotta land, mate, Harry teased Luca whenever he could.

Before the war Luca would never have looked at a woman like Kate. Highborn. *Protestante*. Married. *Santa Maria madre di Dio.* He shook his head in wonder. *Cattolica, protestante?* No difference, now, to him. Wrapping of the same *merda*.

He was changed. So different from Luca of *Lombardia*. He had lasted, had survived much. Each time, he was changed a little. Tobruk. El Alamein. Shot but not killed. Still one piece, but also many pieces.

Then he'd been captured and sent to India. *Difficile. Molto difficile.* After that? *Australia.* He'd laughed when he'd heard, hungry and sick as he was in the Indian POW camp. He was going to *Australia*? *Ridicolo.*

Luca stretched his right leg to relieve a cramp, careful not to move his hand from Grimes's. The light in Australia, though, was like *Italia*. He remembered that. Walking down the gangplank, off the ship in Sydney, soldiers with rifles all around, old soldiers, under a large sky, a huge sun. Blinding, like the sun of *Lombardia*.

Then the POW camp. It was not so bad. They had enough food, at last. He was lucky, also, that he was only in for a year. Then came this *programma*, for POWs to go onto the farms, to work for the Australian farmers. Without the guards.

He remembered the first day. Jumping from the prison train onto the dirt. Grimes pointing his rifle at him, showing him they would be enemies. Luca shook his head, looking at the hand, listening to the man's ragged breathing.

Overhead, a finch flitted across between the trunk tops, from one bank to the other, and Luca was glad for him that he'd survived the fire, not that there'd be many moths or beetles about now for him to eat. Even the cicadas were silenced. That crow would have this finch, if there was nothing else. *Be wary, my friend.*

Luca had a clear view through a gap in the myalls that lined the bank, to the paddock beyond. The light was fading fast. Dr King had not come and this Flying Doctor had little daylight left in which to land. *The bugger*, Harry would say. No, just *bugger*.

CHAPTER 38

The general principle that like begets like is a sound one for breeding, and poor rearing ability should be culled from the flock.

THE WOOLGROWER'S COMPANION, 1906

The homestead kitchen was quiet – despite all the people – in the hope of hearing an aircraft. Harry sat, wincing, at the table, as Mrs Riley worked on his arm, putting on a fresh dressing. Next to them, the map covered much of the table. At the sink, Mrs Walters was making tea, turning the teapot.

Wingnut was looking at the map.

'You reckon he'll be all right?' Harry asked Mrs Riley softly. 'Old Grimesy?'

Kate had half an ear on this. Harry was worried about his uncle. Great-uncle.

Mrs Riley shifted her gaze from the burn to Harry's eyes, inches from hers, their heads almost touching. 'He's a strong fellow, dear.'

'But. Will he, y'know . . . ?'

Mrs Riley looked back to the burn. 'The Flying Doctor is tremendous. Hope for the best, dear.'

Kate put a cup of tea, with saucer, on the table next to Mrs Riley, and gave a mug to the sergeant.

Harry turned towards Kate and spoke to her across the

kitchen. 'Can I go an see him? Grimes? Now? In the paddock?'

'No, son,' Wingnut replied, without looking up. 'When the doc turns up, he might wanna move im up here.'

Harry dropped his head, his eyes back on his arm as Mrs Riley worked.

'We should have shifted him.' Kate was worried about a man lying on the dirt in the creek bed all this time.

Wingnut was firm. 'He mighta broke something. Doc wants em left, usually. We was right to leave him lie.'

Kate frowned. The arse-covering had begun. 'Sergeant,' she said. 'The lights for the runway strip. We'll put a vehicle at each end?'

'Yeah. They come in over the top of lights facing into the wind. Low beam, they want. Not shining in the pilot's eyes. A vehicle at the other end too, with lights on. For him to line up to land.'

'What about the bit in the middle? They want perimeter lights too,' Kate said. 'Orientation to the surroundings, apparently.'

'Yeah.' Wingnut scratched behind an ear, thinking.

'Bonfires,' Harry said.

'No, mate. There's nothin t'burn. Nothin but ash in there now. That right, Mrs D?' Wingnut asked.

'Yes. Johnno checked. The timber's all gone.' The amount of wood they'd need for all those bonfires – two dozen beacons, probably, to line the strip perimeter – was huge. They had no time to shift in all that wood.

'I got an idea,' Harry said.

'Not now, son,' Wingnut said, again without looking up, his eyes fixed on the map on the table.

Kate was glad Harry was still alert, especially with that burn. She'd worry when he started to fade.

Harry put his head down again, and Kate suspected there might be tears. He'd held up so well, until now. She stood behind him and patted his back, a gentle tap out of sight of the others.

'Ya won't let me bloody help.' Harry was crying, ashamed of his stupid tears.

'All right,' Kate said, fighting tears herself. 'What's your idea?'

Only a few minutes later, Kate heard the motorbike and went out onto the verandah.

Robbo had pulled up at the fence. 'Track's clear, Mrs D,' he called.

The 'airstrip' was ready for the Flying Doctor plane. Kate waved a thank you and he was off again. She was headed back into the kitchen when she stopped. Fleming's car was coming up out of the gully, Dr King in the passenger seat.

'About bloody time,' Harry said, beside her on the verandah. 'Mrs F's thumb must have been a mess.'

Kate wondered how she'd hurt it.

Mr Riley joined them and they watched the car approach, Robbo on the motorbike now following them back.

'Can you take him to Mr Grimes, Mr Riley? Robbo will show you where they are.'

Mr Riley hurried across the lawn and motioned the doctor straight out of the car.

Kate waved a cordial greeting at John Fleming and turned to go into the house, hoping he'd be on his way now he'd brought the doctor. But he came in through the gate.

'Mrs Dowd,' Fleming said. Civil enough, yet he went up the stairs and right past her towards the men in the kitchen. She had no choice but to follow him inside her own house.

Fleming ignored her and spoke to Wingnut. 'Give me the short version, if you would, Sergeant,' he said.

'Flying Doctor's due in the next forty-five minutes. Strip's clear. They're gunna land on the road in the paddock. An Mrs D's got lights organised.'

'I think Mrs Dowd has done enough.' Fleming's tone silenced the room.

'What do you mean?' Kate said. 'We didn't start this fire.'

'No doubt the sergeant here will see about that.'

'No,' Kate said again. 'We did not—'

The two-way crackled across the kitchen, cutting her off. '*Mrs D, you on channel?*'

It was Ed. Kate glared at Fleming and picked up the hand-piece. 'Go ahead.'

'*Luca says ya better bring Harry, eh.*'

For a moment, she couldn't speak. Grimes must be very bad. 'We'll bring him. You hear me?'

'*Roger.*'

'Ed? The doctor just left here. With you soon.'

'*Roger that. Over and out.*'

Harry appeared in the hallway, holding his bandaged arm. 'What did he say?' he asked Kate.

'You should go with the men, Harry. To see your uncle.'

Fleming intervened. 'No, son. It's not appropriate.' He turned to Kate. 'The boy won't go with you.' It was an instruction.

Kate looked at her watch. 'He *will*, and we have to leave now. Get the things for the lights, Harry.' The boy shot back into the hall.

'You can't let a boy see his uncle injured in this way,' Fleming said to Kate. 'Not sensible. You understand.' With things back on course, he turned to Wingnut. 'What's this lights idea? Have you checked, Sergeant? The safety of the plane is not for women and children to be playing about with.'

Wingnut hesitated. 'What were you and Harry cooking up, Mrs D?'

In the laundry, Mrs Riley cleared her throat politely.

'We have the lights in hand, thank you,' Kate said.

Fleming appealed again to Wingnut. 'You'd risk the doctor, the pilot and even Grimes?'

The sergeant said nothing, saved by Harry's reappearance. He was dragging a hessian sack behind him across the floor, with another on his shoulder. Whatever they held was bulky but light, and he manoeuvred them easily out the door.

'Back in here, boy!' Fleming's angry voice followed Harry.

Piss off popped into Kate's head. But she was a lady, whatever that was. She went to the doorway and turned back. 'You coming, Sergeant?'

Wingnut followed her, and he didn't look Fleming in the eye.

CHAPTER 39

As the day draws in, a woolgrower should be mindful that a mob will tend to camp on easterly facing slopes, on high ground and clustered together.

THE WOOLGROWER'S COMPANION, 1906

The light was fading and the noise of *cicale* filled the air when Ed's voice carried to Luca.

'Mate. I got the doc.'

Ed came along the creek bed, the greying Dr King behind him, carrying a bag.

The doctor gave Luca a perfunctory nod. He put his bag on the sand, and knelt quickly next to Grimes.

'What time did you find him, Ed?'

Luca replied. 'Before nine the morning.'

'Was he lying like this? Just like this?' Again, he spoke to Ed.

'No,' Luca said. This *medico* was not thinking. 'He is under the roots here. I find him there. We turn him like this.'

'Has he complained of any injuries? Broken bones?' The doctor looked again at Ed.

Ed looked confused. Why ask him?

But Luca understood. Many old soldiers did not like him. Once a POW, always a POW. 'He not speak,' Luca said. 'He say me nothing.'

The doctor pressed a stethoscope gently against the blue cloth of Grimes's shirt.

'I give him the morphine twelve o'clock.' Luca held out the vial.

Dr King sat back and took a syringe from his bag, preparing an injection. He cleaned as best he could a place on Grimes's arm, and inserted the needle. Grimes didn't flinch, just gave a slight rasp from his lips. 'For the pain, again. She is good for you,' Luca explained softly.

Dr King put the syringe away into his bag. 'Very well, Ed. I need to radio in. Can you take me to the truck? Then come back. Get him gently onto that stretcher and over to the road they're going to land on. Box Ridge, yes? Plane's due round seven-fifteen. I hear you'll have to carry him a bit. Track into the strip has trees down on it.'

The doctor stood up and, with his own torch, went back through the dusk to radio in.

In the gathering darkness of the Box Ridge paddock – what would be the airstrip paddock – Kate put down her sack of fire supplies on the ash and shone her torch onto her watch. Just before seven o'clock. They were really stretching 'last light'. She cleared her throat. The heavy smoke of yesterday had gone but the smell of it still hung in the air.

'Harry. You, Robbo and Johnno look after the southern side? Wingnut and I'll do this one.'

'Yep,' Harry's voice came through the darkness. He had his own sack.

Wingnut went ahead of Kate, shining his torch on the blackened paddock in front of them. Best not to stand on a snake in the darkness, even an injured one.

Kate stopped and waited, looking into the dark where Harry must be. Should be. Suddenly a fire flared up behind the shadow of a man and a boy. The figures moved on.

Next to her, Wingnut crouched down and held his lighter to the makeshift flare, the acrid smell of kero more pungent than the stale smoke. The fuel caught, and he hopped back fast. 'Works a treat,' he said, as they moved on along the fence line to place the next one and the next.

Within fifteen minutes, two rows of flares lit the sides of the crude Amiens strip. Kate and Harry walked back towards the southern end, waiting for Ed's truck, listening for the aircraft. The light was fading fast, and the figures at the other end of the strip were rendered tiny, silhouette sticks, black against the vast bowl of the sky.

'Harry,' Kate said softly in the near-darkness. 'You need to be ready.'

'Yeah, I know,' he said. After a pause, he added, 'What for?'

'Mr Grimes is hurt. Very badly.'

Silence.

'He'll feel better when he knows you're there. Even if he doesn't speak.'

Still nothing.

'You need to be careful not to say anything. About—'

'About how crook he is.'

'Yes.'

Kate heard only the sound of the cicadas in the coming night. At least they were back.

The truck shifted down gears and started to slow. 'OK, Mr Grimes,' Luca said, bracing himself against the tray upright. 'I see many fires. Lights for your plane.' Ed was driving, Grimes in the tray on the makeshift stretcher, Luca next to him, talking all the way. To Luca's disgust, the doctor travelled in the cabin with Ed.

When the truck came to a stop, Luca stood up before Ed cut the engine. Two long lines of burning flares stood like an honour guard down each side of the track that would serve as the airstrip. 'Ah! She is beautiful,' he said to Grimes. 'These lights. All for you.'

The painful rasp of Grimes's throat brought Luca back. He squatted down and squeezed a hand gently. 'We get you out now. OK? We must carry you a little but soon? In the plane. Up in the wind.'

Ed climbed up, and together they carefully heaved the stretcher off the truck and lowered the injured man gently down to the dirt. It was heavy going; Grimes must have weighed 180 pounds. Dr King stood by, bag in hand, and made no move to help.

'No, no! Thank you, Doctor. We is fine,' Luca called through the darkness with a smile. He heard Ed snort a laugh.

They set off then; Dr King in the lead lighting the way with his torch, Luca at the front of the stretcher, Ed at the back. Robbo scooted past them towards the truck. 'I gotta move it. For the lights. An into the wind.'

The doctor walked briskly, encumbered only by his Gladstone bag. Luca and Ed were breathing heavily when they approached the first flare. They lowered Grimes onto the ground, about a dozen feet out from the light, and Ed squatted next to him.

Harry came through the dusk, his eyes locked on the stretcher and Grimes. Luca went to him and placed his hands on the boy's cheeks, turning him away from the stretcher, to speak and to prepare him.

'Listen me.' Luca's voice was soft. Harry was shaking. 'Good you see him. But difficult. To look him. Understand?'

'Yes,' he said in a small voice.

'I bring you now?'

Harry nodded.

'Good bloke,' Luca said, and patted his shoulder. 'What is this fire?'

'Dunny rolls in empty tins,' Harry said. 'We soaked em in kero.'

'Ah. She burn good.' He took Harry's hand and led him to Grimes.

Luca squatted next to the injured man. 'Sit, Harry.'

But Harry couldn't move, shocked by the whiteness of his great-uncle's face, and the oozing through the bandages, revealed in bursts by flickers from the flares.

Luca took his arm and applied enough pressure to get the boy onto his knees next to his uncle. 'Take his hand. Gently.'

Harry looked at Luca, horrified, so he levered Harry's hand under Grimes's palm. 'You touch this hand. Yes. Is good.'

Luca squeezed his shoulder, talking all the while. 'You do her lights, Harry?'

The boy said nothing, tears rolling down his cheeks.

Luca spoke for him. 'He do them for you, Mr Grimes. Harry make the fires for your plane.'

Finally Harry leant down, his face close to his great-uncle's.

'Plane!' Kate's voice shot through the darkness. They all listened. Soon, a light aircraft hum carried to them. Then they could make out its navigation lights, green on the right, red on the left as it tracked towards them.

'It's come, eh,' Harry whispered, his voice strangled.

The biplane went right over the top of them, at only seven hundred feet or so, a squat body between twin engines, a tail-wheel bringing up the rear. It came in low above the track and punched its landing lights on: two broad circles of light like something from a space comic. The aircraft kept on coming and then slowly the wings shifted, tipping thirty degrees one way then the other. Luca stood up to watch. Harry stayed kneeling, holding that hand.

The plane lined up to land and came in, lower and lower, nose up, tail down, wavering, held steady by the pilot. It cleared the truck with only feet to spare. With a thump, the wheels connected with the dirt, and the pilot applied the brakes heavily, slowing her up just in time before the gate at the fence. Ash and dust swirled as the plane taxied round.

The engines had barely stopped when the double doors swung open. A man jumped out, medical bag in hand. 'Evening, all. I'm Dr Lang,' he called over the dying engines. He went immediately to squat next to Grimes, throwing Harry, opposite, a brief smile in the flickering light.

Dr King went forward. 'I'll give you my medical assessment. The man is—'

'We'll get the patient on board, and if you'd be good enough to brief me as we go, Doctor?'

The pilot came out of the plane then with a torch, and shone it over Grimes's torso, away from his eyes.

The doctor spoke clearly, slowly. 'Mr Grimes. Evening to you. Flying Doctor Service here. We're going to get you airborne and on to Grafton very soon. All right?' He took Grimes's pulse, talking all the while. 'Big hospital, Grafton Base, isn't it, Smithy?'

The pilot responded quickly. 'Huge. Full of pretty nurses.'

'Must be all that sugar cane,' Dr Lang said.

'Or they eat the jacarandas,' the pilot added, his tone light but his face serious.

It occurred to Kate that they probably had the same routine everywhere they went, to jolly the patient.

'Do you get to fly the plane?' Harry asked the doctor quietly.

'Only when we have no patients on board. And then I let him' – he gestured at the pilot – 'do a bit of the surgery.' He laughed to show he was kidding. 'Morphine?' he said over his shoulder.

'Half an ounce at . . .' Dr King hesitated.

'Six-thirty. Also, the midday.' Luca's voice cut through the last light.

'Quick as we can, Smithy.' Dr Lang turned back to the

injured man, his tone suddenly more relaxed. 'All right, Mr Grimes. Let's get you onto our stretcher and on board.' He leant in to Harry. 'Wish him luck, now, son.'

Harry nodded, unable to speak. He squeezed Grimes's hand and released it only as the stretcher moved away and the patient was loaded into the double doors of the biplane.

Then pilot left them, to do his pre-flight checks. He took a fuel sample from each wing tank in a narrow vial, holding it up in the dim light with a folded white handkerchief behind it.

'What's he looking for?' Harry had taken Kate's hand.

'Water, mate,' Ed said. 'It'd sink, eh, below the fuel, if there's any. Bugger em good, if that got into the fuel line.'

The pilot called across. 'Can you blokes check the strip?'

Robbo climbed onto the motorbike and hit the kick-starter. Lights on, he rode up and then back down the track; one last check for a kangaroo or a stray beast.

With the main doors closed and secured, the pilot climbed in. First one engine then the second fired up, in a burst of noise and dust. From next to his patient, the doctor gave a cheery wave through the window, which Kate fancied was directed at Harry. The plane was turning in a tight circle to line up with the track.

Harry shouted at Kate through the din. 'He's right up against that gateway, eh!' The pilot needed every foot of airstrip he could squeeze out of the paddock. He was taking off into the wind, such as it was, for more lift.

The throttle opened, and the plane moved away along the track, picking up speed and throwing up more and more dust as it went. As its landing lights swept the beacons marking the end of the runway, it lifted off, just clearing the truck.

Kate shook her head – at their speed on the take-off and at this miracle of flight. She'd never flown. Already the biplane, awkward on the ground, grew small and sleek in the sky. It banked, heading eastwards, like a cockatoo before rain.

Kate stayed, standing with Harry, as the black shape became just a light in the sky. She wished Grimes well, for Harry's sake. She knew what it was like to feel alone in the world.

They moved slowly towards the truck and the cars, Wingnut and Mr Riley up ahead. Luca caught up and smiled at her through the last of the light.

CHAPTER 40

The capricious nature of the seasons in our great new land mean that a successful woolgrower is one who is buoyant, hardy and adaptable to all the despair that his calling shall visit upon him.

THE WOOLGROWER'S COMPANION, 1906

The dawn chorus penetrated the half-light of her sleep. Still exhausted, Kate shifted awake, finding the thin cotton of her pillow damp with tears. She'd cried in her sleep: tears of relief and tears of loss.

She pushed her thoughts to the day ahead. Amiens, or some of it, was burnt out: blackened paddocks, downed trees and dead stock. Today she would know better the full extent of the damage, the number of dead and injured sheep. She tried to think of the miracles; of Luca, Ed and Harry. Of her own survival and Pearl's too.

But that took her thoughts to dear Daisy. Kate felt grief and fear well up and threaten to swallow her. She simply could not allow that, not for Pearl, or Daisy or Harry. She tried to imagine what loss lay ahead for tiny Pearl, growing up without her mother.

Something heavy landed hard on her chest and her vision was filled with Donald, his velvety muzzle sniffing at her mouth. He'd escaped from his pillowcase in the laundry and was making the most of it.

'Off, off, now.' She got up and shepherded him out the double doors onto the verandah, then shut them behind him, hoping he hadn't made a mess anywhere. Glad of his distraction, she got herself dressed. Work was always a comfort, helping her get through the days in her life she wanted to forget.

Because Kate was afraid of what she would learn today. Just how bad were Amiens's stock losses? Could they survive?

Nearby a kookaburra laughed and its mates joined in, like a drunken quartet. The ordinariness of the call struck her. The *ack-ack-ack-ack* went on and on, the kookaburra and Kate both glad they were alive. The call reminded Kate of how Luca used to mimic the noise. Dear Luca. He had smiled at her yesterday, had kissed her when he found her after the fire, walking from the dam with Pearl. He knew that she still loved him. Joy in the midst of grief.

The rattle of a teapot from the kitchen startled Kate. Then she realised; it was Mrs Walters, not Daisy, who made tea this morning. Every morning, now. Her throat caught with dread at what lay ahead, and she dug her fingernails into her palms. Today the men would retrieve the fallen tree from the dam, after Ed had gone. He was leaving for Broken Hill early, to deliver the young rams to Mr Perry.

In the kitchen, Kate nodded a hello and Mrs Walters smiled wearily at her across the table of breakfast things. The housekeeper's curls looked a little flat this morning. Kate and she were each a collection of shattered pieces after the fire, holding themselves together.

Kate poured herself some tea and set about making sandwiches for Ed's trip. Mrs Walters took care of two thermoses of tea. 'How far is it to Broken Hill, Mrs Dowd?'

'Just under seven hundred miles, I think. So he'll be there late tonight. Hopefully.'

'And will Ed bring the cheque back?' she asked.

Kate half smiled. Even the housekeeper was determined that Amiens should get paid. They'd only had the deposit so far.

'Yes. I'm sure Mr Perry'll be all right.' Kate couldn't believe him capable of being underhand, like Fleming had been, withholding the cheque. The Broken Hill grazier seemed too kind, too gentlemanly. She hoped she was right about him.

'There's the truck now.' Kate finished the sandwiches and got them into a cake tin, and then into a rucksack with the two thermoses.

Just beyond the fence, Ed was pulling at the tie-down ropes of the stock crate, checking them one last time, where the men had secured the trucking crate to the tray. He came over to Kate with that lopsided gait of his, and took the rucksack over the fence. Ed looked older perhaps, and more pensive. For them both, everything had changed.

'You ready?' Kate asked.

'Mr Riley's expectin me. I'll load the rams quick. Then I'll take it quietly on to Broken Hill.'

'Good.' She was still nervous for the trip, and glad for Ed's foresight. He was the one who'd suggested they move Mr Perry's young rams for safekeeping to the Rileys', in case of a fire. He'd been right.

'Mrs D, the fire? I reckon it were a lightning strike. Dry lightning.'

'But I don't recall any lightning. Not the day of the fire. It was, what, a week before?'

'Six days. We had a whole lotta lightning in that storm on the twenty-fourth.'

She looked at him, confused.

'Lightning can hit a tree and smoulder. For days. Then you get high winds—'

'And the tree burns.' Kate understood. 'Will anyone believe us?'

'They will if we find the bloody tree. I got the boys out lookin.' They both knew there'd be questions asked in the coming days, especially if Grimes died – questions about how the fire started.

'The boys are lined up for the dam,' he said. 'I wanna help em too.'

'I know.' She paused. 'But I think it's best we do it.' Johnno and Spinksy would do the work to pull out the downed dead tree. And the rest.

'Mebbe you're right. Thanks, Mrs D. For everything.' He turned to go.

'Of course. One odd thing. The morning of the fire I saw Grimes up near the stockmen's hut,' Kate said.

Ed swung round.

'It had to be him. It was Fleming's truck, on the track on the Longhope Downs side.'

'He got a truck in there?' he asked.

'Yes. That track must be in better condition than we thought. But I'm more concerned about why he'd be up there. In that rough country. You don't think—'

'That he lit the fire?' Ed said.

The question hung in the air.

'I don't think so. He's a bastard, but he's not troppo.'

'But then it's an odd place to be, isn't it?'

'That's the truth. Longhope Downs had only a few wild scrubbers up in there, far as I knew. No sheep.'

'Perhaps when Grimes is well, we'll know why he was there.'

'*If* he gets well, Mrs D.'

'Yes. Let's hope he does, for Harry's sake. Are you all right, Ed? For all this? For the trip?'

'Yeah.'

'Safe travels, then. Good luck.' She reached out and touched his arm, then he limped away towards the truck.

CHAPTER 41

Metal- or wood-chewing, skittishness and bawling-like bleating, are all symptoms of distress.

THE WOOLGROWER'S COMPANION, 1906

'Sorry to intrude, Mrs Dowd,' Wingnut said, coming across the Amiens lawn. The *Mrs Dowd* didn't bode well. He didn't explain why he'd not rung ahead or even got her on the two-way, as a courtesy, to say he was coming. Either he didn't want the locals to know, as the visit was gossip-worthy, or he didn't want to tip Kate off that he was coming. Neither was good.

'Tea?' she offered automatically. Pearl, ever keen on visitors, appeared from the kitchen and clutched her leg. Kate stroked her head absently.

Wingnut cleared his throat. 'I wanted a quiet word, Mrs D.'

'Of course. Come up.'

'In private,' he said, his eyes on the toddler.

Kate paused then. 'All right. Just a minute.' She picked up Pearl and, hugging her tightly, went into the kitchen, where Mrs Walters was making scones, her hands white with what looked like a flour and water glue.

'The sergeant is here,' Kate said, keeping her voice even. She inclined her head a fraction towards the verandah and the waiting Wingnut, and kissed Pearl's cheek. 'Can you look after this little one for me?'

Mrs Walters took in Kate's seriousness and moved quickly to the sink to wash away the dough. Hands clean, she held them out to Pearl. 'Come along, dear. You're going to help me get the washing off the line.'

A few seconds later Kate heard the whine of the hinge on the back gate, and guessed where Mrs Walters had really gone. The chook house. It was easy to get into the bush from there too. If the sergeant headed that way.

Wingnut was still on the lawn, his back to her, a white piece of paper folded over and sticking out of the back hip pocket of his navy trousers. 'You people were lucky. The fire really did come close.' His eyes were on the row of black trunks that lined the gully.

'We lost Daisy, Sergeant.'

'Yeah. O'course.'

It struck Kate that he hadn't asked about the retrieval of Daisy's body, just as he hadn't counted Daisy as one of those killed by the fire. Ed had been right. He'd said that no death certificate would be issued. *Not usual for Abos, Mrs D.*

'The medical superintendent at Grafton Base rang. The next twenty-four hours are important for the poor bugger. Whether he fights off the infection.'

Kate wasn't sure how she'd tell Harry. But she would tell him. It seemed odd that Wingnut would want to come all the way out from town for that, serious as it was.

'I'm afraid we have no verandah chairs at the moment. One of them we must get out of the dam. The other . . . Would you like to come into the kitchen to sit?'

'No worries, Mrs D. It's about that. The Board's been onto me, see, about your Abo girl, Daisy Nunn. They didn't know she perished in the fire.'

Worry cut through Kate. 'I've just written the letter to

them. It's to go in the mail today.'

'Yeah. I reckoned. Anyhow, they tell me to pick up Pearl.'

Kate kept very still, not wanting Wingnut to see her fear. She just hoped Mrs Walters had taken Pearl on into the bush behind the chooks.

Wingnut turned and looked past the house, past the clothes line, towards the back creek and the chook pen.

'Don't worry, Mrs D. I'm not takin Pearl,' he said.

He must have heard her exhale because he smiled. 'The Board asked me if ya did ya duty by Daisy. I said I reckoned ya did.'

'Thank you.' Kate felt a rush of relief.

'The girl's death probly solves your problem.'

Kate looked at him. 'What do you mean?'

'Y'know Board policy. A half-caste kid can't stay with its Abo mother. It has t'be placed with a white family for proper raising. Not to be blunt, Mrs D, but since the Abo mother's dead, I reckon the Board'll forget about Pearl in a bit. Assumin you raise her. An assumin nobody stirs things up with the Board.'

She held the sergeant's gaze for a long moment. Wingnut was a practical man. It was much simpler and easier to remove the child from his list of things to do than to remove her from Kate. Less paperwork, less trouble. He'd come to tell her as much. Lay low with Pearl, and he would too.

CHAPTER 42

Whilst it may be an opinion unfashionable among men of science, shepherds in the old country would attest that in a small flock, the survivors will bleat, calling to the one of their own, now deceased.

THE WOOLGROWER'S COMPANION, 1906

Ed got back from Broken Hill late the following afternoon. Kate could see by his slow walk that he was worn out.

'No trouble on the trip?' she asked at the fence.

'Nope. It went off well.'

'Good,' Kate said. 'It's all done here too. The resting place and so on.' They couldn't use the little cemetery, where Kate's parents were buried. Her parents wouldn't have approved, let alone the people of the district.

'How did the boys go yesterday?' Ed asked.

'They did the work at the dam, and the little memorial. At the top of the Box Ridge paddock. It's nice up there. You can see right across Amiens.'

He nodded and looked away to the creek.

'Maguire, the postie, asked where it was, so I told him.'

'Yeah?' Ed looked concerned.

'Don't worry. He said there were better places on Amiens for Daisy. Listed them. Always ready with advice!'

Ed smiled, and shook his head. 'I stopped in town, eh.' He

cleared his throat. 'I hear old Grimes is worse. Does Harry know?'

'I've told him, in a roundabout way.'

They stood for a moment in silence, just the high cry of the bats, and the cicadas droning around them.

'Did you see much of Perry's place?'

'A bit. There's a lot to see. Sixty thousand acres.'

'Sixty *thousand*?'

'Not countin the place he got on the Queensland border.'

'Heavens.'

'An he's a good bloke, Perry.' Ed sounded surprised, as if that much country didn't go with reasonableness. 'He'd be a good boss.' He looked at her.

Kate made herself speak. 'I'll give you a reference, Ed.' She'd manage. She had to.

'Thanks, Mrs D. Not now, eh.'

They left it at that.

The telephone rang, shrilling through the homestead, and Kate went to it. 'Mrs Dowd? You need to come and get his things.'

'What's that?' Kate said, trying to place the female voice.

'Keith Grimes's things. I can't let the room with his muck all over it.'

'Ah, Mrs Christopher.' She ran the single men's boarding house in Longhope, a lady with more than enough backbone to handle her lodgers should they stray from her rules. Kate had heard that Grimes had been there since he got back to town.

'Can you get em today, Mrs Dowd?' Mrs Christopher was impatient. 'Tomorrow?'

'But Mr Grimes is in hospital.'

'He was leaving anyway, to move onto Longhope Downs with that boy. And now he's not paying his rent, so these things need to be shifted out. I told Wingnut the same.'

Wingnut? Why was Wingnut consulted? And why ring Kate about Keith Grimes's things?

'Well?' Mrs Christopher's irritation carried down the party line.

'I'm not sure Mr Grimes will want that.'

'I rang Harry's grandmother. A *trunk* call, if you please. She said these things have to go to Harry. So you're it.'

Mrs Grimes had written a short note to Kate, thanking her for looking after Harry while Grimes recovered. But she'd made no mention of his things.

Suddenly, a thought occurred to Kate. 'Are there any papers? Or just clothes?'

'*Puh.*' That was Mrs Christopher's expression of disgust. 'Some tobacco. Which is against the rules, I'll have you know.'

'I'm sorry,' Kate said automatically, wondering immediately why she was apologising for Grimes's pipe-smoking. 'Nothing else?'

'No.' *Damn.* Kate was hoping by some long stroke of luck that Grimes had not signed Jack's divorce statement, so there'd be no concrete evidence of her affair with Luca. Or if he *had* signed, that the copies were still with his things. They were *his* things, of course. But . . .

'You best come collect the items or off they go to St Vincent de Paul's, quick sticks.'

'Please don't—'

Click. Mrs Christopher had hung up.

At dusk, from the kitchen window, Kate saw the Rileys' truck pull up at the homestead fence. Luca got out and stopped at the gate. She went quickly down the steps and across the lawn to him, smiling, self-conscious when she realised she was smoothing her hair for this, a risky social call.

'We walk a little, *Signora*?' he said, pointing.

They went together towards the creek. She was so glad to be with him. Joyous even. Part of her felt that the disapproving district could go to hell. Luca would help her, just as he said before the fire that he would.

'Is funny, no? That the fire, she stop before this valley?' Luca motioned with his hand, outlining the gentle undulation of the house paddock, which remained green, outlined by the black where the fire had stopped.

'Ed had burnt off most everything in these paddocks.'

'Nothing for the fire to eat.'

'Exactly.'

They walked on a bit, then scrambled down the bank into the creek bed, Luca turning to give her a hand.

She felt the warmth of his skin on hers and he enveloped her and kissed her hard, her mouth, her face, her nose, taking her in. 'Ah,' he said, smiling.

He didn't speak, but took her hand in his and put his lips to her fingers, one by one. Then he kissed her again and again. She wanted him badly.

He pulled away from her abruptly, suddenly serious. 'Grimes wrote already, perhaps. The paper for Jack?'

'Perhaps.' Harry seemed to know everything, and what Harry knew, he told Luca.

Luca shrugged. He kissed her again, and Jack felt far away. They stayed there, until the dusk closed in. Only then did Luca lead her back up the bank, to walk hand in hand in the dark along to the homestead. Kate felt a peace she had not known for a long time.

Harry was sitting on the chair armrest as she came up the verandah steps. He swung one leg backwards and forwards. 'You been canoodlin, Mrs D?'

Kate went on past him, hoping the dusk would hide the heat in her face.

CHAPTER 43

The prudent woolgrower remains alive to the promise and bounty of the Merino ewe and her ability to raise twins and triplets.

THE WOOLGROWER'S COMPANION, 1906

The weekend passed quietly enough, with no news of Grimes, good or bad. But on Monday afternoon, Kate was in the office going over the accounts when the telephone rang. At first, she thought it was the boarding house again. She'd not yet been in to collect Mr Grimes's things.

But it was Wingnut. 'Young Harry back from school?' he asked.

Kate's heart sank. 'He's here.'

'Grimes passed away.'

'I'm sorry.'

'Too right. Doctor at Grafton Base just rang me. Said they did all they could. No pain at the end.'

'When?'

'Early this arvo. Tough old coot. Mazin he survived at all.'

Kate sighed. *Poor Harry.*

'You're doin all right, Mrs D. Bringin him up.'

Kate didn't know what to say. But in his job as the Aborigines Board rep, he must have seen a lot of kids having a rough trot. She just hoped this meant Wingnut would look kindly on them if, God forbid, the Board one day instructed him to take Pearl away.

'Give Harry my condolences.' He rang off.

Kate held the big receiver in her hand, steeling herself to tell Harry. He and his uncle – great-uncle – might have been estranged, but they were still blood.

What cannot be said will be wept. Kate's father had said that to her once, after they lost her mother. She'd pretended not to notice her father's eyes wet with tears. He said he learnt it from a Pommie in a trench on the Western Front. Written by a Greek bloke, apparently. Greek or Pom, the writer was right.

She went out onto the verandah. Pearl and Harry were sitting on the edge, Harry with a bikkie in one hand. Pearl reached for his other hand but he gently batted her away.

Kate sat down next to him. He frowned, alarmed at her closeness. 'Wotcha doin?'

She looked out across the paddocks, a gentle breeze ruffling what was left of the cut shrubs round the homestead.

'That was Wingnut,' she said. 'On the telephone.'

Harry's face clouded. 'He's dead, isn't he? Grimesy.'

'Yes.'

Harry nodded, his eyes to the front.

'Wingnut said that they did all they could. That he was not in pain at the end.'

'I reckon dying's gunna hurt like billyo.'

His eyes closed; he seemed older then. This time, when Pearl reached for his hand, he didn't move. Her face lit up, and she set their hands together in her lap, throwing a proud look at Kate.

'I don't care, anyhow, that he's dead,' Harry said, his voice thick. Then his face crumpled as the tears came. Pearl's eyes widened. She pressed her hand against his damp cheek. Even then he didn't shift away, indulging her, like an old pony that's good with children.

'He loved you. He would have told you, if he could speak.'

'He did talk.'

'What?'

'S*ee ya, Harry. Be good*. That's what he said.'

'Are you sure he spoke? When was this?'

'Yeah. On the ground. Fore they took him in the plane.'

It was possible, of course, or perhaps Harry just *hoped* Grimes had said something. Certainly, Grimes spoke to no one else from the fire until his death.

They sat there, the three of them, for a long while. A part of Kate was relieved at Grimes's passing: Harry would surely stay with her now.

Grimes's death was all the talk over the days that followed; in the pubs and at the Country Women's Association, in Dr King's waiting room and at the stock and station agent's. Grimes wasn't liked; he'd lived and worked long enough in the district for people to know him as a bastard. But there was a certain respect for a man who, burnt to a crisp, was tough enough to keep himself alive for days after.

Was it Grimes or the doctors who should take the credit? Most people's money was on the Flying Doctor. Others believed it was Grimes's pig-headedness that had sustained him for those days.

Then there was the business of the Eye-tie. Grimes's low regard for Italians was as well known as his short fuse. He'd lain for hours out in that paddock with only the ex-POW for comfort. No one deserved that. As the days passed, a subtle shift took place.

Nothing becomes a man quite like an early demise. Grimes managed, dead, to overturn the wide disregard in which he'd been held. There was talk that he died trying to save stock. That seemed unlikely to those on Amiens, those who knew him best. But in the still heat of the summer days that followed, from out of that new, misplaced respect grew a thirst for an accounting; somebody was responsible for this good man's death.

'Merciful God. We submit Mr Keith Grimes, our friend, our neighbour, a member of our flock, to your safekeeping.'

Kate waited, predicting the Reverend Popliss's next pronouncement. Yes: the twenty-third psalm. They rose to sing.

The reverend had a solid funeral service and used it over and over; the same hymns and prayers as he had for Kate's father's funeral years before, and possibly even for Kate's mother before that. She couldn't really remember that one.

Her father would certainly have found it funny, this repetition. But Kate could not. She had such sad memories of her father's death. She shivered, even in the oppressive heat of the December afternoon. Today she had to be sensible. She had duties, the children to look after; although one no longer counted himself as a child.

Beside her, Harry wriggled his neck. He did not like ties. They sat, just the two of them, in the front pew, the packed church behind them. The town had turned out: sleazy Mr Nettiford and his poor wife; Wingnut; Mrs Christopher from the boarding house, looking disapprovingly at Kate.

But absent was old Mrs Grimes, Harry's grandmother, too frail to come all the way to Longhope for her brother-in-law's funeral. Kate wondered if that wasn't a blessing. She could not imagine the woman's grief in laying him to rest. Now she had just Harry.

Kate had written to Mrs Grimes, sending her condolences and also offering for Grimes to be buried on Amiens, so Harry could visit the grave. While Harry might not be too keen on the idea now, that might change. When there was no reply to her letter, Kate rang, a trunk call all the way to Sydney. But the old lady made it very clear she didn't want Grimes buried on Amiens. Kate was relieved.

Reverend Popliss cleared his throat, and she tried to concentrate. The eulogy was coming.

Let us, Kate predicted.

'Let us hear a few words about our friend.'

She was surprised when the minister stepped back, away from the lectern, to make room for another speaker. Who knew Grimes well? Apart from Kate and Harry? Ed wouldn't be allowed to speak, given the gossip about him having Aboriginal blood. He and Luca were in the congregation at the back, under the protection of Mr and Mrs Riley. Without the Rileys, they'd no doubt have been ushered out by Reverend Popliss. So who would give the eulogy?

John Fleming took the reverend's place at the lectern. Kate didn't trust him. She squeezed Harry's hand out of nerves.

'It is my honour to speak of Mr Keith Grimes today. We all of us knew Keith. He was in the district for many years. But now he has left us too soon.'

When Fleming threw a look Kate's way, she held her breath.

'Though not a young man, Keith still had many good years ahead of him.' Behind them, there was a gentle shifting in the congregation. 'I have sympathy for young Harry, here. You should know your uncle—'

'Great-uncle,' Harry said loudly. Words spoken for the congregation, as much as for the speaker.

Fleming was indeed thrown off, but only for a second. 'Keith Grimes had a good name. A man of few words, and a fair man too. He knew what he stood for, what he believed in.'

The congregation didn't shuffle at that, there being an unspoken agreement that poor Harry needed a good send-off for his uncle – great-uncle – and no one was about to challenge this more recent version of Keith Grimes.

Fleming frowned and gripped the lectern. 'I wish to say a few words about the tragic nature of his death.'

Kate's eyes narrowed. If Fleming so much as mentioned anything distressing for Harry, she vowed to be on her feet, no matter the embarrassment she'd cause.

Fleming looked down at his notes and went on. 'Keith Grimes loved stock. We all know he did an excellent job with the Amiens flock, after the passing of Ralph Stimson.'

She gritted her teeth; he was giving Grimes credit for all the work that she and Ed had done after her father passed away. John Fleming was indeed a bastard. But as he continued, she realised that not getting recognition for her skill and work was the slightest of her problems.

'I can tell you myself that he kept on doing just that, for the short time he worked for me. Animal husbandry: he had a talent for it.' When he shook his head oddly, Kate had a terrible intuition that he'd practised the speech in front of a mirror.

'Keith Grimes knew a lot about the land, and about stock. He was willing to teach the young, too.' He glanced at Kate with a frown. 'Where there was aptitude and appetite to learn, he'd teach willingly.'

Kate's mouth was set, grim.

'Keith Grimes believed in duty. He served with distinction in the First War, in the Second Division of the AIF, fighting at Gallipoli and then in France.'

Kate knew that. He had served about the same time as her father. One of the things they had in common.

'Keith Grimes believed not just in duty, but in responsibility. Amiens, and then Longhope Downs, were run with a tight hand under him.'

That was for Kate. Fleming was making clear she couldn't keep her men under control.

'He was respecting of his neighbours, never putting them in danger. He had the respect of his men, too.'

'Not the Abos,' Harry said. 'They hated his guts.' Kate dug him in the ribs.

'Keith Grimes died saving animals, trying to save stock from the fire. That's what you should remember, young Harry, about your great-uncle.'

Kate noticed he got it right this time. He must have heard Harry's correction. She sat up straight, expecting the final prayer. But Fleming went on.

'One last thing I want you to know, Harry.' He looked straight at the boy. 'Out of respect for your great-uncle, I'll be seeking the people responsible, directly or indirectly' – he turned to Kate – 'for his death. The people who lit that fire, or those who allowed a fire to happen.'

Kate seethed. Fleming had pointed the finger of blame at her. And if an inquest was not on the cards before, it certainly was now.

CHAPTER 44

It should go unsaid that the woolgrower is the best advertisement for his flock and the magnificence that is the Merino. A wool tie, wool socks and tweed jacket should be his uniform of sorts, worn with bearing proud.

THE WOOLGROWER'S COMPANION, 1906

The next day, Kate was back in Longhope, this time to collect Grimes's things from Mrs Christopher. As she pulled the car in to park in front of the boarding house, she worried at the cost of the petrol for all this toing and froing to town. It seemed wasteful, but then none of the trips could be avoided. Truth be told, Kate hadn't felt comfortable coming anywhere near the boarding house while Grimes was still alive.

Kate took a moment before getting out of the car. She knew Mrs Christopher only slightly, just enough to nod at her in the street. That never took long; the lady was, as Harry had said at breakfast, a battleaxe, and she'd not chat with Kate anyway because of Pearl.

Kate walked carefully, avoiding the scattered jacaranda flowers, forgotten confetti along the narrow path. About to knock, she was surprised when the door swung open quickly and a broom head swept dust over her legs. Mrs Christopher was sweeping.

'I'm sorry,' Kate said automatically.

For a long moment the woman just stared at her, her disapproving expression unchanged from the funeral.

'Ah. *Mrs* Dowd,' she said at last. 'I'll be pleased to be having that room back. Now you take these things, mind. I told my husband Ern: I'm tired of people turning up and not taking everything.'

Kate was confused; who'd been here before her? But Mrs Christopher had already walked away, broom in hand, down the hall. 'Come along then,' she called over her shoulder, and Kate did as she was told.

The woman stopped at an open doorway and pointed into a small, neat room. 'Here you are.'

Mrs Christopher watched as Kate prepared herself. It was never easy to pack up a dead person's things. It was her father's familiar smell that had done Kate in all those years before. But here the scent of furniture polish hung in the air. Kate knew she was nervous too about the witness statement and wanted to find it. Surely she deserved some good luck. She smiled at the landlady, hoping she'd go away, but there was no movement.

The small room was neat as a pin, the single bed made tidily, sheets so tightly tucked Kate bet she could bounce a penny off them. The little dresser was bare (save for a tin of tobacco on top; Mrs Christopher glared at that), the bottom drawer slightly askew. Two fruit boxes leant empty against the dresser. Kate began to take off her gloves.

'Poor Mr Grimes.' Mrs Christopher spoke with such intensity. The expression on the lady's face told her she blamed Kate for his death. Ridiculous gossip had landed responsibility for the fire at her feet.

I didn't cause it! Kate wanted to shout.

'Let me know when you're finished.' Mrs Christopher pointed at the empty boxes. 'Only take what's his, mind.'

Kate let that pass.

'But do *take* those things, for goodness' sake, *Mrs* Dowd.' She shook her head and retreated to the kitchen.

Mrs Christopher seemed to know that she and Jack were separated, and disapproved of that too. Well, *bugger her*. Kate had to think more like Harry.

In the top drawer of the dresser were a few pairs of socks and a short stack of blue shirts, all put away, almost certainly by Grimes. It felt odd, as if Kate was trespassing. It was his hands that had gently folded the shirts and the socks, and placed them in neat order in the drawer. To disrupt them felt like a transgression.

She was doing this for Harry, she reminded herself. She reached for them, emptying the drawer, and moved along. Mr Grimes lived frugally. He had had less than a handful of those blue shirts of which he was so fond, and three pairs of trousers, plus miscellaneous woollen socks and underwear.

Pressing on, she shook off the sense of melancholy that had fallen on her. She would offer the clothes to Ed. He was slightly shorter than Grimes but about the same size and, no doubt, he could take the trousers up. Kate felt a rush of grief. Daisy would have done that for him. Before.

Kate pulled at the bottom drawer. It was empty, apart from a belt that looked quite new, and a small leather case no more than eight inches by four. When she opened it, the aroma of burnt tobacco filled her nostrils. His pipe. She coughed then, and hiccupped, a gulp of grief overtaking her; a swirl of sorrow for Harry, a reliving of her own grief for her father, and a sadness even for Pearl many years hence packing up Kate's things in this way. It takes another's death to make us face our own.

She forced herself to keep going and picked up the shiny belt. Coiled neatly, it was unusual, and looked expensive with its heavy buckle shaped like a ram's head, the sort of belt worn by a cocky who was a regular at the races. Most unlike the

Grimes she knew. But then, do you ever really know people? she wondered. The belt went into the crate with the other things.

Anything else? On her hands and knees, Kate checked under the bed – nothing – and turned sideways for a quick look under the dresser. That's when she saw it: the corner of an envelope, a large one, behind, flush with the wall. That's what was stopping the bottom drawer from closing.

Please. Please let it be the statement. She listened for Mrs Christopher and heard the reassuring sound of crockery being stacked. On her hands and knees on the shiny floorboards, Kate stretched under the dresser and pulled at the envelope. It wouldn't come. She tried shifting one end of the dresser out, away from the wall. That didn't work. The envelope was stuck between the bottom strut and the drawer itself. She took the drawer out entirely and set it gently, silently, on the floor to reach in through the dresser, the sound of her heartbeat loud in her ears. With some tugging it came away, intact, unripped, and she pulled it out.

'Whose is that, Mrs Dowd?'

On her knees Kate whipped around, dropping the envelope.

Barely had the envelope hit the floor when Mrs Christopher scooped it up.

'Ern!' she shouted down the hall. 'Come here!'

Kate got up but stood, stock still. The envelope wasn't hers but she had to get it back.

'*Ern*! She's ready.' Mrs Christopher handed the envelope to Kate.

Kate let out a sigh of relief, hardly believing Mrs Christopher was giving it up. But then she saw: *DOWD* was typewritten across the front of the envelope.

Arms crossed, the landlady eyed the crate. 'At least *you're* taking his things.'

'Have others been here, Mrs Christopher?' *Jack, perhaps?*

'I'm sure that's none of your concern, *Mrs* Dowd. My lodgers like their privacy. I never mention who comes and goes.' She threw another disapproving look and went back to the kitchen, as her husband appeared to carry the crate. He said nothing, just nodded amiably at Kate.

With a genuine thank you to Ern for carrying the fruit box to her car, Kate forced herself to leave slowly, no matter how badly she wanted to rip open the envelope. After a studied cheery wave, she put the car into gear and gently moved off, as if she had not an estranged husband to fight, and a lover – she squirmed calling him that – to protect.

The post office was her next stop. She'd already collected the mail that day, yet to the casual passer-by, Mrs Dowd was looking over a letter in her car outside. Hands shaking, Kate took the envelope from her handbag and leant it against the steering wheel. Should she even open it? It was Jack's, not hers. For sure.

Before, she'd not even have taken it out of Keith Grimes's room. She'd have delivered it up to the old battleaxe Mrs Christopher, with a request that it be sent to Jack's solicitors. That was before. Before her father died. Before the bank manager, Addison, tried to get her thrown off Amiens. Before Jack left her and claimed her money. Before Luca.

She levered a finger into the seal, gently tore the envelope open and pulled out the contents: Grimes's statement for Jack's solicitors, with a cover letter on shorter paper. The letter almost begged Grimes to sign this 'revised draft', with two copies. They were still attached. She flicked through the pages as quickly as her fingers, fat with fear, would allow. The signature page was blank. *He'd not signed*. She and Luca were free – of Jack, at least.

Kate drove from town in the late afternoon, not home to Amiens but to the Rileys'. There was no guarantee that she'd even see Luca. However, she was willing to take that chance. He just might be in from the paddocks.

The Rileys' car was gone. Kate knew that Mrs Riley would be at Amiens at this time of day. Still, she parked outside the empty homestead. Little human activity on a grazing property goes unnoticed. If she parked at Luca's cottage, it'd get back to Jack sooner or later. But here, at the Rileys', they could meet in less danger.

She walked slowly towards the homestead. A dog came round the corner of the fence, barking at her.

'Rusty!' Kate called, and the dog stopped barking, sidling in, tail wagging to welcome a friend. She leant down to pat the dog and he dropped to the dirt, rolling over for Kate to rub his belly.

'*Signora*!'

Luca walked towards her from the cottage, so easy on her eyes. Kate stood up, working hard not to smile. Failing.

'I have some news,' she said, not able to contain her grin. 'Good news.'

They both stood leaning against the fence as Kate explained, each struggling not to reach for the other, the current of attraction and affection palpable to each. Only the broad smile set on Luca's face, and the quick laughter he got from Kate when he spoke, gave away their feelings.

CHAPTER 45

A woolgrower may be surprised to find some of his flock more able, more gifted, more willing to act in the face of danger, than others. Yet, such is the condition of mankind, as much as in his sheep.

THE WOOLGROWER'S COMPANION, 1906

Late the following afternoon, when Kate came in from the paddocks, Mrs Riley's car was in its usual spot: parked outside the Amiens fence.

Kate smiled as she walked towards the homestead. Since the fire Mrs Riley had become as regular as clockwork at Amiens on weekday afternoons. She read endless books to Pearl, loved her to distraction, and, with Mrs Walters and Kate, helped to fill the terrible void of her missing mother as best they could. Together they made more biscuits than any mortal could eat.

Kate sat on the verandah steps and took her boots off, distant sounds of play coming from inside the house.

She followed the giggles. In the dining room, someone had taken a sheet and draped it right over the table, a chair at each end holding it out to make a cubby.

'Mrs Riley?' Kate crouched and lifted the edge of the sheet. The lady was sitting, her legs folded neatly to one side, her stockinged feet just visible from under her silk dress. Next to her sat Pearl. Around them were all of Pearl's toys: her bear, her doll, and the broken train that she had inherited from Harry. Each was seated behind a place set for a tea party.

'Tea?' Pearl asked, holding out a tiny cup. Kate crawled in and sat cross-legged in her jodhpurs, 'sipping' tea, when a male voice carried to them.

'You home, Mrs D?'

The two women looked at each other. 'Wingnut,' Kate said, and Mrs Riley nodded, concerned.

'Mrs D?'

'Coming.' Kate got back out from under the table and went into the kitchen. Wingnut was standing at the top of the verandah steps.

'Mrs Dowd,' Wingnut said.

He doesn't want to be here, Kate thought. She didn't bother with small talk. Mrs Riley appeared. 'Can I offer you some tea, Sergeant Withers?'

'Wouldn't say no. Bit of a drive out here.'

Wingnut sat on one of the newly installed verandah chairs (a loan from the Rileys). Mrs Riley produced a tray of tea things, and then withdrew into the kitchen. She pottered about there, humming, putting away the drying-up, emitting gentle waves of normalcy, of domesticity. Of support.

Wingnut frowned and put sugar into his tea. It was more than well stirred before he spoke. 'There's gunna be an inquest. Into the fire and Keith Grimes's death.'

Kate felt her lungs constrict. 'Is that normal?'

'Not *un*usual. Fire damage. Man's dead. I gotta take a statement from ya. The coroner'll probly need you to give evidence in person, Mrs D. You. Ed, too.'

'Why Ed?' Kate was suddenly afraid.

'Bout ya burnin off. To clear up how it started.'

'We didn't start it.'

'That's what the coroner will want to hear. He's gotta find the facts.'

'Will John Fleming give evidence?'

'Yeah. He volunteered a week or so back. He lost a lot of pasture.'

Because he hadn't burnt off.

'When will it start? This inquest.'

'Sixth o'January.'

Not even a month away.

'I gotta tell ya not to shoot through. Not to leave the district. Nor Ed neither.' Wingnut stood. 'Thanks for the tea, Mrs D.'

The policeman walked quickly back across the lawn, relief in every step.

Mrs Riley came onto the verandah and patted Kate's arm.

'Did you hear that?' Kate asked her.

'I did. You know, dear, perhaps you should talk to our solicitor from Tamworth? These things are best with help. Court things.'

Kate thought about that as the dust from Wingnut's vehicle drifted lazily across the fence. She would need a solicitor for the stupid divorce, too. But she couldn't hire one now. 'You know how people are. If I get a solicitor, it means I'm guilty. It's a given.'

Mrs Riley smiled. 'But why don't you consider it, anyway?'

Kate was sure she didn't need a solicitor. *Doctors are for the dying, and solicitors for the guilty*, her father always said. The locals would assume the worst.

CHAPTER 46

Woolgrowers must be alert to the dangers of certain species of bird to their flock. Crows and eagles will attack eyes, tongues, and the soft flesh of underbelly.

THE WOOLGROWER'S COMPANION, 1906

Mrs Riley, in the Amiens kitchen, was trying to persuade Kate. 'Reginald thinks you three – Ed, Luca and you – should spend time trying to work out how the fire started. Be prepared, as it were.'

Kate was squirming inside, conscious Mrs Riley would finagle any realistic chance to get Luca onto Amiens, for him to see Kate. If that wasn't bad enough, Kate realised then with horror that Mrs Riley, wearing her usual pearls, was *folding their washing*, including Kate's smalls. Mrs Walters worked hard, and Kate did as well, when she was not in the paddocks. But there always seemed to be more to do. So Mrs Riley helped.

'He thinks you could work out which way the fire went. When poor Mr Grimes saved those stock, and so on.' Reginald Riley had a reputation in the district as a brilliant man. But over the months she'd come to know the Rileys well, Kate had realised that *what Reginald thinks* was really what his wife thought. Even now, in 1948, life was complicated for clever women. Complicated, Kate decided, in fact, for all women navigating the pride of each man around them. She was exhausted by it.

Mrs Riley kept on folding, the tick of the wall clock filling the air.

'The coroner will ask, I suppose, if we actually lit a fire that day,' Kate said.

'No doubt Wingnut will get that from you in a statement beforehand too. That's easy enough. Don't let anyone leave, will you, dear? Before the inquest. In case the coroner wants to hear from each man himself.'

'It's a good idea. That we investigate.' Absently, Kate picked up one of the piles of washing, preparing to deliver it to Pearl's room. 'John Fleming seems to want to make me responsible somehow for the fire, and for Grimes's death.'

'Perhaps he doesn't want people to think the fire was his fault.'

Kate thought about that. It was possible. Someone had to bear the blame, and Fleming didn't want it to be him.

'And Ed told me that Mr Nettiford, the fire brigade captain, is the same. He apparently thinks it started on Amiens, a back-burn that got away.'

Mrs Riley patted her arm and that threw Kate. 'You'd heard that already?' She came around the table to Kate and enfolded her, and the washing, in a hug of linen and lavender water.

'They're coming after me,' Kate almost cried.

Mrs Riley looked into her eyes, trying to comfort her. 'You're a lady, dear. A lady doing as she wishes. Menfolk are not used to that.'

'It's as though I must be punished *more*. If I were a bloke, I'm sure they'd turn a blind eye.'

'Have you thought about that solicitor?'

Kate shook her head. 'You know what people'll think.'

Mrs Riley nodded, although Kate could see worry on her face. 'I'm sure everything will come right in the end.' When she touched Kate's cheek, Kate felt a sudden physical need for her own mother.

Early the next morning, she drifted awake, slowly aware of the restful silence inside the homestead, the still-soothing disharmony of birdsong outside. The birds had come back after the fire, bit by bit. *Bird by bird*, Harry put it.

Kate turned over, pulling the thin sheet with her. She had the promise of a day in the paddocks ahead, yet a feeling of unhappiness weighed on her. The inquest. She made herself think of Luca. He would come this morning to work on Amiens. She doubted they'd be able to speak privately the first day, or much at all. But at least he'd be near, and they might steal some time together alone. There was something almost bizarre about her life now; she knew that. The inquest posed real risk, yet she and Luca were now free of Jack. Kate had Grimes's statements. Jack had no evidence now. It seemed that there was nothing to stop them being together. Lightheaded with relief, Kate threw back the sheet and got up.

The smile came again as she pulled a brush through her hair. She touched her fingers to her lips, to her smile. Despite the inquest, for the first time in so many years, Kate was hopeful. Almost.

Ed pulled the truck to a stop close to where the State Forest boundary would have been, and the three of them, Kate and Luca with him, got out. 'We'll start here at the fence line, looking for the lightning tree,' he said. 'And any fire damage we can see over the boundary too.' The fence was burnt; only occasional bits of mangled wire had survived. The trees and shrubs at the base of the cliffs were mostly gone too.

They walked in silence through the ash and stumps. The country got more and more rugged, their going slower, and they did not reach the end of the fire's path.

'We'll be on Longhope Downs soon f'sure.' Ed looked at the map, back the way they'd come and forward, up the escarpment. 'It musta started somewhere further up in the triway. In that rough country. I'd bet my boots on it,' he said. 'Burnt its way outwards from the escarpment. Wind took it down the boundary. Tween us and Fleming.'

'We have to get onto Longhope Downs,' Kate said. 'To look for the tree there. Walk over it as we have here.'

'I don't reckon old Fleming's gunna let us on,' Ed said.

He was right about that. They all knew it.

By the time they got back to the homestead, dusk was approaching. Ed spread the map out onto the truck tray, but it was hard to see in the fading light.

'We were very lucky,' Kate said, looking at the map. Then she realised what she'd said, and she and Ed avoided each other's eyes.

They took their leave then, Ed and Luca, a long, difficult afternoon for them all. Kate watched them, still finding herself enjoying the sight of Luca's back as he went towards the Rileys' truck. He waved at her as he got in, a pensive smile on his face.

He was worried about her. She was worried about her too.

She went to have a shower, to try to wash away the ash and dust from their walk. But the fire had penetrated her thoughts as well as her clothes and skin. The inquest weighed on her. She couldn't shake it. Her mother always said to look on the bright side. *But assume the worst*, her father would add.

CHAPTER 47

It is the prudent woolgrower who shall maintain excellent relations with all such enterprises as shall impinge upon the success of his own, and above all, shall avoid unnecessary contretemps.

THE WOOLGROWER'S COMPANION, 1906

Mrs Walters delivered the post to Kate, who was working in the office. The inquest, now just three weeks away, was more than a distraction, but the running of Amiens had to go on.

Kate cleared a space on the desk, shifting aside her copy of *The Woolgrower's Companion*. It dawned on her that she looked at this book less and less.

From the kitchen, she could hear Maguire talking and she lay low, willing him to be gone. He was nattering on with all the gossip about Mr Buconti, an Italian POW just like Luca, who'd worked unguarded during the war in the Longhope district, under the Rural Employment Scheme. He'd come back to Australia, arriving the week before. But as he was apparently a communist, he'd not been allowed to get off the boat. It seemed both the Catholic Church and others were keen as mustard to keep those blokes out.

Kate concentrated on the post, and the official-looking letter on the top of the bundle. The postmark, stamped on 9 December, jolted her. Jack's solicitor had threatened to start divorce proceedings based on her adultery unless she agreed, by the end of November, to pay him. The fire had intervened but he would be back, she was sure.

However, the letter turned out to be from the bank, and only one paragraph at that. Addison had dressed it up – *we regret to inform you that your application has been unsuccessful* – but it was a flat no to the loan.

Kate shook her head. The bank made her think of Fleming. He still owed her the cheque for the wethers, even if they were dead now. And somehow, Kate had to get them – Luca, Ed and herself – onto Longhope Downs, to search for the lightning tree. She had an idea.

It was only the next day, on the Friday morning, that Kate managed it. Luca appeared early at the Amiens homestead, to go with Kate and Ed to Longhope Downs.

'Ready, *Signora*?' He smiled at her. Kate held his gaze. *I am a brazen hussy*, she thought with delight.

Ed drove them in the Amiens truck, Kate between the men in the cab. She was conscious of the warmth of Luca's leg against her.

'Ya sure Fleming's at the sale yards?' Ed turned the truck in through the big gates onto Longhope Downs.

'That's his routine. From Maguire's chatter, Fleming goes to every Longhope auction then on to Armidale for the night, for some reason.'

The talk stopped then, silenced by the beginnings of the fire damage to Longhope Downs; patches of blackened pasture, the air heavy with the smell of dead sheep. As they drove the mile in from the main road, it got worse. Entire paddocks were bare, with scorched earth, downed trunks and charred stock carcasses.

The black pasture stopped just half a mile from the homestead. It was miraculous to see. The house itself, with its circular drive and its neat green gardens, was intact, an oasis in the wasteland. No wonder Fleming wanted someone to blame. They were lucky they were sound financially.

Elizabeth Fleming was working in that beautiful garden. She came to the drive to meet the truck, peeling off her garden gloves, patting her hair, surprised. She frowned when Luca climbed down from the cabin, but corrected that when she saw Kate.

Even in gardening attire, she was sleek. Elizabeth reminded Kate of the horses at the picnic races, pampered and shining, groomed from mane to fetlock but with an overbred fragility.

'We weren't expecting you,' Elizabeth said askance, twisting her gardening gloves in her hands. 'John will be unhappy.'

'I was in town and thought I might come on here. I wanted a chat with John. He's forgotten to give me a cheque.' Best to put it like that. Elizabeth might even write one out.

She didn't take the bait. 'But John's at the sale yards. He won't be back today.'

Kate produced a disappointed face. She genuinely felt sorry for Elizabeth, stuck, as she was, with Fleming.

'Would you like a cup of tea?' Elizabeth said. The invitation was to Kate. The working men would fend for themselves.

'No. Thank you. I don't want to hold up Ed and Luca. We'll be on our way.'

'I'll tell John. Perhaps he can go to see you.'

Unlikely. With the wethers dead in the fire, Kate was sure he'd never pay her, even though he owed the debt.

'Perhaps.' Kate looked at the gloves in Elizabeth's hands. 'How's your thumb? Better?'

Elizabeth flushed. 'Oh, it was nothing. John insisted, though, that the doctor look at it.'

'Oh.' If it wasn't Elizabeth's thumb, what had tied up Dr King for all those hours while Keith Grimes lay in the creek bed, in need of attention?

Kate smiled and moved towards the truck. Then she turned back. 'One thought, Elizabeth. Do you think we might go out the back road? Through your paddocks towards Amiens? That'd save us going the long way round. It'd cut a good five miles, I think.'

Elizabeth looked doubtful again. 'That's through the fire. Where the fire was, I mean.'

'Is the track blocked?'

'No, no. It's not that. Everyone's been. Wingnut. Mr Nettiford . . .'

'But you'd rather we didn't see the paddocks?'

Elizabeth was caught. 'There's nothing to hide. Of course.'

'Good. Thanks. Sorry to miss John.' Kate left a startled Elizabeth clutching her gardening gloves.

Back in the cab, Kate warned Ed as he let the clutch out, 'Slowly does it.' They mustn't appear too keen to see the Longhope Downs paddocks.

Ed drove them along a track in the direction of the creek and Amiens.

'I'm gunna take us up to the triway. Where Amiens meets Longhope Downs and the State Forest. Then work our way along the boundary, right through the Longhope Downs dead country. See the burn.'

'You think we'll find where it started? Near the triway?'

'I reckon. If we can tell, that is.'

They drove across into the footprint of the fire, leaving the unburnt pasture for the blackened ash. Lands Department map on his lap, Luca marked the force of the blaze from the damage, the *forza*, as he called it. In each paddock the fire damage was more obvious than the last; the shade trees down, burnt away, the pasture gone.

'Soon, the Downs, she end,' Luca said, looking at the map.

'Yeah, mate. I reckon we're just about at the triway.'

'We were right. The fire has to have started close to here. You can see' – Kate pointed through the windscreen – 'the escarpment. It's burnt up to the foot of the rock face to the east but not much on the northern side. On the side away from us. You still sure it was dry lightning, Ed?' she asked.

He nodded.

Luca counted the ways off on his fingers. 'This dry lightning is one. A fire runs away – escape – is two. There is three: someone light her.'

That didn't bear thinking about. That a man would torch the bush, knowing the destruction that must follow. Stock, trees. Human life.

'You don't think . . .' Kate struggled to say out loud what she was still contemplating. 'That Grimes *lit* it. Out of spite or revenge or something?'

Ed shook his head. 'Nuh. He was a bastard, all right. But he wasn't crazy.'

'We need to find the lightning tree, otherwise people might think it was us. What would the tree look like?'

'Chances are she's gone, burnt away,' Ed said. 'A lightning strike up top, smouldering for close on a week? It's gotta slowly burn its way down the trunk, down to the ground.'

'But once it burns down, the tree falls and you lose the lot in the bushfire it starts?'

'Yup. So only if we're lucky will there be any bits left. If it did survive, the lightning tree will have a clean cut from top to bottom. Like it's been split for kindling by a giant.'

They drove on slowly through the blackened paddock, when over a rise a burnt-out shell came into view further along the track. The Longhope Downs truck, its driver's-side door eerily still open. The lights were gone too so it looked oddly wide-eyed, surprised.

Ed pulled up, and they walked round it. The hulk sat low, the tyres burnt away, and there was little left, the heat of the fire so intense that almost everything was destroyed – the interior, much of the bench seat, the dash, all a burnt mess of what had been metal and leather.

At the back, Kate poked with a stick at a long black thing in the tray, and it shifted slightly, showing what was left of an attached canvas mat. 'The fire-beater's here,' she said. A gust of rotting animal reached her and she waved a hand across her nose.

Ed looked in the driver's door. He retrieved a hessian sack from the tray of the Amiens truck and put it on what remained of the driver's seat. Sitting on the sack, he reached for the gear stick, then the clutch.

'In gear?' Luca asked.

'Yeah,' Ed replied.

'He must have *meant* to get out. He didn't leave it idling.'

Ed nodded. 'I reckon you're right, Mrs D. He musta switched the engine off. An the hand brake's on. He meant to stop all right.'

'He parked the truck facing *away* from the fire. For a quick getaway?'

Ed smiled. 'Nerves o'steel, eh. Didn't get the wind up.'

'Where's the waterhole from here? Where you found Grimes.' Kate shaded her eyes against the sun and scanned the course of burnt trees that plotted the creek bed, the boundary between Longhope Downs and Amiens.

Luca walked towards the creek and ran his eyes up and down the line. 'Here,' he pointed. 'I think she is here.' He walked that way and they followed him in.

Kate found the creek bed spooky. The air was still, for one thing, protected from the light breeze. The charred tree trunks reached up into the blue of the sky as if begging.

'You all right, Mrs D?' Ed watched her curiously.

Kate told herself to be sensible, and nodded.

Luca stood, his face solemn, hands on hips and his back to

them, surveying fallen branches and mangled tufts of wool, the waterhole muddied by hooves.

Kate, with her hand to her mouth against the smell, went to him. 'And Grimes was here?'

Luca nodded. 'He come for the water. Burnt on the flat. Then to the water.'

What a terrible thing was a fire. She turned away then and looked about for the stock. 'It's remarkable the sheep survived.'

'The creek bed's deep enough. Dry enough.' Ed shrugged. 'The front passed over em.'

Kate stood still, and took another look around her. It was odd. Something didn't seem right to her.

'*Signora*?' Luca asked.

'It's not what I expected, somehow. Now I've seen where the truck is. Could he have heard the sheep from there?'

Ed frowned, unconvinced, and then climbed up the bank. With him out of sight, Luca grabbed her hand quickly and kissed it. She pulled away, smiling at him, and followed Ed up the bank, taking one last look at Grimes's sanctuary, at the almost neat tangle of stake-like branches on the side of the little waterhole.

Eventually, they got back in the Amiens truck. Ed drove them beyond the hulk and up another small hill. There was no sign of any lightning tree. Once over the crest, the road sloped down, then towards the creek.

'Amiens,' Luca said, and sure enough they could see the woolshed, its neat yards around it, the huge letters spelling out the name stark on its roof. A Southern Cross windmill whirled in the breeze at the top of Riflebutt.

'It looks so peaceful,' Kate said, but her voice caught. She was thinking of Daisy.

The last of the day eked in through the kitchen door, throwing golden light across the map on the table. Ed stood, frowning, his hands and eyes on the map. 'I reckon Grimesy musta seen the smoke from the Longhope Downs homestead buildings. Gone lookin.'

Luca nodded, studying the map. 'He get out to stop. To fight her.'

'Yet his fire-beater was still in the truck tray.' Kate handed over a mug of Mrs Walters's fresh tea to Ed, and then one to Luca, with a smile for him.

'The truck, she look away from the creek bed. He turn her to park.'

Ed frowned. 'That makes sense. He sees the fire burnin. Stops the truck but pulls up, ready to roll.'

'But good to drive away. Why go to the creek?' Luca tapped the large X on the map, showing where he found Grimes.

'I reckon he got stuck, the poor bugger. Trapped, I mean. He sees the fire burnin, hears the stock. Goes to try to save em. When he knows he can't he comes up outa the creek bed and runs for the truck.'

'He is caught. In the fire on the flat,' Luca said, shaking his head just to think of it. 'He is burnt. He crawl back for the water.'

Kate almost dropped her mug. 'I forgot. The spark plugs!'

'Say again?'

'Before the fire, the day we left for Sydney, I went to Hayward's. When I got there, George was on the telephone with John Fleming.'

'I'm not followin, Mrs D,' Ed said.

'The Longhope Downs truck. It has – had – electrical problems. Spark plugs. Could that have started the fire? The electrics? What about the exhaust? A hot exhaust lighting the grass?' Kate asked.

Ed weighed all of that. 'The spark plugs? Doubtful. You'd need a fuel leak as well, I reckon. Or a prang to produce one. We got none of that.'

'What about the truck exhaust?'

'Possible, but a grass fire'd take longer t'get goin. This fire did a lot of damage. An it was big. Nuh, my money's on dry lightning.'

'But maybe this is why Fleming is encouraging the talk that we lit the damn fire. Because *his* clapped-out truck might have had something to do with Grimes's death,' Kate said.

'Did he say anything at all, mate?' Ed asked Luca. 'Grimes? While you was with him?'

Luca exhaled, shaking his head. 'Not the word.' He ran his fingers up and down his throat. 'Is hurt, I think.'

'Bad enough not to talk, ya reckon?' Ed asked, still surprised, even these weeks later.

'He say me nothing.' Luca shrugged again, his expression pained. Kate half smiled at him. It wasn't his fault Grimes couldn't talk.

'You know, Harry swears Grimes spoke to him that night,' Kate said. They looked at her. '*See ya, Harry, and be good.* Something like that.'

Ed smiled wryly. 'Sounds like Grimesy. But why would he speak to Harry and not to Luca or me or the docs?'

'It doesn't make sense,' Kate said.

'Ya reckon Wingnut knows?' Ed asked. 'About the spark plug problem?'

'I don't think anyone knows. Apart from Fleming, Hayward and me. I have to tell him,' Kate said. 'So he can talk to George Hayward.'

'Fleming hide this from Wingnut?' Luca suggested.

'Why hide it, if it didn't start the fire?' Kate asked.

'Doesn't want mud to stick,' Ed said.

CHAPTER 48

When threatened by a fox or other miscreant, sheep will flock together and the new-chum woolgrower may be surprised to hear their noise, a hissing and bleating. In truth, the creatures have no defence other than their numbers.

THE WOOLGROWER'S COMPANION, 1906

Kate drove into town the next morning. Straight to Hayward's. There was no one at the battered desk in the office so she went on into the workshop, surprising a young apprentice in grease-covered overalls.

'Is Mr Hayward in?' Kate asked.

'Nuh,' the boy said, embarrassed to be talking to anyone of the opposite sex.

'Is he back soon?'

The apprentice twisted a spanner in his hands. 'Yeah, I reckon.' He didn't often deal with customers, was Kate's guess.

'I shall return. Like MacArthur.'

He looked at her blankly.

An hour later, her errands done, Kate went back to Hayward's. Both the office and the workshop were empty this time. The smell of smoke drifted in through the open door at the back of the workshop.

She smiled at George Hayward through the door. He seemed shocked to see her. He was burning rubbish in an old 44-gallon drum, one end cut out, repurposed as a burner. Flames reached up into the air between them.

'I wanted a word,' Kate said.

'Yeah?' Hayward poked hard at the fire with a two-foot steel rod, so hard Kate almost stepped back. Was he angry? With her?

'It's about Fleming's truck,' she said.

He kept his eyes on the fire.

'Remember a month or so back, I was in. Fleming was having a go at you on the phone. About the Longhope Downs truck?'

He shook his head. Looked blank.

'About the spark plugs? Wrong part had been sent up from Sydney?'

He shook his head again, eyes on the flames, and Kate realised he would not look at her. 'I tell you what, George. Let's look at your order books. It'll be in there, won't it? Fleming's order for spark plugs.'

'Can't, Mrs Dowd. Sorry,' he said. 'They got thrown out, see. By mistake.'

The man's face was obscured by the waves of heat coming out of the drum. She leant forward to look into the fire. The flames were eating rapidly through the pages of books, the same squat shape and size as she'd seen on the desk at the front. Order books.

'You're burning them,' she said flatly.

He poked hard again at the rubbish and an ember floated up with a cloud of sparks, perilously close to the eaves of his shed.

'Why are you doing this?'

'Nothin personal, Mrs Dowd.'

'Nothing *personal*?'

'It's business. No woman can run a big place like Amiens and survive.'

'But Fleming will survive. That's it, isn't it?'

'The Flemings been here forever.' He shrugged. 'I gotta make a livin.'

'Me too, George Hayward. Me too.' She hoped his shed burnt down.

Kate pulled her car door shut with an angry bang, and wound down the window hard, to let out some of the hot air from the car. The sun-heat of the leather seat seeped through her cotton frock.

Clutch in, she reached forward to turn the key, but jolted back when a large shadow filled her open window.

'Hello, Kate.'

Jack put one elbow proprietarily along the window.

Kate couldn't speak and regretted it. Now he knew she was afraid.

'Did I startle you?' Jack cocked his head. He tapped the window ledge with a tight roll of paper in his fist, a document of some sort.

Kate flicked her eyes about the street. Who might see them? And would anyone help her if they did? She tried to keep her voice even. 'I didn't know you were back in town.'

'*Surprise*,' he said.

'What do you want?'

'What I deserve.'

She swallowed a retort. She'd learnt that well enough. *Don't challenge him. No good comes of it.* Grimes was dead now. Jack had nothing on them.

'I must go,' she said.

'I'm still your husband, Kate.' He smiled, without any humour.

She told herself again, *He has no power over me now.*

'Maybe you're wondering, did Grimes sign? Before he copped it?'

She had the unsigned statement. What did Jack mean?

'It's a terrible thing to wish a man dead, Kate.'

'I never did.'

'No? I hear you did more than wishing.'

'That's nonsense.'

He laughed. 'Not so, my little wallaby. Doesn't matter anyhow, given what I got.' He waved the rolled document. 'Grimes signed, God rest his soul. Eventually . . .'

Kate had a sudden terrible feeling that Jack was speaking the truth. It made sense: the pleading tone in the solicitor's cover letter. There must have been a later version of the statement, a version Grimes had signed. And Jack had it.

'What do you want?' She tried to keep her voice even.

'Like I said. To get what's mine. To tell you in person that Grimes's statement is ready to go. To the judge, I mean.'

Kate felt her palms clammy on the steering wheel. It wasn't possible.

'Speaking of ready: your little Eye-tie better pack his bags. Or bag, I suppose.'

Kate kept her eyes to the front.

'Grimes added a little something to his statement, y'see. For good measure. Canali's a commie, Kate.'

'That's ridiculous. Luca fought for Mussolini.'

'Well, there's an endorsement for you.' Jack laughed. 'Anyhow. Grimes reckons, *reckoned*, Canali and that Buconti bloke were mates. Buconti's the commie they sent home, in case you forgot.'

'That's not true. Luca and Buconti couldn't stand each other.'

'That did occur to me.' Jack leant in, both hands on the car windowsill. 'Look. I'm a reasonable man. Your Eye-tie's a bastard but I don't think he's a commie. Grimes did, though.'

'Well?' Kate said, livid with both Jack and Grimes.

'Before we get to that, I hear you're having trouble getting my money?'

'It's not your money.'

'As miserable as a bandicoot, Kate. But nothing's impossible for a lady grazier like yourself. Isn't that what you were always telling me?'

She gripped the steering wheel, her knuckles white.

'Here's what we're gunna do. You can pay me off over time. Each December when you get the wool cheque. A thousand pounds a year. You can stretch to that.'

Nonsense and he knew it. Still, she was boxed in. She might have to pay. That would be difficult, but –

'Not impossible, eh? I know you so well.' He laughed again.

'You'd destroy Grimes's note? About Luca?'

'Nothing's free, Kate. Your Eye-tie has to pack his bags. Get himself out of the state. After the inquest.'

'Why?'

'It's not good for Harry, to have that bloke around,' Jack said. 'I'm doing this for Grimes. He couldn't stand your little spiv.'

'You're doing this for *you*. Not for Grimes.'

'Maybe. But be assured, my little Kate, I am doing it.'

'What if Luca won't leave?'

'He's needed for the moment anyhow. To give evidence about poor bloody Grimes. I wanna make sure you're in the clear. We don't want my golden goose locked up, do we?'

'And then?'

'End of the inquest? If he doesn't shoot through, he's gunna be back on a boat to Eye-tie land.'

Kate dropped her head forward. She knew she was beaten.

'That's the spirit. Just so you know: I'm helpin Biggsy for a coupla weeks. I'll see ya round.' He stood up suddenly and banged the top of the car twice. 'On ya horse, then.'

He walked off, the statement still rolled in his fist. Kate sat, breathing hard. It took her two goes to steady her shaking hands enough to turn the key in the ignition.

CHAPTER 49

This writer begs the indulgence of his readers, to consider this personally held opinion: he is much struck, as regards the introduction of fauna and flora to our great land, that every such species yet introduced has brought with it eventual calamity.

THE WOOLGROWER'S COMPANION, 1906

Kate drove home slowly. Jack had shaken her to her core. Grimes had signed, which was bad enough. Jack had his statement, one that would be embarrassing in court for Kate, and also for the dear Rileys and Luca. But this note was much worse than embarrassing. If Luca was even accused of being a communist, he might well be deported. It didn't help that he'd annoyed the local Catholic priest who'd tried to get him to attend mass.

As the car rattled across the grid, it was as if Jack himself had taken hold of her shoulders. She felt sick with fear, terrified of what he might do, to her and to Luca. Though it broke her heart, she had to convince Luca to go.

What she feared most was that he would refuse.

The day dragged by. Kate made it into the garden early that afternoon, as if that, of itself, might bring Luca to her sooner. She worked on cutting back the yellow trumpet vine.

Her mother had planted the vine, so Kate felt disloyal getting rid of it. But with its big bell-shaped flowers, it was just too shiny, too dissimilar from the sombre shades of bush flowers. Different. Un-Australian. Which, it occurred to her, was why Luca would be deported if accused. He was not a local. He was someone who spoke funny and looked funny. So he was suspect. Different was all it took.

She threw a cut piece of vine aside, annoyed that she could not get Jack and his cruelty out of her head. The vine had grown back in the few weeks since she'd last had a go at it, creeping along the fence, leaping like a spider on a web across from the tank stand, and quietly but steadily heading for the gate. Kate went to the source and cut each outpost that had colonised the fence.

The last of the vine was resisting her pull when the Rileys' truck came up out of the gully. From the truck cabin, Luca smiled when he saw her. Kate took a deep breath. This would be difficult. He would want to take Jack on.

Luca braked and turned off the engine. As he got out, Kate moved along the fence to shut the gate – so that he couldn't come in.

'*Signora*,' he said, eyeing her across the closed gate. 'She is good – you is good?'

She couldn't reply.

'Kate,' he said, looking at her curiously.

'Jack. He's here. In town, I mean.'

'Ah,' he said, indifferent.

'But, Luca—'

He turned then to look at her, his face full of concern. For her. *Dear God*, he was the one who should be worried.

'Grimes signed the statement. Jack has them.'

'Is difficult for Mr Riley.' Luca looked down and scuffed a boot into the dirt. She could tell he would never knowingly hurt the Rileys.

'There's more. About you.'

'I?'

'Grimes wrote something. On the statement. That you're a communist. A friend of Buconti's.'

'This is the lie.'

'A terrible lie. And Jack knows.' Kate stared at the clippers in her gloved hand, ashamed of her husband. 'Jack says you must leave the state, or he will give the letter to Wingnut.'

He stared at her as if she was mad.

'They'll send you back to Italy. Don't you see?'

'*Communisti di merda.*'

Kate knew he swore. It struck her with force and clarity that she wanted Jack to die, and the strength of her hatred made her afraid.

'How this is possible?' Luca said. 'his is dead. The people like him now?'

It was true. Ironically, this communist smear might not have worked if Grimes was still alive. It could have been challenged, shown for a lie. Yet dead, his word was sacrosanct.

'Grimes never liked Buconti either,' Kate said.

'No one like Buconti.'

She didn't smile. An accusation might still be enough. The Catholic Church was keen to deport all communists.

Luca leant his elbows on the gate cross-piece. This was too close for Kate and she paced, backwards and forwards, on the other side of the fence.

'Jack says you can stay in town until the inquest is over.' She looked away, embarrassed. 'But then you must go.'

'*He says.*'

Kate stopped and swung towards him. 'You must leave town then. Go from here now. You can't come to Amiens. Not while Jack's about.'

Surprised, Luca straightened up.

'Don't you see? Jack is out to get you.'

'Because he say, I must go?' he shot back, in a rare show of anger.

Kate's face fell. He would not go; he would not understand. 'You can't be here. You can't come here.' She was terrified of what she knew Jack would do.

A flash of anger crossed Luca's face. Perhaps because she was telling him what to do, or because he thought she was a coward, for not standing up to Jack. Probably both.

CHAPTER 50

Predators may emerge at the most unexpected of times and with the direst of consequences. Woolgrowers must be especially alert to feral pigs.

THE WOOLGROWER'S COMPANION, 1906

Kate thought of her father often in the week that followed. He used to say, when times were bad, that the sword of Damocles hung over him. Kate couldn't remember who Damocles was, but she felt sorry for him, and a little bit envious. At least when the sword fell, it would have been quick.

Kate pulled her thoughts back to the present. She had to get through Christmas lunch at the Rileys'. Luca would surely be there. It would be painful for both of them.

The children, at least, were looking forward to lunch, Pearl actively trying to dress quickly to get to 'Biss', her name for Mrs Riley. She'd registered there'd be presents involved. And that excitement made Kate happy, that at least for a moment she and Pearl weren't missing Daisy.

Kneeling in front of Pearl, Kate helped wriggle a small hand into the armhole. 'That's it. Now the other one.' It took little coaxing. Pearl loved the dress: a pale green and white checked muslin smocked across the bodice; a gathered skirt with tiny green flowers hand-embroidered, scattered about. It must have taken Mrs Riley hours and hours to make on her treadle Singer.

Pearl resisted when Kate tried to turn her away to do the buttons at the back, her eyes on the novelty of Kate's lipstick. Kate had done her hair with more care than usual too. *It's not for Luca*, she had assured her reflection in the gaudy bathroom mirror.

'Quick sticks. Let's get you buttoned up.' While Kate pulled each handmade loop around its shiny button orb, Pearl looked down at the smocking.

'Pretty,' she said.

'Very pretty,' Kate agreed, taking her hand. 'Now let's see if that Harry looks just as smart.'

That Harry was seated at the kitchen table looking, in fact, very smart, with combed hair. A comic in one hand, he tugged at his neck with the other. 'I hate ties,' he said, to no one in particular.

Mrs Walters appeared, with her handbag and another dillybag suspiciously full of boxes. *Presents.*

'You look very nice, Mrs Dowd.' She smiled at Kate shyly.

Kate smiled back and smoothed the skirt of her dress. It felt unfamiliar now, to be in a tizzy frock. This one she'd not worn in years, not since she and Jack were courting. It struck her that, at twenty-five, she'd outgrown frippery.

'Off we go.' Kate shepherded them out. Once in the car, Pearl hummed something. It sounded like 'Santa Claus is Comin' to Town'. Harry took it up then, probably to annoy the grown-ups.

'Best behaviour, Harry and Pearl, please,' Kate said, as she steered the car up the drive towards the house. The Rileys had the gates to the homestead garden open in their honour.

Mrs Riley came down the steps, beaming her happiness, her face pink and shiny from the heat of the kitchen and the cooking. Mr Riley was right behind her, looking only a shade less thrilled.

And there in the hall doorway was Luca, his face impassive. Kate's head said that was to be expected, but her heart fell. It would be a long day.

Ahead, Mr Riley guided the children along.

'Reginald's only just back,' Mrs Riley explained. 'He took over a ham I cooked for Elizabeth. She's not well, really, in herself. After . . . you know.'

'After what?'

Mrs Riley whispered, 'She lost a baby. Miscarried the day of the fire.'

Kate gasped. 'Poor Elizabeth!'

'That's why the doctor was with her. John wasn't back and she was quite ill.'

'Oh gosh. Why keep it a secret?'

Mrs Riley shook her head. 'John's very private. I fear he sees it as their failure. The miscarriage.'

Kate took a moment to absorb such sad news. She bitterly regretted asking Elizabeth about the stupid thumb.

Later, they sat at the Rileys' dining room table, watching as Mr Riley carved the roast ham.

'Pearl. Can you please sit down? We're going to have lunch.'

Outside, a dog barked, and soon after Mrs Riley's voice carried in to them from the kitchen. 'Reginald, dear,' she called.

'Almost finished,' he said, his eyes on the ham.

'I'm afraid I must have you *now*, dearest.'

Mr Riley put his carving knife and fork down, and departed, leaving the dining room in awkward silence. From the kitchen, snatches of urgent whisper floated in. Kate wondered if there'd been a culinary mishap.

A dog barked again, then another. Harry got up and went

to the window. 'Somebody come,' he said, peering through the white net curtains. His voice changed. 'You better go, Mrs D. It's Jack.'

Kate got up quickly, Luca too. Her throat tightened, afraid of Jack, afraid for Luca. 'Look after Pearl, Mrs Walters. Stay inside. You too, Harry.' She went into the kitchen.

There, Mrs Riley spoke softly. 'Reginald will talk to him, dear. Best you stay here. Don't you think?' She took Kate's arm and patted it.

From the kitchen, Kate could see Mr Riley on his lawn, chatting away amiably, all the time in the world to pass. On the other side of the homestead fence, Jack stood, silent, arms crossed, legs astride, looking up at the house. Kate could not speak for her shame.

Then Jack made to come through the gate and Mr Riley held it gently against him. He said something to Jack, firm, serious, and they stood, each with a hand on the gate.

Jack went to force the gate, and it was then that Kate saw a figure cross the verandah and move down the steps. Luca. She slipped free of Mrs Riley and followed.

Jack saw Luca, then Kate. 'That'd be bloody right!' he said scornfully.

'Now, son.' Mr Riley's voice was gentle, and Kate wasn't sure if he spoke to Jack or Luca or both. 'Let's be sensible.'

Just as he spoke, Pearl ran across the lawn, giggling at her escape from a frantic Mrs Walters, who was right behind her, her face pale. Pearl skipped straight between Mr Riley and the gate he held firm. She climbed up, her feet on the lower cross-piece.

Jack spoke only to Luca. 'Next bloody time, mate. I'm looking forward to it.' He turned and strode away.

Kate was aghast. Jack would think the worst, seeing her with Luca. 'You must leave,' she said to him quietly. 'After the inquest.'

Luca spoke finally. 'Sorry for you,' he said, offhand, before he went back inside. The resignation in his voice almost made her cry.

After Jack left, Mrs Riley insisted that they go ahead with Christmas lunch, but the meal was strained, the only conversation between Mrs Riley and her husband; she worrying that the food wasn't hot enough, he reassuring her. Later, in the kitchen as they were washing up, Kate tried to apologise for Jack, but Mrs Riley was quietly sympathetic, more concerned about Kate's Christmas Day than her own. 'You know, dear, I'm not sure if it helps at all but I want to tell you something about Mr Dowd.'

Kate stopped drying up and looked at her across the big Tindale kitchen.

'He's quite serious about a young lady. An English girl who's governessing in the Islands.'

Kate considered that and started drying again.

'The next part is gossip, dear, and you know I don't go in for it.'

'Please tell me.'

'He's told her that he's well off.' The older lady looked at her across the kitchen.

'He needs to divorce,' Kate said, suddenly understanding.

'And he needs—'

'Money.'

CHAPTER 51

The humane destruction of injured animals is sometimes the unfortunate duty of the woolgrower. He may indeed be envious of such French persons as perfected that terrible instrument the guillotine, which was tested first on the necks of sheep.

THE WOOLGROWER'S COMPANION, 1906

Never show the buggers you're afraid: one of her father's sayings. That's what she would try to do today at the inquest. In her best dress and hat, Kate stood up very straight, the morning sun warm on her back. She gripped her handbag and went purposefully up through the people milling about on the steps of the Longhope Courthouse.

'Mrs Dowd,' a voice called, breathless. Kate turned, surprised; Mrs Nettiford from the haberdashery was speaking to her, unprompted. She was dressed up, like Kate, in hat and gloves.

Kate felt for her. Poor lady, with a husband like that. If only she knew.

'They had to shift the inquest,' Mrs Nettiford said. 'Because of all the people. It's over at the RSL hall.' She went past, then stopped and turned, hesitating. 'Would you like to walk with me?'

Kate saw she was hoping she'd say no. 'I'm all right. I don't want to keep you from the shop.'

'Aw.' At last Mrs Nettiford looked embarrassed. 'Jenny, our eldest's holding the fort today. So I can watch.'

Kate thought suddenly of those women of the French Revolution, the ones that came every day, chatting and knitting, spectators to the guillotine beheadings. All Kate's resolve not to show that she was afraid had evaporated.

They walked in silence the couple of hundred yards around the corner to the RSL. It seemed to take a long time. Once there, Mrs Nettiford held the door for her, and Kate went into the noisy entrance hall.

Much of the talk stopped then, a lull so sudden that Kate wondered if the proceedings had begun. But the quiet faces were turned to her. She was grateful for Mrs Nettiford's company and glanced back. But Mrs Nettiford was gone.

Kate walked on, in through the open doors to the main hall, and stopped at the back. There were people everywhere, standing, sitting, talking, every one of the RSL's chairs pressed into use. Kate estimated there must be two hundred and fifty people. Even Jack was there; his back to her, fortunately. She could not bear to look at him. At the front were three trestle tables set end to end and one chair off by itself, no doubt for the witnesses.

She looked about madly for an empty chair.

Wingnut sat at another table facing the front, the square of his shoulders solid through his blue police uniform. He waved at her, gesturing her forward, and pointing at an empty seat in the front row on the other side from him. Kate made her way there, conversations stopping as she passed. She told herself it didn't matter and smiled a thank you as she slid into the seat, glad to be taking cover.

A man in a suit came into the hall from the front and sat at one end of the long table, and the hum of conversation dropped a notch but didn't stop. This must be the coroner's clerk: sixty-odd, with thick black-rimmed glasses and a large stomach, the kind that took years to build. An older woman scurried in and sat at the other end. Like the coroner and the clerk, she was no doubt up specially from Armidale, forty miles to the south.

'All rise!' the clerk shouted over the crowd. 'All rise!'

The movement and shuffling of the two hundred and fifty people filled the hall, with little conversation. Another man, robed and with half-glasses, entered from the front. Kate winced, recognising him. It was the Armidale magistrate who had heard the bank's application to enforce its mortgage over Amiens, back in 1945. He'd thrown it out then, after some strong-arming by Wingnut. But Kate hadn't liked him, and she suspected he didn't like her.

The coroner went directly to the middle of the long table, and sat lightly.

The clerk waited until a straggler in the crowd found a seat. 'In the matter of the inquiry into the fire and death of one person –'

Kate thought of Daisy. Ed had been right about that too. He'd predicted the coroner wouldn't examine her death.

'– in the Longhope district of New England, on or about November thirtieth 1948, the coroner's court of New England is in session. Your Worship.'

The crowd waited patiently. The coroner cleared his throat. 'Ladies and gentlemen, I thank you for your attendance. The court sits in special session, as a court of coronial inquiry.'

Kate stared at him.

'That does not mean, for the uninitiated, that we're here to try anyone.' There was some shifting about in the crowd. He stopped then and looked at them, for the first time, over his half-glasses.

'I am duty-bound to make findings of fact and to bring any appropriate charges arising therefrom. If grounds are found for charges to be brought.'

A ripple of anticipation went through the audience.

Kate went cold. Is that what they'd come for? They wanted charges?

'Sergeant Withers is here in a dual capacity, as Officer in Charge of the Investigation as well as Counsel Assisting the Coroner. He has taken witness statements . . .' The coroner held out a short list and the clerk was up on his feet, to ferry it to the court reporter.

Kate well remembered the awkward morning just after Christmas, when Wingnut had come out to take her statement, and Ed's. He'd spoken to each of her men, too; all except Robbo, who was away, shifting stock. Wingnut's probing questions had made her defensive.

'Before we commence, I offer my condolences to the family and friends of the departed. There will be many of you here today. I give you my solemn promise that I will find out where and how this fire started, its area of origin' – he looked straight at Kate – 'and how this good man died.'

'Mrs Dowd?'

Kate jumped. 'Yes?'

'You are one of the witnesses who will come before the inquiry.' He peered at her over his half-glasses. 'Dowd . . . Dowd . . . Do I know you, Mrs Dowd? Been in front of me before?'

'Yes,' she said quietly.

'When was that? Remind me,' he said, tapping a finger against his papers.

Kate's mouth went dry. Everyone knew, except the coroner. 'In December '45, your Worship.'

'And?' His response was loud, as if compensating for her.

'It was the bank. Sir.'

'The bank?'

Wingnut saved her. 'It were over a mortgage, your Worship. In 1945. A dispute with a bank. Mrs Dowd's sheep place, Amiens, was the security.'

The coroner frowned, until his clerk leant over and spoke softly to him. 'Ah.' He moved on, scanning the pages in front of him. 'Who else is on my list . . . ? Mr John Fleming, Longhope Downs?'

'Yes.' Fleming's voice came from behind Kate.

'Thank you,' the coroner said. 'Edward Storch, Amiens?'

Kate was stricken. She'd thought Ed would be called after her, days into the inquest. He'd not come into town.

Wingnut turned and looked across at Kate. 'Where's Ed?'

'Working. But I can get him in. Soon as we know when he's needed,' she whispered.

'Tell the coroner then,' Wingnut said.

'He's working, your . . . sir,' Kate stumbled. Wingnut had asked if he was coming and Kate had said yes. She had thought Wingnut would tell her today *when* Ed should come in. 'I can get him, your Worship. He's available.'

'*Available*,' the coroner repeated, to a titter from the crowd, as he wrote a note. Kate felt her face burn.

'Those of you who've been before me in the past' – and he stopped then to look at Kate over his glasses – 'will know I take no nonsense. I get to the facts and as carefully and quickly as possible. Sitting as a coroner, I can ask anything I believe on reasonable grounds to be relevant, to establish the manner and cause of death, and cause and origin of the fire. Understood?'

There was silence from the crowd. This was the sort of thing they'd come for.

'A coronial inquiry is an inquisitorial process, not an adversarial one. All witnesses are my witnesses, and all evidence is given under oath. There is no cross-examination other than by Counsel Assisting, and any solicitor or other person representing the family of the deceased, or an interested person.'

He looked at his notes. 'But I see the family has not appointed anyone.' He smiled fleetingly, apparently pleased no lawyer was going to clutter up his inquest. Kate wondered if

Harry's grandmother had even replied. She must be suffering terribly.

The coroner looked out sternly across the silent crowd. 'I am here for two purposes only: firstly, to establish the circumstances of the fire, and secondly, the identity of the deceased, as well as when, where and how he came by his death. From those, I shall decide whether to bring manslaughter or other charges.'

Kate flinched.

'This is my courtroom and anyone who wants to stay will do as I say or will be out on his ear. Understood?' The hall was silent. He turned to look at Wingnut. 'Sergeant, please enter the statements into the record.'

The sergeant stood up at his table. 'I tender statements from relevant witnesses, being Mr Leonard Nettiford, Mr John Fleming, Mr Luca Canali and Mrs Katherine Dowd, as well as Mrs Dowd's men.'

'Thank you, Sergeant. Is the captain of the fire brigade present?'

The haberdasher jumped to his feet. 'Yes, your Worship. I exercised my rights as captain to request the inquest under your good self.'

Truly a ratbag, Nettiford was behind the inquest. Kate bet he wasn't alone.

'Thank you, Captain. I was confirming your presence. Your comments just now will not form part of the record.'

Nettiford looked confused and Kate was too. The procedure was bewildering.

'We'll now call the sergeant in your capacity as witness. Mr Andrews?'

'The inquest calls Sergeant Withers.' The clerk's voice boomed across the hall.

Wingnut got up again and went across the front of the hall to the witness chair. Surrounded by silence, Kate felt very alone.

CHAPTER 52

In these times of rapid and voracious scientific advancement, the woolgrower is grateful for the passing of such ancient times as necessitated the sacrifice of lambs.

THE WOOLGROWER'S COMPANION, 1906

It was the sight of Wingnut with his hand on the Bible that Kate remembered afterwards. For all the coroner's claims that it was not a trial, it felt like one, only worse. Mrs Riley had been right. Kate should not have ignored her advice about getting a solicitor.

'Particulars of the deceased, Sergeant, and place of death.'

Wingnut read from his notebook. 'Mr Keith Ian Grimes, aged fifty-nine, then manager of Longhope Downs. Mr Grimes died at the Grafton Base hospital, six days after injuries sustained in a bushfire that took place on sheep properties Amiens and Longhope Downs in this district. Reports of smoke in the triway were made by radio from the State Forest fire tower at Longhope just before twelve noon on Tuesday, November thirtieth. The smoke was carrying north-west with strong prevailing winds.'

The coroner turned to his clerk. 'Bring the map.'

The clerk disappeared through the side door next to the stage. Returning with a Lands Department map on an easel tripod, he placed it next to the witness chair, at forty-five degrees.

'Show us what's what, Sergeant.' The coroner draped an arm over the back of his chair, his suit jacket parting over his stomach.

Wingnut went over to the map and pointed. 'Amiens is here, Longhope Downs there, and the main road here, your Worship.'

'Can you mark where Mr Grimes was found in the creek bed? And the location of his truck?'

Wingnut checked his notebook for the coordinates and make a mark. 'That's it, your Worship.'

'Can you draw the imprint of the fire for me on the map?'

Wingnut paused.

Kate wanted to say that *they'd* mapped it, she and Ed and Luca, but this coroner would not take kindly to volunteers.

'I'd defer to the fire brigade captain on that, your Worship. To Mr Nettiford.'

'Fair enough. We'll get to the captain. Stock losses?'

'About a thousand-odd on Longhope Downs, and about two hundred on Amiens.'

'Two hundred? We'll need to confirm that for the record. I don't believe the number was known when statements were taken by the sergeant.' The coroner looked across at Kate in the audience. 'Mrs Dowd?'

'Yes, sir.'

'You'll have someone with you who can confirm those losses?'

'It's correct, sir,' Kate said. 'The figure is right.'

'I'm not asking you to confirm it now. I'm telling you that when evidence is given on Amiens's stock losses, that number will need to be addressed by a qualified person. '

Kate felt her face grow hot.

'Perhaps your Mr Storch? When he's next *available*.'

Kate felt her face burn even more, but fought to appear unruffled.

'Fire losses, Sergeant? Sheds, et cetera?'

'Longhope Downs lost the truck in the blaze. Completely destroyed. Fencing on both places suffered, pretty much in proportion to the stock losses.'

'Cause of Mr Grimes's death, Sergeant? Your summary, if you please.'

'Complications arising from third-degree burns, your Worship.'

'Thank you, Sergeant. That's all for now as witness.'

Wingnut came back to his seat at the table, but avoided Kate's eye.

'Now, Sergeant. In your capacity as Counsel Assisting, let's move on to the fire itself. From the statements, please summarise the views on the area of origin of the fire.'

This physical shifting around, and that of Wingnut's roles, made no sense to Kate.

Wingnut stood again, and looked at his notes. 'Mrs Dowd, Mr Storch – head stockman of Amiens – Mr Fleming and the captain are all of the view, in their statements, that the fire started in the vicinity of the triway. The triway, your Worship, is the area where the three properties converge at the one point: Longhope Downs, Amiens and the State Forest.'

'On which of the three properties is the area of origin?'

'There is no agreement in the statements. With one exception, none of the witnesses has evidence on that.'

Chatter broke out across the room: someone knew for sure where the fire started.

'The exception, Sergeant?'

'The observation log of the fire tower in the State Forest, being the fire tower which reported the outbreak on the thirtieth, your Worship. The log entry identifies the first known sighting of the fire as Amiens.'

CHAPTER 53

When handling, mustering or drenching, the woolgrower must remain alert to the need for rest in his flock. Under duress, the sheep will take only short naps, either standing or sitting.

THE WOOLGROWER'S COMPANION, 1906

Dr King swore the oath and sat down in the witness chair. A young doctor in the First War, he was now in his late fifties, yet looked older. She'd seen it with her father, too. Kate often thought that the men who'd fought carried it with them.

The coroner spoke. 'Before I ask the doctor to begin, any person who wishes to leave the room at this point, I should advise to do so now.'

The crowd quietened with anticipation.

'Dr King, what time did you examine Mr Grimes?'

'Just after 1800 hours, your Worship.'

'Where was Mr Grimes?'

'In the creek bed, in the position already indicated by the sergeant. He was lying on the sandy creek floor, on a shirt of some kind, his head propped up. Mr Canali there was with him.'

'What was his condition?'

'He was badly burnt. Burns to forty per cent of his body. Large areas of skin had been burnt away, mainly from the back.'

The room was completely silent.

'How did you treat Mr Grimes?'

'I administered morphine, and oversaw the shifting of the patient to the paddock where the Flying Doctor aircraft landed.'

'Can you give a summary of the Grafton Base hospital report as to the cause of death? From the medical superintendent there?'

'The report appears complete. The deceased succumbed to infection, as a result of third-degree burns sustained in a grass fire.'

'In your medical opinion, d'you think Mr Grimes was injured in the creek bed, where they found him, or had he got himself there after?'

'My assessment is that the deceased was injured by the fire front on open ground. The few sheep in the gully survived.'

Kate wasn't used to this process, this stating of the obvious. Grimes *must* have been burnt in the open. Even she could tell that. The real question was why he didn't stay put with the stock, and risked that run across the flat ahead of the fire.

'Would you look at the truck marked on the map, and the creek bed and stock position also marked. The injuries you observed: are they consistent with the deceased being injured between the creek bed and the truck?'

'Yes. It was perhaps a tragic mistake on his part. If he'd stayed in the creek bed with the stock, he might well have been spared.'

Kate opened the packed lunch alone in her car. She soon set the sandwich aside. It was tasty – cold mutton on buttered bread with pickle – she just had no appetite. Mrs Walters had put in some Anzac bikkies too, as a special treat, but they went untouched. They were a bit on the burnt side.

Kate cradled her cup of tea from the thermos. A pattering of rain on the car roof broke into her thoughts. There was a bit of breeze around now, after a hot, still morning. Perhaps they might get some rain. A good thing. There was only one more session before the end of the day. Kate just had to stay calm and listen and think of questions she should ask, no matter how scary the coroner. Then she must decide what to do.

As she went up the steps to the RSL hall after lunch, a gentle hand took her arm. 'Hello, Kate, dear. I'm sorry I'm a little late.' It was Mrs Riley, dressed for town, like Kate, but with pearls in place as well.

Kate was almost brought to tears by the kindness. 'I didn't know you were coming.'

Mrs Riley smiled. 'Reginald heard about this morning. So we're here for moral support. I've brought my knitting.' She held up a dillybag in her spare hand and Kate thought again of guillotines.

Mrs Riley led her through the crowd. Wingnut did a quick double-take on seeing Mrs Riley, but he waved them over nonetheless. By the time they'd worked their way through the crowd to him, he'd shifted an unhappy spectator from the front row to make room.

'Afternoon, ladies,' he said.

'Sergeant,' Mrs Riley said, with a certain frost. She clearly believed that the policeman had not done enough so far to help Kate in this process. She sat, produced her knitting and began, one of those people who could knit without looking.

Kate was turning to sit, but then stared. Luca had arrived. On his arm was a lady in a sky-blue dress, tightly fitted at the waist and around her ample bosom. Her dyed red hair was fashionably rolled, and a large matching cartwheel hat was carefully pinned in place at an angle.

Luca led the woman to a pair of seats just in front of Fleming, and he waited for her to sit first. How very gallant of him. Kate half wondered if that hat brim might not block Fleming's view.

Realising with horror that she was still standing, Kate sat.

'Who's that with Luca?' she asked Mrs Riley quietly.

The older lady's eyes were on her knitting, as she was counting stitches. 'I believe Mr Nettiford will give evidence now, dear.'

No answer, but it struck Kate that Mrs Riley was very well informed.

'My name is Leonard Alfred Henry Nettiford, rank of captain, Longhope volunteer brigade.' A haircut had been had for the occasion, and he sat up ramrod straight.

'What's your line of work, Captain? Outside the volunteer brigade?'

'I established a haberdashery business in March 1937. We supply the district with all its linen, dress materials and other haberdashery needs.' Mr Nettiford glanced into the crowd. To Kate, he seemed nervous. She was going to be too.

'Let's get going. I see from your statement that this is the biggest fire in recent years?'

'Yes, sir. All of the volunteer brigades in the district were called up.'

'How long did you fight it?'

'Siren went off in Longhope just after midday on Tuesday the thirtieth of November. The last of the brigades downed tools late the following day.'

'Where was the smoke first seen?'

'The State Forest fire tower reported it. From what they call the triway. It's rough country up there.'

'Can you put up the outline of the fire?'

The captain did so. He glanced at the crowd again as he went back to his seat.

'More acres were lost on Longhope Downs than Amiens. Why would that be?'

'Wind.'

More fuel! Kate wanted to shout. *Fleming didn't burn it off.*

The coroner, though, was digging. 'Just wind?'

'Yes, and bad luck – for Mr Fleming, I mean.'

Mrs Riley looked at Kate. She knew Mr Nettiford would never criticise Fleming, a good customer. Longhope Downs kitted out their stockmen there. Maybe it was Fleming that Nettiford kept looking at.

'The sergeant has listed four possible causes of the fire from the statements: burning off; arson; ignition by a vehicle exhaust pipe; and ignition from an earlier lightning strike. Your views on each, if you please, Captain.'

Kate held her breath.

Nettiford swallowed. 'There's no evidence I've seen to rule out any of em.'

The mutters from the crowd told the coroner that was a surprise.

'Is there any evidence for one over the others?'

'I doubt the lightning strike theory, your Worship.' Nettiford shifted in the witness chair. 'It is true that a dry lightning storm went through six days before. But a tree'd have to be hit by lightning, smoulder for days and then be fanned.' He shook his head.

'Those high winds the day of the fire do it?'

Nettiford frowned. 'It's possible.' He wasn't enthusiastic.

'Vehicle exhaust pipe?'

The hall was very quiet. Was Grimes implicated in his own death?

'Not in my opinion, because the wind drives the direction. Wind, along with slope and aspect.'

In his opinion, Kate thought.

'Fire burns faster uphill?'

'Yes. And north- and west-facing slopes burn faster and hotter as they're more affected by the sun.'

'But we got a creek flat. No slope. So where does that leave us? The remaining likely causes must be a back-burn escape and arson?'

'Yes, your Worship,' Nettiford said grudgingly.

From the hum of chatter in the hall, and the glances her way, no one believed arson. No; this had to be a fire that got away. An *Amiens* back-burn that got away.

The coroner cleared his throat. 'We'll need to sit late today to get through the scheduled witnesses. There'll be a short afternoon adjournment and then we continue.' He was on his feet, then gone.

'Come along, dear. Let's have a cup of tea ourselves.' Mrs Riley gathered her knitting things sedately. Kate saw that her slow pace was by design. They wouldn't move until the last of the crowd had left the hall. The shorthand lady smiled at Kate with an odd expression, and she realised with a pang that it was pity.

Luca and the woman had left ahead of them, their departure causing a frisson of interest through the crowd. She certainly was unusual. Kate tried not to be jealous, but failed. That woman wasn't Luca's type anyway, Kate told herself. And she didn't look very bright. Neither of these thoughts helped.

Spots of rain fell as Kate and Mrs Riley went down the steps of the RSL hall. The afternoon sky was overcast with thick, dark cloud, deepening to grey-green in the east. She just hoped the prospect of a good downpour might drive some of the court audience to an early departure, so they didn't get stuck in town.

'Now, where is dear Reginald?' Mrs Riley frowned, scanning the street. 'Ah!' She spotted their car, parked under one of the tall acacias that lined the centre of the road.

Kate vented as they walked, Mrs Riley's arm looped through hers. 'Why do you think they seem to object to our burning off? It's so much better than just throwing a match in things once in a blue moon, like Fleming.'

'You're a lady, dear. If you do things at all differently, they don't like it.' Mrs Riley patted Kate's arm.

'I'm being punished for defying Fleming and Nettiford, even though *I didn't*. They hated my father and now me. Blood will tell.'

When Mrs Riley said nothing, Kate was embarrassed. 'I'm whingeing now, aren't I?'

'Whinge away.' She smiled. 'Here's Reginald.'

He'd parked the car one spot back from the tree itself. In that space, under the shelter of the wide branches, tea was served. Mr Riley had three fold-up chairs and a card table set out, complete with a cloth on the table, a thermos and cups, and raisin scones.

'Hello, Kate, dear,' Mr Riley said, as though they were at the picnic races. 'I do hope this rain holds off for us.'

Kate was overcome at their kindness. She sank into one of the chairs and was issued with a cup of steaming tea, while Mrs Riley made small talk. She didn't mention the trial at all – *the inquest*, Kate corrected herself in her head – but only her knitting, and the need to get more raisins on the way home. Then she paused and took Kate's hand.

'Kate, dear. Reginald has a suggestion for you.'

Kate nodded automatically. She was grateful, but she was so tired it was hard to consider anything more in her mind.

'Go ahead, dearest,' Mrs Riley said, and smiled her encouragement to her husband. 'Tell Kate.'

Mr Riley began. 'Perhaps you might need some help, Mrs Dowd. With this court business.'

'She knows that, dearest.'

'Perhaps you should ask—'

'Patrick Williams. You should ask him to help.' Mrs Riley did the job.

'Who?' Kate said.

'Remember the Williamses? Boy and a girl? Mr Williams was the government surveyor in Longhope.'

Kate didn't.

'Well, anyway, Patrick Williams did law at Sydney University. Such a clever boy.'

'He's a solicitor?' Kate asked.

'Yes. He has his own practice now, in Tamworth. Patrick is very good. Catholic, but excellent. He does our legal work. Conveyancing and so on. We think you should ask him,' Mrs Riley said.

'He's due here late this afternoon,' Mr Riley added, beaming. 'He was coming anyway. For us.'

Kate wondered if this Patrick fellow really happened to be coming today, or whether it was a 'coincidence' organised by Mrs Riley. But Kate didn't mind. She needed help badly.

'Scone, dear? They're Reginald's.'

'They're very good, Mr Riley,' Kate said.

He looked embarrassed.

'Eat up, dear. You'll need some nourishment for the rest of the afternoon ahead.'

But Mrs Riley was wrong. When Kate returned to the hall for the afternoon sitting, it was largely deserted; just the court reporter sliding her notebooks into a case, and the clerk packing up the coroner's papers. Even bloody Jack was gone. Kate was grateful for that mercy. Just the sight of him made her angry, now.

'Is it not on this afternoon?' she asked the clerk.

He shook his head. 'There's been an inch of rain at Tenterfield. The coroner headed home to Armidale soon as he heard, in case the water goes over the bridge. He'll be back tomorrow if the road's open.'

Kate felt a weight lift off her shoulders. A reprieve.

'Now you can meet Patrick, dear,' Mrs Riley whispered at her elbow. 'All the sooner.'

CHAPTER 54

The prudent woolgrower knows not just his fleece, its tensile strength and fibres, but also that inevitable body of laws and regulation which might stretch its leery hand even into the most remote of domains. Never be ashamed to seek the counsel of a man of the law, where resources allow.

THE WOOLGROWER'S COMPANION, 1906

Kate followed the Rileys home from town in her own car, Mr Riley driving sedately so she could keep up. She hoped this Patrick fellow would come to something. Sure enough, as they drove up the track towards the Tindale homestead, there was an unknown car parked in front of the gates.

But waiting on the verandah was a lone young woman, no older than Kate, with bright red lipstick and a firm handshake.

'Enid, dear.' Mrs Riley greeted her with a kiss. 'But where's Patrick?'

'He sends his apologies. He didn't want to get cut off by the rain. I'm expendable,' she quipped.

Kate liked her, and the rather fashionable dress she wore so beautifully. It looked bought. Everything Kate wore was homemade.

'This is Patrick's sister, Kate, dear. She works in the office for him.'

Tea for all appeared and they sat. Mrs Riley poured, and put the teapot on the table under a cosy shaped like an English cottage. The spout peeked out of a thatched roof. 'Not that we're disappointed to see you, but lovely Kate – Mrs Dowd – needs a solicitor.'

'I'm a solicitor,' Enid said calmly.

'Really, dear?' Mrs Riley was lost in admiration. 'I thought you did the typing for Patrick.'

'I did – I do – but I qualified as a solicitor four years ago.'

'Well, congratulations, dear. Are you able to work on your own?'

'Oh, yes.'

There was a long pause as Kate guessed the Rileys were contemplating whether they should encourage her to consult Enid, this *rather new* solicitor, and a girl to boot. Kate didn't mind. She needed someone who knew their way around that nasty coroner. She was certainly willing to give this Enid-of-the-bright-lipstick a go.

The Rileys had discreetly withdrawn into the house. Kate was on her third cup of tea and had answered Enid's hundred questions – most importantly, that they'd not found a lightning tree.

'Have you done this kind of work before, then?' Kate asked. Enid seemed to know something about inquests. She wondered if she knew about divorces too.

Enid smiled wryly. 'I worked in the Crown Law office after I qualified. For four years, until just recently. I saw quite a bit of this. Loved it.'

'But now you're working for Patrick?'

'I got married. A girl has to leave the Public Service when she marries.'

Kate felt sorry for her. She'd hate to be forced to leave her livelihood. 'Can you help me, do you think?'

Enid looked again at her notebook and frowned. 'At an

inquest, the family of the deceased can be represented. That's not you.'

'No.'

'But there's also an "interested person". That includes any person whose act or omission, or that of his servant or agent, may have caused or contributed to the death.'

'But if we say that, won't we be acknowledging I did contribute?'

'Simply applying isn't an admission.'

'But to be honest, I don't *want* a solicitor,' Kate said. 'It'll make people think I'm guilty, or that I'm hiding something. You know?'

'The coroner is used to solicitors, Mrs Dowd. Don't forget: he has the power to bring charges, and to set bail.'

'You mean you think he'd actually charge me?'

Enid had no time to reply. 'Kate, dear? May we borrow you?' Mrs Riley's head appeared round the kitchen door.

Kate smiled an apology and took her cup into the kitchen.

Inside, Mrs Riley spoke softly to her. 'Reginald rang Patrick, dear. Just to see if he could come back. You know, a *man*, to work on the inquest.'

Kate recognised that the old coroner was likely to be unhappy about a female solicitor; this Patrick might be a bit more palatable to him.

'I'm so sorry, dear. Patrick's tied up all week with a murder trial – can you imagine? – in Tamworth. Some lady killed her poor husband.'

Kate felt a rush of sympathy for that lady.

'But Patrick said you're welcome to Enid for the week. Better than nothing, he said.'

Kate went back onto the verandah. 'I'm sorry. I was asking you, do you think they'd charge me?'

Enid made a dent in that bright red lipstick when she bit her lip. 'From what I've heard – and bear in mind this is all based on my understanding of what you've told me this afternoon – I think there's a possibility that you might indeed be charged with an offence or offences. The least offence – assuming you were to be charged at all – would be permitting a fire to escape, causing injury to the property of another.'

'That's the least? What if I was charged with that?'

'The penalty? For a first offence, as in your case, it's a fine of up to a hundred pounds, or imprisonment for up to a year, or both.'

Kate couldn't speak.

'It's wise to proceed accordingly, Mrs Dowd.' Enid changed tack. 'Do you remember what questions the sergeant asked you? When he took your statement?'

'It was about the day of the fire. Where I was, what I did—' Kate stopped.

'Were you full and frank with him?'

'He asked about the men, too, what I'd asked them to do that day. If I knew Grimes would be in the boundary paddocks. He asked me that several times in different ways.'

Enid saw the sidestep. 'No omissions?'

Kate didn't answer.

CHAPTER 55

One of the ablest of employees, the noblest and the most loyal, is a woolgrower's hound. Born of instinct to work stock with natural power, eschewing teeth over influence, the sheep dog is as much a part of success as a man's choice of companion.

THE WOOLGROWER'S COMPANION, 1906

That night, Kate went to bed knowing she would not sleep. She could not get from her head the fear of what would happen to Harry and Pearl. If she was convicted, she might go to prison. Pearl would be lost, to the labyrinth of homes and institutions for Aboriginal children, and to fostering, and on to the Child Welfare Department for adoption. Harry, too, might fall into the hands of the same department.

She was conscious that Addison lurked as well. Under the terms of Amiens's mortgage to the bank, for her to be *charged* with a crime was an 'event of default'. She'd learnt this years before, when Addison had tried to get her off Amiens. If an event of default happened, the bank had the right to accelerate repayment – to immediately require the entire mortgage to be repaid – and then to sell Amiens if she failed to pay.

She lay in the dark listening to the gentle sleep of the house itself, the creak and shrink of timber cooling in the night. But she could not find comfort even in these familiar sounds. Instead, she turned over and over thoughts of what may come, hoping for nothingness, for the blessed relief of sleep, comforted only by knowing that it must come, eventually.

Early on the Friday morning, Kate was grateful for the gentle birdsong of the dawn chorus, magpie calls and the chink of crockery in the kitchen. Mrs Walters. Gunner, on sleeping sentry duty outside her room, thumped his tail, happy to see her. She squatted next to him, and with a hand on his ears, she looked out across the paddocks, overcast with thick, low cloud. It even smelt like rain, and the Bureau was forecasting more showers. She wondered if the coroner had been able to get in from Armidale or whether the road was blocked.

It was good to think about something ordinary, and a bit more rain would help things start to come alive again. She looked hard at the sky. She didn't want to get trapped in town today if Quart Pot Creek rose and went over the little bridge, while she was a fixture at the damn inquest. But getting stuck in Longhope would be worth it for the rain.

Town. The inquest. She hoped the coroner would accept Enid. So much was at stake.

Gunner pushed his wet nose into her hand and banged his tail again on the wooden boards of the verandah. She pulled softly at his ears, and he dropped and rolled, folding quick as a deck chair to expose his tummy for rubbing. Kate stood up and leant against the verandah upright to drag her toes softly across the dog's warm spotted belly.

'Katie!' Pearl's voice filtered out of the homestead.

Kate pushed the enormity of what she faced out of her head and went in to Pearl, standing up in her cot.

'Hello, darling girl,' she said, and kissed the top of her head, the hair ticklish against her lips.

'Hunner,' Pearl said, smiling. Gunner knew to stay outside, just his head extending into the room.

Kate lifted Pearl out of the cot. *Children and dogs*, she thought: *the only good things in the world.* She would be composed today at the inquest. She had to be.

CHAPTER 56

A ram will almost always charge a challenger that approaches within fifteen feet. The prudent woolgrower, if charged unexpectedly, should look to the assistance of topography, for perambulation uphill remains much more difficult for a sheep than for a man.

THE WOOLGROWER'S COMPANION, 1906

Kate went to face the inquest that day with her reinforcements – Mrs Riley and Enid.

Audience numbers in the RSL hall were down, which pleased Kate. What didn't please her was Luca appearing again with that woman. The *lady* was in a dark green dress, possibly *poured* into it. Once more, to her relief, Luca avoided Kate's eye. He sat in his usual seat, just in front of Fleming. Jack was there too, on the other side of the room. He didn't see Kate.

The coroner planted himself in his chair.

'This is the resumption of the inquiry into the death of Mr Keith Ian Grimes,' the clerk called.

Enid rose and stood in front of the coroner's table.

He didn't look up. 'Take your seat, please. Quickly. Members of the public may observe but not interfere with the business of the inquiry.'

'If it please your Worship, I have an application to make.' Enid's voice was brisk.

He looked up then, and his glare would have stopped a ram. 'And you are?'

'Mrs Enid Morrison, of Williams and Fish Solicitors.'

'Which are you? Mr Williams or Mr Fish? I believe you're wasting my time, young lady.' His eyes went back to his papers.

'Certainly not, your Worship. I wish to make an application on behalf of an interested person. For her representation.'

The coroner sat up at the *her* and looked from Enid to Wingnut. The sergeant shook his head. He knew nothing about this. 'Which particular interested person, then?'

'Mrs Katherine Louise Dowd, of Amiens station, proximate to the place of death of the deceased, Mr Keith Grimes, which matter is before this inquest.'

'I'm aware of whose death is before this inquest, young lady,' the coroner growled. 'How can I hear you?'

'I am admitted to the Supreme Court of New South Wales, your Worship.'

'You're admitted?' He snorted a laugh as if she was mad. 'Serious?' He leant around Enid again, this time to find Kate. 'Mrs Dowd, really?'

Kate nodded.

He shook his head. 'All right. You'll want to have the transcript from yesterday?'

'Yes, your Worship.'

The court recognises Miss – Mrs whatever her name is.'

'Morrison, your Worship. Mrs Enid Morrison.'

'All right. Get this girl's name, Andrews, and find her a chair, will you?'

The clerk disappeared through the side door, and the coroner turned back to Enid. 'I'll remind you that you are limited to questions relevant to your client's interests. No more than that. Do I make myself clear?'

'Thank you, your Worship. If it please the court, Mrs Dowd wishes to apply to the court for witnesses to be called.'

The coroner scowled as the clerk returned with a chair. 'More people, Mrs Morrison? What do you think this is, the Country Women's Association?'

Enid's face didn't change. 'The witnesses are relevant to the findings of fact that the inquest must make, your Worship.'

'Who is it?'

'In the first instance, Mr George Hayward of Hayward's fuel station, Longhope.'

'The relevance of Mr Hayward to the proceedings?'

'Mr Hayward undertook repairs to the Longhope Downs truck over the course of its working life, and has information relevant to the condition of the vehicle at the time of the fire.' Enid had told Kate it was still worth raising the truck's electrics at the inquest, even though they were unlikely to have caused the fire. *Raise everything that might put doubt in the coroner's mind that the fire started on Amiens.*

'What are you saying, Mrs Morrison? That a man drove out to a fire in a truck that wasn't mobile?'

The titterers did their best, although there wasn't much heart in it. This was a development the few remaining people in the crowd had not expected. Fleming himself sat very still.

'We believe the vehicle has a repair history most relevant to the matters before the inquest.'

The coroner rolled his eyes. 'All right, then. Ask him to organise a time with the clerk.'

'Your Worship, we seek your assistance in this regard.'

He looked at Enid over his half-glasses. 'Because . . . ?'

'We believe Mr Hayward would require a summons to appear.'

There was a ripple of surprise. The locals were now wise to the fact George Hayward didn't want to give evidence.

'Do we, indeed.' The coroner sighed and turned to his clerk. 'See to it, will you, Andrews.'

'Your Worship.'

He took his glasses off and shook his head. 'Mrs Morrison.'

'We also wish to apply for certain other statements to be taken or witnesses to appear.'

'Being . . . ?'

'If it please your Worship, the stockmen and other employees of Mrs Kate Dowd. To give evidence to the effect that no burning off took place at Amiens on the day of the fire.'

He didn't look at her.

She went on. 'No formal statements were taken before the inquest from these witnesses, and we submit this evidence is central to one of the potential causes of the fire.'

It occurred to Kate that the coroner knew full well about this gap in the record.

'I'll consider it.'

'Thank you, your Worship.' Enid sat at the table in her newly acquired seat, the coroner's eyes on her behind as she did so.

Kate leant forward to whisper, 'Did he say yes? To getting my men to give evidence?'

'Not clear,' Enid said. '*Shhh.*'

Next Mr Nettiford was called back. Nervous, he shifted about and looked into the crowd.

'Captain, in your opinion, might the fire itself have been prevented?'

'A fire ban was in place. Back-burning would have been a breach of the law.'

'You can leave the law to me, Captain.'

'O'course. Apologies. Your Majesty,' he flustered, and a titter went through the crowd.

'I'm not so elevated, Captain. "Your Worship" is the appropriate address.'

'Yes, your Worship,' Nettiford said, his ears pink.

'Where do you think Mr Grimes suffered those burns? In the paddock?'

Nettiford cleared his throat again. 'I believe he were caught in the open. He must have balled up against a tree trunk or a tussock, when the fire front passed over him. A grass fire, mind. He'd never have survived in a bushfire or a forest fire.'

'You'll be aware that I am duty-bound to consider what steps, if any, might have been taken to prevent the death of the deceased. In your view, Captain, was Mr Grimes's death preventable?'

Nettiford shrugged. 'He saved them sheep. If he'd got away or stayed put in the creek bed, he mighta survived.'

'I want to return now to your assessment as to the cause of the fire, and the area of origin.'

There was silence in the room.

'From the statement, it was your opinion then, based on that first reporting from the lookout in the State Forest fire tower, that the area of origin of the fire was some point on Amiens, and that it was likely a back-burning had been lit on that property, uncontained and so permitted to escape?'

Nettiford didn't reply, his eyes on the crowd, not the coroner.

'Captain? Is that still your evidence? That the area of origin of the fire was on Amiens? A back-burning there?'

Nettiford looked down. 'I don't believe it's possible to say for certain, your Worship.'

Kate forced herself not to react but the crowd chattered, their disappointment evident. They'd expected better from the captain.

Spots of rain pinged on the iron roof of the RSL hall. Then the raindrops turned to a drumbeat and more good luck followed: the coroner suspended the inquiry until after the weekend.

Jack nodded to Kate as she left the hall, his face a mask of concern. He was worried about his money. She could not look at him.

⋆

Enid came to stay at Amiens. There was more rain forecast and she didn't want to get caught in Tamworth. 'I doubt that the coroner would agree to stay proceedings until I could get back. Best we not risk it,' she'd told Kate.

They could discuss and plan, as well. So on the Friday night, Kate set Enid up in the office, to work. 'Are you sure you don't need anything else?' she asked.

Enid shook her head. 'I'll get through yesterday's transcript.' She patted the short stack of typed pages the clerk had given to her. 'All right?'

Kate nodded, mutely terrified that Enid would become more convinced, not less, that there would be charges. She went back to the kitchen. Pearl was already asleep, the homestead quiet, Mrs Walters retired for the night after putting the toddler to bed. They were close now, those two, and for that Kate was so grateful. Another person who loved her dear Pearl.

Kate took out the Amiens journal and tried to write up the day. But it had been spent – wasted – at the silly inquest. While she'd done no work in the paddocks, she had much to record and she started to write. Harry appeared from the hall.

'You look as happy as a bastard on Father's Day,' he said.

'Harry!' He'd picked up some terrible sayings from the shearers.

Enid appeared in the kitchen. 'Can we chat?'

Chat? She followed Enid into the office.

Enid's eyes were on the pages in front of her. Then she looked straight at Kate. 'The transcript from the first day is worrying.'

Kate realised she was still clutching the tea towel.

'In his written statement, Nettiford was quite clear that the fire brigade believed the area of origin of the fire to be an unknown location on Amiens, as a result of back-burning that got away. Mr Fleming has reinforced that possibility in his evidence, when he mentioned the previous back-burnings that his men had observed on Amiens from Longhope Downs.'

'But we weren't back-burning that day. Or even a week before it. We'd never back-burn in those winds.'

'I understand. Fortunately, Mr Nettiford – for reasons which I can't understand as yet – without any prompting, has backtracked a little on that today.'

'Nettiford was nervous about Fleming in the audience. Fleming is a big customer.'

'Less certainty that the fire started on Amiens doesn't benefit Mr Fleming, of course.'

That was true. Kate was worried and not thinking clearly. She got up and started straightening the books on the shelves, too anxious to sit still.

'That fire lookout.' Enid frowned suddenly. 'Is it manned round the clock?'

'I believe so. Why do you ask?'

'They must log their observations. Note them down.'

'A logbook. Where's the logbook? Mr Riley will know. I'll ask him.'

'Good.'

'But overall, what do you think?'

'For you to be entirely free from the risk of any charge, the coroner must find what's called an accidental death. In this case, that means he must find that the fire did not start on Amiens and that you did not otherwise contribute to Mr Grimes's death.'

'So what do we do . . . ?'

'Present all credible evidence to establish that no fire was lit on Amiens on that day. Establish that on the day of the fire you were not in the vicinity of the triway.'

Kate's face fell and she looked down at her hands.

Enid paused, choosing her words carefully. 'Is that a statement you could make?'

'Not really. I was down in that boundary paddock out towards the triway. At the stockmen's hut. First thing.'

'What were you doing?'

'Nothing. Just checking the hut. I do it every couple of months.'

'You'd choose to go when a bushfire was likely?'

Kate looked away, caught in her lie.

'That puts you much closer to the likely site of the start of the fire.'

'Look, it had nothing to do with the fire. Why I was there.'

'So why were you there? Was it an assignation? Are you afraid for the reputation of the other party? For your good name?'

Kate almost laughed. Good name?

'A simple question from the coroner about your day's activities will uncover that you were there.'

'I understand. But it's nothing. Truly.'

Enid wasn't convinced. 'It's very important that you recognise the risks. The least charge is the one I described yesterday afternoon. An offence of permitting a fire to escape from your property, which fire caused damage.'

'That's the least? There's a worse risk?'

'It's unlikely. Most unlikely.'

'What is it?' Kate watched Enid's face.

'Manslaughter.'

Kate was silenced.

'Manslaughter by criminal negligence is the offence. It would be very difficult to establish. The prosecution would need to prove what's called "wicked negligence". It'd need to be found that you set a back-burn on the day, knowing that Mr Grimes would likely be in the affected paddocks.'

Kate tried to take that in. 'But . . . what if they did somehow prove it? At a trial?'

'The penalty? Imprisonment. Up to twenty-five years.'

CHAPTER 57

The prudent woolgrower shall bear in mind that a mere crow may do as much damage to a lamb as a dingo.

THE WOOLGROWER'S COMPANION, 1906

Kate and Enid worked hard over the weekend, looking at the map and planning what Enid called their strategy.

'You mean my *defence*?' Kate had asked.

'No, not yet. You're not charged, and if we're careful, you won't be.'

Kate didn't share Enid's confidence in the legal system. By Sunday night, her head was reeling from the information she'd given and discussed and taken apart and put back together. She had trouble getting to sleep that night. Every cry from a curlew brought her back to wakefulness. She finally got to sleep, but then the dog started up, and Kate was awake at once.

Jack?

Gunner was gone from the verandah outside her bedroom, off after something in the outbuildings, judging by the direction of the barking. Kate got up, casting about for some joddies in the darkness. They must be in the washing. She'd just have to stay in her pyjama pants. In the hall, she met Mrs Walters in her dressing gown, with Harry behind her. A sleepy Enid appeared as well. Kate waved them back to bed.

'I'm comin with ya.' Harry cradled the shotgun in his arms.

'No,' Kate said. 'It's probably just a snake making him bark.'

'So I can shoot it?'

'No,' she said again. When he didn't shift, she gave in. 'You can only come if you don't bring that.'

He didn't move.

'I mean it,' she said.

Harry went to the office to return the gun. She made a note to herself to hide the key for the rack.

Mrs Walters offered Kate the kitchen torch. 'You sure you don't want the shotgun, dear?'

'No.' But she looked about for something, anything, and had to make do with one of the tennis racquets from the umbrella stand. Harry was back, empty-handed. Grumbling, he took a racquet as well, and then in the garden he picked up a hoe and gave her his tennis racquet.

They went out into the night. Kate trained the torch on the track. That small circle of light was their only protection against a snakebite. *Stupid to get bitten by a snake on your way to kill another one.* The barking had kept up – not a frenzy, just a persistent woof every minute or so. Whatever it was, it was still there.

Kate was glad there was a bit of moon. She could make out the blackness of the meat shed, and the faint pasture all around it. In the daylight, those paddocks were yellowed and thirsty.

She looked across to her right, to the gully and the little cemetery beyond.

Then the dog broke out into vicious barking close by, behind the meat house. Gunner must have the thing bailed up.

'Ready?' Kate said. She switched hands, putting one racquet in her right and the torch and the spare racquet in the left. She felt like an idiot. She should have left the second racquet in the garden. She and Harry followed the barking around the corner of the meat house.

'Evenin.'

Kate shrieked and dropped a racquet, just saving the torch, mad with herself for screaming. Gunner took off, leaping and barking anew.

The voice had come from atop a vehicle. This man had hidden his ute behind the meat house and was standing now on its roof. Kate shone the torch at him.

'G'day, Mrs Dowd.' His tone was conversational, despite the dog and the night and the sneaking.

'Who are you?' Kate squinted to make out his features in the small circle of light. She could hardly believe her eyes. It was one of the Wilson boys. 'Bill? You work at the bank.' She didn't understand it.

'Yeah. I come t'see ya.'

'In the middle of the bloody night?' Harry put in.

Gunner stopped barking, sensing Kate and Harry weren't afraid.

'I got somethin ya want.'

'So. What is it?' Kate was tired. It was gone midnight and the Wilson boy – supposedly the smartest one of the lot – was standing on a ute behind her meat house, and she was holding a tennis racquet.

'Gunna cost ya,' he said. 'What I know.'

Kate saw red. 'You go on your way. As if I'll be paying you a penny. Off you go!'

He didn't move. 'Or what? Ya gunna hit me with your tennis racquets?'

'I'm not paying you anything.'

She must have sounded serious.

'Orright. Call yer dog off, Mrs D. An I'll shoot through.'

She yelled and Gunner slunk over to her. Harry squatted, holding the dog's collar to stop him from getting a jaw hold on their visitor's leg.

Dog secure, the Wilson boy jumped from the ute to the dirt, and then got in, starting the ignition. He turned the vehicle neatly to come to a stop by Kate, his arm out of the open window, dust floating lazily across the beams of lights punching into the dark.

'You got no mates and a lot of enemies, Mrs D. But I can help ya.'

Maybe he really did know something? 'I don't keep cash in the house.'

'Don't want no cash.'

'What do you want? Even assuming I'm willing to pay.'

'Yer ram. The good one.'

'Minute Man? He's worth a lot.'

'So is what I got.'

Kate shook her head.

'I'll give ya a coupla days t'think about it. Be back then. If ya lucky.'

CHAPTER 58

A purebred's pedigree is not worth its parchment if the animal itself proves wilful and ill-tempered.

THE WOOLGROWER'S COMPANION, 1906

At breakfast the next morning, Enid didn't ask about their night-time visitor and Kate didn't volunteer anything. She wanted to know what he knew first. She'd lain awake after the Wilson boy left, staring into the dark, trying to imagine what he could know that would be valuable. His father had bits of country all over the district. Was it something old Mr Wilson had heard around the traps? Or something from the bank?

The inquest would begin again in a matter of hours, and Enid was all business.

'One thing you will need to consider is whether you want to give evidence,' Enid said on the drive in. 'You'll be called last, after all the other witnesses. The coroner will want to put to you his conclusions based on the evidence he has heard. *If* you do.'

Kate's mind was on the charges, on the Wilson boy and what he might have. 'Don't I *have* to give evidence?'

'Not necessarily. You may refuse on the grounds that you might incriminate yourself.'

Kate glanced across at Enid. 'That'll go down well in the district.'

'Don't reject it out of hand. We can speak more on the benefits and disadvantages.'

Kate smiled at her. She liked Enid, who was everything Kate guessed a good solicitor would be: thoughtful, measured, objective. And with an eye for a great lip colour. But for all of that, Kate knew one thing Enid did not: if Kate refused to give evidence, she might as well have handed the town a confession.

The clerk had barely finished opening the day's proceedings when Enid was on her feet.

'Mrs Morrison,' the coroner said without pleasure.

'If it please the court, your Worship, Mrs Dowd wishes to apply to the court for certain evidence to be brought before the inquest.'

'Namely?'

'The observation logbooks maintained by the Longhope State Forest fire lookout.'

A murmur went through the hall. Most knew that the lookouts did indeed keep a log.

'They're relevant to the matters before the inquest, your Worship,' Enid pressed.

The coroner's face turned from impartial to a frown at that moment. 'Sergeant, in your capacity as Counsel Assisting, please make enquiries of the volunteer brigade, for production of the logbook or books for November thirtieth 1948. Thank you, Mrs Morr—'

'Your Worship, I submit that the relevant period is from and including the twenty-fourth to the thirtieth of November 1948. To include the date of the dry lightning storm six days before the fire.'

'*Alleged*, Mrs Morrison. Alleged dry lightning storm,' he growled.

'Yes, your Worship.' Enid sat down.

⋆

The coroner didn't look at Luca, seated stiffly in the witness chair. 'Name?'

'Luca Roberto Canali.'

He was nervous, Kate could tell: the hint of sheen to his face, his tight posture.

'You Eye-talian?' The coroner fixed a beady gaze on Luca.

'*Sì*.'

'You'll speak English, if you please.'

'Yes,' Luca said.

'Address?'

'Tindale. I work for the Mr Riley.'

'We don't need you for much, Mr Canali.'

Luca nodded.

'For the record, can you confirm that the place where you found Mr Grimes is as marked on the map?'

Luca looked carefully, and then brought his finger to the black pin on the map. '*Sì*. In the creek bed. On the side of Longhope Downs.'

Kate pushed her fingernails into her palms, to force away tears. Because Luca was defending her. The boundary ran down the centre of the creek bed, officially, according to the Lands Department. Luca was making it clear that Grimes had lain injured on Longhope Downs, not Amiens. It was the truth, yet a truth she'd not thought about until now.

'Keith Grimes was burnt where, Mr Canali?'

'*Sì*. Here' – Luca patted his torso, then his legs – 'and here.'

'You reckon he'd been injured long, when you found him?'

He shrugged. 'The fire, she come in the afternoon. He burn then. I find him at the morning. The next.'

'You sat with him till the Flying Doctor got there?'

Luca nodded, his face solemn.

'You have to speak, Mr Canali. No nodding.'

Luca looked at him, confused.

'SPEAK. SAY THE WORDS.' The coroner gestured with a hand from his mouth.

'Yes.'

'What time would that have been?'

Luca put his head on one side. 'She come – the plane come – before the night. Seven-fifteen, it is. The night.'

'What did you do for him? In that time?'

Luca shook his head, remembering. 'We have just the rum at first. Ed, he take this to us. Water also. We wrap him with the bandage.'

'Why didn't you move him to the homestead?'

'We wait for the doctor. They say.'

'Dr King?'

'Yes. We think he come soon, you know? But it is a long time.'

In the audience, Dr King shifted uncomfortably.

'Did he talk to you? Did Mr Grimes say anything?'

Luca shook his head. 'No, sir.' He tapped his throat. 'Words is not possible for him.'

The coroner frowned. 'Did he know you were there?'

'*Sì*. Yes.'

'Why are you sure?'

'I hold the hand. He tell me when he want more water, like this.' He squeezed one hand with his other.

The coroner raised his eyebrows. 'What did you do, while you waited for the doctor? Almost twelve hours in the paddock with him?'

'I talk.'

'But you said he couldn't speak.'

'Yes. I talk at him. The noise is good for them. For the soldiers waiting for the *medico*, is good to hear voice.'

Afterwards, Luca returned to his seat through a silent crowd. Kate was pleased for him, and afraid. Enid had warned her it would be Fleming next. Then Kate.

As John Fleming swore on the Bible, he looked very much the successful grazier that he was: polished riding boots, wool jacket and wool tie.

The coroner began. 'Mr Fleming—' But he stopped and listened, as a few drops of rain stung the corrugated iron roof of the RSL hall.

'Mr Fleming, I want to reassure you that no one is on trial here, least of all your good self. My task is to find the facts, and your evidence is very important.'

'I'm pleased to assist this inquiry, your Worship.'

'I'd be grateful if you would identify yourself for the record.'

'I'm John Edward Fleming, of Longhope Downs Pastoral Company.'

Fleming spoke firmly, with authority. Kate remembered then that Jack had always admired him. Everything about him was patrician, and he carried his pedigree in the marrow of his bones, with an educated accent and bearing to match. He was everything Jack wanted to be.

'Background?'

'I was born on Longhope Downs and went to school at Shore in Sydney. I've run the place since my father, John Senior, was killed in an accident when I was twenty-three.'

Kate hadn't realised Fleming had been so young, the same age as her when she lost her own father. Credit to him that he'd managed to keep the place afloat at that age. *He had no debt.* Her father's voice was in her head. *You did the same but with a big mortgage.*

The *click-click-click* of Mrs Riley's knitting needles reminded Kate where she was.

'When was the last time you saw Keith Grimes?' The coroner peered at Fleming over his glasses.

'The morning of the twenty-ninth. I witnessed his signature for him on a legal document.'

Kate almost flinched. Grimes *had* signed.

'So that was where?'

'At the homestead. He came up with the document just before I left for the monthly auction. I assisted him with that, then left for town.'

'What were the events of the day of the fire itself?'

Fleming cleared his throat. 'Mr Grimes was in charge, of course. I was in Armidale on business.'

A ripple of surprise went through the crowd. With the fire risk at its highest in months, Fleming had gone off to Armidale? It struck Kate that poor Elizabeth had been alone that morning. That she must have been in a bad way after the miscarriage, for the doctor to go to her and then stay all those hours.

Fleming seemed compelled to explain. 'Keith Grimes is – was – a very experienced manager. I felt entirely comfortable leaving him in charge.'

'When did you last speak?'

'I rang him just after 7 am. Said I'd be back later that day. He was off on his rounds in the truck.'

'His rounds being . . . ?'

'It depends. He often started down by the main road, then on to the woolshed – we had shearing coming – and he'd finish up in the paddocks along the boundary with Amiens. To keep a watchful eye.'

'For burning off?'

Kate leant forward to Enid, who shook her head and whispered, 'We can't really challenge the coroner himself. It'd be tricky.'

Fleming went on. 'Yes, for burning off, and Mr Grimes'd found fence holes on the Amiens boundary, on occasion.'

'So he may have been finishing his rounds then? To end up in the creek between Longhope Downs and Amiens?'

'Yes.'

'Have you walked over the burnt-out parts of Longhope Downs?'

Fleming nodded, his mouth set.

'Where is the area of origin of the fire? In your opinion?'

Enid was on her feet then. 'With no disrespect to Mr Fleming, your Worship, he has no special expertise in fire.'

'Mr Fleming and his family have fought bushfires for generations. You'll take your seat, Miss.' He glared her down.

'It's my opinion that a back-burn on Amiens may have got away.'

Kate shook her head.

'Had you seen back-burns on Amiens recently?'

'I sent my men out each time. Just in case one got away on them.'

'Had you warned Mrs Dowd about back-burning in recent months?'

'I did. Several times.'

A swell of astonishment shifted through the crowd.

'Might you have dates for those warnings?'

Fleming frowned. 'I checked my journals. I spoke to Mrs Dowd personally to warn her against back-burning on the tenth and the twenty-fourth of November. I believe the captain visited Mrs Dowd to warn her as well. On the twenty-third.'

Kate forced herself to appear unmoved as surprise ran through the hall at this information. So many warnings.

'Your Worship, one more thing,' Fleming said. 'I had Mr Grimes speak to Mrs Dowd as well, to instruct her to stop back-burning. That was the second of November.'

The hall erupted. Grimes himself had warned her about back-burning, and now he was dead.

'Quiet! Silence in the court!' The coroner was up, shouting across the noise.

As order was restored, Fleming spoke. 'I believe Keith saw smoke on the Longhope Downs–Amiens boundary and went to it. He must have heard the stock in the creek and tried to save them.'

Enid jumped up. 'Speculation, your Worship. Mr Fleming has no knowledge of these matters.'

'Thank you, Mrs Morrison. Accepted. Mr Fleming, a reminder that you may respond only to the questions put to you. Not otherwise.'

Enid took her seat.

'For the record, Mr Fleming, was your truck sound?'

'Hayward would know the ins and outs but I don't recall any problems.'

Liar. Kate wanted Enid to object, but she knew there was nothing they could do now. If they got Hayward to give evidence, then Enid had said she'd 'put Fleming's denial to him then'.

'Do you think his death might have been prevented?'

'He must have decided to save those stock.' Fleming shrugged. 'Put them before himself.'

The coroner looked up from his notes at Fleming, as if checking he'd heard right. He tried again. 'Might the fire itself have been prevented?'

'All I can tell you is what I saw after it had burnt through, and what I saw in the weeks leading up to it.'

'I regret that you have suffered stock and pasture losses. Were any of those losses from the Longhope Downs part of the triway?'

'No, your Worship. It's rough country, that area. Not cleared. I don't believe even Mrs Dowd runs mobs in there.'

Enid rose.

'Yes, Mrs Morrison. Speculation. We'll remove from the record. Thank you, Mr Fleming. I'll adjourn—'

'Your Worship, I have another point.' Enid was still on her feet as Fleming went back to his seat.

'Of course you do, Mrs Morrison.' He took his glasses

off and rubbed the bridge of his nose, eyes closed. 'What is it?'

'I'd like to propose a view, your Worship. A visit to the site of the fire.'

The coroner stopped rubbing and frowned. 'I'm aware of the meaning of a view, Miss.' Frown in place, he glanced across at his clerk, who was flipping through pages.

Enid pressed her case. 'A view will give your Worship an opportunity to see for yourself the creek bed, and the location of the truck.'

He leant back then, pot belly exposed as he draped one arm over the back of his chair, glasses in hand.

'You've heard a number of variations in person, and, under questioning, divergence from the evidence presented by Counsel Assisting at the start of the inquest. I put to your Worship that a view would enable a reconciliation of those discrepancies.'

He glared at her.

'Apologies, your Worship. Those *potential differences*.'

He nodded, less unhappy with that on the record. 'I'll consider it,' he said, gathering his papers ahead of the tea break.

Ed's time as witness was so brief Kate worried the coroner had already decided not to believe him. He sat, stiff and upright, on the edge of the witness chair, awkward in a tie and too-large jacket (kindly lent by Mr Riley).

'Were you present on Amiens on November thirtieth 1948?'

'Yes, sir.'

'*Your Worship*, son.'

Ed nodded nervously.

'Did you or anyone you saw set a fire on Amiens or its environs on that date?'

'No, your Worship.'

'Any questions, Mrs Morrison?'

Enid looked startled. That was it? But she was happy for him to accept Ed's evidence. 'No questions, your Worship.'

'That'll be all.'

There were no more witnesses. It would be Kate's turn tomorrow.

CHAPTER 59

Sheep should be left overnight to empty out before removal to the slaughterhouse.

THE WOOLGROWER'S COMPANION, 1906

The hard upright of the witness chair pressed against Kate's back. Enid had warned her over and over. *He may try to unsettle you. Don't take the bait.*

Kate kept saying that in her head. *He may make you wait. That's to embarrass you into speaking. Don't fall for it.*

Finally, the coroner spoke. 'Mrs Dowd. This may be difficult for you. You must tell me if you'd like to stop. Do you understand?'

Kate nodded, and then remembered. 'Yes, your Worship.' She clasped her hands in her lap to stop them shaking.

'For the record, you're Mrs Katherine Louise Dowd of Amiens Station, Longhope?'

'Yes.'

'On the morning of November thirtieth last year, who was present at the Amiens homestead?'

'Myself, Pearl Stimson, our domestic Daisy, and Harry—'

'Who's Pearl Stimson? What's her age?'

'Pearl is my sister, your Worship. She's three.'

'Three?' He looked at Kate with curiosity.

'My father's child . . .' She trailed off and there was a murmur in the audience. The town knew.

'Harry Grimes was there too. He's thirteen.'

'Where was Edward Storch?' The coroner looked at his list.

'Ed went into town early that day. He took Mrs Walters – our housekeeper – in to do the shopping and to deliver some rams to the Rileys. In case of a fire.'

The coroner looked at his notes. 'It's fortunate that you lost so little, Mrs Dowd.'

'We lost . . .' *We lost Daisy*, she felt she should say. But Enid had warned her they didn't want two deaths investigated.

'So eventually Mr Canali came and took you to the dam. Is that correct?'

'Yes. The fire looked as though it would reach the homestead. We had to go.'

'So you all went?'

'Except Harry. Harry Grimes. He'd gone to search for his pony. So Mr Canali took us to the dam and went back to look for Harry.'

'The fire kept coming down the boundary, didn't it? It went close to the dam?'

Kate nodded. Suddenly the fire was with her. She could almost feel Daisy's presence.

'Mrs Dowd?'

It was the conversation in the crowd that awakened Kate. She heard them, a worried thrum.

'Mrs Dowd? The fire went close to the dam?'

'Yes.'

'I want to talk about your burning off,' the coroner said. 'Is it the case that you were warned to stop?'

'We followed a process of regular burns, depending on the country and the pasture. Some burn as we do. Others burn everything and then nothing at all. I don't think personally that's as good as careful fire management.' *So there.*

The coroner scowled and Enid pursed those red lips. *Don't annoy him.*

'Were you back-burning at any time on November thirtieth?'

'No. We'd not burnt off for weeks. It was too dry.'

'Did you stop because you were advised to stop?'

'I run my own place, your Worship.'

Enid frowned.

'You don't think it's sensible to hear from your elders and betters, Mrs Dowd?'

Elders and betters? Kate's eyes narrowed.

Enid dropped a folder of papers on the floor behind her table with a bang. *Apologies*, she mouthed, but it was an intended diversion. For Kate.

The coroner looked at his watch. 'We'll adjourn here for lunch.'

Kate's hands were shaking again. She had only brief spouts of bravery. Was that bravado?

Enid spoke softly to her as they left the hall together. 'We cannot discuss the facts of your evidence during the adjournment. Do you understand?'

Kate's hands were still shaking when she sat in the fold-up chair next to the Rileys' car.

'It'll all be over soon,' Mrs Riley said, and patted her arm.

Kate was just relieved that Luca was not with them. Then, frighteningly, terribly, against her will, she began to cry, her breathing interrupted by stifled sobs, wet tears running down her cheeks.

'My dear.' Mrs Riley found a pressed white handkerchief in her husband's suit pocket.

Kate took it and wiped her nose. The hankie smelled of starch. She stopped her tears and blew her nose. Opposite her, Mrs Riley set down her tea and squeezed her hand. 'Well done, dear.'

'You're female. So it's important – *very important* – that you come across as credible, reliable,' Enid said. 'They'll believe you're capable of madly burning off when you shouldn't, of your men running amok, if you seem the slightest bit flighty.'

'I understand.'

'They have to forget you're a lady. To have them do that, you *must* appear calm.'

Kate was tired at even the thought of giving further evidence.

Enid looked at her watch. 'We better get back.' She took Kate's arm, only letting it go as they went up the steps. 'Remember, calm. Not emotional. Don't annoy him.'

Kate returned to that hard witness chair.

'Mrs Dowd. Ready?' The coroner looked across at the court reporter. 'Where were we up to?'

The shorthand lady looked back and read aloud: '*I run my own place.*'

'Now, what about Harry Grimes, Mrs Dowd? Had you told him not to leave the homestead?'

'Yes.'

'He left anyway?'

'Harry was worried about Ben, his pony,' Kate said. 'I told him that Ed – Ed Storch – would have opened the gates on all the paddocks as he left Amiens early that morning.'

'When did you know Harry was missing?'

'Mr Canali arrived. That's when I couldn't find Harry.'

'You went to the dam anyway?'

'We might all have perished. We had to go.'

'Who went?'

'Daisy, myself and Pearl. Mr Canali got us to the dam and then left immediately.'

'To look for Harry?'

'Yes.'

'Were your men burning off that morning?'

'What? No. Absolutely not.'

'By your own statement, even a small boy disobeys you, Mrs Dowd. I put it to you that your men may have done the same.'

Enid pressed her lips together. *Calm. Not emotional.*

'No one was back-burning that day,' Kate said firmly.

'Mrs Dowd, a history of ill-advised back-burning on Amiens has been established.'

'We stopped in good time, your Worship.'

'I see from the statements that not all of your men have confirmed there was no burning off on the day of the fire. Is Robert Yorke still in your employ?'

'Yes. Robbo – Robert – Yorke was away the day the sergeant came.'

'I'll have him summonsed. To ensure he's *available*.'

Enid was on her feet. 'No need, your Worship. Mr Yorke will be happy to attend without summons. Perhaps you might wish to speak to him if you were to conduct a view?'

The coroner took off his glasses and shook his head. 'Mrs Morrison, for your information, I have indeed determined to conduct a view. Tomorrow at 10 am. Take your seat.'

Enid sat and glanced back at Kate. *This is good. You just need to hold on. Keep calm.*

'Mrs Dowd, is it the case that you had shearers on Amiens in November?'

Kate was unnerved. 'Yes. Of course.'

'Did you have a fight in the shed, Mrs Dowd? At one point?'

Kate saw then that he was setting her up as having no control over the place – not over Harry, not over the men.

'Mrs Dowd?'

'There was a fight, yes. That's not unusual with shearers, your Worship.'

'If you could limit your remarks to facts, I'd be grateful, Mrs Dowd.' He made a note. 'So how did you stop this fight?'

Kate looked down at her hands. 'Keith Grimes did.'

There was an outbreak of chatter.

'Keith Grimes stopped it,' the coroner repeated. 'Your former manager?'

'Yes.'

'Lucky he happened to drop in.'

Enid's red lips pursed.

'Your activities on the morning of the fire, Mrs Dowd,' the coroner began.

Kate tensed.

'What did you do?'

'We cut down the trees round the house.'

'Please start from first thing. What time did you get up, when did you have breakfast? Each thing you did from then on until you left for the dam.'

Enid was up. 'I'm not sure this is relevant, your Worship.'

'Not *relevant*, Mrs Morrison? When this inquiry must establish whether a fire was deliberately lit? Or allowed to be lit? Or allowed to escape? It's highly relevant, I believe. Proceed, Mrs Dowd.'

Kate said nothing.

'Mrs Dowd? It's a simple question. Please list your activities the morning of the fire. Quite straightforward.'

'I was up early. Had breakfast at six. I went up—' She stopped.

'Go on.'

'I went up to the stockmen's hut.'

'Where's that? Can you point to it on the map?'

Kate knew she moved too slowly, that it would make things worse, but still she found it hard to get up and take the few steps to the map on its tripod. She reached out to land her finger on the triway.

Exclamations broke out then. She had put herself in the area where the fire had started on that very morning.

'What were you doing, Mrs Dowd?' The coroner's voice was hard and clear across the room.

'Checking. That the paddock was clear of stock.'

'From the location you have marked, this is approaching the escarpment. Is that correct?'

'Yes.'

'And also from the location, the hut must be within the triway area, which I understand from previous witnesses is generally heavily timbered. Is the stockmen's hut area an exception? Cleared? Have trees been felled?'

'Just round the old yards, which are close to the hut.'

The coroner tipped his head to one side, looking at the map. He began leafing through his notes, searching for something. 'If memory serves . . . Ah. Here we are.'

He cleared his throat. 'Mr Fleming gave evidence that *It's rough country, that area. Not cleared. I don't believe even Mrs Dowd runs mobs in there.*'

Enid stood quickly. 'Your Worship—'

'Yes, yes, Mrs Morrison. I can assure you this forms no part of the official record. But I put it to you, Mrs Dowd: is the Amiens side of the triway cleared for grazing?'

'No.'

'Had you run stock in there within a month, say, of the day of the fire?'

'No.'

Enid was up again. 'Your Worship—'

'Sit down, Mrs Morrison. Sit. Down.'

Enid did so, concern across her face.

'How did you get up there, Mrs Dowd?'

'In the car.'

'So how did you propose to clear this stock that you might have found? With the car?'

The crowd tittered with nervous excitement.

'Do you carry a spare tank of petrol, Mrs Dowd? In your vehicle?'

'Yes, but—'

Enid almost shouted. 'That is not relevant, your Worship.'

'Your objection is noted, Mrs Morrison. That'll be all, Mrs Dowd. For now. Until after the view.'

Wrung out, Kate went back to her seat. Jack, in the audience, caught her eye.

'Before we finish. Mrs Morrison, I have news of Mr Hayward. A family member has been taken ill, and he's been obliged to travel to the bedside.'

'A family member, your Worship?' Enid asked flatly.

'He's shot through,' Kate murmured to Mrs Riley.

'His mother, if you must know, Mrs Morrison. I'm sure even you had a mother once. But Mr Hayward provided a statement before he left, as to the facts you wished to have on the record, as regards repairs to the Longhope Downs truck. The clerk will provide you with a copy of that now.'

Enid took it from the clerk and held the statement to one side. Kate leant forward and they both read. It was a single page.

The parts books were accidentally thrown out jumped out at Kate. Then: *no recollection of any electrical problem.*

'The statement is appreciated, your Worship. But we need to hear from Mr Hayward himself.'

'You've got what you're getting.'

'Your Worship, on a related matter, I still seek permission to view the logbooks. The observation logs of the Longhope State Forest fire lookout for the period of—'

'I know the dates, Mrs Morrison. No logbooks have yet been made available to the inquest by the State Forest lookout. There seems to be some difficulty in locating them. Efforts continue, I understand.'

'Missing logbooks, your Worship? I do hope that these records have not suffered the same fate as the order books of Mr Hayward. That of accidental destruction, your Worship.'

'I don't appreciate your tone, young lady.' He spoke sharply, looking hard at Enid over his half-glasses.

'My apologies, your Worship,' Enid said. 'I am mindful that few witnesses remain before the conclusion of the inquest.'

'I am also *mindful*,' he frowned.

CHAPTER 60

The woolgrower should only accept assistance when proffered, if he be certain of the giver. For a ravening wolf may come cloaked in the fleece of a sheep.

THE WOOLGROWER'S COMPANION, 1906

It had been a long, long day. Kate sat with Enid on the verandah, each with a mug of tea from Mrs Walters. The post lay untouched in Kate's lap. Too much time had been spent going over the events of the morning, her head swirling with her evidence and the coroner's apparent belief that she was a liar, and somehow responsible for the fire. Now she had the next day and the 'view' to think about.

'It was bad, wasn't it, Enid?' she said.

'Yes.'

'But he hasn't asked to see the hut, has he?'

'The coroner? No. But he could, tomorrow. Why is that such a bad thing?'

Kate said nothing.

Enid was also thinking ahead. 'Your last man, Mr Yorke, will be available tomorrow? We need him. It's essential he give evidence.'

'Robbo? Yes. He's gone to Armidale to pick up a part. He'll be back late tonight.'

'I think I'll turn in, then.' Enid left, just as Harry appeared to keep Kate company while she waited. The black of the night reached in to them, Harry's socked feet near Kate's chair as he lay on the verandah.

'Ya reckon it'll be after bloody midnight again? Before he shows up?'

'Let's just hope he comes.' Kate watched the gully for car lights. Behind her, all the homestead was dark, Mrs Walters and Pearl long in bed.

'Why d'they fly like loonies?' He was watching the bats flitting about the homestead.

'It's not as crazy as it looks. Dad said it was insects. They change course when they see one. To catch it.'

'Daisy reckoned . . .' Harry stopped.

'Tell me,' Kate said.

He shook his head and they sat in silence, listening. The bats' noise was bird-like, a high-pitched call.

Kate stood up and looked hard again at the gully. Sure enough, vehicle lights cut into the blackness, towards the homestead.

Harry got up too, yawning, and Kate flicked the big outside lights on. Bill Wilson was in his ute again, but there was no truck or horse trailer. 'Where's he gunna put the ram? Passenger seat?' Harry asked.

Out of the ute and in the light, Bill Wilson seemed even younger than Kate remembered. It could have been his clothes. She was used to seeing him in a shirt and tie at the bank. Tonight, he was dressed like the dozens of graziers anywhere across the country: riding boots, moleskin trousers, kangaroo-skin belt, plain work shirt.

He smiled awkwardly at them, a bit green to be pulling this sort of caper. Kate wondered if Bill's father was in on all this. He was rough around the edges and fond of a beer. But even for old Mr Wilson it seemed a bit wild, trying to swap information for a ram.

'What are you selling then?' Kate said, annoyed she had to be buying.

He cleared his throat. 'You wanted to borrow, eh? From the bank.'

Would he know why? Kate wondered. That it was for the divorce? Might he broadcast that? A bargain was one thing; blackmail was quite another.

'Addison never sent that to Sydney. Your application. It's still on the file. He just wrote *do not submit*.'

'But I got a letter from him,' Kate said. 'Sydney rejected my application.'

The boy smiled. 'That's what he wrote to ya.'

'So? Addison lied. That's not worth a ram. What else have you got?'

'Someone sent it anyway, your application. Addison's secretary, apparently. She saw it and just put it in the bag for Sydney.'

Kate looked at him. *God bless Mrs End.*

'An Sydney approved it. Addison's a bit of a bastard.'

'You don't say,' Harry put in.

That was useful information to Kate, in its own way. It meant she just might have money, if she wanted to pay Jack off to go away for good. Her choice, not his blackmail. There was that word again. And she'd certainly let Addison know she knew, when she next needed something from him.

'Good to know, young man. Still not worth a ram.'

'Hold ya horses, eh. There's more.'

Kate leant against the fence, hoping against hope that this wasn't a wild goose chase.

'You been sniffin round Hayward's. Lookin for the order book for the Longhope Downs truck parts.'

'How do you know that?'

'I'm mates with Earlsy. Hayward's apprentice.'

Earlsy must be the shy young man in the workshop.

'You were askin Hayward about the Longhope Downs truck.'

'And?'

'Fleming wanted a new truck. He got a loan from the bank. An it's there on the file. Addison wrote it. *Problem with electrics*, it says. In Addison's hand.'

Useful. To a point. 'Still not worth a ram.'

'I been savin the best for last. I can't say it in front of the boy.' He jerked his head at Harry.

Kate sent him off. 'You go back to the house. Now, you hear me?'

'Not bloody likely.' Harry bristled.

'You go or I will ask Bill here to go instead.' Her voice cut through the night.

Harry still didn't shift.

'*I will.*'

Her tone did it. Harry frowned and moved off slowly to the verandah steps, standing there with his arms crossed. She waved him inside. He stood watching them through the kitchen window, but at least he couldn't hear.

'You better not be wasting my time, young man.' Kate sounded like the awful coroner speaking to Enid, and decided to be kinder. 'All right. What is it?'

'It's about Grimesy.'

She watched him.

'Everyone reckons he were savin those sheep, eh.'

'What else would he be doing?'

'He were stealin, Mrs D. Duffin sheep.'

CHAPTER 61

It is a lamentable fact of life that malefactors may avail themselves of the chattels of their betters.

THE WOOLGROWER'S COMPANION, 1906

Kate's blood pounded in her ears. 'I don't believe it. Grimes wasn't a thief.'

'I can tell you for a fact he were.' The Wilson boy was adamant.

'How do you know?'

'A mate was buyin sheep off him. Regular. Amiens sheep and Longhope Downs sheep.'

Kate was silenced. Things suddenly added up: Fleming complaining about losing stock to holes in the boundary fence; sheep in a creek bed; why the savvy Grimes would risk being caught in the open in a bushfire. And why after the fire he would speak to Harry, on the quiet, but no one else.

Bill Wilson smiled and shook his head. 'Fleming reckoned he were losin em to you blokes.' He laughed.

Kate's mind raced. 'The branches like stakes in the creek . . .'

Wilson nodded. 'Grimes had a yard tucked down there. Just temporary. A holdin pen.'

'And he had water. But it's hardly worth it, the few sheep he could keep in the creek.'

The boy smiled again. 'That were only small beer. Most of em he put in your old yards, up by the escarpment. He'd truck em out of there at night through the State Forest.'

Kate's mouth opened. The morning of the fire: the truck she saw from the stockmen's hut retreating into the Longhope Downs bush.

'No one for miles up there. An you got good ewes, Mrs D. Better than Longhope Downs, I can tell you that.'

'Can you now?'

The boy blushed, and Kate knew her guess was right: Wilson Senior, this boy's father, was almost certainly buying the stock that Grimes stole. That might not be a bad thing. The Wilsons would keep this quiet.

The kitchen door banged. Harry was coming back.

Bill quickly went towards his vehicle, surprising Kate.

'What about the ram?' Harry asked from beside her. She threw him a dirty look.

Bill scuffed at the pasture with a boot. 'No charge, eh.'

'Really?' Kate said, despite herself.

'Me big sister found out. She won't let me take yer ram. Made me tell yez anyway.'

Kate smiled. 'Thank you. Both.'

The Wilson boy rolled his eyes and went off.

At first light, Kate, Ed and Enid were heading down the creek from the Amiens side.

'Mrs D, I'll go m'self,' Ed said. 'Lookin for Robbo.'

'Robbo's missing?' Enid asked.

'Well, he's not back, anyway. Not yet.'

'But he must give evidence today,' Enid said. 'He's the last of your men needed to confirm there was no back-burning the day of the fire.'

'I know. I'm sure he'll turn up in time,' Kate said.

Ed did not appear so confident.

They went down the bank one by one, to the clearing by the muddy waterhole.

Ed said nothing for a bit, walking all around the creek bed, squatting beside the long straight-ish branches strewn about.

'Uprights. Bugger me. Sorry, ladies. I can't believe I didn't bloody see it.' Ed shook his head.

'We just weren't looking for yards or anything like that,' Kate said.

'Explains why Grimes were out of the truck. He wasn't fightin the fire. He were—'

'Down here kicking the yard posts away. Getting rid of the evidence.'

'Not a hero. A bloody thief. Usin our bloody yards.' Ed shook his head in disgust. 'I bet he *could* talk too. After the fire.'

Kate was annoyed, but with herself, for not putting things together.

'You gunna tell the coroner, Mrs D? He'd wanna see the old yards up by the stockmen's hut too, then.'

She paused. 'No. We just have to keep searching for the lightning tree.'

'What? The tree may be gone. Is likely to be gone. You *must* disclose this,' Enid said. 'I'd advise you – strongly advise you – to consider it. It will almost certainly get you off the hook. This explains why Grimes was there. Why he took such a risk.'

'I can't let them see the yards,' Kate said.

'Then just disclose what we've found here. That he was stealing the sheep in the creek.'

'I *can't* tell people this,' Kate said, and headed for the creek bank.

A short time later, they were on the road, Kate driving Enid to Longhope Downs for the 'view', where the coroner would see for himself the site of the fire, the creek bed and the burnt-out truck.

Enid was uncommonly quiet. Usually, she would coach Kate on the expected proceedings of the day ahead. But they were over the Quart Pot Creek bridge before she spoke. 'Ed's not following in the truck?'

'No. He's gone to search for Robbo. Try to get him back to Amiens by this afternoon, when the coroner will come.'

There was another long silence. Kate wasn't looking forward to the afternoon. Luca would be at Amiens then too. They had not spoken since she sent him away after Jack's threat, apart from the awkwardness at Christmas lunch. At least Jack was nowhere to be seen – not on Longhope Downs, and not on Amiens in the afternoon. Witnesses only today, the coroner had stipulated.

Her thoughts were interrupted by Enid. 'I know I've said this already, but I will say it again.'

'I must tell the coroner?' Kate said.

'Of course. The sheep stealing explains why Mr Grimes was there. Regardless of the cause of the fire, this information shows why he took such unnecessary, almost irrational risk. It helps you enormously.'

Kate shifted a little in her seat. 'I understand that is your advice.'

'But . . . ?'

'You're in the bush,' Kate said. 'There are other considerations.'

'There is a very real risk that you will have criminal charges brought against you. Prison time *is* a possibility. Do you understand? Prison.'

Worried as Kate was, she felt sorry for Enid. It turns out she was flappable after all. 'I understand.'

'Then please explain for me. I cannot think of a reason not to disclose this. Even in the bush.'

Kate considered. The gun-metal grey of the eucalypts

blurred past them at the side of the road. She trusted Enid, and she could not endanger her. 'There are two reasons. The real reason has nothing to do with the fire and I can't tell you about that. The lesser one? It probably seems silly to a townie.'

'Go on.'

'Out here, a child's character is determined by blood. He has no choice. It's the character of his or her family. He might escape it but, sooner or later, he'll do what the district expects of him. Whether that's good or bad.'

'You're talking about Harry.'

'Because his only male relative is a thief,' Kate said, 'if this gets out, Harry'll always be a thief to this district.'

'You don't know that would happen.'

'I do. It's a bit of my own experience. My father was an upstart, and he didn't help himself either – cutting corners, damming creeks, falling out with all the locals, good families included.'

'I don't understand,' Enid said.

'Over time, I was accepted by the good families in the district, even if he never was. Then, well, things happened. Now I'm back where he started. The locals mostly like that. No one should get above their place.'

'But you have Amiens.'

'True, but that makes it worse. I'm undeserving, like my upstart father. Much worse, because I'm female. These people are waiting, hoping, for me to lose the place. Blood will tell, crimes of the fathers and all that.'

'So that's it? You think Harry's name will be tarnished by association? *That's* why you won't tell the coroner Grimes was a thief?'

'Yes.'

Enid's red lips were sceptical, and she spoke forcefully. 'Whatever your reasons, I must say to you that the coroner will already have doubts about your credibility after yesterday.'

'I still can't disclose.'

Enid stared at Kate, as if she was seeing her for the first time.

A little less than an hour later, Kate and Enid stood on the neat lawns of the Longhope Downs homestead, waiting for the coroner. Kate had parked outside the fence, next to the police car.

'What are they doing?' Enid asked, looking up at the house. Voices and the clink of crockery carried from within.

'Having tea without us.' Kate moved into the shade. 'Making a point.'

It was already hot, and Kate wondered how the coroner and his large tummy would cope walking a mile or more across paddocks in the heat. She looked into Elizabeth's garden. It was neat, and all flowers, not a veggie in sight, nor a bowerbird for that matter. No children to make a mess of it. *Poor Elizabeth.*

The coroner appeared at last, followed by his clerk and the lady court reporter, then John Fleming, Wingnut and Mr Nettiford. Behind them, Elizabeth Fleming stopped on the verandah, her face pale.

Kate smiled at Elizabeth and got a slight wave in return.

Kate and Enid followed the two cars – the police vehicle and Fleming's – in the Amiens car, out through the Longhope Downs farm buildings and slowly towards the black edge of the fire's footprint.

The vehicles stopped at the burnt-out hulk of the Longhope Downs truck, and the passengers got out, silenced by the wreck before them. The court reporter carried her notebook and pencil in front of her, to record any question asked and the answer given. The coroner walked around the truck, the others behind him. He said nothing.

'Mr Fleming?' The coroner looked around. 'Take me to the creek bed, will you. To where Mr Grimes was found.'

They followed Fleming and the coroner across the flat, walking on scarred ground. Kate counted six weeks since the fire. Even with the rain they'd had since, there were few signs of fresh growth. It would take a long time to all come back.

They went down the creek bank single file, and into the sandy bed. Once on the sand, the coroner walked the length of the clearing, the natural dead end made by the downed tree by which Grimes had lain. He looked backwards and forwards, scratched his head, then walked it again.

There was little conversation, and that was a good thing. No assumptions could be planted or fertilised. Kate hoped there would be more to say in the afternoon, when the coroner came to visit Amiens to speak to Robbo. It could just as easily have been done in town, but Kate had agreed to the visit. It might make the coroner feel more sympathy for her if he met Harry. She was desperate; she knew that.

The view was over almost as soon as it had begun, and the trio of vehicles returned to the Longhope Downs homestead.

Kate expected Wingnut would drive ahead, take the coroner back to town for lunch before their visit to Amiens. But they stayed on the verandah, and eventually Kate left with Enid. 'They must be having them to lunch,' Kate explained.

'That's inappropriate,' Enid said crossly.

'You reckon?' Kate teased, turning the car down the avenue of blackened poplars. She just hoped Robbo had been unearthed.

CHAPTER 62

While a sheep's faculty of sight may not be as sharp as that of his two-legged master, the powers of visual perception of our oldest domesticated animal is still sufficient for its purposes.

THE WOOLGROWER'S COMPANION, 1906

Kate steered the car off from the main road onto Amiens, opening up that wonderful view. Despite her problems, she savoured that sight. Her father, for all the years she could remember, would pull the car to a stop here and look out over his land with a small smile.

Even as a little girl, she knew what it was that he felt. Pleasure in the view, yes, but also pride; pride that he had made this, built this place from a small soldier-settler holding into the biggest sheep property in the district. He'd made few friends doing it, so sharp were his practices. He couldn't care less. *The harder I work, the luckier I get*, he'd say when someone or other exclaimed how fortunate he was.

Kate wondered, as she looked out at that same view, if she felt pride. *Not really.* Duty, she was sure of that, a knowledge that she had to keep Amiens whole, keep it operating and solvent and safe, for Pearl and Harry and herself.

Where did Luca come into that? She simply didn't know.

Kate didn't stop the car, just drove it slowly over the grid, each rung jolting them out of the morning they'd had.

Ed and the truck were waiting for them when they reached the homestead.

'You haven't found Robbo?' Kate asked.

'Not yet. I'll go down t'see if the boys know anything at the woolshed yards.'

'Don't tell me I told you so,' Kate said to Ed, as she and Enid headed into the house.

'Wouldn't dream of it, Mrs D.'

Harry appeared. 'Well done,' Kate said, as he came in the kitchen door. She'd told him to be home sharpish from school. 'But you're wet,' she said, shocked.

'A bit.' He shrugged and started rattling bikkie tins until he found one with something in it.

'You mustn't swim in the dam any more. You *know* that.' It was a whisper.

'Well, I did, eh,' he said, and disappeared into the hall. To the bathroom, Kate hoped, to get a towel.

Enid had her notes spread on the kitchen table, and she spoke to Kate. 'We should plan now – in case Mr Yorke is not located, and for each possible outcome tomorrow.'

'Tomorrow?'

'I expect the coroner will present his findings of fact then, and . . .' Enid paused.

'Any charges,' Kate finished for her.

'Exactly. We need to be prepared.'

The Amiens truck reappeared just before four. Out through the kitchen window, Kate saw Ed shake his head at her. Behind him, up out of the gully came the police car: Wingnut with the coroner, his clerk and the court reporter. Kate had no Robbo.

Mrs Walters prepared tea things, and Harry appeared then in the kitchen, hair combed and nearly dry.

'Thank you,' Kate said, grateful. 'Now, be good.' He rolled

his eyes. Together, they went out onto the verandah as the men and the court reporter got out of the police car, frowns in place, and made their way across the lawn. All for the missing Robbo.

The coroner came up the stairs and held out his hand to Harry. 'My condolences, young man.' He accepted a cup from Mrs Walters and turned back to talk to the boy.

Kate willed Robbo to appear, but her hopes were fading.

'I wouldn't do that,' Kate heard the coroner say. Whatever *that* was, it was serious; Harry went inside.

She was relieved when he was soon back, with his new cricket bat. The coroner took it and ran a hand along its smooth willow. 'Linseed oil,' he said sagely. 'You sand it back and apply the linseed. None on the splice, mind. Then go on knocking in with your mallet.'

'Haven't got a mallet, eh,' Harry said. 'I been usin a ball.'

'Ball'll still do the trick,' the coroner said, handing the bat back to Harry. Kate wished he'd held on to it. Where the hell was Robbo?

'I take it your bloke's not coming, Mrs Dowd,' the coroner said.

'Here they are!' Harry yelled at an approaching vehicle. Still carrying the bat, he ran down to the fence, towards the truck. *Thank heavens.* Luca was driving, and she could see a passenger on board. Robbo.

'Yes, here they are,' Kate said, as if she'd been expecting this joint and timely entrance all along.

Enid went down to the fence, spoke briefly to Robbo and led them back. Her face told Kate something was wrong. It was a study in conscious implacability. Her court battle face. Luca came up the verandah stairs, Robbo behind him, head down.

Then Kate understood. Robbo was knocked about, his face cut above one eye, and the same eye was black. A wave of stale alcohol carried with him. He must have been on a blinder. What a time for him to do it.

The coroner's lips pursed as he got down to business. 'You're Robert Yorke, I take it? What happened to you?'

Robbo shrugged, avoiding his gaze.

'I'll waste no more time. Sergeant Withers will get a formal statement, but answer this: are you aware of back-burning, or fires lit intentionally or otherwise, on Amiens or its environs on November thirtieth?'

'No, sir. No back-burning for a couple of months now,' Robbo said.

'And no person has exerted pressure or influence of any kind to sway your evidence?'

'No.' Robbo was aghast.

'Sergeant?' The coroner looked around for Wingnut. 'Let's get back to town. Nice to meet you, Harry.' He headed for the police car.

Enid spoke to Kate on the verandah as the police car disappeared.

'You need to be prepared for all possibilities tomorrow. The coroner will present his findings of fact first. Then he'll bring any charges.'

'You mean, in his report?' Kate asked.

'No. He'll read them aloud.'

'That's how I'll find out about charges? He'll *read them out*?' Kate was shocked.

'I'm afraid so.'

Kate's head was spinning. 'Wingnut might arrest me? In the room?'

'Yes. Please reconsider. It's not too late to approach the coroner. To reveal why you believe Grimes was there that day. Have the Wilson boy summonsed.'

Kate shook her head slowly. 'I can't do that.'

'If you're charged, you'll be tried.' Enid spoke intensely. 'You'll lose Harry and Pearl and Amiens and your liberty. *Please* reconsider.'

Later, Kate went in search of Pearl and found her with the housekeeper in the laundry. She kissed the top of Pearl's head. 'Have you been good for Mrs Walters?'

The toddler considered. 'Very, *very* good.'

Kate smiled. 'Let's walk round the garden.' She pulled on some riding boots over her stockings, and put Pearl into a too-big pair of Harry's old boots. It felt so good to wander with her, to be outside with her little sister, after the long, full days of the inquest spent in the hall.

Her mind turned to the next day and the coroner's findings. Charges, if they were to come.

'Bird!' Pearl pointed. Overhead, Daisy's lorikeets shrieked and scattered. They'd come back only a day or so after the fire, and Kate was tearful every time she saw them. Pearl had not mentioned Daisy as often. Kate got a lump in her throat when she thought about it.

Harry appeared on the verandah, a pencil in his hand. 'G'day,' he said. 'You two lookin for snakes?'

Pearl frowned and gripped Kate's hand.

'Don't tease her, Harry,' she said.

'How do ya think it went today?' he asked.

Kate shrugged. 'It all gets finished up tomorrow, apparently. There might be, well, charges.'

'You mean a cost?'

'No. I may be charged. Criminal negligence.'

'Enid reckon that's gunna happen?'

'It might.' Kate looked off to the scorched paddock that led to the gully. 'So I must take you and Pearl to Mrs Riley tonight. In case. You can go to school from there.'

'Nope.'

'What?'

'I'm not goin. This is where I live an that's that. Pearl can stay here with me and Mrs W.'

'Pearl has to go. You know, in case . . .' She stopped, not wanting to mention the Aborigines Welfare Board in front of her.

'Ya reckon they would?'

'If there are charges, they'd have to.'

Harry understood. 'All right. But *I'm* stayin here.'

Driving at night in the bush was an odd thing for Kate; she loved it and hated it, this diving into an inkwell, her car lights the only artificial light in the liquid blackness. She drove slowly, wary of kangaroos and alert to the precious cargo asleep on the back seat. There was little moon, just a dusting of stars.

She kept her eyes peeled too for any other car, fearful of who it might be. It was no way to live, with this constant fear that Jack would appear. Her sensible self knew it was irrational; he'd not be out towards Tindale in the middle of the night. But she was still afraid, wanting comfort. Wanting Luca.

Everything came back to Luca. She'd probably not see him tonight at the Riley homestead, but she hoped she would. That lady he was with? Had he turned to her? Kate could not believe it. She *would* not believe it, stifling her urge to assume the worst.

The road in to the Rileys' took the visitor past the workmen's accommodation. Luca's cottage was in darkness. Maybe he would be at the main house after all. She drove on up the long drive.

The homestead was lit up like a Christmas tree, and Kate felt a surge of pleasure to come to a house where she was welcome. The Rileys came down the steps towards her, each of them beaming.

'Where's young Harry, then?' Mr Riley asked, his voice a whisper, his eyes on the sleeping Pearl.

'He preferred to stay at home. Hold the fort, and so on.'

'Reginald will carry Pearl in for you, dear,' Mrs Riley whispered.

Kate followed them inside, along the hall to the spare bedroom at the back. She stopped in the doorway, wide-eyed. A nursery of sorts was set up, complete with a cot and a short line of dolls. It all looked both new and expensive.

'I hope you don't think that's too forward of me. I had Nettifords' order the cot a month or so ago. Just in case you needed more help, dear.'

Kate's eyes filled with tears, and she couldn't speak. She hugged Mrs Riley.

'Tea, Mrs Dowd?' It seemed Mr Riley could never quite bring himself to call her Kate, no matter how fond he was of her.

'Thank you, but no. I'd best get back to Harry and Mrs Walters.' *In case Jack appears.*

'I'm sure everything will be all right tomorrow,' Mrs Riley said.

'Even if nothing happens, what must people think of this?' Kate said.

'That's one of the benefits of getting old. One stops worrying what others think.'

Back on Amiens, Kate got herself ready for bed in the silent homestead. The nights were quieter now than before the fire. With the trees cut down, there were no branches to brush against the corrugated iron like the swish of a witch's broom; no pair of fighting possums to drop with a bang, scratching their way down the roof in a wrestle for territory. As a little girl, Kate had liked to imagine a lady possum sitting off to one side, filing her nails and looking through her long lashes for the latest on the fight.

Instead, the unfamiliar silence blanketed the homestead and weighed on Kate. She tried to sleep but her head was full of worry. For the inquest findings the next day. For Luca. For Pearl. Eventually, she got up and went onto the verandah with a knee rug. Gunner greeted her with a stretch and a yawn, pleased to have her company in the early hours.

Kate took herself to one of the borrowed wicker chairs. She curled up, tucking herself into the rug, as Gunner dropped on the verandah boards at her feet. She wondered where Luca was at that very moment. Was he with that woman? She tried to stop herself but it was too late. Tears of tiredness, of worry and loss, welled in her eyes and made their way down her cheeks.

Gunner was soon asleep, snuffling and whimpering through doggy dreams. In her long wakefulness, Kate watched the bats flit in and out around the homestead in the dim starlight, as if nothing ever changed, when really everything had changed. When the dawn came on that clear, still January morning, she woke in the chair stiff and cold, dreading the day ahead.

She'd dressed especially carefully, sombrely. Enid had warned her from the start of the inquest: *look demure*. Kate had laughed. Jack used to complain that she dressed like a Sunday school teacher. So. Her navy-blue dress today. The same one that she had worn to her father's funeral three years before.

Mrs Walters tried to press some toast on her, but it just made Kate feel ill. She said her farewells to the housekeeper and Harry, vetoing Harry's attempts to get the day off school and come with her. While she appreciated the thought, school was school.

So off he went towards the stables, to saddle his new pony, Bert (a gift from the generous Rileys).

Kate and Enid were silent as they got into the car, the odd stillness of the place pressing in. Amiens seemed deserted, empty without Pearl and Daisy. As Kate turned the car out towards the main road, with the burnt-out paddocks on either side of the track, she saw them: green shoots had begun to push through, improbably bright against the fire-black landscape.

The stock was gone too. Ed had moved the remaining sheep into the unburnt paddocks, to give their wool time to wash out by next year's shearing. But they all knew that was a long shot. Their wool would be discoloured. The question was, by how much. That would push the price down.

There was a time when that sort of problem would have given her sleepless nights. But she had to let go – even of Amiens, now. There was something more important. Kate knew she was taking a huge risk in choosing not to tell the coroner that Grimes was a thief. Enid's silence reminded her of the jeopardy she faced.

But it was a gamble Kate had to take. *Let it be all right*, she said to herself over and over, as the miles to Longhope rolled by. Glinting grey in the morning light, tall eucalypts lined the road like sentries.

CHAPTER 63

Especial care must be taken when working with mobs in large numbers. A fright and a crush against a fence may cause great loss of sheep.

THE WOOLGROWER'S COMPANION, 1906

'But it's *Thursday*,' Kate said, perplexed by all the cars. She drove slowly along the main street of Longhope, looking for a park. 'Graziers usually come to town on Fridays.'

When Enid said nothing, it dawned on Kate. 'They've come specially, haven't they? To see the end of the inquest?'

'Perhaps.' Enid looked down at the notes in her lap. Her bright red lipstick was in place, even on this worst of days.

With all these cars, Kate was not sorry to park a street away from the RSL. She patted the car for good luck as they left, hoping that she would be back at the end of the day and reminded herself not to worry. Enid had explained that the coroner had powers to bring charges, and then to set bail too. Enid was ready to apply for bail, if Kate was charged.

They walked along the footpath towards the hall, towards chatting couples and groups of three or four. Conversations stopped as Kate and Enid passed, just as they had on the day the inquest started. Kate's father would have greeted each warmly and loudly, shaming them into speaking to him. But she didn't have his gumption, or his smarts. She had boxed herself in and now the odds were overwhelmingly against her, after her stupid answer to why she was up near the stockmen's hut. She carried that weight, stopping at the bottom of the RSL steps to straighten up, summon her courage and enter the crowded hall.

Luca was waiting against the wall opposite the entrance, and he came to her, spruced and worried. She felt a rush of gratitude and relief. He was alone, without that woman.

'Come, *Signora*.' Luca shepherded her through the packed hall, his fingers warm and light on her arm, Enid behind them.

Wingnut nodded at her and she at him. He'd kept her usual seats at the front, but, oddly, he ushered her into the witness chair. Kate sat, straight away unhappy, wishing she'd had the guts to resist, not automatically *do as she was told*. While the chair had been turned a little so it mostly faced the front, it put her on display. Mrs Riley arrived then, looking determinedly unworried – although momentarily alarmed at Kate in that chair out by itself. But she mustered a calming smile as she sat down.

Kate tried not to look at the audience, but one person stood out. Luca's lady friend *was* there after all, in bright red with a hat to match. He must have installed her earlier. Kate looked down at her work-worn hands.

The clerk stood. 'All rise,' he said over the hum of anticipation. It was like church; an expectation of ceremony.

The coroner appeared, walking slowly up to his table. Usually he bounded in. He sat, cleared his throat and turned over the pages of his file.

Just then, Mr Nettiford approached the clerk and whispered to him, showing him a leather-bound logbook. The clerk listened, asked something, then went up to the coroner. The three converged in conversation.

Nettiford opened the logbook on the table in front of the coroner and swivelled it around so that he could read it. He nodded slowly. There was a quick and quiet dialogue back and forth, Nettiford responding to questions. The intense discussion went on until the restlessness in the audience passed from quiet curiosity to impatient chatter. The noise seemed to annoy the coroner and he glanced up, frowning, from time to time. Whatever the captain had to say was also annoying the coroner; he shook his head unhappily. Finally, leaving that leather logbook open in front of him, he waved Nettiford away, back to his seat.

The clerk stood briefly to hush the audience.

The coroner cleared his throat. 'Ladies and gentlemen. Let me begin by thanking you for your patience as we enter the last day of the inquiry. A man has died. It was incumbent upon me to establish not only the identification of the deceased person, and the date and place of death, but the manner and cause of death, and also, most notably, whether a known person or persons may have contributed to the death, and whether charges must be brought.'

Kate sat very still, and from the rest of the hall there was not a sound.

'Before I move on to my findings of fact, I mark as an exhibit a logbook of the Longhope State Forest fire lookout, which logbook includes certain entries for November thirtieth 1948, being the day of the fire.'

Enid mouthed to Kate, 'Don't get your hopes up.'

The coroner continued. 'For the purpose of the transcript, I note that the logbook contains entries for the period from November first 1948 up to and including January twelfth 1949.'

Nettiford must have gone to the State Forest lookout himself, to press them for the logbook for the coroner.

'I note, also for the record, one entry in particular.'

Kate glanced across at Enid for comfort, but the solicitor's face was still, her eyes locked on the coroner.

'The entry for November twenty-fourth 1948.'

A murmur went through the crowd at the date: almost a week *before* the fire. Kate clenched her hands into fists, not wanting to hope.

'It is noted that the lookout on duty on the twenty-fourth made an entry just before 11 am. *Lightning strikes observed to the north-north-east in the triway area.* Then a further entry is made at approximately twelve noon. *Possible smoke observed from the vicinity of the earlier lightning strikes. Likely strike a tree or trees at the foot of the escarpment.* Finally, at 5 pm: *No further smoke observed.*'

There were mutterings from the crowd. There might be something to that lightning strike theory after all.

'I also mark as an exhibit a report dated yesterday and prepared by Captain Nettiford, concerning the inspection, carried out in the triway above the foot of the escarpment, of an acacia tree at the farthest end of the fire footprint, split by lightning—'

The full house gave up any pretence of quiet as the understanding spread. The lightning tree: Nettiford had found it.

The people who might now lose money on an unexpected result were not happy and there was only a handful of winners in the hall. Enid, ever cautious, continued to watch the coroner. The clerk, on his feet against the noise, got the crowd back to a semblance of order.

The coroner paused, the report in his hands, and looked out over his glasses. 'The full report will shortly be available. But today, I will announce my key finding of fact, as follows. First, it is the finding of this inquiry that the bushfire commencing in the Longhope district on November thirtieth 1948 was by cause or causes unknown.'

In the hubbub that followed, Kate remembered Enid. She looked across at Kate and smiled, her court face gone.

Kate didn't know if Nettiford had meant to help her or was simply responding, at last, to the request from the coroner. But whatever the motive, his finding the lightning tree had saved her.

Kate remembered little from the rest of the morning. Just the coroner's final pronouncement: 'I record the death of Mr Keith Grimes to be accidental.'

She was free.

CHAPTER 64

In some cases, it has been found that very trifling changes in the pasture and environs of a flock may give rise to a resulting difference in weight, and the woolgrower would do well to pay heed to such difference.

THE WOOLGROWER'S COMPANION, 1906

Mrs Riley's eyes brimmed with relief at the close of the inquiry. As she kissed Kate's cheek, a tear transferred.

Kate was dimly aware of Luca behind her, his arm under hers. They moved then, Mrs Riley an icebreaker through the crowd, clearing a path for Enid, then Luca with Kate in her wake.

'Smile,' Enid said softly, and Kate tried, looking at the throng of well-wishers. They now seemed all of the mind that she could never have been responsible for the fire.

The hot room suddenly swam about her. Immediately Luca was there, holding her up, lowering her into an aisle chair. He squatted in front of her, and she sat like that, a buzz of interest across the still-crowded room. Kate thought she saw Jack's face, disapproving, his eyes not on Kate but on Luca before her. She realised with a jolt that he'd want his money now, money she didn't have.

'I doubt she's eaten much for days, poor poppet.' Mrs Riley's voice seemed far away. Luca helped her up.

Outside, Kate felt the sudden glare of the sunlight.

'Best wishes, Mrs Dowd,' a voice called to her. It was the coroner, almost unrecognisable with something like a smile on his face. He waved at her, a set of long court papers rolled up in his fist.

Kate gasped when it hit her. That paper – the paper used for the statements – was *long*. It was always long.

'What is it?' Enid asked.

Kate couldn't speak. The statement that Jack had waved about at her was too short. He was bluffing.

She smiled, looking around for Luca, but he was gone.

'I'll go to the Rileys' for the afternoon, then back to yours later, ahead of the train tomorrow,' Enid said. 'But are you all right?'

'Right as rain,' Kate managed. She meant it, trying hard not to cry as Mrs Riley hugged her tight before they left.

On the drive home alone to Amiens, relief overwhelmed her. Without Enid to talk to, Kate struggled to stay awake in the warmth of the car on that long straight road. When her head nodded forward, Kate braked, turning the car off the road into the dirt scrabble at the side. Dust drifted over the car and she watched it pass.

She'd lived with the fear of charges for so many weeks that now she struggled to believe the inquest was over. Her head wanted to lie back against the upholstery, so she got out and leant against the car. Ahead of her across a wire fence, a ring-barked tree supported clustered pink and grey galahs on its uppermost branches.

The galahs spotted her and started up, its raucous heckles cutting through the still afternoon.

She looked along the road to get her bearings. She was so tired she wasn't even sure how far she'd come from town. A dip into a gully. A creek. Quart Pot Creek. Nearly home.

She took the water bag off the car and poured a little into

the cap top. With her legs wide, she tilted her head forward and tipped the contents into her hair at the back of her neck, trapping it there, trying to wake herself up. Drops spattered at her feet, dark circles in the dirt.

She was awake then, awake and angry that she had been wrongly accused, that so many were willing to assume she must have been at fault. Why *should* it be? Why should a woman alone automatically be without intelligence or wisdom or judgement?

She put the cap back on the water bag, the bag back on the radiator, and got into the driver's seat, leaving the galahs. She needed to be more like them. Unapologetic. But they were a mob, with safety in numbers, and she was alone. Bloody Luca was off with that woman, and Kate had been too embarrassed to ask Mrs Riley who she was.

CHAPTER 65

The woolgrower is blessed indeed by the marvellous powers of Merino manure. A lamb might produce four pounds of effluent daily, each pound low in the chemical element nitrogen, so immediately useful to fertilise its pasture.

THE WOOLGROWER'S COMPANION, 1906

'I have gossip,' Harry said, as he came up the verandah stairs late that afternoon. Kate wondered what he'd heard. He dropped himself into the chair opposite her.

'Lots of news,' he added. 'I can't tell ya all of it, but.'

'Why not?'

'Aw, you'll see. Anyhow, first. Fleming's hard up. He's a two-up bloke and a big better on the horses.'

'Heavens. I doubt that.' It occurred to Kate, though, that it *could* explain why he didn't buy the paddock from her, why he hadn't paid her for the sheep, why he always seemed to be short of money. It was stacking up.

'Fair dinkum. Started when he was a boy at Shore. An he loses.'

'How do you know?' Fighting annoyance, she accepted a cup of tea from Mrs Walters. If Harry was right, she really would never get paid for those wethers. 'It's not possible.'

He leant towards her and tapped the side of his nose. 'I were on litter patrol today.'

'So?'

'I made myself scarce to get out of it. Anyway, guess what I heard behind the thunderboxes?' Harry laughed. 'Tim Maguire gabbing with Mattie.'

'You shouldn't eavesdrop. We've spoken about this.'

'No secrets in a country town, I hear. Anyway, there was a dust-up on Longhope Downs a while back.'

'What do you mean?' Kate was suddenly worried for Elizabeth.

'Just before Christmas a two-up bloke come from Armidale. Fleming played. Only he didn't have the dosh to pay this bloke the night he lost. So the bloke come to Longhope Downs to get his money.'

'That can't be right.'

'Tim heard Maguire telling his mum. The postie were at Longhope Downs when the two-up bloke appeared, stroppy as all get-out and rearing to have a go.'

'Fleming's really a gambler?'

'He goes once a month. After the auction. Set ya clock by it, apparently.'

Kate suddenly understood why Fleming was away before the fire. Playing two-up in Armidale. And he'd had the nerve to lecture *her* on farm management and prudence and being careful, when he's the one with the debts? And the gambling problem.

'Mrs Fleming knew the two-up bloke, according to Maguire. So it musta happened before.'

Fleming was short of money. More secrets.

'Tim Maguire shouldn't be telling anyone these things.'

'Like father, like son, eh. Got a big mouth.'

That made Kate think of Jack. He was sure to come out to Amiens soon, to push her for money now that the inquest was over.

'Harry, can you help me with something? When Jack comes?'

'It'll cost ya,' he said automatically. But he listened. Kate was just finishing when they heard a vehicle.

Rumbling up out of the gully came the Rileys' truck; Luca at the wheel, Enid in the passenger seat. Kate stood and smoothed her hair. She had so much still to do – overcome the Board, deal with Jack – she wasn't sure she knew what to say to Luca yet.

He climbed down from the truck cab, hat in hand, and walked up with Enid to the homestead verandah. As he came up the stairs, he tucked in his shirt. That stark white against his olive skin made him look the business. Kate shook that thought out of her head.

He waited awkwardly on the verandah as Enid went inside to pack.

'I need to thank you,' Kate said. 'For finding Robbo.'

'Is hard for him.' Luca waggled his spare hand as if holding a bottle. 'He try but Jack want to buy him the beer.'

'What?'

'Robbo explain me. He bring Jack back to Longhope from Armidale. A lift, is it called? Then Jack say he must buy the beer for Robbo.'

It occurred to Kate that whatever Jack touched seemed to go bad. He wouldn't have meant any harm, but she could see him offering to shout a round at the pub, insisting that Robbo be man enough to drink *just one beer*. Then they'd have had another.

'Jack must be the only one in the district who doesn't know Robbo has a grog problem.'

'Perhaps.'

'How did you find Robbo anyway?'

'I go in the pub. First one, then the next.' He shrugged. 'To the end.'

'Well. Thank you.' She smiled at him and there was an uncomfortable silence.

Luca turned his hat in his hands.

'I pay my friend today,' he said. 'The lady.'

'The lady?' Kate wanted to kick herself for even asking. It was none of her business and she should not assume the worst. *Remember?*

'I must pay her. She is a lady of the night, this lady.'

'A what?'

'*Sì*. She is from the *bordello*.'

Kate's eyes widened.

'Mr Nettiford is her—' His face creased as he sought the right word. '*Cliente*. He is her *cliente*.'

She had no words.

'My friend tell me about her. About Mr Nettiford. So I bring her.' He nodded, looking worried. Kate realised he wanted to explain. He wanted her to know why the woman was there, with him.

'I pay her.' As he took in her expression, realisation took hold, and his face conveyed his own shock. 'No, no. I pay her. *Sì*. But I not pay her for—'

'I understand,' Kate said, saving him.

He laughed then, a deep-throated guffaw.

'You brought her to show Nettiford you knew . . . ?'

'*Sì*.'

'That's why he helped, why he found the logbook and went looking for the lightning tree?'

'Perhaps.'

Kate looked at him, aghast at what he'd done for her. 'Thank you.'

He smiled back, a smile so wide she felt the heat come to her face.

The sound of a car engine floated to them.

Harry appeared at the kitchen window. 'It's Biggsy's vehicle. It's gotta be Jack.'

'Ah.' Luca was pleased at the prospect.

'No, no!' Kate said, horrified. 'I must do this alone. But can you wait? Out of sight?' Luca looked disappointed. 'Please. Just go round the side. The woodpile? Chop some kindling?' She smiled at him.

'But I listen. I come.'

'And you'll have an axe,' she quipped, with false levity. She might need reinforcements. He went slowly, still relishing the prospect of a run-in with Jack. One she wanted to avoid.

Kate went into the kitchen to Harry. 'You ready?'

He patted his pocket.

'Can you get it? Do you have the key? Jack has to know I'm serious. And please ask Enid to stay out of sight for a bit. Tell her it's Jack.'

Harry disappeared immediately as Kate went outside. She stood at the top of the steps, clasping her hands to stop them shaking.

'*Mrs* Dowd,' Jack said, coming through the gate. He stopped on the lawn, legs astride, arms folded.

She said nothing, afraid her voice would show her up.

'Cup of tea'd be polite, Kate,' he chided.

She shook her head. The gentle sound of splitting wood carried from the back of the house. She was glad Luca was there, even if Jack didn't know it.

Harry appeared then, cradling a shotgun, and Jack's eyebrows went up. 'Is that necessary, Kate?'

'Yes. It is.'

'You'd have a boy do your dirty work?'

'The gun's for me.' She was relieved to hear her voice was calm. She took the shotgun from Harry.

Jack's jaw set. 'This is bull. You know what I'm here for. You pay me or I'm going ahead.'

She said nothing, remembering Enid's advice. *Nerves will make people want to fill silences. Let them.*

Jack tried again. 'They'll all know about your Eye-tie, little commie that he is. He'll be shipped back.'

'I've already made a cheque out for you.'

That took Jack by surprise. 'Well, then. Why didn't you say so.'

Harry went past her, took a folded cheque from his pocket, and handed it to Jack. He ran back up the steps to stand behind Kate on the verandah.

Jack had unfolded the cheque and was stunned into a momentary silence.

'It's only five hundred.' He looked up at her. 'Don't bloody think you're going to get away with—'

She held up a hand from the gun, to quieten him. 'You don't have Grimes's statement.'

'I do,' he said, too quickly.

She shook her head.

'The wrong size paper, Jack. You should have known that. Legal paper is long. Not the shorter stuff your solicitors type their letters on.'

He was silent, wary.

'So why am I paying you? Because you need a new start. A new life. I want that to go well.'

'You'll have to give me more than this to get rid of me,' he said, regrouping.

'I don't have to give you anything. It's you who needs the money.' She realised she was sounding like Fleming.

Jack looked at her, calculations rolling through his mind and across his face.

'You told her you had money, didn't you? Your fiancée? Just like you told my mother you had money.'

His face coloured.

'Well, now you have that money. But if you come back – if you so much as put a foot on Amiens or even in Longhope – I will find her. I'll tell her then, show her that you lied to her. That all of your money came from me.'

For the first time, Jack looked uncertain.

'Go now. Get off Amiens.'

He didn't move so she cocked the shotgun, ready to fire. She heard Harry shift nervously behind her.

When Jack began to refold the cheque, she knew she had him. He threw a look of contempt at them both and went out of the gate to the car.

He moved the vehicle off fast, throwing dust and dirt over the fence towards the homestead.

'Once an idiot, always . . .' Harry observed.

The car accelerated away.

'Oof.' Harry winced as it bottomed in the gully with a crunch.

Luca's tuneless whistling carried to them, and he came round the side of the house.

Kate passed him the shotgun with relief. He broke open the breech to unload it but looked at them in surprise. 'She is empty.'

Harry shook his head. 'I didn't load it, eh. Mrs D mighta shot the bastard.'

Luca laughed. 'All is good?'

'Yes,' Kate said.

'I don't get it.' Harry looked at Kate. 'If old Jack don't have the paper Grimesy signed, the one Fleming witnessed, and *you* don't have it, who does?'

She smiled. 'I have an idea. I'm going to start with Wingnut.'

CHAPTER 66

Naturalists will attest to this most unfortunate law of nature: that certain rams possess a temperament disagreeable surely even to themselves.

THE WOOLGROWER'S COMPANION, 1906

A week had passed since Jack had left and there'd been no sign of him since. Kate hoped for the best. She'd wanted to get rid of Jack herself, without help from Luca. She had guessed Jack's pride might just take her sending him packing. But he'd never have coped with Luca doing it. Men were like rams.

She'd been to see Wingnut. Her hunch had been right. He said he'd taken Grimes's signed statements at the boarding house, to send them to the next of kin. But in his mess of an office, he'd mislaid them for a time. He'd refused to tell Kate what he'd done with them once he found them.

'How's Ed gettin t'the station?' Harry asked from the end of the kitchen table, homework open in front of him.

Kate was watching Pearl put most of the mushed-up fruit from her flat-bottomed feeder bowl on the table or herself. She coaxed the spoon from Pearl and used it to wipe up the debris from round her mouth.

'Luca's giving him a lift,' Kate said. She glanced up at the big kitchen clock. The train was at five, and it was just after half past three. It was hard to believe. Ed was leaving Amiens.

Gunner barked. 'I reckon they're here,' Harry said, getting his hat on the way out.

Kate wiped Pearl's face and hands with a wet washer and kissed the top of her head. 'Come outside, little one. You need to give Ed a big hug.'

Concern filled Pearl's face.

Kate was about to say, 'He's not going away.' But he was, and poor Pearl already missed her mum so much. Kate hugged the toddler tight, kissed her cheek, and led her by the hand to the office. There, she scooped up a cheque for Ed's wages. 'Do you want to carry the envelope?'

Pearl accepted her task solemnly and they went together, back through the kitchen and across the lawn towards Ed, who was at the fence, and Luca, who was climbing out of the Rileys' car.

'*Signora.*' Luca nodded a sort of formal greeting at her, and she smiled back at him, each looking too long. She made herself remember these moments, brimming with the promise of all that lay ahead.

Then Pearl went to Ed and attached herself to one of his trouser legs, holding the envelope up to him. He took it, rubbed her head and smiled at them all, his farewell party. Kate saw a restfulness about Ed's face. This was the right thing, that he was going.

'Good luck, mate,' Harry said. Ed held out his hand and they shook. Kate wondered if Harry would cry, but he managed not to. She was proud of him.

Mrs Walters appeared at the kitchen door and Pearl ran off to her across the lawn.

'Thank you, Ed. For everything,' Kate said. He looked away, pleased and embarrassed. 'We'll be out your way, from time to time. So, you know. To see you.' She said no more. He understood.

In that lull, Luca gave Ed a small box. 'A present, also. I do this. I make her.'

Ed took off the lid and held a small bust, a child's head and shoulders, carved in wood. Pearl. 'She is for Daisy,' Luca said. 'Please say my greeting to her.'

Luca knows.

Kate was caught out, shock across her face.

Harry laughed hard. 'No flies on old Luca.' Pearl appeared at Harry's feet, and he scooped her up.

Ed, ever unflappable, moved on as before. He had a train to catch. 'Thanks, Mrs D.' He held out his hand and she shook it, smiling, biting back her own tears. She hoped he and Daisy would be safe.

'Be careful,' she said, as Ed and Luca headed for the Rileys' car, and the train station.

Kate thought back to Ed, coming to her long before the fire, asking her to help them.

They knew that the Board had singled Daisy out as a troublemaker, an agitator, when she was neither of these. It was Kate who'd asked for Daisy's wages. But the Board would punish Daisy, would want to make an example of her throughout her life. Pearl would be taken into the system of Homes and fostering, and eventually adopted by a white family, the memories of her birth mother obliterated.

Ed had come up with the idea. Kate would put some food and provisions in the remote stockmen's hut up by the escarpment. Daisy would disappear, the day before Ed was due to go to Broken Hill with the stock, and Kate would report her missing. Daisy would hide, waiting overnight in the stockmen's hut. The next day, when Ed shipped the young rams to Mr Perry, in secret Daisy would travel with him, to her family at Broken Hill.

A respectable time later, Ed would leave Amiens to join her. Daisy would see Pearl only rarely, and in secret. With some luck, they'd be all right, Daisy and Ed, but the Board would still search for her.

Kate felt responsible for much that had happened, so she'd agreed to help them. Harry, ever the eavesdropper, had overheard enough of one conversation between Kate and Ed to confront them. Risky as it was – relying on a thirteen-year-old to keep a secret – it seemed they had no choice, so from then he was in on it.

Then when it seemed a fire would come, the idea of Daisy's 'death' came too. She had a chance to be completely free of the Board. The risks and the sacrifices were enormous for all of them. Kate had to rely on Ed and Daisy's belief that if Daisy 'died' in the fire, there'd be no death certificate as she was Aboriginal. Ed was certain – 'never is, Mrs D' – just as he was certain the policeman would not insist on viewing the body. When the fire came, and Kate and Daisy narrowly escaped the falling tree trunk in the dam, Daisy realised that's how she would die. Afterwards, Ed asked Amiens's Aboriginal stockmen to pretend both to retrieve a body from the dam and to build a 'resting place'; window-dressing for the curious Maguires of the district.

The fire unwittingly offered many second chances; for Harry, for Kate with Luca, and for Daisy a new life no longer controlled by the Board. Kate worried that they might all be discovered, but it was only the worry of doing something wrong for the right ends. That she could bear. She would at last be helping redress the wrongs. But when Grimes was revealed as a thief, she'd had a terrible choice to make. If she'd disclosed he was duffing sheep, the coroner might have wanted to see the old yards and start digging around, asking questions of all the stockmen. The secret of Daisy's escape would be in peril. So Kate chose not to say anything, telling herself she'd fight any charges at a trial, rather than put Daisy at risk.

Luca would tell her later that it took him a long time to suspect that Daisy might be alive, and then only because he knew Kate and Ed so well. He had seen Kate grieve for her father, and this was different. She'd seen no point in jeopardising him with the knowledge. There were no guarantees for Daisy, and such a terrible cost. To start again as someone else. To suffer the unbearable separation from her child. But perhaps – perhaps – Daisy's sacrifice might keep Pearl safe from the Board.

CHAPTER 67

For the woolgrower, the turn of the seasons and the array of assaults upon his endeavours require both constancy and zeal.

THE WOOLGROWER'S COMPANION, 1906

Kate had one last piece of unfinished business. But it was not until the end of February that she was able to take Harry to Sydney to see his grandmother. She wanted to try to smooth over the cracks that had appeared when Grimes died, among other things.

On the bus to Narrabeen, Kate glanced across at Harry. He was as tall as her already. She was so proud of him. He'd grow into a fine man. A kind man. Everything that Jack was not.

Jack himself had taken the bait and banked the cheque. His solicitors had written to Kate soon after with divorce papers on the grounds of abandonment: Jack's of Kate. It seemed he would toe the line: he wanted his money, and he wanted his young lady. He needed one for the other.

Harry was angling persistently for another trip to Luna Park, with all its enticing amusements. Kate was resisting. They needed to see Mrs Grimes. After the train to Sydney, an overnight at the Country Women's Association hostel in Potts Point, and the early bus from Central, it was a relief to finally be there.

They found Mrs Grimes in the aviary. The bird noise was immense, the *skrarrrrk-skrarrrrk* of sulphur-crested cockatoos all around them. Harry's grandmother took no time to send him away, 'so the adults can speak'. He was off onto the lawn with another present, a puzzle this time.

With Harry out of the way, Mrs Grimes returned to her task: attaching a white shaft of dried cuttlefish onto the side of a cockatoo's cage. From behind the wire, the bird eyed them suspiciously.

'I wanted to apologise. For not telling you when I was here last time.'

'That your husband had left you?' She was blunt.

'Yes.' Kate felt the heat of shame in her face.

'You know, Mrs Dowd, I made a trunk call to tell Keith that I'd decided to allow Harry to stay with you. I rang him at the boarding house. But I got Mrs Christopher instead.'

'Oh.' Kate suddenly understood. 'And she told you.'

'I don't like falsehoods, Mrs Dowd, even by omission.'

'I regret not telling you very much. It was cowardly.' The cockatoo inside the cage began to bob up and down in agreement.

'You don't like birds, do you, Mrs Dowd?' Mrs Grimes said.

'Oh, I do,' Kate said, hesitant.

'But . . .'

'I'm from the bush, Mrs Grimes. I don't like to see anything in a cage.'

'Ah.' The old lady nodded. 'I remember now. It's your husband who doesn't like birds.'

Kate paused, almost afraid to ask. 'You've met Jack?' He had to have been looking for Grimes's signed statement.

Mrs Grimes nodded. 'He came to see me. Just after Keith died.'

The white cockatoo in the cage bounced up and down on its perch.

'What did he want?'

The old lady looked through the cage, past the bird and directly at Kate. 'What you want, Mrs Dowd. Keith's statement. His papers for the court.'

Does she have them?

'After Keith died, a bit after, I got the statement from the police. Just in the post, one day.'

So Kate's guess had been right.

'I'm sorry to say, Mrs Dowd, that I read them over and over. Those papers. I felt it wasn't right, you understand. What Keith was doing. Getting involved in other people's business.'

But where are they?

'I wasn't sure what to do with them. But then you were coming today, so I decided to use them,' she said. The old lady smiled, pointing at the bottom of the birdcage. It was lined with typed paper, hardly recognisable under the droppings and broken seed husks. But in one corner, Kate could make out a signature she knew. *Keith Grimes.*

'*Bloody hell, Narelle,*' the cockatoo screeched.

'Someone taught him that,' Mrs Grimes said, ashamed. 'I don't know who.'

'*Bloody hell, Narelle.*'

The screeches followed Kate out as she went to get Harry.

The finalising of Kate's divorce took longer than she expected, but 'no more than usual', Enid reassured Kate, through immaculate red lips. Jack behaved, signing the necessary papers on time and without objection. Kate's new life was gathering steam. For, mad as it seemed after the sadness of her first marriage, and more than a year after the fire, Kate nonetheless now looked forward to marrying Luca. They had to overcome a stumbling block: who would perform the ceremony? No priest could do so. Kate was not Catholic, and was now a divorcee.

Help came unprompted and from an unexpected quarter.

Reverend Popliss wrote to Kate, volunteering to marry the happy couple under certain conditions. A whistle-stop ceremony without music was to be held on a Tuesday at seven in the morning. Harry's theory was that this timing would prevent any parishioners or the organist getting wind of it, as the church would be deserted.

Kate accepted gratefully, surprised at the minister's broad-mindedness. Things became clearer after the hasty dress rehearsal. As Reverend Popliss hurried them out of the church, Kate saw Mr Riley quietly slip him a cheque 'to cover the repairs to the church roof'.

It struck Kate that she was very fortunate. Dear Daisy and Ed did not have the luxury of a family like the Rileys to smooth their path.

On the morning of her wedding, Kate felt keenly the absence of her parents, of Daisy. So it was with an odd mix of sadness, excitement and even alarm that Kate went up the steps of the Longhope church on Mr Riley's arm, a flower girl just ahead of them. Pearl took her duties extremely seriously, after rigorous coaching from Mrs Walters.

Pearl walked down the silent aisle, pacing as if for a duel, her small posy gripped tightly. When Mr Riley patted Kate's hand, she thought of her father doing the same thing years before when she married Jack. This, though, was so different – joyous and hopeful – and she went towards Luca, who was positively bursting with pride.

She loved him deeply, and knew him much better than she'd ever known Jack. Luca was kind and calm and happy and hard-working, and he wanted her, not Amiens. *Although the thirty thousand acres won't go astray*, Harry always said if given the chance.

As they passed the front pew, Mrs Riley, Mrs Walters and Harry beamed at them.

Luca stood at the altar, his face filled with tenderness. They'd been through so much, and they trusted each other and themselves. Kate felt she understood life better now, too: a struggle relieved by brief bouts of happiness, that joy as rare as rain in the bush, and just as life-giving. Enough to go on.

EPILOGUE

After the fire

When the intense heat lifted, they knew that the fire front had passed. Clinging together, weeping and hiccupping tears of relief, Kate and Daisy supported Pearl between them. They waded slowly out of the deep water, past the downed trunk that had almost killed them when it fell. They dropped to rest just out of the water, and held each other, not quite believing that they had escaped. Pearl shifted about, her head tucked in under her mother's chin.

In the dam, the top of one wicker chair stuck out above the water. The other chair was gone, pinned to the dam floor, crushed under the fallen trunk. Kate was shocked at how close the dead tree had come to them. 'We were so lucky,' she said in a whisper.

'Cept for me, eh.' Daisy almost smiled.

Slowly, it dawned on Kate what Daisy meant. She stared at the trunk where it disappeared below the water. The dam surface was otherwise still and weirdly peaceful, now that the front had passed.

'I'm unna that tree, eh, Missus.'

Kate squeezed Daisy's hand. *It might work. It has to.*

They sat for a time, neither wanting to speak or to move, to think of what must come.

'You take her now, Missus,' Daisy said, stroking Pearl's hair.

It took a while before Kate could speak. 'Are you sure?' Her voice was very soft.

Daisy sighed, a breath of sadness and fear. She lifted her chin up, away from her child's head. 'I gotta, Missus. They'll take Pearl from yez if I stay. They never let me marry Ed. An mebbe Mum's still . . . still alive.'

A tear ran down Kate's cheek. 'I'll look after Pearl for you. Till you . . .' Kate's voice trailed off and Daisy looked down at her hands. Neither of them knew what the future held.

'I'll do my very best, Daisy. I promise,' Kate said, her voice cracking. 'Luca will too. If he'll have me.'

A fleeting smile crossed Daisy's face, a flash of happiness for Kate through her tears.

Pearl stood up, her head above Daisy's. Fascinated, she touched the tears on her mother's cheeks.

'Littlie,' Daisy said. 'You be good, eh?'

Pearl's brow wrinkled in confusion.

Daisy turned to Kate. 'I reckon you should go ahead of me, Missus. When someone comes searchin, they'll see yez first. I'll be back a bit. Watching yez.'

Kate wept, unable to speak. Slowly, she got to her feet.

Daisy put Pearl's hands to her face, and spoke softly. 'You go with the missus, orright, Pearl? She's gunna take care of ya for now.'

Daisy got up onto her haunches and hugged Pearl tightly, so tightly. She breathed in everything that her child was. 'S'orright,' she said. 'Truly. S'orright.'

Pearl started to cry and clung to her mother.

Gently, so gently, as tears flowed down her face, Daisy unwound Pearl's little hand from her neck and put her in Kate's arms.

'I'll be watchin yez now.' Daisy wrapped both Pearl and

Kate in a tight hug, then slowly released them, her fingers lingering on Pearl's arm.

Crying quietly, Kate took a few steps away towards the track, and looked back.

Daisy nodded, encouraging her to go on. Kate turned and walked up the track as it rose. Pearl cried too, her arms round Kate's neck outstretched behind, reaching for her mother as they moved further and further away.

Daisy stood, made immobile by grief, but she fought her sobs, for Pearl's sake wanting to make no sound.

Kate retreated slowly, the figure growing smaller and smaller over the black hill until it seemed that there was nothing more.

Daisy could no longer pretend that she could see them. She collapsed to her knees, weeping for her child and for her life. No sound intruded, no bird or sheep alive across the blackness of the fire's aftermath, just the ripple of a smoky breeze on the dam's surface.

At last, when her crying slowed, Daisy got to her feet and headed for the bush. With her first steps, she took care to tread on rocks until she was out of the mud, to leave no telltale footprint. She reached the safety of the unburnt bush, heading overland to the stockmen's hut, and on to a new life with Ed. An uncertain life – but a life, at least, of their making.

AUTHOR'S NOTE

Like my first novel, *The Woolgrower's Companion*, this standalone sequel is fiction. But both books grew from family stories, especially those of my grandmother, Gladys Wyndham Mueller-Chateau, 1906–2009. While these books are not her own story, they were inspired by her. She spent most of her life on her family's sheep property in northern New South Wales, including through the Second World War, when Italian prisoners were assigned there as unguarded labour to help get the wool clip in.

The guide to woolgrowing that Kate consults, *The Woolgrower's Companion, 1906*, does not exist, apart from in my imagination. I chose 1906 to honour my grandmother; the year of her birth.

Some of the material covered is confronting. For authenticity, I have been obliged to use terms which are offensive, like 'Abos' or 'Aborigines', rather than 'the Aboriginal people'.

The town of Longhope is fictitious but Myall Creek is not. It was the site of the massacre of approximately thirty unarmed Wirrayaraay people – men, women and children – on 10 June 1838. The hangings of seven Europeans for the massacre was the only time in Australia's frontier wars that those responsible were tried and hanged. A memorial was built in 2000, bringing together descendants of survivors and perpetrators.

The site is on Australia's National Heritage List: https://www.myallcreek.org

The Myall Creek massacre is tragically not unique. It was one of at least 240 massacres of Aboriginal people that occurred during the spread of pastoral settlement in Australia. The University of Newcastle has created a digital map which you can view here: https://c21ch.newcastle.edu.au/colonialmassacres/map.php

For information on Reconciliation Week, Sorry Day, and activities in your area, please go to: https://www.reconciliation.org.au

ATTRIBUTIONS

The source for the extract in chapter 15 is from the 1947 Aborigines Welfare Board Annual Report, which is available online from the remarkable National Library of Australia resource that is Trove: *Annual report of the Aborigines Welfare Board for the year ended 30th June 1947*. Sydney: Govt. Printer, 1941–48. http://nla.gov.au/nla.obj-53818904

Aboriginal people endure the tragedy of generations of children removed from families. The Royal Commission report is truly 'a tribute to the strength and struggles of many thousands of Aboriginal and Torres Strait Islander people affected by forcible removal'. Go to: https://www.humanrights.gov.au/publications/bringing-them-home-report-1997

The character Enid Morrison is named in honour of Sibyl Enid Morrison, the first woman to practise at the New South Wales Bar. For more information, see the wonderful dissertation by Joan O'Brien available on the Women Lawyers of NSW website: https://womenlawyersnsw.org.au/wp-content/uploads/History-of-Women-in-Legal-Profession.pdf

RESOURCES

Preparedness is key to survival in a bushfire. Check your preparations against best practice guidance from the **CSIRO** here: https://blog.csiro.au/bushfire-resilience-preparing-yourself-and-your-property/

Fire brigade warnings can be found here: https://www.rfs.nsw.gov.au/fire-information/fires-near-me/

The **Royal Flying Doctor Service** provides evacuations, much like the one you see in this book. Less well known are the essential regular on-site RFDS medical and dental clinics in remote Australian locations. See what they do and how to support them here: https://www.flyingdoctor.org.au/what-we-do/

Raising orphan wallaroos and other indigenous wildlife is a job only for specialists, and the network of trained volunteers at **WIRES** do a remarkable job. For more information on their work and to support them, go to: https://www.wires.org.au/

Like Kate, farmers and graziers have the interests of their land at heart, and more and more bush and city people alike are working to protect the environment and save our future. Please join a local group that aligns with your area or interests to help fight climate change. For ideas, take a look at the member organisations of **Climate Action Network Australia**: https://www.cana.net.au/our_members

ACKNOWLEDGEMENTS

I acknowledge the traditional custodians of the Australian lands on which I have lived and worked, and on which I learn. I pay my respects to all Elders, past and present.

I acknowledge with grateful thanks all those who have so willingly shared their expertise: Richie Brittingham, Tim Butcher, Tim Clark, Barbara Ellis, Dr Katherine Ellinghaus, Paul Freeburn, Jocelyn Granville, Professor Victoria Haskins, Dr Colin James, Joanna Jenkins, Dr Jennifer Jones, Dr Stephen Langford, Vickii Lett, Justin Leonard, Gian Luca Manca, Relle Mott, Stephen O'Mally, Ruth and Bruce Rhoades, Dr Gundi Rhoades, Professor Peter Stanley, Katie Vandine and Donna Ward. All mistakes, of course, are mine.

I thank also Aunty Judi Wickes for so kindly sharing both her academic research and her experience of certificates of exemption.

I am deeply indebted to Aunty Kerry Reed-Gilbert, a woman of the Wiradjuri Nation, from whom I have learnt so much. I thank her, and I am so grateful for all her cultural guidance, her gentle suggestions and her keen eye.

I thank my generous first readers: Relle Mott, Joanna Jenkins, Melissa Gribble, Christine Gallagher, Sarah Covey Mitchell, Sharon Foo, Janet Haynes, Wendy Grigg, Naomi Weinberg and Ros Higgins.

I thank Beverley Cousins, my remarkable editor at Penguin Random House Australia. I also thank, at PRH, each and all of Catherine Hill, Claire Gatzen, Heidi Camilleri and Bella Arnott-Hoare.

Finally, I thank my terrific agent, Stephanie Koven.

RECIPES

The Amiens kitchen is a happy one, a hub for all the work, activities and happenings of the place. I treasure memories from my own childhood of the country women who filled their kitchens with people, cake and tea. A recipe mainstay for bush women is the most current *Country Women's Association Cookbook*, which I swear by. The CWA has helped country communities from its beginnings, and continues to do so.

I am also lucky enough to have a copy of the 1941 edition of the cookbook, full of sensible housekeeping advice and excellent recipes of the era. Below for you are some much-loved recipes from my family's collection, along with some 1941 recipes, much as Kate would have made them.

FROM MY FAMILY

Nan McGaw's Christmas Cake

1 cup brown sugar, 170g margarine, 5 eggs, 2½ cups sifted plain flour, ½ teaspoon salt, 2 teaspoons mixed spice, 1 standard wine glass spirits, 500g mixed dried fruit, 250g chopped dried cherries, ¼ cup chopped almonds if liked.

Put the fruit and cherries in a bowl with the spirits and soak overnight.

Beat the margarine to a cream, then add the sugar gradually; beat well. Add the eggs one at a time; beat well.

Then add the flour, salt and spices, alternating with the drained fruit and almonds, if using.

Bake in a lined tin with two layers of aluminium foil on top of the cake for 1 hour at 150°C, then remove the foil and bake for a further 1½ to 2 hours at 120°C till cooked through.

Diny's Lemon Delicious Pudding

1 tablespoon butter or margarine, ¾ cup caster sugar, 2 tablespoons plain flour, juice and rind of 2 good-sized lemons, 2 eggs, 1 cup milk.

Beat the butter/margarine and sugar to a cream. Add the flour and mix in gently, then stir in the lemon juice and grated rind.

Separate the yolks from the egg whites and add to the mixture, reserving the whites. Add the milk and mix in carefully – it will be rather watery. Beat the egg whites until very stiff, then fold into the mixture.

Pour into a heatproof dish, placed in a pan of hot water. Bake at 180°C for ½ hour, or until set and browned nicely.

Serve with custard or ice cream.

Isabel's Date Loaf

¾ cup caster sugar, 1 teaspoon cinnamon, 2 cups self-raising flour, 1 cup chopped dates, 1 tablespoon butter, 1 cup hot water, 1 beaten egg, 1 teaspoon bicarbonate of soda dissolved in water.

Sift the sugar, cinnamon and flour into a bowl.

Put the dates, butter and water into a saucepan. Place over heat and gently bring to the boil.

In a separate bowl, mix the egg and soda. Add to the date mixture and stir well. Add all of this to the flour mixture and stir well – it will be sticky.

Half-fill 2 cylinder date roll tins (greased and floured) or 2 medium loaf tins. Bake for 45 minutes to 1 hour in moderate oven.

Serve plain or buttered for afternoon tea.

Nana Borwick's Shortbread

This recipe came from Scotland to Australia with my great-grandmother in 1886.

Rub together in a bowl: 1¼ cups sifted plain flour, ¼ cup cornflour, ¾ cup caster sugar, 110g butter (never use margarine).

Press into 2 round sponge cake tins. Decorate by dragging a fork across and slightly pricking the surface.

Bake for ½ hour at 150°C (no more). It will be pale in colour when cooked. Cut diagonally across while hot, and allow to cool in the tins.

FROM THE 1941 CWA COOKBOOK

Lamingtons

5 ozs butter, 5 ozs sugar, 10 ozs self-raising flour, 2 eggs, 4 tablespoons milk, a few drops vanilla.

Cream the butter and sugar, add the beaten eggs with the milk and vanilla, and lastly the sifted flour.

Grease a flattish dish, pour the mixture into it and bake for 30 minutes in a moderate oven. Turn out onto a cooling rack and leave until the next day, then cut onto squares and ice with the following: 3 ozs butter, 1 tablespoon cocoa, 8 ozs icing sugar, a few drops vanilla.

Cream the butter and icing sugar, then add the cocoa mixed with a little hot water and the vanilla. Ice the squares (cakes) all over, then roll them in browned coconut.

Crumpets

2 cups flour, 2 teaspoons baking powder, ¼ teaspoon salt, 1 teaspoon sugar.

Mix with enough milk to make a creamy batter and then stir in the stiffly beaten whites of 2 eggs. Allow to stand for 7 or 8 minutes. Fry in a little butter in a pan.

When well honeycombed, turn and brown the other side. Butter hot and serve.

Fudge

3 cups sugar, 1 cup milk, 1 tablespoon butter, 1 tablespoon cocoa, 1 teaspoon vanilla.

Melt the sugar, milk and butter. Add the cocoa. Boil for 15 minutes.

Take off, add the vanilla and stir till creamy. Pour onto a buttered plate and leave till set, then cut into blocks.

Rainbow Cake

2 cups flour, ½ lb butter, ¾ cup sugar, 6 eggs, small cup milk, 2 teaspoons cream of tartar, 1 teaspoon bicarbonate of soda, ½ teaspoon salt, 2 ozs cocoa or chocolate, 1 teaspoon cochineal.

Beat the butter and sugar to a cream. Add to the yolks of the eggs and beat well.

Sift the flour, soda and cream of tartar together; add to the yolks of the eggs, sugar and butter with milk alternately, and then the salt.

Fold in the whites of the eggs, well beaten.

Divide the mixture into three parts: one unchanged, one colour with cocoa and the third with cochineal.

Place in sandwich tins, cook in a moderate oven, put lemon cheese or strawberry jam between, and ice to taste.

BOOK CLUB QUESTIONS

1. At the beginning of the book, Kate believes that she no longer loves Luca, and importantly, that her exclusive duty must be to Daisy and to Pearl. Do you think every person owes a duty to self? Do you think such a duty might be a kind of self-care?
2. 'There are no secrets in a small town.' Do you think it is possible to keep a secret in a small community? How does the writer reveal that town's secrets? How many can you find?
3. Small towns are often associated with a strong and supportive community. Which, of the local people (men or women) who helped Kate, did you like particularly?
4. Kate has around her a number of strong and supportive women: Daisy, Mrs Riley, Mrs Walters, Enid, and even the Wilson sister, who pressures her little brother to reveal to Kate what he knows but does not allow him to charge her for that information. Do you think that support among women has changed? Has women's willingness to help other women, whether officially, quietly or even subversively, grown stronger since 1948?
5. In the book, many graziers operate back-burning programs not dissimilar to that followed by Kate and Ed. But Kate is singled out for criticism from John Fleming. Why do you think she is the focus of his attention? Is it

simply her gender or are there other factors that threaten him as well?

6. Kate works hard with Ed to care for her land and her stock. Fleming dismisses her approach to the protection of her land as being 'soft'. But today most Australians, farmers and graziers included, feel strongly about protecting the environment. Do you think it's a peculiarly Australian thing to feel such a strong connection to land and environment?
7. *The Burnt Country* and *The Woolgrower's Companion* are often described by readers as cinematic. Do you agree? Who would you choose to play Kate? Luca? Daisy?
8. Kate suffers harassment from Nettiford, the fire captain, and endures routine 'mansplaining' from Fleming and Maguire, among others. Do you think this is realistic? Might it happen today?
9. At the end of the novel, Kate agrees to pay her estranged husband, Jack, a small amount of money, so long as he stays away from the district. Do you think he will stick to that condition? Do you think she should have paid him anything?
10. The book contains a number of surprises: that Grimes is a sheep thief, and that Daisy and Ed (with help from Kate) faked Daisy's death. Did you expect either of these surprises? If so, what made you suspicious?
11. Kate believes that she cannot reveal to the district that Grimes is a sheep thief because Harry would then be marked as a thief himself. Do you think people still make those kinds of associations, between one generation and the next?
12. Daisy, with Ed's support, decides to make a terrible sacrifice to protect Pearl. She will fake her own death to prevent the Aborigines Welfare Board from putting Pearl into foster care and ultimately on the path to adoption. Do you think she made the right choice?

13. Kate's experience in the bushfire helps her to see that she is prepared to fight to be with Luca after all. Do you think the local people will be generally accepting of her marriage to a former prisoner of war?
14. It is Luca who first points out to Kate that her land gives her power. Do you think that after they marry, Kate will transfer Amiens into joint ownership with Luca? Do you think Kate should maintain sole ownership? How do you think Luca might react to whatever Kate decides to do?
15. *The Burnt Country* is a stand-alone sequel to Joy Rhoades's debut novel, *The Woolgrower's Companion*. If you've read that book, how do you think Kate changed in the three years before Luca returned?

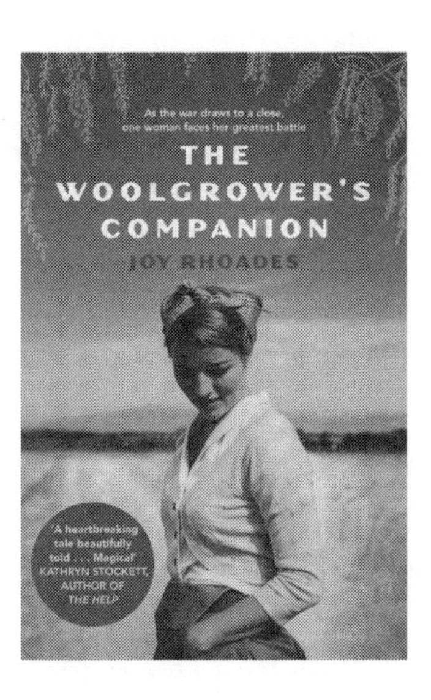

'A wonderful new voice in literary rural fiction' ***Australian Women's Weekly***

Australia 1945. Kate Dowd has led a sheltered life on Amiens, her family's sprawling sheep station in northern New South Wales. The horrors of war have for the most part left her untouched. But with her father succumbing to wounds he's borne since the Great War, the management of the farm is increasingly falling on Kate's shoulders.

With only the sheep-rearing book *The Woolgrower's Companion* to guide her, Kate rises to the challenge. However, the arrival of two Italian POW labourers unsettles not only the other workers, but Kate too – especially when she finds herself drawn to the enigmatic Luca Canali.

Then she receives devastating news. The farm is near bankrupt and the bank is set to repossess. Given just eight weeks to pay the debt, Kate is now in a race to save everything she holds dear.

'A heart-breaking tale beautifully told . . . This compelling story of war and love, of family and prejudice is magical' Kathryn Stockett, author of *The Help*

'This sweeping epic set in rural New South Wales is about love, family and testing our mettle – and it's compulsively readable. Just the thing for those lazy summer days'
Marie Claire

'Joy Rhoades' Kate Dowd is Elizabeth-Bennet-meets-The-Drover's-Wife . . . an accomplished debut' ***Saturday Age***